lastly in the advanced intellectual atmosphere of her ~~~~~ circle. In May, 1814, she met Percy Bysshe Shelley, and in July of that year eloped with him to the Continent. Two years later, after the death of Shelley's wife, the poet and Mary were able to marry. It was in Switzerland in 1816, as a result of a story-writing competition among the Shelleys and Lord Byron, that Mary began *Frankenstein*, her first and most famous novel. Published in 1816, it was followed by such works as *Valperga* (1823), *The Last Man* (1826), *Lodore* (1835), and *Falkner* (1837). In 1823, after the death of her husband, she returned to England; there she devoted herself to the upbringing of her son and the securing of his right to the Shelley family title. She died in 1851.

MARY SHELLEY

Did I request thee, Maker, from my clay
To mould me Man, did I solicit thee
From darkness to promote me?
        Paradise Lost, X, 743-45

With an Afterword by
Harold Bloom

Revised and Updated Bibliography

A SIGNET CLASSIC

NEW AMERICAN LIBRARY

New York and Scarborough, Ontario

FRANKENSTEIN

stein for one of their series, ~~requesting~~ ~~me~~ ~~to~~
furnish them with some account of the origin of the story.
I am the more willing to comply because I shall thus give a
general answer to the question so very frequently asked me
—how I, then a young girl, came to think of and to dilate
upon so very hideous an idea. It is true that I am very averse
to bringing myself forward in print, but as my account will
only appear as an appendage to a former production, and as
it will be confined to such topics as have connection with my
authorship alone, I can scarcely accuse myself of a personal intrusion.

It is not singular that, as the daughter of two persons of
distinguished literary celebrity, I should very early in life
have thought of writing. As a child I scribbled, and my
favourite pastime during the hours given me for recreation
was to "write stories." Still, I had a dearer pleasure than this,
which was the formation of castles in the air—the indulging
in waking dreams—the following up trains of thought, which
had for their subject the formation of a succession of imaginary incidents. My dreams were at once more fantastic
and agreeable than my writings. In the latter I was a close
imitator—rather doing as others had done than putting down
the suggestions of my own mind. What I wrote was intended
at least for one other eye—my childhood's companion and
friend; but my dreams were all my own; I accounted for
them to nobody; they were my refuge when annoyed—my
dearest pleasure when free.

I lived principally in the country as a girl and passed a
considerable time in Scotland. I made occasional visits to the
more picturesque parts, but my habitual residence was on

the blank and dreary northern shores of the Tay, near Dundee.
Blank and dreary on retrospection I call them; they were
not so to me then. They were the aerie of freedom and the
pleasant region where unheeded I could commune with the
creatures of my fancy. I wrote then, but in a most common-
place style. It was beneath the trees of the grounds belonging
to our house, or on the bleak sides of the woodless mountains
near, that my true compositions, the airy flights of my imagination, were born and fostered. I did not make myself the
heroine of my tales. Life appeared to me too common-place
an affair as regarded myself. I could not figure to myself
that romantic woes or wonderful events would ever be my
lot; but I was not confined to my own identity, and I could
people the hours with creations far more interesting to me
at that age than my own sensations.

After this my life became busier, and reality stood in
place of fiction. My husband, however, was from the first
very anxious that I should prove myself worthy of my parent-
age and enrol myself on the page of fame. He was forever
inciting me to obtain literary reputation, which even on my
own part I cared for then, though since I have become infinitely indifferent to it. At this time he desired that I should
write, not so much with the idea that I could produce anything worthy of notice, but that he might himself judge how
far I possessed the promise of better things hereafter. Still
I did nothing. Travelling, and the cares of a family, occupied
my time; and study, in the way of reading or improving my
ideas in communication with his far more cultivated mind
was all of literary employment that engaged my attention.

In the summer of 1816 we visited Switzerland and became
the neighbours of Lord Byron. At first we spent our pleasant
hours on the lake or wandering on its shores; and Lord
Byron, who was writing the third canto of *Childe Harold*,
was the only one among us who put his thoughts upon paper.
These, as he brought them successively to us, clothed in all
the light and harmony of poetry, seemed to stamp as divine
the glories of heaven and earth, whose influences we partook
with him.

But it proved a wet, ungenial summer, and incessant rain
often confined us for days to the house. Some volumes of
ghost stories translated from the German into French fell
into our hands. There was the *History of the Inconstant*

Lover, who, when he thought to clasp the bride to whom he
~~...~~ his vows, found himself in the arms of the pale
~~...~~ the tale of

step was ~~...~~
advanced to the couch of the blooming you~~...~~,
healthy sleep. Eternal sorrow sat upon his face as he bent
down and kissed the forehead of the boys, who from that
hour withered like flowers snapped upon the stalk. I have
not seen these stories since then, but their incidents are as
fresh in my mind as if I had read them yesterday.

"We will each write a ghost story," said Lord Byron, and
his proposition was acceded to. There were four of us. The
noble author began a tale, a fragment of which he printed at
the end of his poem of Mazeppa. Shelley, more apt to em-
body ideas and sentiments in the radiance of brilliant imagery
and in the music of the most melodious verse that adorns our
language than to invent the machinery of a story, commenced
one founded on the experiences of his early life. Poor Polidori
had some terrible idea about a skull-headed lady who was
so punished for peeping through a key-hole—what to see I
forget: something very shocking and wrong of course; but
when she was reduced to a worse condition than the renowned Tom of Coventry, he did not know what to do with
her and was obliged to dispatch her to the tomb of the
Capulets, the only place for which she was fitted. The illustrious poets also, annoyed by the platitude of prose, speedily
relinquished their uncongenial task.

I busied myself *to think of a story*—a story to rival those
which had excited us to this task. One which would speak to
the mysterious fears of our nature and awaken thrilling
horror—one to make the reader dread to look round, to
curdle the blood, and quicken the beatings of the heart. If
I did not accomplish these things, my ghost story would be
unworthy of its name. I thought and pondered—vainly. I

felt that blank incapability of invention which is the greatest misery of authorship, when dull Nothing replies to our anxious invocations. "Have you thought of a story?" I was asked each morning, and each morning I was forced to reply with a mortifying negative.

Everything must have a beginning, to speak in Sanchean phrase; and that beginning must be linked to something that went before. The Hindus give the world an elephant to support it, but they make the elephant stand upon a tortoise. Invention, it must be humbly admitted, does not consist in creating out of void, but out of chaos; the materials must, in the first place, be afforded: it can give form to dark, shapeless substances but cannot bring into being the substance itself. In all matters of discovery and invention, even of those that appertain to the imagination, we are continually reminded of the story of Columbus and his egg. Invention consists in the capacity of seizing on the capabilities of a subject and in the power of moulding and fashioning ideas suggested to it.

Many and long were the conversations between Lord Byron and Shelley to which I was a devout but nearly silent listener. During one of these, various philosophical doctrines were discussed, and among others the nature of the principle of life, and whether there was any probability of its ever being discovered and communicated. They talked of the experiments of Dr. Darwin (I speak not of what the doctor really did or said that he did, but, as more to my purpose, of what was then spoken of as having been done by him), who preserved a piece of vermicelli in a glass case till by some extraordinary means it began to move with voluntary motion. Not thus, after all, would life be given. Perhaps a corpse would be reanimated; galvanism had given token of such things: perhaps the component parts of a creature might be manufactured, brought together, and endued with vital warmth.

Night waned upon this talk, and even the witching hour had gone by before we retired to rest. When I placed my head on my pillow I did not sleep, nor could I be said to think. My imagination, unbidden, possessed and guided me, gifting the successive images that arose in my mind with a vividness far beyond the usual bounds of reverie. I saw—with shut eyes, but acute mental vision—I saw the pale student of unhallowed arts kneeling beside the thing he had

̵ ̵ I saw the hideous phantasm of a man stretched

powerful engine, show

mation woul

in the belief that the silence of the gr

ever the transient existence of the hideous corpse which he had looked upon as the cradle of life. He sleeps; but he is awakened; he opens his eyes; behold, the horrid thing stands at his bedside, opening his curtains and looking on him with yellow, watery, but speculative eyes.

I opened mine in terror. The idea so possessed my mind that a thrill of fear ran through me, and I wished to exchange the ghastly image of my fancy for the realities around. I see them still: the very room, the dark parquet, the closed shutters with the moonlight struggling through, and the sense I had that the glassy lake and white high Alps were beyond. I could not so easily get rid of my hideous phantom; still it haunted me. I must try to think of something else. I recurred to my ghost story—my tiresome, unlucky ghost story! Oh! If I could only contrive one which would frighten my reader as I myself had been frightened that night!

Swift as light and as cheering was the idea that broke in upon me. "I have found it! What terrified me will terrify others; and I need only describe the spectre which had haunted my midnight pillow." On the morrow I announced that I had *thought of a story*. I began that day with the words "It was on a dreary night of November," making only a transcript of the grim terrors of my waking dream.

At first I thought but of a few pages, of a short tale, but Shelley urged me to develop the idea at greater length. I certainly did not owe the suggestion of one incident, nor scarcely of one train of feeling, to my husband, and yet but for his incitement it would never have taken the form in which it was presented to the world. From this declaration I must except the preface. As far as I can recollect, it was entirely written by him.

And now, once again, I bid my hideous progeny go forth and prosper. I have an affection for it, for it was the offspring of happy days, when death and grief were but words which found no true echo in my heart. Its several pages speak of many a walk, many a drive, and many a conversation, when I was not alone; and my companion was one who, in this world, I shall never see more. But this is for myself; my readers have nothing to do with these associations.

I will add but one word as to the alterations I have made. They are principally those of style. I have changed no portion of the story nor introduced any new ideas or circumstances. I have mended the language where it was so bald as to interfere with the interest of the narrative; and these changes occur almost exclusively in the beginning of the first volume. Throughout they are entirely confined to such parts as are mere adjuncts to the story, leaving the core and substance of it untouched.

London, October 15, 1831

by Dr. Darwin and some of the p... ...
many, as not of impossible occurrence. I shall not be supposed as according the remotest degree of serious faith
to such an imagination; yet, in assuming it as the basis of
a work of fancy, I have not considered myself as merely
weaving a series of supernatural terrors. The event on which
the interest of the story depends is exempt from the dis-
advantages of a mere tale of spectres or enchantment. It was
recommended by the novelty of the situations which it de-
velops, and however impossible as a physical fact, affords a
point of view to the imagination for the delineating of human
passions more comprehensive and commanding than any
which the ordinary relations of existing events can yield.

I have thus endeavoured to preserve the truth of the elementary principles of human nature, while I have not
scrupled to innovate upon their combinations. The *Iliad,* the
tragic poetry of Greece, Shakespeare in the *Tempest* and
Midsummer Night's Dream, and most especially Milton in
Paradise Lost conform to this rule; and the most humble
novelist, who seeks to confer or receive amusement from his
labours, may, without presumption, apply to prose fiction a
license, or rather a rule, from the adoption of which so many
exquisite combinations of human feeling have resulted in the
highest specimens of poetry.

The circumstance on which my story rests was suggested
in casual conversation. It was commenced partly as a source
of amusement, and partly as an expedient for exercising any
untried resources of mind. Other motives were mingled with
these as the work proceeded. I am by no means indifferent
to the manner in which whatever moral tendencies exist in

the sentiments or characters it contains shall affect the reader; yet my chief concern in this respect has been limited to the avoiding the enervating effects of the novels of the present day, and to the exhibition of the amiableness of domestic affection, and the excellence of universal virtue. The opinions which naturally spring from the character and situation of the hero are by no means to be conceived as existing always in my own conviction; nor is any inference justly to be drawn from the following pages as prejudicing any philosophical doctrine of whatever kind.

It is a subject also of additional interest to the author that this story was begun in the majestic region where the scene is principally laid and in society which cannot cease to be regretted. I passed the summer of 1816 in the environs of Geneva. The season was cold and rainy, and in the evenings we crowded around a blazing wood fire and occasionally amused ourselves with some German stories of ghosts which happened to fall into our hands. These tales excited in us a playful desire of imitation. Two other friends (a tale from the pen of one of whom would be far more acceptable to the public than anything I can ever hope to produce) and myself agreed to write each a story founded on some supernatural occurrence.

The weather, however, suddenly became serene; and my two friends left me on a journey among the Alps and lost, in the magnificent scenes which they present, all memory of their ghostly visions. The following tale is the only one which has been completed.

Marlow, September, 1817

the commencement of an enterprise which you have been with such evil forebodings. I arrived here yesterday, and my first task is to assure my dear sister of my welfare and increasing confidence in the success of my undertaking.

I am already far north of London, and as I walk in the streets of Petersburgh, I feel a cold northern breeze play upon my cheeks, which braces my nerves and fills me with delight. Do you understand this feeling? This breeze, which has travelled from the regions towards which I am advancing, gives me a foretaste of those icy climes. Inspirited by this wind of promise, my daydreams become more fervent and vivid. I try in vain to be persuaded that the pole is the seat of frost and desolation; it ever presents itself to my imagination as the region of beauty and delight. There, Margaret, the sun is forever visible, its broad disk just skirting the horizon and diffusing a perpetual splendour. There—for with your leave, my sister, I will put some trust in preceding navigators—there snow and frost are banished; and, sailing over a calm sea, we may be wafted to a land surpassing in wonders and in beauty every region hitherto discovered on the habitable globe. Its productions and features may be without example, as the phenomena of the heavenly bodies undoubtedly are in those undiscovered solitudes. What may not be expected in a country of eternal light? I may there discover the wondrous power which attracts the needle and may regulate a thousand celestial observations that require only this voyage to render their seeming eccentricities consistent forever. I shall satiate my ardent curiosity with the sight of a part of the world never before visited, and may tread a land never before imprinted by the foot of man. These are

Trying to gain something from new land

my enticements, and they are sufficient to conquer all fear of danger or death and to induce me to commence this laborious voyage with the joy a child feels when he embarks in a little boat, with his holiday mates, on an expedition of discovery up his native river. But supposing all these conjectures to be false, you cannot contest the inestimable benefit which I shall confer on all mankind, to the last generation, by discovering a passage near the pole to those countries, to reach which at present so many months are requisite; or by ascertaining the secret of the magnet, which, if at all possible, can only be effected by an undertaking such as mine.

These reflections have dispelled the agitation with which I began my letter, and I feel my heart glow with an enthusiasm which elevates me to heaven, for nothing contributes so much to tranquillize the mind as a steady purpose —a point on which the soul may fix its intellectual eye. This expedition has been the favourite dream of my early years. I have read with ardour the accounts of the various voyages which have been made in the prospect of arriving at the North Pacific Ocean through the seas which surround the pole. You may remember that a history of all the voyages made for purposes of discovery composed the whole of our good Uncle Thomas' library. My education was neglected, yet I was passionately fond of reading. These volumes were my study day and night, and my familiarity with them increased that regret which I had felt, as a child, on learning that my father's dying injunction had forbidden my uncle to allow me to embark in a seafaring life.

These visions faded when I perused, for the first time, those poets whose effusions entranced my soul and lifted it to heaven. I also became a poet and for one year lived in a paradise of my own creation; I imagined that I also might obtain a niche in the temple where the names of Homer and Shakespeare are consecrated. You are well acquainted with my failure and how heavily I bore the disappointment. But just at that time I inherited the fortune of my cousin, and my thoughts were turned into the channel of their earlier bent.

Six years have passed since I resolved on my present undertaking. I can, even now, remember the hour from which I dedicated myself to this great enterprise. I commenced by inuring my body to hardship. I accompanied the whale-fishers on several expeditions to the North Sea; I vol-

Failed in some-- dreamer

untarily endured cold, famine, thirst, and want of sleep; I
 ~~had harder~~ than the common sailors during the day

And now, dear ~~Margaret~~,
plish some great purpose? My life might have been passed in
ease and luxury, but I preferred glory to every enticement
that wealth placed in my path. Oh, that some encouraging
voice would answer in the affirmative! My courage and my
resolution is firm; but my hopes fluctuate, and my spirits are
often depressed. I am about to proceed on a long and difficult voyage, the emergencies of which will demand all my
fortitude: I am required not only to raise the spirits of
others, but sometimes to sustain my own, when theirs are
failing.

This is the most favourable period for travelling in Russia.
They fly quickly over the snow in their sledges; the motion
is pleasant, and, in my opinion, far more agreeable than that
of an English stagecoach. The cold is not excessive, if you
are wrapped in furs—a dress which I have already adopted,
for there is a great difference between walking the deck
and remaining seated motionless for hours, when no exercise
prevents the blood from actually freezing in your veins. I
have no ambition to lose my life on the post-road between
St. Petersburgh and Archangel.

I shall depart for the latter town in a fortnight or three
weeks; and my intention is to hire a ship there, which can
easily be done by paying the insurance for the owner, and to
engage as many sailors as I think necessary among those
who are accustomed to the whale-fishing. I do not intend
to sail until the month of June; and when shall I return?
Ah, dear sister, how can I answer this question? If I succeed,
many, many months, perhaps years, will pass before you and
I may meet. If I fail, you will see me again soon, or never.

Farewell, my dear, excellent Margaret. Heaven shower

down blessings on you, and save me, that I may again and
again testify my gratitude for all your love and kindness.

Your affectionate brother,
R. Walton

LETTER 2

To Mrs. Saville, England

Archangel, 28th March, 17—

How slowly the time passes here, encompassed as I am
by frost and snow! Yet a second step is taken towards my
enterprise. I have hired a vessel and am occupied in collecting my sailors; those whom I have already engaged appear to be men on whom I can depend and are certainly
possessed of dauntless courage.

But I have one want which I have never yet been able to
satisfy, and the absence of the object of which I now feel
as a most severe evil. I have no friend, Margaret: when I
am glowing with the enthusiasm of success, there will be none
to participate my joy; if I am assailed by disappointment,
no one will endeavour to sustain me in dejection. I shall
commit my thoughts to paper, it is true; but that is a poor
medium for the communication of feeling. I desire the
company of a man who could sympathize with me, whose
eyes would reply to mine. You may deem me romantic,
my dear sister, but I bitterly feel the want of a friend. I
have no one near me, gentle yet courageous, possessed of a
cultivated as well as of a capacious mind, whose tastes are
like my own, to approve or amend my plans. How would
such a friend repair the faults of your poor brother! I am
too ardent in execution and too impatient of difficulties. But
it is a still greater evil to me that I am self-educated: for
the first fourteen years of my life I ran wild on a common
and read nothing but our Uncle Thomas' books of voyages.
At that age I became acquainted with the celebrated poets
of our own country; but it was only when it had ceased to
be in my power to derive its most important benefits from

such a conviction that I perceived the necessity of becoming
_____ _____ more languages than that of my native

among merchants and ___

to the dross of human nature, beat even in these rugged
bosoms. My lieutenant, for instance, is a man of wonderful
courage and enterprise; he is madly desirous of glory, or
rather, to word my phrase more characteristically, of ad-
vancement in his profession. He is an Englishman, and in
the midst of national and professional prejudices, unsoftened
by cultivation, retains some of the noblest endowments of
humanity. I first became acquainted with him on board a
whale vessel; finding that he was unemployed in this
city, I easily engaged him to assist in my enterprise.

The master is a person of an excellent disposition and is
remarkable in the ship for his gentleness and the mildness
of his discipline. This circumstance, added to his well-known
integrity and dauntless courage, made me very desirous to
engage him. A youth passed in solitude, my best years spent
under your gentle and feminine fosterage, has so refined the
groundwork of my character that I cannot overcome an
intense distaste to the usual brutality exercised on board
ship: I have never believed it to be necessary, and when I
heard of a mariner equally noted for his kindliness of heart
and the respect and obedience paid to him by his crew, I
felt myself peculiarly fortunate in being able to secure his
services. I heard of him first in rather a romantic manner,
from a lady who owes to him the happiness of her life.
This, briefly, is his story. Some years ago he loved a young
Russian lady of moderate fortune, and having amassed a
considerable sum in prize-money, the father of the girl consented to the match. He saw his mistress once before the
destined ceremony; but she was bathed in tears, and throw-
ing herself at his feet, entreated him to spare her, confessing

at the same time that she loved another, but that he was poor, and that her father would never consent to the union. My generous friend reassured the suppliant, and on being informed of the name of her lover, instantly abandoned his pursuit. He had already bought a farm with his money, on which he had designed to pass the remainder of his life; but he bestowed the whole on his rival, together with the remains of his prize-money to purchase stock, and then himself solicited the young woman's father to consent to her marriage with her lover. But the old man decidedly refused, thinking himself bound in honour to my friend, who, when he found the father inexorable, quitted his country, nor returned until he heard that his former mistress was married according to her inclinations. "What a noble fellow!" you will exclaim. He is so; but then he is wholly uneducated: he is as silent as a Turk, and a kind of ignorant carelessness attends him, which, while it renders his conduct the more astonishing, detracts from the interest and sympathy which otherwise he would command.

Yet do not suppose, because I complain a little or because I can conceive a consolation for my toils which I may never know, that I am wavering in my resolutions. Those are as fixed as fate, and my voyage is only now delayed until the weather shall permit my embarkation. The winter has been dreadfully severe, but the spring promises well, and it is considered as a remarkably early season, so that perhaps I may sail sooner than I expected. I shall do nothing rashly: you know me sufficiently to confide in my prudence and considerateness whenever the safety of others is committed to my care.

I cannot describe to you my sensations on the near prospect of my undertaking. It is impossible to communicate to you a conception of the trembling sensation, half pleasurable and half fearful, with which I am preparing to depart. I am going to unexplored regions, to "the land of mist and snow," but I shall kill no albatross; therefore do not be alarmed for my safety or if I should come back to you as worn and woeful as the "Ancient Mariner." You will smile at my allusion, but I will disclose a secret. I have often attributed my attachment to, my passionate enthusiasm for, the dangerous mysteries of ocean to that production of the most imaginative of modern poets. There is something at

def. of Romantic soul

work in my soul which I do not understand. I am practically industrious—painstaking, a workman to execute with per-

every opportunity: I may receive your letters on some occasions when I need them most to support my spirits. I love you very tenderly. Remember me with affection, should you never hear from me again.

romantic crazy
but good soul

Your affectionate brother,
Robert Walton

LETTER 3

To Mrs. Saville, England

Why regret now?

July 7th, 17—

My dear Sister,

I write a few lines in haste to say that I am safe—and well advanced on my voyage. This letter will reach England by a merchantman now on its homeward voyage from Archangel; more fortunate than I, who may not see my native land, perhaps, for many years. I am, however, in good spirits: my men are bold and apparently firm of purpose, nor do the floating sheets of ice that continually pass us, indicating the dangers of the region towards which we are advancing, appear to dismay them. We have already reached a very high latitude; but it is the height of summer, and although not so warm as in England, the southern gales, which blow us speedily towards those shores which I so ar-

little regret of trip?

dently desire to attain, breathe a degree of renovating warmth which I had not expected.

No incidents have hitherto befallen us that would make a figure in a letter. One or two stiff gales and the springing of a leak are accidents which experienced navigators scarcely remember to record, and I shall be well content if nothing worse happen to us during our voyage.

Adieu, my dear Margaret. Be assured that for my own sake, as well as yours, I will not rashly encounter danger. I will be cool, persevering, and prudent.

But success *shall* crown my endeavours. Wherefore not? Thus far I have gone, tracing a secure way over the pathless seas, the very stars themselves being witnesses and testimonies of my triumph. Why not still proceed over the untamed yet obedient element? What can stop the determined heart and resolved will of man?

My swelling heart involuntarily pours itself out thus. But I must finish. Heaven bless my beloved sister!

R. W.

LETTER 4

To Mrs. Saville, England

August 5th, 17—

So strange an accident has happened to us that I cannot forbear recording it, although it is very probable that you will see me before these papers can come into your possession.

Last Monday (July 31st) we were nearly surrounded by ice, which closed in the ship on all sides, scarcely leaving her the sea-room in which she floated. Our situation was somewhat dangerous, especially as we were compassed round by a very thick fog. We accordingly lay to, hoping that some change would take place in the atmosphere and weather.

About two o'clock the mist cleared away, and we beheld, stretched out in every direction, vast and irregular plains of

Finally — Problem reality

equalities of the ice.

This appearance excited our unqualified wonder. We were, as we believed, many hundred miles from any land; but this apparition seemed to denote that it was not, in reality, so distant as we had supposed. Shut in, however, by ice, it was impossible to follow his track, which we had observed with the greatest attention.

About two hours after this occurrence we heard the ground sea, and before night the ice broke and freed our ship. We, however, lay to until the morning, fearing to encounter in the dark those large loose masses which float about after the breaking up of the ice. I profited of this time to rest for a few hours.

In the morning, however, as soon as it was light, I went upon deck and found all the sailors busy on one side of the vessel, apparently talking to someone in the sea. It was, in fact, a sledge, like that we had seen before, which had drifted towards us in the night on a large fragment of ice. Only one dog remained alive; but there was a human being within it whom the sailors were persuading to enter the vessel. He was not, as the other traveller seemed to be, a savage inhabitant of some undiscovered island, but a European. When I appeared on deck the master said, "Here is our captain, and he will not allow you to perish on the open sea."

On perceiving me, the stranger addressed me in English, although with a foreign accent. "Before I come on board your vessel," said he, "will you have the kindness to inform me whither you are bound?"

You may conceive my astonishment on hearing such a question addressed to me from a man on the brink of destruction and to whom I should have supposed that my vessel would have been a resource which he would not have

meet observed Frankenstein

exchanged for the most precious wealth the earth can afford. I replied, however, that we were on a voyage of discovery towards the northern pole.

Upon hearing this he appeared satisfied and consented to come on board. Good God! Margaret, if you had seen the man who thus capitulated for his safety, your surprise would have been boundless. His limbs were nearly frozen, and his body dreadfully emaciated by fatigue and suffering. I never saw a man in so wretched a condition. We attempted to carry him into the cabin, but as soon as he had quitted the fresh air he fainted. We accordingly brought him back to the deck and restored him to animation by rubbing him with brandy and forcing him to swallow a small quantity. As soon as he showed signs of life we wrapped him up in blankets and placed him near the chimney of the kitchen stove. By slow degrees he recovered and ate a little soup, which restored him wonderfully.

Two days passed in this manner before he was able to speak, and I often feared that his sufferings had deprived him of understanding. When he had in some measure recovered, I removed him to my own cabin and attended on him as much as my duty would permit. I never saw a more interesting creature: his eyes have generally an expression of wildness, and even madness, but there are moments when, if anyone performs an act of kindness towards him or does him any the most trifling service, his whole countenance is lighted up, as it were, with a beam of benevolence and sweetness that I never saw equalled. But he is generally melancholy and despairing, and sometimes he gnashes his teeth, as if impatient of the weight of woes that oppresses him.

When my guest was a little recovered I had great trouble to keep off the men, who wished to ask him a thousand questions; but I would not allow him to be tormented by their idle curiosity, in a state of body and mind whose restoration evidently depended upon entire repose. Once, however, the lieutenant asked why he had come so far upon the ice in so strange a vehicle.

His countenance instantly assumed an aspect of the deepest gloom, and he replied, "To seek one who fled from me."

"And did the man whom you pursued travel in the same fashion?"

"Yes."

...would indeed be very impertinent and inhuman in me to trouble you with any inquisitiveness of mine."

"And yet you rescued me from a strange and perilous situation; you have benevolently restored me to life."

Soon after this he inquired if I thought that the breaking up of the ice had destroyed the other sledge. I replied that I could not answer with any degree of certainty, for the ice had not broken until near midnight, and the traveller might have arrived at a place of safety before that time; but of this I could not judge.

From this time a new spirit of life animated the decaying frame of the stranger. He manifested the greatest eagerness to be upon deck to watch for the sledge which had before appeared; but I have persuaded him to remain in the cabin, for he is far too weak to sustain the rawness of the atmosphere. I have promised that someone should watch for him and give him instant notice if any new object should appear in sight.

Such is my journal of what relates to this strange occurrence up to the present day. The stranger has gradually improved in health but is very silent and appears uneasy when anyone except myself enters his cabin. Yet his manners are so conciliating and gentle that the sailors are all interested in him, although they have had very little communication with him. For my own part, I begin to love him as a brother, and his constant and deep grief fills me with sympathy and compassion. He must have been a noble creature in his better days, being even now in wreck so attractive and amiable.

I said in one of my letters, my dear Margaret, that I should find no friend on the wide ocean; yet I have found a man who, before his spirit had been broken by misery, I should have been happy to have possessed as the brother of my heart.

I shall continue my journal concerning the stranger at intervals, should I have any fresh incidents to record.

August 13th, 17—

My affection for my guest increases every day. He excites at once my admiration and my pity to an astonishing degree. How can I see so noble a creature destroyed by misery without feeling the most poignant grief? He is so gentle, yet so wise; his mind is so cultivated, and when he speaks, although his words are culled with the choicest art, yet they flow with rapidity and unparalleled eloquence.

He is now much recovered from his illness and is continually on the deck, apparently watching for the sledge that preceded his own. Yet, although unhappy, he is not so utterly occupied by his own misery but that he interests himself deeply in the projects of others. He has frequently conversed with me on mine, which I have communicated to him without disguise. He entered attentively into all my arguments in favour of my eventual success and into every minute detail of the measures I had taken to secure it. I was easily led by the sympathy which he evinced to use the language of my heart, to give utterance to the burning ardour of my soul, and to say, with all the fervour that warmed me, how gladly I would sacrifice my fortune, my existence, my every hope, to the furtherance of my enterprise. One man's life or death were but a small price to pay for the acquirement of the knowledge which I sought, for the dominion I should acquire and transmit over the elemental foes of our race. As I spoke, a dark gloom spread over my listener's countenance. At first I perceived that he tried to suppress his emotion; he placed his hands before his eyes, and my voice quivered and failed me as I beheld tears trickle fast from between his fingers; a groan burst from his heaving breast. I paused; at length he spoke, in broken accents: "Unhappy man! Do you share my madness? Have you drunk also of the intoxicating draught? Hear me; let me reveal my tale, and you will dash the cup from your lips!"

Such words, you may imagine, strongly excited my curi-

osity; but the paroxysm of grief th~~~
overcame his weakened ~~~
and tranquil con~~~
posure

~~~, out
~~~ ~~~ of my de-
~~~ for a more intimate
~~~ than had ever fallen to my
~~~ my conviction that a man could boast
~~~ppiness who did not enjoy this blessing.

"I agree with you," replied the stranger; "we are un-fashioned creatures, but half made up, if one wiser, better, dearer than ourselves—such a friend ought to be—do not lend his aid to perfectionate our weak and faulty natures. I once had a friend, the most noble of human creatures, and am entitled, therefore, to judge respecting friendship. You have hope, and the world before you, and have no cause for despair. But I—I have lost everything and cannot begin life anew."

As he said this his countenance became expressive of a calm, settled grief that touched me to the heart. But he was silent and presently retired to his cabin.

Even broken in spirit as he is, no one can feel more deeply than he does the beauties of nature. The starry sky, the sea, and every sight afforded by these wonderful regions seem still to have the power of elevating his soul from earth. Such a man has a double existence: he may suffer misery and be overwhelmed by disappointments, yet when he has retired into himself, he will be like a celestial spirit that has a halo around him, within whose circle no grief or folly ventures.

Will you smile at the enthusiasm I express concerning this divine wanderer? You would not if you saw him. You have been tutored and refined by books and retirement from the world, and you are therefore somewhat fastidious; but this only renders you the more fit to appreciate the extraordinary merits of this wonderful man. Sometimes I have endeavoured to discover what quality it is which he pos-

F extraordinary

sesses that elevates him so immeasurably above any other person I ever knew. I believe it to be an intuitive discernment, a quick but never-failing power of judgment, a penetration into the causes of things, unequalled for clearness and precision; add to this a facility of expression and a voice whose varied intonations are soul-subduing music.

Warning for overreacher

August 19, 17—

Yesterday the stranger said to me, "You may easily perceive, Captain Walton, that I have suffered great and unparalleled misfortunes. I had determined at one time that the memory of these evils should die with me, but you have won me to alter my determination. You seek for knowledge and wisdom, as I once did; and I ardently hope that the gratification of your wishes may not be a serpent to sting you, as mine has been. I do not know that the relation of my disasters will be useful to you; yet, when I reflect that you are pursuing the same course, exposing yourself to the same dangers which have rendered me what I am, I imagine that you may deduce an apt moral from my tale, one that may direct you if you succeed in your undertaking and console you in case of failure. Prepare to hear of occurrences which are usually deemed marvellous. Were we among the tamer scenes of nature I might fear to encounter your unbelief, perhaps your ridicule; but many things will appear possible in these wild and mysterious regions which would provoke the laughter of those unacquainted with the ever-varied powers of nature; nor can I doubt but that my tale conveys in its series internal evidence of the truth of the events of which it is composed."

You may easily imagine that I was much gratified by the offered communication, yet I could not endure that he should renew his grief by a recital of his misfortunes. I felt the greatest eagerness to hear the promised narrative, partly from curiosity and partly from a strong desire to ameliorate his fate if it were in my power. I expressed these feelings in my answer.

"I thank you," he replied, "for your sympathy, but it is useless; my fate is nearly fulfilled. I wait but for one event, and then I shall repose in peace. I understand your feeling," continued he, perceiving that I wished to interrupt

Sharing my warning

impact of exotic setting　　*fatalism in F*

least make notes. This manuscript will doubtless afford you the greatest pleasure; but to me, who know him and who hear it from his own lips—with what interest and sympathy shall I read it in some future day! Even now, as I commence my task, his full-toned voice swells in my ears; his lustrous eyes dwell on me with all their melancholy sweetness; I see his thin hand raised in animation, while the lineaments of his face are irradiated by the soul within. Strange and harrowing must be his story, frightful the storm which embraced the gallant vessel on its course and wrecked it—thus!

I am by birth a Genevese, and my family is one of the most distinguished of that republic. My ancestors had been for many years counsellors and syndics, and my father had filled several public situations with honour and reputation. He was respected by all who knew him for his integrity and indefatigable attention to public business. He passed his younger days perpetually occupied by the affairs of his country; a variety of circumstances had prevented his marrying early, nor was it until the decline of life that he became a husband and the father of a family.

As the circumstances of his marriage illustrate his character, I cannot refrain from relating them. One of his most intimate friends was a merchant who, from a flourishing state, fell, through numerous mischances, into poverty. This man, whose name was Beaufort, was of a proud and unbending disposition and could not bear to live in poverty and oblivion in the same country where he had formerly been distinguished for his rank and magnificence. Having paid his debts, therefore, in the most honourable manner, he retreated with his daughter to the town of Lucerne, where he lived unknown and in wretchedness. My father loved Beaufort with the truest friendship and was deeply grieved by his retreat in these unfortunate circumstances. He bitterly deplored the false pride which led his friend to a conduct so little worthy of the affection that united them. He lost no time in endeavouring to seek him out, with the hope of persuading him to begin the world again through his credit and assistance.

Beaufort had taken effectual measures to conceal himself, and it was ten months before my father discovered his abode. Overjoyed at this discovery, he hastened to the house, which was situated in a mean street near the Reuss. But when he entered, misery and despair alone welcomed him. Beaufort had saved but a very small sum of money from the wreck of his fortunes, but it was sufficient to provide him with sustenance for some months, and in the meantime he hoped to procure some respectable employment in a merchant's house. The interval was, consequently, spent in inaction; his grief only became more deep and rankling when he had leisure for reflection, and at length it took so fast hold of his mind that at the end of three months he lay on a bed of sickness, incapable of any exertion.

His daughter attended him with the greatest tenderness, but she saw with despair that their little fund was rapidly decreasing and that there was no other prospect of support. But Caroline Beaufort possessed a mind of an uncommon mould, and her courage rose to support her in her adversity. She procured plain work; she plaited straw and by various means contrived to earn a pittance scarcely sufficient to support life.

Several months passed in this manner. Her father grew worse; her time was more entirely occupied in attending him; her means of subsistence decreased; and in the tenth month her father died in her arms, leaving her an orphan and a beggar. This last blow overcame her, and she knelt by Beaufort's coffin weeping bitterly, when my father entered the chamber. He came like a protecting spirit to the poor girl, who committed herself to his care; and after the interment of his friend he conducted her to Geneva and placed her under the protection of a relation. Two years after this event Caroline became his wife.

There was a considerable difference between the ages of my parents, but this circumstance seemed to unite them only closer in bonds of devoted affection. There was a sense of justice in my father's upright mind which rendered it necessary that he should approve highly to love strongly. Perhaps during former years he had suffered from the late-discovered unworthiness of one beloved and so was disposed to set a greater value on tried worth. There was a show of gratitude and worship in his attachment to my mother, differing wholly from the doting fondness of age, for it was inspired by reverence for her virtues and a desire to be the means of, in some degree, recompensing her for the

sorrows she had endured, but whi—
to his behaviour

⋯⋯⋯ all ⋯⋯⋯ately after their union they

⋯pleasant climate of Italy, and the change of scene and interest attendant on a tour through that land of wonders, as a restorative for her weakened frame.

From Italy they visited Germany and France. I, their eldest child, was born at Naples, and as an infant accompanied them in their rambles. I remained for several years their only child. Much as they were attached to each other, they seemed to draw inexhaustible stores of affection from a very mine of love to bestow them upon me. My mother's tender caresses and my father's smile of benevolent pleasure while regarding me are my first recollections. I was their plaything and their idol, and something better—their child, the innocent and helpless creature bestowed on them by heaven, whom to bring up to good, and whose future lot it was in their hands to direct to happiness or misery, according as they fulfilled their duties towards me. With this deep consciousness of what they owed towards the being to which they had given life, added to the active spirit of tenderness that animated both, it may be imagined that while during every hour of my infant life I received a lesson of patience, of charity, and of self-control, I was so guided by a silken cord that all seemed but one train of enjoyment to me.

For a long time I was their only care. My mother had much desired to have a daughter, but I continued their single offspring. When I was about five years old, while making an excursion beyond the frontiers of Italy, they passed a week on the shores of the Lake of Como. Their benevolent disposition often made them enter the cottages of the poor. This, to my mother, was more than a duty; it was a necessity, a passion—remembering what she had suffered, and how she had been relieved—for her to act in her turn the guardian angel to the afflicted. During one of their walks a poor cot in the foldings of a vale attracted their notice as being singularly disconsolate, while the number of half-clothed children gathered about it spoke of penury in its worst shape. One day, when my father had gone by himself to Milan, my mother, accompanied by me, visited this abode. She found a peasant and his wife, hard working, bent down by care and labour, distributing a scanty meal to five hungry babes. Among these there was one which attracted my mother far above all the rest. She appeared of a different stock. The four others were dark-eyed, hardy little vagrants; this child was thin and very fair. Her hair was the brightest living gold, and despite the poverty of her clothing, seemed to set a crown of distinction on her head. Her brow was clear and ample, her blue eyes cloudless, and her lips and the moulding of her face so expressive of sensibility and sweetness that none could behold her without looking on her as of a distinct species, a being heaven-sent, and bearing a celestial stamp in all her features.

The peasant woman, perceiving that my mother fixed eyes of wonder and admiration on this lovely girl, eagerly communicated her history. She was not her child, but the daughter of a Milanese nobleman. Her mother was a German and had died on giving her birth. The infant had been placed with these good people to nurse: they were better off then. They had not been long married, and their eldest child was but just born. The father of their charge was one of those Italians nursed in the memory of the antique glory of Italy—one among the *schiavi ognor frementi*, who exerted himself to obtain the liberty of his country. He became the victim of its weakness. Whether he had died or still lingered in the dungeons of Austria was not known. His property was confiscated; his child became an orphan and a beggar. She continued with her foster parents and bloomed in their rude abode, fairer than a garden rose among dark-leaved brambles.

When my father returned from Milan, he found playing with me in the hall of our villa a child fairer than pictured cherub—a creature who seemed to shed radiance from her looks and whose form and motions were lighter than the chamois of the hills. The

_____ Elizabeth. The passionate and almost reverential attachment with which all regarded her became, while I shared it, my pride and my delight. On the evening previous to her being brought to my home, my mother had said playfully, "I have a pretty present for my Victor— tomorrow he shall have it." And when, on the morrow, she presented Elizabeth to me as her promised gift, I, with childish seriousness, interpreted her words literally and looked upon Elizabeth as mine—mine to protect, love, and cherish. All praises bestowed on her I received as made to a possession of my own. We called each other familiarly by the name of cousin. No word, no expression could body forth the kind of relation in which she stood to me —my more than sister, since till death she was to be mine only.

CHAPTER 2

We were brought up together; there was not quite a year difference in our ages. I need not say that we were strangers to any species of disunion or dispute. Harmony was the soul of our companionship, and the diversity and contrast that subsisted in our characters drew us nearer together. Elizabeth was of a calmer and more concentrated disposition; but, with all my ardour, I was capable of a more intense application and was more deeply smitten with the thirst for knowledge. She busied herself with following the aerial creations of the poets; and in the majestic and wondrous scenes which surrounded our Swiss home—the sublime shapes of the mountains, the changes of the seasons, tempest and calm, the silence of winter, and the life and turbulence of our Alpine summers—she found ample scope for admiration and delight. While my companion contemplated with a serious and satisfied spirit the magnificent appearances of things, I delighted in investigating their causes. The world was to me a secret which I desired to divine. Curiosity, earnest research to learn the hidden laws of nature, gladness akin to rapture, as they were unfolded to me, are among the earliest sensations I can remember.

On the birth of a second son, my junior by seven years, my parents gave up entirely their wandering life and fixed themselves in their native country. We possessed a house in Geneva, and a *campagne* on Belrive, the eastern shore of the lake, at the distance of rather more than a league from the city. We resided principally in the latter, and the lives of my parents were passed in considerable seclusion. It was my temper to avoid a crowd and to attach myself fervently to a few. I was indifferent, therefore, to my schoolfellows in general; but I united myself in the bonds

36

isolated, few class, relating around

of the closest friendship to ~~~~

~~~~ ~~~~ blood to

~~~~ from the hands of the infidels.

No human being could have passed a happier childhood than myself. My parents were possessed by the very spirit of kindness and indulgence. We felt that they were not the tyrants to rule our lot according to their caprice, but the agents and creators of all the many delights which we enjoyed. When I mingled with other families I distinctly discerned how peculiarly fortunate my lot was, and gratitude assisted the development of filial love.

My temper was sometimes violent, and my passions vehement; but by some law in my temperature they were turned not towards childish pursuits but to an eager desire to learn, and not to learn all things indiscriminately. I confess that neither the structure of languages, nor the code of governments, nor the politics of various states possessed attractions for me. It was the secrets of heaven and earth that I desired to learn; and whether it was the outward substance of things or the inner spirit of nature and the mysterious soul of man that occupied me, still my inquiries were directed to the metaphysical, or in its highest sense, the physical secrets of the world.

Meanwhile Clerval occupied himself, so to speak, with the moral relations of things. The busy stage of life, the virtues of heroes, and the actions of men were his theme; and his hope and his dream was to become one among those whose names are recorded in story as the gallant and adventurous benefactors of our species. The saintly soul of Elizabeth shone like a shrine-dedicated lamp in our peaceful home. Her sympathy was ours; her smile, her soft voice, the sweet glance of her celestial eyes, were ever there to bless and animate us. She was the living spirit of love to soften and attract; I might have become sullen in my study,

live like angels as kids

38 MARY W. SHELLEY

rough through the ardour of my nature, but that she was there to subdue me to a semblance of her own gentleness. And Clerval—could aught ill entrench on the noble spirit of Clerval? Yet he might not have been so perfectly humane, so thoughtful in his generosity, so full of kindness and tenderness amidst his passion for adventurous exploit, had she not unfolded to him the real loveliness of beneficence and made the doing good the end and aim of his soaring ambition.

I feel exquisite pleasure in dwelling on the recollections of childhood, before misfortune had tainted my mind and changed its bright visions of extensive usefulness into gloomy and narrow reflections upon self. Besides, in drawing the picture of my early days, I also record those events which led, by insensible steps, to my after tale of misery, for when I would account to myself for the birth of that passion which afterwards ruled my destiny I find it arise, like a mountain river, from ignoble and almost forgotten sources; but, swelling as it proceeded, it became the torrent which, in its course, has swept away all my hopes and joys.

Natural philosophy is the genius that has regulated my fate; I desire, therefore, in this narration, to state those facts which led to my predilection for that science. When I was thirteen years of age we all went on a party of pleasure to the baths near Thonon; the inclemency of the weather obliged us to remain a day confined to the inn. In this house I chanced to find a volume of the works of Cornelius Agrippa. I opened it with apathy; the theory which he attempts to demonstrate and the wonderful facts which he relates soon changed this feeling into enthusiasm. A new light seemed to dawn upon my mind, and bounding with joy, I communicated my discovery to my father. My father looked carelessly at the title page of my book and said, "Ah! Cornelius Agrippa! My dear Victor, do not waste your time upon this; it is sad trash."

If, instead of this remark, my father had taken the pains to explain to me that the principles of Agrippa had been entirely exploded and that a modern system of science had been introduced which possessed much greater powers than the ancient, because the powers of the latter were chimerical, while those of the former were real and practical, under such circumstances I should certainly have thrown

Agrippa said, and...

...wild fancies

...those writers with delight; they appeared to me treasures known to few besides myself. I have described myself as always having been imbued with a fervent longing to penetrate the secrets of nature. In spite of the intense labour and wonderful discoveries of modern philosophers, I always came from my studies discontented and unsatisfied. Sir Isaac Newton is said to have avowed that he felt like a child picking up shells beside the great and unexplored ocean of truth. Those of his successors in each branch of natural philosophy with whom I was acquainted appeared even to my boy's apprehensions as tyros engaged in the same pursuit.

The untaught peasant beheld the elements around him and was acquainted with their practical uses. The most learned philosopher knew little more. He had partially unveiled the face of Nature, but her immortal lineaments were still a wonder and a mystery. He might dissect, anatomize, and give names; but, not to speak of a final cause, causes in their secondary and tertiary grades were utterly unknown to him. I had gazed upon the fortifications and impediments that seemed to keep human beings from entering the citadel of nature, and rashly and ignorantly I had repined.

But here were books, and here were men who had penetrated deeper and knew more. I took their word for all that they averred, and I became their disciple. It may appear strange that such should arise in the eighteenth century; but while I followed the routine of education in the schools of Geneva, I was, to a great degree, self-taught with regard to my favourite studies. My father was not scientific, and I was left to struggle with a child's blindness, added to a student's thirst for knowledge. Under the guidance of my new preceptors I entered with the greatest diligence into the search of the philosopher's stone and the elixir of life; but the latter soon obtained my undivided attention. Wealth was an inferior object, but what glory would attend the discovery if I could banish disease from the human frame and render man invulnerable to any but a violent death!

Nor were these my only visions. The raising of ghosts or devils was a promise liberally accorded by my favourite authors, the fulfilment of which I most eagerly sought; and if my incantations were always unsuccessful, I attributed the failure rather to my own inexperience and mistake than to a want of skill or fidelity in my instructors. And thus for a time I was occupied by exploded systems, mingling, like an unadept, a thousand contradictory theories and floundering desperately in a very slough of multifarious knowledge, guided by an ardent imagination and childish reasoning, till an accident again changed the current of my ideas.

When I was about fifteen years old we had retired to our house near Belrive, when we witnessed a most violent and terrible thunderstorm. It advanced from behind the mountains of Jura, and the thunder burst at once with frightful loudness from various quarters of the heavens. I remained, while the storm lasted, watching its progress with curiosity and delight. As I stood at the door, on a sudden I beheld a stream of fire issue from an old and beautiful oak which stood about twenty yards from our house; and so soon as the dazzling light vanished, the oak had disappeared, and nothing remained but a blasted stump. When we visited it the next morning, we found the tree shattered in a singular manner. It was not splintered by the shock, but entirely reduced to thin ribbons of wood. I never beheld anything so utterly destroyed.

Before this I was not unacquainted with the more obvious laws of electricity. On this occasion a man of great research in natural philosophy was with us, and excited by this catastrophe, he entered on the explanation of a theory which he had formed on the subject of electricity and galvanism, which was at once new and astonishing to me. All that he said threw greatly into the shade Cornelius Agrippa, Albertus Magnus, and Paracelsus, the lords of my imagination; but by some fatality the overthrow of these men disinclined me to pursue my accustomed studies. It seemed to me as if nothing would or could ever be known. All that

irony of "creator"

worthy of my consideration.

Thus strangely are our souls constructed, and by such slight ligaments are we bound to prosperity or ruin. When I look back, it seems to me as if this almost miraculous change of inclination and will was the immediate suggestion of the guardian angel of my life—the last effort made by the spirit of preservation to avert the storm that was even then hanging in the stars and ready to envelop me. Her victory was announced by an unusual tranquillity and gladness of soul which followed the relinquishing of my ancient and latterly tormenting studies. It was thus that I was to be taught to associate evil with their prosecution, happiness with their disregard.

It was a strong effort of the spirit of good, but it was ineffectual. Destiny was too potent, and her immutable laws had decreed my utter and terrible destruction.

reflects rationalization on destiny

trys to go to rational science bc unbelievable

doesn't know

get marriage

CHAPTER 3

title

agitate

When I had attained the age of seventeen my parents resolved that I should become a student at the university of Ingolstadt. I had hitherto attended the schools of Geneva, but my father thought it necessary for the completion of my education that I should be made acquainted with other customs than those of my native country. My departure was therefore fixed at an early date, but before the day resolved upon could arrive, the first misfortune of my life occurred—an omen, as it were, of my future misery.

Elizabeth had caught the scarlet fever; her illness was severe, and she was in the greatest danger. During her illness many arguments had been urged to persuade my mother to refrain from attending upon her. She had at first yielded to our entreaties, but when she heard that the life of her favourite was menaced, she could no longer control her anxiety. She attended her sickbed; her watchful attentions triumphed over the malignity of the distemper—Elizabeth was saved, but the consequences of this imprudence were fatal to her preserver. On the third day my mother sickened; her fever was accompanied by the most alarming symptoms, and the looks of her medical attendants prognosticated the worst event. On her deathbed the fortitude and benignity of this best of women did not desert her. She joined the hands of Elizabeth and myself. "My children," she said, "my firmest hopes of future happiness were placed on the prospect of your union. This expectation will now be the consolation of your father. Elizabeth, my love, you must supply my place to my younger children. Alas! I regret that I am taken from you; and, happy and beloved as I have been, is it not hard to quit you all? But these are not thoughts befitting me; I will endeavour to resign myself

42

Big strong connection w/ Liz

Mom dies, sympathy

cheerfully to death ...

...eye can have been extinguished and the sound of a voice so familiar and dear to the ear can be hushed, never more to be heard. These are the reflections of the first days; but when the lapse of time proves the reality of the evil, then the actual bitterness of grief commences. Yet from whom has not that rude hand rent away some dear connection? And why should I describe a sorrow which all have felt, and must feel? The time at length arrives when grief is rather an indulgence than a necessity; and the smile that plays upon the lips, although it may be deemed a sacrilege, is not banished. My mother was dead, but we had still duties which we ought to perform; we must continue our course with the rest and learn to think ourselves fortunate whilst one remains whom the spoiler has not seized. *Continues.*

My departure for Ingolstadt, which had been deferred by these events, was now again determined upon. I obtained from my father a respite of some weeks. It appeared to me sacrilege so soon to leave the repose, akin to death, of the house of mourning and to rush into the thick of life. I was new to sorrow, but it did not the less alarm me. I was unwilling to quit the sight of those that remained to me, and above all, I desired to see my sweet Elizabeth in some degree consoled.

She indeed veiled her grief and strove to act the comforter to us all. She looked steadily on life and assumed its duties with courage and zeal. She devoted herself to those whom she had been taught to call her uncle and cousins. Never was she so enchanting as at this time, when she recalled the sunshine of her smiles and spent them upon us. She forgot even her own regret in her endeavours to make us forget.

affection

love for circle

The day of my departure at length arrived. Clerval spent the last evening with us. He had endeavoured to persuade his father to permit him to accompany me and to become my fellow student, but in vain. His father was a narrow-minded trader and saw idleness and ruin in the aspirations and ambition of his son. Henry deeply felt the misfortune of being debarred from a liberal education. He said little, but when he spoke I read in his kindling eye and in his animated glance a restrained but firm resolve not to be chained to the miserable details of commerce.

We sat late. We could not tear ourselves away from each other nor persuade ourselves to say the word "Farewell!" It was said, and we retired under the pretence of seeking repose, each fancying that the other was deceived; but when at morning's dawn I descended to the carriage which was to convey me away, they were all there— my father again to bless me, Clerval to press my hand once more, my Elizabeth to renew her entreaties that I would write often and to bestow the last feminine attentions on her playmate and friend.

I threw myself into the chaise that was to convey me away and indulged in the most melancholy reflections. I, who had ever been surrounded by amiable companions, continually engaged in endeavoring to bestow mutual pleasure—I was now alone. In the university whither I was going I must form my own friends and be my own protector. My life had hitherto been remarkably secluded and domestic, and this had given me invincible repugnance to new countenances. I loved my brothers, Elizabeth, and Clerval; these were "old familiar faces," but I believed myself totally unfitted for the company of strangers. Such were my reflections as I commenced my journey; but as I proceeded, my spirits and hopes rose. I ardently desired the acquisition of knowledge. I had often, when at home, thought it hard to remain during my youth cooped up in one place and had longed to enter the world and take my station among other human beings. Now my desires were complied with, and it would, indeed, have been folly to repent. *No connection*

I had sufficient leisure for these and many other reflections during my journey to Ingolstadt, which was long and fatiguing. At length the high white steeple of the town met

knowledge sub for friends?

my eyes. I alighted and was cond_____
apartment to spend _____

_____ questions

_____ branches of science
_____ natural philosophy. I replied carelessly, and
partly in contempt, mentioned the names of my alchemists
as the principal authors I had studied. The professor stared.
"Have you," he said, "really spent your time in studying
such nonsense?"

I replied in the affirmative. "Every minute," continued
M. Krempe with warmth, "every instant that you have
wasted on those books is utterly and entirely lost. You
have burdened your memory with exploded systems and
useless names. Good God! In what desert land have you
lived, where no one was kind enough to inform you that
these fancies which you have so greedily imbibed are a
thousand years old and as musty as they are ancient? I
little expected, in this enlightened and scientific age, to find
a disciple of Albertus Magnus and Paracelsus. My dear sir,
you must begin your studies entirely anew."

So saying, he stepped aside and wrote down a list of
several books treating of natural philosophy which he desired me to procure, and dismissed me after mentioning that
in the beginning of the following week he intended to commence a course of lectures upon natural philosophy in its
general relations, and that M. Waldman, a fellow professor,
would lecture upon chemistry the alternate days that he
omitted.

I returned home not disappointed, for I have said that
I had long considered those authors useless whom the professor reprobated; but I returned not at all the more in-
clined to recur to these studies in any shape. M. Krempe
was a little squat man with a gruff voice and a repulsive
countenance; the teacher, therefore, did not prepossess me
in favour of his pursuits. In rather a too philosophical and

connected a strain, perhaps, I have given an account of the conclusions I had come to concerning them in my early years. As a child I had not been content with the results promised by the modern professors of natural science. With a confusion of ideas only to be accounted for by my extreme youth and my want of a guide on such matters, I had retrod the steps of knowledge along the paths of time and exchanged the discoveries of recent inquirers for the dreams of forgotten alchemists. Besides, I had a contempt for the uses of modern natural philosophy. It was very different when the masters of the science sought immortality and power; such views, although futile, were grand; but now the scene was changed. The ambition of the inquirer seemed to limit itself to the annihilation of those visions on which my interest in science was chiefly founded. I was required to exchange chimeras of boundless grandeur for realities of little worth.

Such were my reflections during the first two or three days of my residence at Ingolstadt, which were chiefly spent in becoming acquainted with the localities and the principal residents in my new abode. But as the ensuing week commenced, I thought of the information which M. Krempe had given me concerning the lectures. And although I could not consent to go and hear that little conceited fellow deliver sentences out of a pulpit, I recollected what he had said of M. Waldman, whom I had never seen, as he had hitherto been out of town.

Partly from curiosity and partly from idleness, I went into the lecturing room, which M. Waldman entered shortly after. This professor was very unlike his colleague. He appeared about fifty years of age, but with an aspect expressive of the greatest benevolence; a few grey hairs covered his temples, but those at the back of his head were nearly black. His person was short but remarkably erect and his voice the sweetest I had ever heard. He began his lecture by a recapitulation of the history of chemistry and the various improvements made by different men of learning, pronouncing with fervour the names of the most distinguished discoverers. He then took a cursory view of the present state of the science and explained many of its elementary terms. After having made a few preparatory ex-

periments, he concluded with a n...
chemistry, the terms of...

"Th...

...They ... ...discovered how the ... the nature of the air we breathe. They ... acquired new and almost unlimited powers; they can command the thunders of heaven, mimic the earthquake, and even mock the invisible world with its own shadows."

Such were the professor's words—rather let me say such the words of the fate—enounced to destroy me. As he went on I felt as if my soul were grappling with a palpable enemy; one by one the various keys were touched which formed the mechanism of my being; chord after chord was sounded, and soon my mind was filled with one thought, one conception, one purpose. So much has been done, exclaimed the soul of Frankenstein—more, far more, will I achieve; treading in the steps already marked, I will pioneer a new way, explore unknown powers, and unfold to the world the deepest mysteries of creation.

I closed not my eyes that night. My internal being was in a state of insurrection and turmoil; I felt that order would thence arise, but I had no power to produce it. By degrees, after the morning's dawn, sleep came. I awoke, and my yesternight's thoughts were as a dream. There only remained a resolution to return to my ancient studies and to devote myself to a science for which I believed myself to possess a natural talent. On the same day I paid M. Waldman a visit. His manners in private were even more mild and attractive than in public, for there was a certain dignity in his mien during his lecture which in his own house was replaced by the greatest affability and kindness. I gave him pretty nearly the same account of my former pursuits as I had given to his fellow professor. He heard with attention the little narration concerning my studies and smiled at the names of Cornelius Agrippa and Paracelsus, but without the contempt that M.

Krempe had exhibited. He said that "These were men to whose indefatigable zeal modern philosophers were indebted for most of the foundations of their knowledge. They had left to us, as an easier task, to give new names and arrange in connected classifications the facts which they in a great degree had been the instruments of bringing to light. The labours of men of genius, however erroneously directed, scarcely ever fail in ultimately turning to the solid advantage of mankind." I listened to his statement, which was delivered without any presumption or affectation, and then added that his lecture had removed my prejudices against modern chemists; I expressed myself in measured terms, with the modesty and deference due from a youth to his instructor, without letting escape (inexperience in life would have made me ashamed) any of the enthusiasm which stimulated my intended labours. I requested his advice concerning the books I ought to procure.

"I am happy," said M. Waldman, "to have gained a disciple; and if your application equals your ability, I have no doubt of your success. Chemistry is that branch of natural philosophy in which the greatest improvements have been and may be made; it is on that account that I have made it my peculiar study; but at the same time, I have not neglected the other branches of science. A man would make but a very sorry chemist if he attended to that department of human knowledge alone. If your wish is to become really a man of science and not merely a petty experimentalist, I should advise you to apply to every branch of natural philosophy, including mathematics."

He then took me into his laboratory and explained to me the uses of his various machines, instructing me as to what I ought to procure and promising me the use of his own when I should have advanced far enough in the science not to derange their mechanism. He also gave me the list of books which I had requested, and I took my leave.

Thus ended a day memorable to me; it decided my future destiny.

philosophy, and particularly chemistry, in the most comprehensive sense of the term, became nearly my sole occupation. I read with ardour those works, so full of genius and discrimination, which modern inquirers have written on these subjects. I attended the lectures and cultivated the acquaintance of the men of science of the university, and I found even in M. Krempe a great deal of sound sense and real information, combined, it is true, with a repulsive physiognomy and manners, but not on that account the less valuable. In M. Waldman I found a true friend. His gentleness was never tinged by dogmatism, and his instructions were given with an air of frankness and good nature that banished every idea of pedantry. In a thousand ways he smoothed for me the path of knowledge and made the most abstruse inquiries clear and facile to my apprehension. My application was at first fluctuating and uncertain; it gained strength as I proceeded and soon became so ardent and eager that the stars often disappeared in the light of morning whilst I was yet engaged in my laboratory.

As I applied so closely, it may be easily conceived that my progress was rapid. My ardour was indeed the astonishment of the students, and my proficiency that of the masters. Professor Krempe often asked me, with a sly smile, how Cornelius Agrippa went on, whilst M. Waldman expressed the most heartfelt exultation in my progress. Two years passed in this manner, during which I paid no visit to Geneva, but was engaged, heart and soul, in the pursuit of some discoveries which I hoped to make. None but those who have experienced them can conceive of the enticements of science. In other studies you go as far as others have gone before you, and there is nothing more to know; but in a scientific pursuit there is continual food for discovery and wonder. A mind of moderate capacity which closely pursues one study must infallibly arrive at great proficiency in that study; and I, who continually sought the attainment of one object of pursuit and was solely wrapped up in this, improved so rapidly that at the end of two years I made some discoveries in the improvement of some chemical instruments, which procured me great esteem and admiration at the university. When I had arrived at this point and had become as well acquainted with the theory and practice of natural philosophy as depended on the lessons of any of the professors at Ingolstadt, my residence there being no longer conducive to my improvements, I thought of returning to my friends and my native town, when an incident happened that protracted my stay.

One of the phenomena which had peculiarly attracted my attention was the structure of the human frame, and, indeed, any animal endued with life. Whence, I often asked myself, did the principle of life proceed? It was a bold question, and one which has ever been considered as a mystery; yet with how many things are we upon the brink of becoming acquainted, if cowardice or carelessness did not restrain our inquiries. I revolved these circumstances in my mind and determined thenceforth to apply myself more particularly to those branches of natural philosophy which relate to physiology. Unless I had been animated by an almost supernatural enthusiasm, my application to this study would have been irksome and almost intolerable. To examine the causes of life, we must first have recourse to death. I became acquainted with the science of anatomy, but this was not sufficient; I must also observe the natural decay and corruption of the human body. In my education my father had taken the greatest precautions that my mind should be impressed with no supernatural horrors. I do not ever remember to have trembled at a tale of superstition or to have feared the apparition of a spirit. Darkness had no effect upon my fancy, and a churchyard was to me merely the receptacle of bodies deprived of life, which, from being the seat of beauty and strength, had become food for the worm. Now I was led to examine the cause and progress of this decay and forced to spend days and nights in vaults and charnel-houses. My attention was fixed upon every object the most insupportable to

weird getting a bit sick — loss
connections w/ humanity feelings

the delicacy of the h...

...ng so many men

...who had directed their inquiries towards the same science, that I alone should be reserved to discover so astonishing a secret.

Remember, I am not recording the vision of a madman. The sun does not more certainly shine in the heavens than that which I now affirm is true. Some miracle might have produced it, yet the stages of the discovery were distinct and probable. After days and nights of incredible labour and fatigue, I succeeded in discovering the cause of generation and life; nay, more, I became myself capable of bestowing animation upon lifeless matter.

The astonishment which I had at first experienced on this discovery soon gave place to delight and rapture. After so much time spent in painful labour, to arrive at once at the summit of my desires was the most gratifying consummation of my toils. But this discovery was so great and overwhelming that all the steps by which I had been progressively led to it were obliterated, and I beheld only the result. What had been the study and desire of the wisest men since the creation of the world was now within my grasp. Not that, like a magic scene, it all opened upon me at once: the information I had obtained was of a nature rather to direct my endeavours so soon as I should point them towards the object of my search than to exhibit that object already accomplished. I was like the Arabian who had been buried with the dead and found a passage to life, aided only by one glimmering and seemingly ineffectual light.

I see by your eagerness and the wonder and hope which your eyes express, my friend, that you expect to be informed of the secret with which I am acquainted; that cannot be; listen patiently until the end of my story, and you will easily perceive why I am reserved upon that subject. I will not

the discovery

lead you on, unguarded and ardent as I then was, to your destruction and infallible misery. Learn from me, if not by my precepts, at least by my example, how dangerous is the acquirement of knowledge and how much happier that man is who believes his native town to be the world, than he who aspires to become greater than his nature will allow.

When I found so astonishing a power placed within my hands, I hesitated a long time concerning the manner in which I should employ it. Although I possessed the capacity of bestowing animation, yet to prepare a frame for the reception of it, with all its intricacies of fibres, muscles, and veins, still remained a work of inconceivable difficulty and labour. I doubted at first whether I should attempt the creation of a being like myself, or one of simpler organization; but my imagination was too much exalted by my first success to permit me to doubt of my ability to give life to an animal as complex and wonderful as man. The materials at present within my command hardly appeared adequate to so arduous an undertaking, but I doubted not that I should ultimately succeed. I prepared myself for a multitude of reverses; my operations might be incessantly baffled, and at last my work be imperfect, yet when I considered the improvement which every day takes place in science and mechanics, I was encouraged to hope my present attempts would at least lay the foundations of future success. Nor could I consider the magnitude and complexity of my plan as any argument of its impracticability. It was with these feelings that I began the creation of a human being. As the minuteness of the parts formed a great hindrance to my speed, I resolved, contrary to my first intention, to make the being of a gigantic stature, that is to say, about eight feet in height, and proportionably large. After having formed this determination and having spent some months in successfully collecting and arranging my materials, I began.

No one can conceive the variety of feelings which bore me onwards, like a hurricane, in the first enthusiasm of success. Life and death appeared to me ideal bounds, which I should first break through, and pour a torrent of light into our dark world. A new species would bless me as its creator and source; many happy and excellent natures would owe their being to me. No father could claim the gratitude of his child so completely as I should deserve theirs. Pursuing these reflections. I thought that if

...pe to which I had dedicated myself; and the moon gazed on my midnight labours, while, with unrelaxed and breathless eagerness, I pursued nature to her hiding-places. Who shall conceive the horrors of my secret toil as I dabbled among the unhallowed damps of the grave or tortured the living animal to animate the lifeless clay? My limbs now tremble, and my eyes swim with the remembrance; but then a resistless and almost frantic impulse urged me forward; I seemed to have lost all soul or sensation but for this one pursuit. It was indeed but a passing trance, that only made me feel with renewed acuteness so soon as, the unnatural stimulus ceasing to operate, I had returned to my old habits. I collected bones from charnel-houses and disturbed, with profane fingers, the tremendous secrets of the human frame. In a solitary chamber, or rather cell, at the top of the house, and separated from all the other apartments by a gallery and staircase, I kept my workshop of filthy creation; my eyeballs were starting from their sockets in attending to the details of my employment. The dissecting room and the slaughter-house furnished many of my materials; and often did my human nature turn with loathing from my occupation, whilst, still urged on by an eagerness which perpetually increased, I brought my work near to a conclusion.

The summer months passed while I was thus engaged, heart and soul, in one pursuit. It was a most beautiful season; never did the fields bestow a more plentiful harvest or the vines yield a more luxuriant vintage, but my eyes were insensible to the charms of nature. And the same feelings which made me neglect the scenes around me caused me also to forget those friends who were so many miles absent, and whom I had not seen for so long a time. I knew my silence disquieted them, and I well remembered the words of my father: "I know that while you are pleased with yourself you will think of us with affection, and we shall hear regularly from you. You must pardon me if I regard any interruption in your correspondence as a proof that your other duties are equally neglected."

I knew well therefore what would be my father's feelings, but I could not tear my thoughts from my employment, loathsome in itself, but which had taken an irresistible hold of my imagination. I wished, as it were, to procrastinate all that related to my feelings of affection until the great object, which swallowed up every habit of my nature, should be completed.

I then thought that my father would be unjust if he ascribed my neglect to vice or faultiness on my part, but I am now convinced that he was justified in conceiving that I should not be altogether free from blame. A human being in perfection ought always to preserve a calm and peaceful mind and never to allow passion or a transitory desire to disturb his tranquillity. I do not think that the pursuit of knowledge is an exception to this rule. If the study to which you apply yourself has a tendency to weaken your affections and to destroy your taste for those simple pleasures in which no alloy can possibly mix, then that study is certainly unlawful, that is to say, not befitting the human mind. If this rule were always observed; if no man allowed any pursuit whatsoever to interfere with the tranquillity of his domestic affections, Greece had not been enslaved, Caesar would have spared his country, America would have been discovered more gradually, and the empires of Mexico and Peru had not been destroyed.

But I forget that I am moralizing in the most interesting part of my tale, and your looks remind me to proceed.

My father made no reproach in his letters and only took notice of my silence by inquiring into my occupations more particularly than before. Winter, spring, and summer passed away during my labours; but I did not watch the blossom or the expanding leaves—sights which before always yielded me supreme delight—so deeply was I engrossed in my occupation. The leaves of that year had withered before my work drew near to a close, and now every day showed me more plainly how well I had succeeded. But my enthusiasm was checked by my anxiety, and I appeared rather like one doomed by

guilt already eating at him knows

should be complete.

looking ahead to
finishing as a release
like — birth or ejaculation

covering
up problems
losing
self.

Is knowledge
worth
it?

CHAPTER 5

It was on a dreary night of November that I beheld the accomplishment of my toils. With an anxiety that almost amounted to agony, I collected the instruments of life around me, that I might infuse a spark of being into the lifeless thing that lay at my feet. It was already one in the morning; the rain pattered dismally against the panes, and my candle was nearly burnt out, when, by the glimmer of the half-extinguished light, I saw the dull yellow eye of the creature open; it breathed hard, and a convulsive motion agitated its limbs.

How can I describe my emotions at this catastrophe, or how delineate the wretch whom with such infinite pains and care I had endeavoured to form? His limbs were in proportion, and I had selected his features as beautiful. Beautiful! Great God! His yellow skin scarcely covered the work of muscles and arteries beneath; his hair was of a lustrous black, and flowing; his teeth of a pearly whiteness; but these luxuriances only formed a more horrid contrast with his watery eyes, that seemed almost of the same colour as the dun-white sockets in which they were set, his shrivelled complexion and straight black lips.

The different accidents of life are not so changeable as the feelings of human nature. I had worked hard for nearly two years, for the sole purpose of infusing life into an inanimate body. For this I had deprived myself of rest and health. I had desired it with an ardour that far exceeded moderation; but now that I had finished, the beauty of the dream vanished, and breathless horror and disgust filled my heart. Unable to endure the aspect of the being I had created, I rushed out of the room and continued a long time traversing my bedchamber, unable to compose my mind to sleep. At length lassitude succeeded to the tumult I had before endured, and I

Disappointed

threw myself on the bed in

…horror, a cold dew covered my forehead, my teeth chattered, and every limb became convulsed; when, by the dim and yellow light of the moon, as it forced its way through the window shutters, I beheld the wretch—the miserable monster whom I had created. He held up the curtain of the bed; and his eyes, if eyes they may be called, were fixed on me. His jaws opened, and he muttered some inarticulate sounds, while a grin wrinkled his cheeks. He might have spoken, but I did not hear; one hand was stretched out, seemingly to detain me, but I escaped and rushed downstairs. I took refuge in the courtyard belonging to the house which I inhabited, where I remained during the rest of the night, walking up and down in the greatest agitation, listening attentively, catching and fearing each sound as if it were to announce the approach of the demoniacal corpse to which I had so miserably given life.

Oh! No mortal could support the horror of that countenance. A mummy again endued with animation could not be so hideous as that wretch. I had gazed on him while unfinished; he was ugly then, but when those muscles and joints were rendered capable of motion, it became a thing such as even Dante could not have conceived. inferno

I passed the night wretchedly. Sometimes my pulse beat so quickly and hardly that I felt the palpitation of every artery; at others, I nearly sank to the ground through languor and extreme weakness. Mingled with this horror, I felt the bitterness of disappointment; dreams that had been my food and pleasant rest for so long a space were now become a hell to me; and the change was so rapid, the overthrow so complete!

Morning, dismal and wet, at length dawned and discovered to my sleepless and aching eyes the church of In-

first meeting → mon reaction

golstadt, its white steeple and clock, which indicated the sixth
hour. The porter opened the gates of the court, which had
that night been my asylum, and I issued into the streets, pacing
them with quick steps, as if I sought to avoid the wretch
whom I feared every turning of the street would present to
my view. I did not dare return to the apartment which I inhabited, but felt impelled to hurry on, although drenched
by the rain which poured from a black and comfortless sky.

I continued walking in this manner for some time, endeavouring by bodily exercise to ease the load that weighed
upon my mind. I traversed the streets without any clear
conception of where I was or what I was doing. My heart
palpitated in the sickness of fear, and I hurried on with irregular steps, not daring to look about me:

> Like one who, on a lonely road,
>   Doth walk in fear and dread,
> And, having once turned round, walks on,
>   And turns no more his head;
> Because he knows a frightful fiend
>   Doth close behind him tread.*

Continuing thus, I came at length opposite to the inn at
which the various diligences and carriages usually stopped.
Here I paused, I knew not why; but I remained some minutes
with my eyes fixed on a coach that was coming towards me
from the other end of the street. As it drew nearer I observed
that it was the Swiss diligence; it stopped just where I was
standing, and on the door being opened, I perceived Henry
Clerval, who, on seeing me, instantly sprung out. "My dear
Frankenstein," exclaimed he, "how glad I am to see you! How
fortunate that you should be here at the very moment of my
alighting!"

Nothing could equal my delight on seeing Clerval; his
presence brought back to my thoughts my father, Elizabeth,
and all those scenes of home so dear to my recollection. I
grasped his hand, and in a moment forgot my horror and
misfortune; I felt suddenly, and for the first time during many
months, calm and serene joy. I welcomed my friend, therefore, in the most cordial manner, and we walked towards
my college. Clerval continued talking for some time about our

*Coleridge's "Ancient Mariner."

mutual friends and his own good f———
to come to I———

———earning,
————rtake a voyage of dis-
———nd of knowledge."

"It gives me the greatest delight to see you; but tell me how you left my father, brothers, and Elizabeth."

"Very well, and very happy, only a little uneasy that they hear from you so seldom. By the by, I mean to lecture you a little upon their account myself. But, my dear Frankenstein," continued he, stopping short and gazing full in my face, "I did not before remark how very ill you appear; so thin and pale; you look as if you had been watching for several nights."

"You have guessed right; I have lately been so deeply engaged in one occupation that I have not allowed myself sufficient rest, as you see; but I hope, I sincerely hope, that all these employments are now at an end and that I am at length free."

Free of self?

I trembled excessively; I could not endure to think of, and far less to allude to, the occurrences of the preceding night. I walked with a quick pace, and we soon arrived at my college. I then reflected, and the thought made me shiver, that the creature whom I had left in my apartment might still be there, alive and walking about. I dreaded to behold this monster, but I feared still more that Henry should see him. Entreating him, therefore, to remain a few minutes at the bottom of the stairs, I darted up towards my own room. My hand was already on the lock of the door before I recollected myself. I then paused, and a cold shivering came over me. I threw the door forcibly open, as children are accustomed to do when they expect a spectre to stand in waiting for them on the other side; but nothing appeared. I stepped fearfully in: the apartment was empty, and my bedroom was also freed from its hideous guest. I could hardly believe that so great a good fortune could have befallen me, but when I became assured that my enemy had indeed fled, I clapped my hands for joy and ran down to Clerval.

We ascended into my room, and the servant presently brought breakfast; but I was unable to contain myself. It was not joy only that possessed me; I felt my flesh tingle with excess of sensitiveness, and my pulse beat rapidly. I was unable to remain for a single instant in the same place; I jumped over the chairs, clapped my hands, and laughed aloud. Clerval at first attributed my unusual spirits to joy on his arrival, but when he observed me more attentively, he saw a wildness in my eyes for which he could not account, and my loud, unrestrained, heartless laughter frightened and astonished him.

"My dear Victor," cried he, "what, for God's sake, is the matter? Do not laugh in that manner. How ill you are! What is the cause of all this?"

"Do not ask me," cried I, putting my hands before my eyes, for I thought I saw the dreaded spectre glide into the room; "*he* can tell. Oh, save me! Save me!" I imagined that the monster seized me; I struggled furiously and fell down in a fit.

Poor Clerval! What must have been his feelings? A meeting, which he anticipated with such joy, so strangely turned to bitterness. But I was not the witness of his grief, for I was lifeless and did not recover my senses for a long, long time.

This was the commencement of a nervous fever which confined me for several months. During all that time Henry was my only nurse. I afterwards learned that, knowing my father's advanced age and unfitness for so long a journey, and how wretched my sickness would make Elizabeth, he spared them this grief by concealing the extent of my disorder. He knew that I could not have a more kind and attentive nurse than himself; and, firm in the hope he felt of my recovery, he did not doubt that, instead of doing harm, he performed the kindest action that he could towards them.

But I was in reality very ill, and surely nothing but the unbounded and unremitting attentions of my friend could have restored me to life. The form of the monster on whom I had bestowed existence was forever before my eyes, and I raved incessantly concerning him. Doubtless my words surprised Henry; he at first believed them to be the wanderings of my disturbed imagination

_____ was a di-

_____on contributed greatly to my con-

valescence. I felt also sentiments of joy and affection revive in my bosom; my gloom disappeared, and in a short time I became as cheerful as before I was attacked by the fatal passion.

"Dearest Clerval," exclaimed I, "how kind, how very good you are to me. This whole winter, instead of being spent in study, as you promised yourself, has been consumed in my sick room. How shall I ever repay you? I feel the greatest remorse for the disappointment of which I have been the occasion, but you will forgive me."

"You will repay me entirely if you do not discompose yourself, but get well as fast as you can; and since you appear in such good spirits, I may speak to you on one subject, may I not?"

I trembled. One subject! What could it be? Could he allude to an object on whom I dared not even think?

"Compose yourself," said Clerval, who observed my change of colour, "I will not mention it if it agitates you; but your father and cousin would be very happy if they received a letter from you in your own handwriting. They hardly know how ill you have been and are uneasy at your long silence."

"Is that all, my dear Henry? How could you suppose that my first thought would not fly towards those dear, dear friends whom I love and who are so deserving of my love?"

"If this is your present temper, my friend, you will perhaps be glad to see a letter that has been lying here some days for you; it is from your cousin, I believe."

CHAPTER 6

Clerval then put the following letter into my hands. It was from my own Elizabeth:

My dearest Cousin,

You have been ill, very ill, and even the constant letters of dear kind Henry are not sufficient to reassure me on your account. You are forbidden to write—to hold a pen; yet one word from you, dear Victor, is necessary to calm our apprehensions. For a long time I have thought that each post would bring this line, and my persuasions have restrained my uncle from undertaking a journey to Ingolstadt. I have prevented his encountering the inconveniences and perhaps dangers of so long a journey, yet how often have I regretted not being able to perform it myself! I figure to myself that the task of attending on your sickbed has devolved on some mercenary old nurse, who could never guess your wishes nor minister to them with the care and affection of your poor cousin. Yet that is over now: Clerval writes that indeed you are getting better. I eagerly hope that you will confirm this intelligence soon in your own handwriting.

Get well—and return to us. You will find a happy, cheerful home and friends who love you dearly. Your father's health is vigorous, and he asks but to see you, but to be assured that you are well; and not a care will ever cloud his benevolent countenance. How pleased you would be to remark the improvement of our Ernest! He is now sixteen and full of activity and spirit. He is desirous to be a true Swiss and to enter into foreign service, but we cannot part with him, at least until his elder brother return to us. My uncle is not pleased with the idea of a military career in a distant country, but Ernest never had your powers of application. He looks upon study as an odious fetter; his time is spent in the open air, climb-

more paren-
child s...

ing the hills or rowing on the lak...
come an idler unless we ...
enter on the prof...
Little ...

...ound
...ken place in
...ber on what occasion
...family? Probably you do not;
...story, therefore, in a few words. Ma-
...z, her mother, was a widow with four children,
...whom Justine was the third. This girl had always been
the favourite of her father, but through a strange per-
versity, her mother could not endure her, and after the
death of M. Moritz, treated her very ill. My aunt observed
this, and when Justine was twelve years of age, prevailed
on her mother to allow her to live at our house. The
republican institutions of our country have produced
simpler and happier manners than those which prevail in
the great monarchies that surround it. Hence there is less
distinction between the several classes of its inhabitants;
and the lower orders, being neither so poor nor so despised, their manners are more refined and moral. A servant in Geneva does not mean the same thing as a
servant in France and England. Justine, thus received in
our family, learned the duties of a servant, a condition
which, in our fortunate country, does not include the
idea of ignorance and a sacrifice of the dignity of a human being.

Justine, you may remember, was a great favourite of
yours; and I recollect you once remarked that if you were
in an ill humour, one glance from Justine could dissipate it, for the same reason that Ariosto gives concerning
the beauty of Angelica—she looked so frank-hearted and
happy. My aunt conceived a great attachment for her, by
which she was induced to give her an education superior
to that which she had at first intended. This benefit was
fully repaid; Justine was the most grateful little creature
in the world: I do not mean that she made any profes-
sions; I never heard one pass her lips, but you could see
by her eyes that she almost adored her protectress. Although her disposition was gay and in many respects

More
simil...
issues

Why Appearance

inconsiderate, yet she paid the greatest attention to every gesture of my aunt. She thought her the model of all excellence and endeavoured to imitate her phraseology and manners, so that even now she often reminds me of her.

When my dearest aunt died everyone was too much occupied in their own grief to notice poor Justine, who had attended her during her illness with the most anxious affection. Poor Justine was very ill, but other trials were reserved for her.

One by one, her brothers and sister died; and her mother, with the exception of her neglected daughter, was left childless. The conscience of the woman was troubled; she began to think that the deaths of her favourites was a judgment from heaven to chastise her partiality. She was a Roman Catholic, and I believe her confessor confirmed the idea which she had conceived. Accordingly, a few months after your departure for Ingolstadt, Justine was called home by her repentant mother. Poor girl! She wept when she quitted our house; she was much altered since the death of my aunt; grief had given softness and a winning mildness to her manners which had before been remarkable for vivacity. Nor was her residence at her mother's house of a nature to restore her gaiety. The poor woman was very vacillating in her repentance. She sometimes begged Justine to forgive her unkindness but much oftener accused her of having caused the deaths of her brothers and sister. Perpetual fretting at length threw Madame Moritz into a decline, which at first increased her irritability, but she is now at peace forever. She died on the first approach of cold weather, at the beginning of this last winter. Justine has returned to us, and I assure you I love her tenderly. She is very clever and gentle and extremely pretty; as I mentioned before, her mien and her expressions continually remind me of my dear aunt.

I must say also a few words to you, my dear cousin, of little darling William. I wish you could see him; he is very tall of his age, with sweet laughing blue eyes, dark eyelashes, and curling hair. When he smiles, two little dimples appear on each cheek, which are rosy with health. He has already had one or two little *wives*, but Louisa Biron is his favourite, a pretty little girl of five years of age.

Now, dear Victor, I dare say you wish to be indulged in a little gossip concerning the good people of Geneva. The pretty Miss Mansfield has already received the con-

gratulatory visits on her approachi~
young Englishman, John M~
Manon, married ~
autumn ~

~ cousin;
~ conclude. Write,
~e word will be a blessing to
~anks to Henry for his kindness, his
~, and his many letters; we are sincerely grateful.
Adieu! My cousin, take care of yourself, and, I entreat
you, write!

Elizabeth Lavenza

Geneva, March 18th, 17—

"Dear, dear Elizabeth!" I exclaimed when I had read her letter. "I will write instantly and relieve them from the anxiety they must feel." I wrote, and this exertion greatly fatigued me; but my convalescence had commenced, and proceeded regularly. In another fortnight I was able to leave my chamber.

One of my first duties on my recovery was to introduce Clerval to the several professors of the university. In doing this, I underwent a kind of rough usage, ill befitting the wounds that my mind had sustained. Ever since the fatal night, the end of my labours, and the beginning of my misfortunes, I had conceived a violent antipathy even to the name of natural philosophy. When I was otherwise quite restored to health, the sight of a chemical instrument would renew all the agony of my nervous symptoms. Henry saw this and had removed all my apparatus from my view. He had also changed my apartment, for he perceived that I had acquired a dislike for the room which had previously been my laboratory. But these cares of Clerval were made of no avail when I visited the professors. M. Waldman inflicted torture when he praised, with kindness and warmth, the astonishing progress I had made in the sciences. He soon perceived that I disliked the subject, but not guessing the real cause, he attributed my feelings to modesty and changed the subject from my improvement to the science itself, with a desire, as I evidently saw, of drawing me out. What could I do? He meant to please, and he tormented me. I felt as if he had placed carefully, one by one, in my view those instruments which were to be afterwards used in putting me to a slow and cruel death. I writhed under his words yet dared not exhibit the pain I felt. Clerval, whose eyes and feelings were always quick in discerning the sensations of others, declined the subject, alleging, in excuse, his total ignorance; and the conversation took a more general turn. I thanked my friend from my heart, but I did not speak. I saw plainly that he was surprised, but he never attempted to draw my secret from me; and although I loved him with a mixture of affection and reverence that knew no bounds, yet I could never persuade myself to confide to him that event which was so often present to my recollection but which I feared the detail to another would only impress more deeply.

M. Krempe was not equally docile; and in my condition at that time, of almost insupportable sensitiveness, his harsh, blunt encomiums gave me even more pain than the benevolent approbation of M. Waldman. "D—n the fellow!" cried he. "Why, M. Clerval, I assure you he has outstripped us all. Ay, stare if you please; but it is nevertheless true. A youngster who, but a few years ago, believed in Cornelius Agrippa as firmly as in the Gospel, has now set himself at the head of the university; and if he is not soon pulled down, we shall all be out of countenance. Ay, ay," continued he, observing my face expressive of suffering, "M. Frankenstein is modest, an excellent quality in a young man. Young men should be diffident of themselves, you know, M. Clerval; I was myself when young, but that wears out in a very short time."

M. Krempe had now commenced a eulogy on himself, which happily turned the conversation from a subject that was so annoying to me.

Clerval had never sympathized in my tastes for natural science, and his literary pursuits differed wholly from those which had occupied me. He came to the university with the design of making himself complete master of the Oriental languages, as thus he should open a field for the plan of life he had marked out for himself. Resolved to pursue no inglorious career, he turned his eyes towards the East as affording scope for his spirit of

repaid my labours. Their melancholy is soothing, and their joy elevating, to a degree I never experienced in studying the authors of any other country. When you read their writings, life appears to consist in a warm sun and a garden of roses, in the smiles and frowns of a fair enemy, and the fire that consumes your own heart. How different from the manly and heroical poetry of Greece and Rome!

Summer passed away in these occupations, and my return to Geneva was fixed for the latter end of autumn; but being delayed by several accidents, winter and snow arrived, the roads were deemed impassable, and my journey was retarded until the ensuing spring. I felt this delay very bitterly, for I longed to see my native town and my beloved friends. My return had only been delayed so long from an unwillingness to leave Clerval in a strange place before he had become acquainted with any of its inhabitants. The winter, however, was spent cheerfully, and although the spring was uncommonly late, when it came its beauty compensated for its dilatoriness.

The month of May had already commenced, and I expected the letter daily which was to fix the date of my departure, when Henry proposed a pedestrian tour in the environs of Ingolstadt, that I might bid a personal farewell to the country I had so long inhabited. I acceded with pleasure to this proposition: I was fond of exercise, and Clerval had always been my favourite companion in the rambles of this nature that I had taken among the scenes of my native country.

We passed a fortnight in these perambulations; my health and spirits had long been restored, and they gained additional strength from the salubrious air I breathed, the natural incidents of our progress, and the conversation of my friend. Study had before secluded me from the intercourse of my

praises of fried

fellow creatures and rendered me unsocial, but Clerval called forth the better feelings of my heart; he again taught me to love the aspect of nature and the cheerful faces of children. Excellent friend! How sincerely did you love me and endeavour to elevate my mind until it was on a level with your own! A selfish pursuit had cramped and narrowed me until your gentleness and affection warmed and opened my senses; I became the same happy creature who, a few years ago, loved and beloved by all, had no sorrow or care. When happy, inanimate nature had the power of bestowing on me the most delightful sensations. A serene sky and verdant fields filled me with ecstasy. The present season was indeed divine; the flowers of spring bloomed in the hedges, while those of summer were already in bud. I was undisturbed by thoughts which during the preceding year had pressed upon me, notwithstanding my endeavours to throw them off, with an invincible burden.

Henry rejoiced in my gaiety and sincerely sympathized in my feelings; he exerted himself to amuse me, while he expressed the sensations that filled his soul. The resources of his mind on this occasion were truly astonishing; his conversation was full of imagination, and very often, in imitation of the Persian and Arabic writers, he invented tales of wonderful fancy and passion. At other times he repeated my favourite poems or drew me out into arguments, which he supported with great ingenuity.

We returned to our college on a Sunday afternoon; the peasants were dancing, and everyone we met appeared gay and happy. My own spirits were high, and I bounded along with feelings of unbridled joy and hilarity.

Loves nature

My dear Victor,

You have probably waited impatiently for a letter to fix the date of your return to us, and I was at first tempted to write only a few lines, merely mentioning the day on which I should expect you. But that would be a cruel kindness, and I dare not do it. What would be your surprise, my son, when you expected a happy and glad welcome, to behold, on the contrary, tears and wretchedness? And how, Victor, can I relate our misfortune? Absence cannot have rendered you callous to our joys and griefs, and how shall I inflict pain on my long-absent son? I wish to prepare you for the woeful news, but I know it is impossible; even now your eye skims over the page to seek the words which are to convey to you the horrible tidings.

William is dead! That sweet child, whose smiles delighted and warmed my heart, who was so gentle, yet so gay! Victor, he is murdered!

I will not attempt to console you, but will simply relate the circumstances of the transaction.

Last Thursday (May 7th) I, my niece, and your two brothers went to walk in Plainpalais. The evening was warm and serene, and we prolonged our walk farther than usual. It was already dusk before we thought of returning, and then we discovered that William and Ernest, who had gone on before, were not to be found. We accordingly rested on a seat until they should return. Presently Ernest came and inquired if we had seen his brother; he said that he had been playing with him, that William had run away to hide himself, and that he vainly sought for him, and afterwards waited for him a long time, but that he did not return.

This account rather alarmed us, and we continued to search for him until night fell, when Elizabeth conjectured that he might have returned to the house. He was not there. We returned again, with torches, for I could not rest when I thought that my sweet boy had lost himself and was exposed to all the damps and dews of night; Elizabeth also suffered extreme anguish. About five in the morning I discovered my lovely boy, whom the night before I had seen blooming and active in health, stretched on the grass livid and motionless; the print of the murderer's finger was on his neck.

He was conveyed home, and the anguish that was visible in my countenance betrayed the secret to Elizabeth. She was very earnest to see the corpse. At first I attempted to prevent her, but she persisted, and entering the room where it lay, hastily examined the neck of the victim, and clasping her hands, exclaimed, "Oh, God! I have murdered my darling child!"

She fainted, and was restored with extreme difficulty. When she again lived, it was only to weep and sigh. She told me that that same evening William had teased her to let him wear a very valuable miniature that she possessed of your mother. This picture is gone and was doubtless the temptation which urged the murderer to the deed. We have no trace of him at present, although our exertions to discover him are unremitted; but they will not restore my beloved William!

Come, dearest Victor; you alone can console Elizabeth. She weeps continually and accuses herself unjustly as the cause of his death; her words pierce my heart. We are all unhappy, but will not that be an additional motive for you, my son, to return and be our comforter? Your dear mother! Alas, Victor! I now say, thank God she did not live to witness the cruel, miserable death of her youngest darling!

Come, Victor; not brooding thoughts of vengeance against the assassin, but with feelings of peace and gentleness, that will heal, instead of festering, the wounds of our minds. Enter the house of mourning, my friend, but with kindness and affection for those who love you, and not with hatred for your enemies.

> Your affectionate and afflicted father,
> Alphonse Frankenstein

Geneva, May 12th, 17—

Clerval, who had watched ~~~
letter, was sur~~~

~~~ ion. Tears also
~~~ as he read the account of my

"I can offer you no consolation, my friend," said he; "your disaster is irreparable. What do you intend to do?"

"To go instantly to Geneva; come with me, Henry, to order the horses."

During our walk Clerval endeavoured to say a few words of consolation; he could only express his heartfelt sympathy. "Poor William!" said he. "Dear lovely child, he now sleeps with his angel mother! Who that had seen him bright and joyous in his young beauty but must weep over his untimely loss! To die so miserably, to feel the murderer's grasp! How much more a murderer, that could destroy such radiant innocence! Poor little fellow! One only consolation have we; his friends mourn and weep, but he is at rest. The pang is over, his sufferings are at an end forever. A sod covers his gentle form, and he knows no pain. He can no longer be a subject for pity; we must reserve that for his miserable survivors."

Clerval spoke thus as we hurried through the streets; the words impressed themselves on my mind, and I remembered them afterwards in solitude. But now, as soon as the horses arrived, I hurried into a cabriolet and bade farewell to my friend.

My journey was very melancholy. At first I wished to hurry on, for I longed to console and sympathize with my loved and sorrowing friends; but when I drew near my native town, I slackened my progress. I could hardly sustain the multitude of feelings that crowded into my mind. I passed through scenes familiar to my youth but which I had not seen for nearly six years. How altered everything might be during that time! One sudden and desolating change had taken place; but a thousand little circumstances might have by degrees worked other alterations, which, although they were done more tranquilly, might not be the less decisive. Fear overcame me; I dared not advance, dreading a thousand nameless evils that made me tremble, although I was unable to define them.

I remained two days at Lausanne in this painful state of mind. I contemplated the lake; the waters were placid, all around was calm, and the snowy mountains, "the palaces of nature," were not changed. By degrees the calm and heavenly scene restored me, and I continued my journey towards Geneva.

The road ran by the side of the lake, which became narrower as I approached my native town. I discovered more distinctly the black sides of Jura and the bright summit of Mont Blanc. I wept like a child. "Dear mountains! My own beautiful lake! How do you welcome your wanderer? Your summits are clear; the sky and lake are blue and placid. Is this to prognosticate peace or to mock at my unhappiness?"

I fear, my friend, that I shall render myself tedious by dwelling on these preliminary circumstances, but they were days of comparative happiness, and I think of them with pleasure. My country, my beloved country! Who but a native can tell the delight I took in again beholding thy streams, thy mountains, and more than all, thy lovely lake!

Yet, as I drew nearer home, grief and fear again overcame me. Night also closed around, and when I could hardly see the dark mountains, I felt still more gloomily. The picture appeared a vast and dim scene of evil, and I foresaw obscurely that I was destined to become the most wretched of human beings. Alas! I prophesied truly, and failed only in one single circumstance, that in all the misery I imagined and dreaded, I did not conceive the hundredth part of the anguish I was destined to endure.

It was completely dark when I arrived in the environs of Geneva; the gates of the town were already shut, and I was obliged to pass the night at Secheron, a village at the distance of half a league from the city. The sky was serene, and as I was unable to rest, I resolved to visit the spot where my poor William had been murdered. As I could not pass through the town. I was obliged to

my head. It was echoed from Salêve, the Juras, and the Alps of Savoy; vivid flashes of lightning dazzled my eyes, illuminating the lake, making it appear like a vast sheet of fire; then for an instant everything seemed of a pitchy darkness, until the eye recovered itself from the preceding flash. The storm, as is often the case in Switzerland, appeared at once in various parts of the heavens. The most violent storm hung exactly north of the town, over that part of the lake which lies between the promontory of Belrive and the village of Copêt. Another storm enlightened Jura with faint flashes, and another darkened and sometimes disclosed the Môle, a peaked mountain to the east of the lake.

While I watched the tempest, so beautiful yet terrific, I wandered on with a hasty step. This noble war in the sky elevated my spirits; I clasped my hands and exclaimed aloud, "William, dear angel! This is thy funeral, this thy dirge!" As I said these words, I perceived in the gloom a figure which stole from behind a clump of trees near me; I stood fixed, gazing intently; I could not be mistaken. A flash of lightning illuminated the object and discovered its shape plainly to me; its gigantic stature, and the deformity of its aspect, more hideous than belongs to humanity, instantly informed me that it was the wretch, the filthy demon to whom I had given life. What did he there? Could he be (I shuddered at the conception) the murderer of my brother? No sooner did that idea cross my imagination than I became convinced of its truth; my teeth chattered, and I was forced to lean against a tree for support. The figure passed me quickly, and I lost it in the gloom. Nothing in human shape could have destroyed that fair child. *He* was the murderer! I could not doubt it. The mere presence of the idea was an irresistible proof of the fact. I thought of pursuing the devil, but it would have been in vain, for another flash discovered him to me hanging among the rocks of the nearly perpendicular ascent of Mont Salêve, a hill that bounds Plainpalais on the south. He soon reached the summit and disappeared.

I remained motionless. The thunder ceased, but the rain still continued, and the scene was enveloped in an impenetrable darkness. I revolved in my mind the events which I had until now sought to forget: the whole train of my progress towards the creation, the appearance of the work of my own hands alive at my bedside, its departure. Two years had now nearly elapsed since the night on which he first received life, and was this his first crime? Alas! I had turned loose into the world a depraved wretch whose delight was in carnage and misery; had he not murdered my brother?

No one can conceive the anguish I suffered during the remainder of the night, which I spent, cold and wet, in the open air. But I did not feel the inconvenience of the weather; my imagination was busy in scenes of evil and despair. I considered the being whom I had cast among mankind and endowed with the will and power to effect purposes of horror, such as the deed which he had now done, nearly in the light of my own vampire, my own spirit let loose from the grave and forced to destroy all that was dear to me.

Day dawned, and I directed my steps towards the town. The gates were open, and I hastened to my father's house. My first thought was to discover what I knew of the murderer and cause instant pursuit to be made. But I paused when I reflected on the story that I had to tell. A being whom I myself had formed, and endued with life, had met me at midnight among the precipices of an inaccessible mountain. I remembered also the nervous fever with which I had been seized just at the time that I dated my creation, and which would give an air of delirium to a tale otherwise so utterly improbable. I well knew that if any other had communicated such a relation to me, I should have looked upon it as the ravings of insanity. Besides, the strange nature of the animal would elude all pursuit, even if I were so far credited as to persuade my relatives to commence it. And then of what use would be pursuit? Who could arrest a creature capable of scaling the overhanging sides of Mont Salêve? These reflections determined me, and I resolved to remain silent.

link monster wl himself, decides to keep secret

It was about five in the m~~orning~~

...~~g by the coffin of~~ her dead father. Her garb was rustic and her cheek pale, but there was an air of dignity and beauty that hardly permitted the sentiment of pity. Below this picture was a miniature of William, and my tears flowed when I looked upon it. While I was thus engaged, Ernest entered; he had heard me arrive and hastened to welcome me. He expressed a sorrowful delight to see me. "Welcome, my dearest Victor," said he. "Ah! I wish you had come three months ago, and then you would have found us all joyous and delighted. You come to us now to share a misery which nothing can alleviate; yet your presence will, I hope, revive our father, who seems sinking under his misfortune; and your persuasions will induce poor Elizabeth to cease her vain and tormenting self-accusations. Poor William! He was our darling and our pride!"

Tears, unrestrained, fell from my brother's eyes; a sense of mortal agony crept over my frame. Before, I had only imagined the wretchedness of my desolated home; the reality came on me as a new and a not less terrible disaster. I tried to calm Ernest; I inquired more minutely concerning my father and her I named my cousin.

"She most of all," said Ernest, "requires consolation; she accused herself of having caused the death of my brother, and that made her very wretched. But since the murderer has been discovered——"

"The murderer discovered! Good God! How can that be? Who could attempt to pursue him? It is impossible; one might as well try to overtake the winds or confine a mountain stream with a straw. I saw him too; he was free last night!"

"I do not know what you mean," replied my brother in accents of wonder, "but to us the discovery we have made completes our misery. No one would believe it at first; and

got another suspect — Justine

even now Elizabeth will not be convinced, notwithstanding all the evidence. Indeed, who would credit that Justine Moritz, who was so amiable and fond of all the family, could suddenly become capable of so frightful, so appalling a crime?" *Borys more probs*

"Justine Moritz! Poor, poor girl, is she the accused? But it is wrongfully; everyone knows that; no one believes it, surely, Ernest?"

"No one did at first, but several circumstances came out that have almost forced conviction upon us; and her own behaviour has been so confused as to add to the evidence of facts a weight that, I fear, leaves no hope for doubt. But she will be tried today, and you will then hear all."

He related that, the morning on which the murder of poor William had been discovered, Justine had been taken ill and confined to her bed for several days. During this interval one of the servants, happening to examine the apparel she had worn on the night of the murder, had discovered in her pocket the picture of my mother, which had been judged to be the temptation of the murderer. The servant instantly showed it to one of the others, who, without saying a word to any of the family, went to a magistrate; and, upon their deposition, Justine was apprehended. On being charged with the fact, the poor girl confirmed the suspicion in a great measure by her extreme confusion of manner.

This was a strange tale, but it did not shake my faith, and I replied earnestly, "You are all mistaken; I know the murderer. Justine, poor, good Justine, is innocent."

At that instant my father entered. I saw unhappiness deeply impressed on his countenance, but he endeavoured to welcome me cheerfully, and after we had exchanged our mournful greeting, would have introduced some other topic than that of our disaster, had not Ernest exclaimed, "Good God, Papa! Victor says that he knows who was the murderer of poor William."

"We do also, unfortunately," replied my father; "for indeed I had rather have been forever ignorant than have discovered so much depravity and ingratitude in one I valued so highly."

"My dear father, you are mistaken; Justine is innocent."

"If she is, God forbid that she should suffer as guilty. She

U says J innocent — won't prove th...

is to be tried today, and I hope. I ...
will be acquitted."

This speec...

... convinced
... ...ument of presumption
... I had let loose upon the world?
... ...on joined by Elizabeth. Time had altered her
... I last beheld her; it had endowed her with loveliness surpassing the beauty of her childish years. There was the same candour, the same vivacity, but it was allied to an expression more full of sensibility and intellect. She welcomed me with the greatest affection. "Your arrival, my dear cousin," said she, "fills me with hope. You perhaps will find some means to justify my poor guiltless Justine. Alas! Who is safe, if she be convicted of crime? I rely on her innocence as certainly as I do upon my own. Our misfortune is doubly hard to us; we have not only lost that lovely darling boy, but this poor girl, whom I sincerely love, is to be torn away by even a worse fate. If she is condemned, I never shall know joy more. But she will not, I am sure she will not; and then I shall be happy again, even after the sad death of my little William."

"She is innocent, my Elizabeth," said I, "and that shall be proved; fear nothing, but let your spirits be cheered by the assurance of her acquittal."

"How kind and generous you are! Everyone else believes in her guilt, and that made me wretched, for I knew that it was impossible; and to see everyone else prejudiced in so deadly a manner rendered me hopeless and despairing." She wept.

"Dearest niece," said my father, "dry your tears. If she is, as you believe, innocent, rely on the justice of our laws, and the activity with which I shall prevent the slightest shadow of partiality."

Never will admit

CHAPTER 8

We passed a few sad hours until eleven o'clock, when the
trial was to commence. My father and the rest of the family
being obliged to attend as witnesses, I accompanied them to
the court. During the whole of this wretched mockery of
justice I suffered living torture. It was to be decided whether
the result of my curiosity and lawless devices would cause
the death of two of my fellow beings: one a smiling babe
full of innocence and joy, the other far more dreadfully murdered, with every aggravation of infamy that could make the
murder memorable in horror. Justine also was a girl of
merit and possessed qualities which promised to render her
life happy; now all was to be obliterated in an ignominious
grave, and I the cause! A thousand times rather would I have
confessed myself guilty of the crime ascribed to Justine, but
I was absent when it was committed, and such a declaration
would have been considered as the ravings of a madman and
would not have exculpated her who suffered through me.

The appearance of Justine was calm. She was dressed in
mourning, and her countenance, always engaging, was rendered, by the solemnity of her feelings, exquisitely beautiful.
Yet she appeared confident in innocence and did not tremble,
although gazed on and execrated by thousands, for all the
kindness which her beauty might otherwise have excited was
obliterated in the minds of the spectators by the imagination
of the enormity she was supposed to have committed. She
was tranquil, yet her tranquillity was evidently constrained;
and as her confusion had before been adduced as a proof
of her guilt, she worked up her mind to an appearance of
courage. When she entered the court she threw her eyes
round it and quickly discovered where we were seated. A
tear seemed to dim her eye when she saw us, but she quick-

78

Innocent

ly recovered herself, and a look of ...
to attest her utter guil.....

The tri.....

... not
... en afterwards
... that she did there, but she
... and only returned a confused and un-
... answer. She returned to the house about eight
o'clock, and when one inquired where she had passed the
night, she replied that she had been looking for the child
and demanded earnestly if anything had been heard concerning him. When shown the body, she fell into violent hys-
terics and kept her bed for several days. The picture was
then produced which the servant had found in her pocket; and
when Elizabeth, in a faltering voice, proved that it was the
same which, an hour before the child had been missed, she
had placed round his neck, a murmur of horror and indignation filled the court.

Justine was called on for her defence. As the trial had
proceeded, her countenance had altered. Surprise, horror,
and misery were strongly expressed. Sometimes she struggled with her tears, but when she was desired to plead,
she collected her powers and spoke in an audible although
variable voice.

"God knows," she said, "how entirely I am innocent. But
I do not pretend that my protestations should acquit me; I
rest my innocence on a plain and simple explanation of the
facts which have been adduced against me, and I hope the
character I have always borne will incline my judges to a
favourable interpretation where any circumstance appears
doubtful or suspicious."

She then related that, by the permission of Elizabeth, she
had passed the evening of the night on which the murder
had been committed at the house of an aunt at Chêne, a
village situated at about a league from Geneva. On her return,
at about nine o'clock, she met a man who asked her if she had
seen anything of the child who was lost. She was alarmed by

this account and passed several hours in looking for him, when the gates of Geneva were shut, and she was forced to remain several hours of the night in a barn belonging to a cottage, being unwilling to call up the inhabitants, to whom she was well known. Most of the night she spent here watching; towards morning she believed that she slept for a few minutes; some steps disturbed her, and she awoke. It was dawn, and she quitted her asylum, that she might again endeavour to find my brother. If she had gone near the spot where his body lay, it was without her knowledge. That she had been bewildered when questioned by the market-woman was not surprising, since she had passed a sleepless night and the fate of poor William was yet uncertain. Concerning the picture she could give no account.

"I know," continued the unhappy victim, "how heavily and fatally this one circumstance weighs against me, but I have no power of explaining it; and when I have expressed my utter ignorance, I am only left to conjecture concerning the probabilities by which it might have been placed in my pocket. But here also I am checked. I believe that I have no enemy on earth, and none surely would have been so wicked as to destroy me wantonly. Did the murderer place it there? I know of no opportunity afforded him for so doing; or, if I had, why should he have stolen the jewel, to part with it again so soon?

"I commit my cause to the justice of my judges, yet I see no room for hope. I beg permission to have a few witnesses examined concerning my character, and if their testimony shall not overweigh my supposed guilt, I must be condemned, although I would pledge my salvation on my innocence."

Several witnesses were called who had known her for many years, and they spoke well of her; but fear and hatred of the crime of which they supposed her guilty rendered them timorous and unwilling to come forward. Elizabeth saw even this last resource, her excellent dispositions and irreproachable conduct, about to fail the accused, when, although violently agitated, she desired permission to address the court.

"I am," said she, "the cousin of the unhappy child who was murdered, or rather his sister, for I was educated by and have lived with his parents ever since and even long before his birth. It may therefore be judged indecent in me

Could this turn tide

to come forward on this occasi...
creature about ...

...r own mother

...ner that excited the admira-
...new her, after which she again lived in my
...le's house, where she was beloved by all the family. She was warmly attached to the child who is now dead and acted towards him like a most affectionate mother. For my own part, I do not hesitate to say that, notwithstanding all the evidence produced against her, I believe and rely on her perfect innocence. She had no temptation for such an action; as to the bauble on which the chief proof rests, if she had earnestly desired it, I should have willingly given it to her, so much do I esteem and value her."

A murmer of approbation followed Elizabeth's simple and powerful appeal, but it was excited by her generous inter-ference, and not in favour of poor Justine, on whom the public indignation was turned with renewed violence, charg-ing her with the blackest ingratitude. She herself wept as Elizabeth spoke, but she did not answer. My own agitation and anguish was extreme during the whole trial. I believed in her innocence; I knew it. Could the demon who had (I did not for a minute doubt) murdered my brother also in his hellish sport have betrayed the innocent to death and ignominy? I could not sustain the horror of my situation, and when I perceived that the popular voice and the coun-tenances of the judges had already condemned my unhappy victim, I rushed out of the court in agony. The tortures of the accused did not equal mine; she was sustained by in-nocence, but the fangs of remorse tore my bosom and would not forgo their hold. Has she ig going to clove

I passed a night of unmingled wretchedness. In the morn-ing I went to the court; my lips and throat were parched. I dared not ask the fatal question, but I was known, and the officer guessed the cause of my visit. The ballots had been

megalomania + guilt

thrown; they were all black, and Justine was condemned.

I cannot pretend to describe what I then felt. I had before experienced sensations of horror, and I have endeavoured to bestow upon them adequate expressions, but words cannot convey an idea of the heart-sickening despair that I then endured. The person to whom I addressed myself added that Justine had already confessed her guilt. "That evidence," he observed, "was hardly required in so glaring a case, but I am glad of it; and, indeed, none of our judges like to condemn a criminal upon circumstantial evidence, be it ever so decisive."

This was strange and unexpected intelligence; what could it mean? Had my eyes deceived me? And was I really as mad as the whole world would believe me to be if I disclosed the object of my suspicions? I hastened to return home, and Elizabeth eagerly demanded the result.

"My cousin," replied I, "it is decided as you may have expected; all judges had rather that ten innocent should suffer than that one guilty should escape. But she has confessed."

This was a dire blow to poor Elizabeth, who had relied with firmness upon Justine's innocence. "Alas!" said she. "How shall I ever again believe in human goodness? Justine, whom I loved and esteemed as my sister, how could she put on those smiles of innocence only to betray? Her mild eyes seemed incapable of any severity or guile, and yet she has committed a murder."

Soon after we heard that the poor victim had expressed a desire to see my cousin. My father wished her not to go but said that he left it to her own judgment and feelings to decide. "Yes," said Elizabeth, "I will go, although she is guilty; and you, Victor, shall accompany me; I cannot go alone." The idea of this visit was torture to me, yet I could not refuse.

We entered the gloomy prison chamber and beheld Justine sitting on some straw at the farther end; her hands were manacled, and her head rested on her knees. She rose on seeing us enter, and when we were left alone with her, she threw herself at the feet of Elizabeth, weeping bitterly. My cousin wept also.

"Oh, Justine!" said she. "Why did you rob me of my last consolation? I relied on your innocence, and although I was then very wretched, I was not so miserable as I am now."

evil around → good → evil

"And do you also believe...

confess, but I confessed a lie. I confessed, that I might obtain absolution; but now that falsehood lies heavier at my heart than all my other sins. The God of heaven forgive me! Ever since I was condemned, my confessor has besieged me; he threatened and menaced, until I almost began to think that I was the monster that he said I was. He threatened excommunication and hell fire in my last moments if I continued obdurate. Dear lady, I had none to support me; all looked on me as a wretch doomed to ignominy and perdition. What could I do? In an evil hour I subscribed to a lie; and now only am I truly miserable."

She paused, weeping, and then continued, "I thought with horror, my sweet lady, that you should believe your Justine, whom your blessed aunt had so highly honoured and whom you loved, was a creature capable of a crime which none but the devil himself could have perpetrated. Dear William! Dearest blessed child! I soon shall see you again in heaven, where we shall all be happy; and that consoles me, going as I am to suffer ignominy and death."

"Oh, Justine! Forgive me for having for one moment distrusted you. Why did you confess? But do not mourn, dear girl. Do not fear. I will proclaim, I will prove your innocence. I will melt the stony hearts of your enemies by my tears and prayers. You shall not die! You, my playfellow, my companion, my sister, perish on the scaffold! No! No! I never could survive so horrible a misfortune."

Justine shook her head mournfully. "I do not fear to die," she said; "that pang is past. God raises my weakness and gives me courage to endure the worst. I leave a sad and bitter world; and if you remember me and think of me as of one unjustly condemned, I am resigned to the fate awaiting

Why still try may as well give up

me. Learn from me, dear lady, to submit in patience to the will of heaven!"

During this conversation I had retired to a corner of the prison room, where I could conceal the horrid anguish that possessed me. Despair! Who dared talk of that? The poor victim, who on the morrow was to pass the awful boundary between life and death, felt not, as I did, such deep and bitter agony. I gnashed my teeth and ground them together, uttering a groan that came from my inmost soul. Justine started. When she saw who it was, she approached me and said, "Dear sir, you are very kind to visit me; you, I hope, do not believe that I am guilty?"

I could not answer. "No, Justine," said Elizabeth; "he is more convinced of your innocence than I was, for even when he heard that you had confessed, he did not credit it."

"I truly thank him. In these last moments I feel the sincerest gratitude towards those who think of me with kindness. How sweet is the affection of others to such a wretch as I am! It removes more than half my misfortune, and I feel as if I could die in peace now that my innocence is acknowledged by you, dear lady, and your cousin."

Thus the poor sufferer tried to comfort others and herself. She indeed gained the resignation she desired. But I, the true murderer, felt the never-dying worm alive in my bosom, which allowed of no hope or consolation. Elizabeth also wept and was unhappy, but hers also was the misery of innocence, which, like a cloud that passes over the fair moon, for a while hides but cannot tarnish its brightness. Anguish and despair had penetrated into the core of my heart; I bore a hell within me which nothing could extinguish. We stayed several hours with Justine, and it was with great difficulty that Elizabeth could tear herself away. "I wish," cried she, "that I were to die with you; I cannot live in this world of misery."

Justine assumed an air of cheerfulness, while she with difficulty repressed her bitter tears. She embraced Elizabeth and said in a voice of half-suppressed emotion, "Farewell, sweet lady, dearest Elizabeth, my beloved and only friend; may heaven, in its bounty, bless and preserve you; may this be the last misfortune that you will ever suffer! Live, and be happy, and make others so."

And on the morrow Justine died. Elizabeth's heart-rending eloquence failed to move the judges from their settled conviction in the criminal...

[illegible]

...ne so shining home—all was the work of my thrice-accursed hands! Ye weep, unhappy ones, but these are not your last tears! Again shall you raise the funeral wail, and the sound of your lamentations shall again and again be heard! Frankenstein, your son, your kinsman, your early, much-loved friend; he who would spend each vital drop of blood for your sakes, who has no thought nor sense of joy except as it is mirrored also in your dear countenances, who would fill the air with blessings and spend his life in serving you—he bids you weep, to shed countless tears; happy beyond his hopes, if thus inexorable fate be satisfied, and if the destruction pause before the peace of the grave have succeeded to your sad torments!

Thus spoke my prophetic soul, as, torn by remorse, horror, and despair, I beheld those I loved spend vain sorrow upon the graves of William and Justine, the first hapless victims to my unhallowed arts.

Nothing to do
horrible
brother

V → monster

CHAPTER 9

Nothing is more painful to the human mind than, after the feelings have been worked up by a quick succession of events, the dead calmness of inaction and certainty which follows and deprives the soul both of hope and fear. Justine died, she rested, and I was alive. The blood flowed freely in my veins, but a weight of despair and remorse pressed on my heart which nothing could remove. Sleep fled from my eyes; I wandered like an evil spirit, for I had committed deeds of mischief beyond description horrible, and more, much more (I persuaded myself) was yet behind. Yet my heart overflowed with kindness and the love of virtue. I had begun life with benevolent intentions and thirsted for the moment when I should put them in practice and make myself useful to my fellow beings. Now all was blasted; instead of that serenity of conscience which allowed me to look back upon the past with self-satisfaction, and from thence to gather promise of new hopes, I was seized by remorse and the sense of guilt, which hurried me away to a hell of intense tortures such as no language can describe.

This state of mind preyed upon my health, which had perhaps never entirely recovered from the first shock it had sustained. I shunned the face of man; all sound of joy or complacency was torture to me; solitude was my only consolation—deep, dark, deathlike solitude.

My father observed with pain the alteration perceptible in my disposition and habits and endeavoured by arguments deduced from the feelings of his serene conscience and guiltless life to inspire me with fortitude and awaken in me the courage to dispel the dark cloud which brooded over me. "Do you think, Victor," said he, "that I do not suffer also? No one could love a child more than I loved your brother"

isolated, can't bear happiness for guilt

—tears came into his eyes as he spoke

duty to the survivors that w…

ing their unhapp…

It i…

…could

…pair and endeavour

…we we retired to our house at Belrive. This
…nge was particularly agreeable to me. The shutting of the
gates regularly at ten o'clock and the impossibility of remaining on the lake after that hour had rendered our residence within the walls of Geneva very irksome to me. I was
now free. Often, after the rest of the family had retired for
the night, I took the boat and passed many hours upon the
water. Sometimes, with my sails set, I was carried by the
wind; and sometimes, after rowing into the middle of the
lake, I left the boat to pursue its own course and gave way
to my own miserable reflections. I was often tempted, when
all was at peace around me, and I the only unquiet thing
that wandered restless in a scene so beautiful and heavenly—if I except some bat, or the frogs, whose harsh and interrupted croaking was heard only when I approached the
shore—often, I say, I was tempted to plunge into the silent
lake, that the waters might close over me and my calamities
forever. But I was restrained, when I thought of the heroic
and suffering Elizabeth, whom I tenderly loved, and whose
existence was bound up in mine. I thought also of my father
and surviving brother; should I by my base desertion leave
them exposed and unprotected to the malice of the fiend
whom I had let loose among them?

At these moments I wept bitterly and wished that peace
would revisit my mind only that I might afford them consolation and happiness. But that could not be. Remorse extinguished every hope. I had been the author of unalterable
evils, and I lived in daily fear lest the monster whom I had
created should perpetrate some new wickedness. I had an
obscure feeling that all was not over and that he would still

commit some signal crime, which by its enormity should almost efface the recollection of the past. There was always scope for fear so long as anything I loved remained behind. My abhorrence of this fiend cannot be conceived. When I thought of him I gnashed my teeth, my eyes became inflamed, and I ardently wished to extinguish that life which I had so thoughtlessly bestowed. When I reflected on his crimes and malice, my hatred and revenge burst all bounds of moderation. I would have made a pilgrimage to the highest peak of the Andes, could I when there have precipitated him to their base. I wished to see him again, that I might wreak the utmost extent of abhorrence on his head and avenge the deaths of William and Justine.

Our house was the house of mourning. My father's health was deeply shaken by the horror of the recent events. Elizabeth was sad and desponding; she no longer took delight in her ordinary occupations; all pleasure seemed to her sacrilege toward the dead; eternal woe and tears she then thought was the just tribute she should pay to innocence so blasted and destroyed. She was no longer that happy creature who in earlier youth wandered with me on the banks of the lake and talked with ecstasy of our future prospects. The first of those sorrows which are sent to wean us from the earth had visited her, and its dimming influence quenched her dearest smiles.

"When I reflect, my dear cousin," said she, "on the miserable death of Justine Moritz, I no longer see the world and its works as they before appeared to me. Before, I looked upon the accounts of vice and injustice that I read in books or heard from others as tales of ancient days or imaginary evils; at least they were remote and more familiar to reason than to the imagination; but now misery has come home, and men appear to me as monsters thirsting for each other's blood. Yet I am certainly unjust. Everybody believed that poor girl to be guilty, and if she could have committed the crime for which she suffered, assuredly she would have been the most depraved of human creatures. For the sake of a few jewels, to have murdered the son of her benefactor and friend, a child whom she had nursed from its birth, and appeared to love as if it had been her own! I could not consent to the death of any human being, but certainly I should have thought such a creature unfit to remain in the society of men.

But she was innocent. I know, I feel sh...
are of the same opinion...
when...

...course with the extremest agony. I, ... deed, but in effect, was the true murderer. Elizabeth read my anguish in my countenance, and kindly taking my hand, said, "My dearest friend, you must calm yourself. These events have affected me, God knows how deeply; but I am not so wretched as you are. There is an expression of despair, and sometimes of revenge, in your countenance that makes me tremble. Dear Victor, banish these dark passions. Remember the friends around you, who centre all their hopes in you. Have we lost the power of rendering you happy? Ah! While we love, while we are true to each other, here in this land of peace and beauty, your native country, we may reap every tranquil blessing—what can disturb our peace?"

And could not such words from her whom I fondly prized before every other gift of fortune suffice to chase away the fiend that lurked in my heart? Even as she spoke I drew near to her, as if in terror, lest at that very moment the destroyer had been near to rob me of her.

Thus not the tenderness of friendship, nor the beauty of earth, nor of heaven, could redeem my soul from woe; the very accents of love were ineffectual. I was encompassed by a cloud which no beneficial influence could penetrate. The wounded deer dragging its fainting limbs to some untrodden brake, there to gaze upon the arrow which had pierced it, and to die, was but a type of me.

Sometimes I could cope with the sullen despair that overwhelmed me, but sometimes the whirlwind passions of my soul drove me to seek, by bodily exercise and by change of place, some relief from my intolerable sensations. It was during an access of this kind that I suddenly left my home,

and bending my steps towards the near Alpine valleys, sought
in the magnificence, the eternity of such scenes, to forget
myself and my ephemeral, because human, sorrows. My
wanderings were directed towards the valley of Chamounix.
I had visited it frequently during my boyhood. Six years had
passed since then: *I* was a wreck, but nought had changed
in those savage and enduring scenes.

I performed the first part of my journey on horseback.
I afterwards hired a mule, as the more sure-footed and least
liable to receive injury on these rugged roads. The weather
was fine; it was about the middle of the month of August,
nearly two months after the death of Justine, that miserable
epoch from which I dated all my woe. The weight upon my
spirit was sensibly lightened as I plunged yet deeper in the
ravine of Arve. The immense mountains and precipices
that overhung me on every side, the sound of the river raging
among the rocks, and the dashing of the waterfalls around
spoke of a power mighty as Omnipotence—and I ceased to
fear or to bend before any being less almighty than that
which had created and ruled the elements, here displayed in
their most terrific guise. Still, as I ascended higher, the
valley assumed a more magnificent and astonishing character.
Ruined castles hanging on the precipices of piny mountains,
the impetuous Arve, and cottages every here and there peeping forth from among the trees formed a scene of singular
beauty. But it was augmented and rendered sublime by the
mighty Alps, whose white and shining pyramids and domes
towered above all, as belonging to another earth, the habitations of another race of beings.

I passed the bridge of Pélissier, where the ravine, which
the river forms, opened before me, and I began to ascend the
mountain that overhangs it. Soon after, I entered the valley
of Chamounix. This valley is more wonderful and sublime,
but not so beautiful and picturesque as that of Servox, through
which I had just passed. The high and snowy mountains
were its immediate boundaries, but I saw no more ruined
castles and fertile fields. Immense glaciers approached the
road; I heard the rumbling thunder of the falling avalanche
and marked the smoke of its passage. Mont Blanc, the supreme and magnificent Mont Blanc, raised itself from the
surrounding *aiguilles,* and its tremendous dome overlooked
the valley.

emotions + nature

A tingling long-lost sense of pleas——
during this j————

————— a more
————— ———ew myself on the grass,
————— ——wn by horror and despair.

At length I arrived at the village of Chamounix. Exhaustion succeeded to the extreme fatigue both of body and of mind which I had endured. For a short space of time I remained at the window watching the pallid lightnings that played above Mont Blanc and listening to the rushing of the Arve, which pursued its noisy way beneath. The same lulling sounds acted as a lullaby to my too keen sensations; when I placed my head upon my pillow, sleep crept over me; I felt it as it came and blessed the giver of oblivion.

√ very emotional

CHAPTER 10

I spent the following day roaming through the valley. I stood beside the sources of the Arveiron, which take their rise in a glacier, that with slow pace is advancing down from the summit of the hills to barricade the valley. The abrupt sides of vast mountains were before me; the icy wall of the glacier overhung me; a few shattered pines were scattered around; and the solemn silence of this glorious presence-chamber of imperial nature was broken only by the brawling waves or the fall of some vast fragment, the thunder sound of the avalanche or the cracking, reverberated along the mountains, of the accumulated ice, which, through the silent working of immutable laws, was ever and anon rent and torn, as if it had been but a plaything in their hands. These sublime and magnificent scenes afforded me the greatest consolation that I was capable of receiving. They elevated me from all littleness of feeling, and although they did not remove my grief, they subdued and tranquillized it. In some degree, also, they diverted my mind from the thoughts over which it had brooded for the last month. I retired to rest at night; my slumbers, as it were, waited on and ministered to by the assemblance of grand shapes which I had contemplated during the day. They congregated round me; the unstained snowy mountaintop, the glittering pinnacle, the pine woods, and ragged bare ravine, the eagle, soaring amidst the clouds —they all gathered round me and bade me be at peace.

Where had they fled when the next morning I awoke? All of soul-inspiring fled with sleep, and dark melancholy clouded every thought. The rain was pouring in torrents, and thick mists hid the summits of the mountains, so that I even saw not the faces of those mighty friends. Still I would penetrate their misty veil and seek them in their

cloudy retreats. What were r̶a̶i̶
was brou̶g̶h̶t̶

to go with-
acquainted with the path, and
presence of another would destroy the solitary grandeur
of the scene.

The ascent is precipitous, but the path is cut into continual
and short windings, which enable you to surmount the per-
pendicularity of the mountain. It is a scene terrifically desolate. In a thousand spots the traces of the winter avalanche
may be perceived, where trees lie broken and strewed on the
ground, some entirely destroyed, others bent, leaning upon
the jutting rocks of the mountain or transversely upon other
trees. The path, as you ascend higher, is intersected by ravines
of snow, down which stones continually roll from above;
one of them is particularly dangerous, as the slightest sound,
such as even speaking in a loud voice, produces a concussion
of air sufficient to draw destruction upon the head of the
speaker. The pines are not tall or luxuriant, but they are
sombre and add an air of severity to the scene. I looked
on the valley beneath; vast mists were rising from the rivers
which ran through it and curling in thick wreaths around
the opposite mountains, whose summits were hid in the uniform clouds, while rain poured from the dark sky and added
to the melancholy impression I received from the objects
around me. Alas! Why does man boast of sensibilities superior to those apparent in the brute; it only renders them
more necessary beings. If our impulses were confined to
hunger, thirst, and desire, we might be nearly free; but now
we are moved by every wind that blows and a chance word
or scene that that word may convey to us.

We rest; a dream has power to poison sleep.
We rise; one wand'ring thought pollutes the day.
We feel, conceive, or reason; laugh or weep,

Embrace fond woe, or cast our cares away;
It is the same: for, be it joy or sorrow,
The path of its departure still is free.
Man's yesterday may ne'er be like his morrow;
Nought may endure but mutability!

It was nearly noon when I arrived at the top of the ascent. For some time I sat upon the rock that overlooks the sea of ice. A mist covered both that and the surrounding mountains. Presently a breeze dissipated the cloud, and I descended upon the glacier. The surface is very uneven, rising like the waves of a troubled sea, descending low, and interspersed by rifts that sink deep. The field of ice is almost a league in width, but I spent nearly two hours in crossing it. The opposite mountain is a bare perpendicular rock. From the side where I now stood Montanvert was exactly opposite, at the distance of a league; and above it rose Mont Blanc, in awful majesty. I remained in a recess of the rock, gazing on this wonderful and stupendous scene. The sea, or rather the vast river of ice, wound among its dependent mountains, whose aerial summits hung over its recesses. Their icy and glittering peaks shone in the sunlight over the clouds. My heart, which was before sorrowful, now swelled with something like joy; I exclaimed, "Wandering spirits, if indeed ye wander, and do not rest in your narrow beds, allow me this faint happiness, or take me, as your companion, away from the joys of life."

As I said this I suddenly beheld the figure of a man, at some distance, advancing towards me with superhuman speed. He bounded over the crevices in the ice, among which I had walked with caution; his stature, also, as he approached, seemed to exceed that of man. I was troubled; a mist came over my eyes, and I felt a faintness seize me; but I was quickly restored by the cold gale of the mountains. I perceived, as the shape came nearer (sight tremendous and abhorred!) that it was the wretch whom I had created. I trembled with rage and horror, resolving to wait his approach and then close with him in mortal combat. He approached; his countenance bespoke bitter anguish, combined with disdain and malignity, while its unearthly ugliness rendered it almost too horrible for human eyes. But I scarcely observed this; rage and hatred had at first deprived me of utterance, and I recovered only to overwhelm him with words expressive of furious detestation and contempt.

only dissoluble by the annihilation of one of us. You purpose to kill me. How dare you sport thus with life? Do your duty towards me, and I will do mine towards you and the rest of mankind. If you will comply with my conditions, I will leave them and you at peace; but if you refuse, I will glut the maw of death, until it be satiated with the blood of your remaining friends."

"Abhorred monster! Fiend that thou art! The tortures of hell are too mild a vengeance for thy crimes. Wretched devil! You reproach me with your creation; come on, then, that I may extinguish the spark which I so negligently bestowed."

My rage was without bounds; I sprang on him, impelled by all the feelings which can arm one being against the existence of another.

He easily eluded me and said, "Be calm! I entreat you to hear me before you give vent to your hatred on my devoted head. Have I not suffered enough, that you seek to increase my misery? Life, although it may only be an accumulation of anguish, is dear to me, and I will defend it. Remember, thou hast made me more powerful than thyself; my height is superior to thine, my joints more supple. But I will not be tempted to set myself in opposition to thee. I am thy creature, and I will be even mild and docile to my natural lord and king if thou wilt also perform thy part, the which thou owest me. Oh, Frankenstein, be not equitable to every other and trample upon me alone, to whom thy justice, and even thy clemency and affection, is most due. Remember that I am thy creature; I ought to be thy Adam, but I am rather the fallen angel, whom thou drivest from joy for no misdeed. Everywhere I see bliss, from which I alone am irrevocably excluded. I was benevolent and good;

misery made me a fiend. Make me happy, and I shall again be virtuous."

"Begone! I will not hear you. There can be no community between you and me; we are enemies. Begone, or let us try our strength in a fight, in which one must fall."

"How can I move thee? Will no entreaties cause thee to turn a favourable eye upon thy creature, who implores thy goodness and compassion? Believe me, Frankenstein, I was benevolent; my soul glowed with love and humanity; but am I not alone, miserably alone? You, my creator, abhor me; what hope can I gather from your fellow creatures, who owe me nothing? They spurn and hate me. The desert mountains and dreary glaciers are my refuge. I have wandered here many days; the caves of ice, which I only do not fear, are a dwelling to me, and the only one which man does not grudge. These bleak skies I hail, for they are kinder to me than your fellow beings. If the multitude of mankind knew of my existence, they would do as you do, and arm themselves for my destruction. Shall I not then hate them who abhor me? I will keep no terms with my enemies. I am miserable, and they shall share my wretchedness. Yet it is in your power to recompense me, and deliver them from an evil which it only remains for you to make so great, that not only you and your family, but thousands of others, shall be swallowed up in the whirlwinds of its rage. Let your compassion be moved, and do not disdain me. Listen to my tale; when you have heard that, abandon or commiserate me, as you shall judge that I deserve. But hear me. The guilty are allowed, by human laws, bloody as they are, to speak in their own defence before they are condemned. Listen to me, Frankenstein. You accuse me of murder, and yet you would, with a satisfied conscience, destroy your own creature. Oh, praise the eternal justice of man! Yet I ask you not to spare me; listen to me, and then, if you can, and if you will, destroy the work of your hands."

"Why do you call to my remembrance," I rejoined, "circumstances of which I shudder to reflect, that I have been the miserable origin and author? Cursed be the day, abhorred devil, in which you first saw light! Cursed (although I curse myself) be the hands that formed you! You have made me wretched beyond expression. You have left me no power to consider whether I

descends to hide itself behind your snowy precipices and illuminate another world, you will have heard my story and can decide. On you it rests, whether I quit forever the neighbourhood of man and lead a harmless life, or become the scourge of your fellow creatures and the author of your own speedy ruin."

As he said this he led the way across the ice; I followed. My heart was full, and I did not answer him, but as I proceeded, I weighed the various arguments that he had used and determined at least to listen to his tale. I was partly urged by curiosity, and compassion confirmed my resolution. I had hitherto supposed him to be the murderer of my brother, and I eagerly sought a confirmation or denial of this opinion. For the first time, also, I felt what the duties of a creator towards his creature were, and that I ought to render him happy before I complained of his wickedness. These motives urged me to comply with his demand. We crossed the ice, therefore, and ascended the opposite rock. The air was cold, and the rain again began to descend; we entered the hut, the fiend with an air of exultation, I with a heavy heart and depressed spirits. But I consented to listen, and seating myself by the fire which my odious companion had lighted, he thus began his tale.

CHAPTER 11

"It is with considerable difficulty that I remember the original era of my being; all the events of that period appear confused and indistinct. A strange multiplicity of sensations seized me, and I saw, felt, heard, and smelt at the same time; and it was, indeed, a long time before I learned to distinguish between the operations of my various senses. By degrees, I remember, a stronger light pressed upon my nerves, so that I was obliged to shut my eyes. Darkness then came over me and troubled me, but hardly had I felt this when, by opening my eyes, as I now suppose, the light poured in upon me again. I walked and, I believe, descended, but I presently found a great alteration in my sensations. Before, dark and opaque bodies had surrounded me, impervious to my touch or sight; but I now found that I could wander on at liberty, with no obstacles which I could not either surmount or avoid. The light became more and more oppressive to me, and the heat wearying me as I walked, I sought a place where I could receive shade. This was the forest near Ingolstadt; and here I lay by the side of a brook resting from my fatigue, until I felt tormented by hunger and thirst. This roused me from my nearly dormant state, and I ate some berries which I found hanging on the trees or lying on the ground. I slaked my thirst at the brook, and then lying down, was overcome by sleep.

"It was dark when I awoke; I felt cold also, and half frightened, as it were, instinctively, finding myself so desolate. Before I had quitted your apartment, on a sensation of cold, I had covered myself with some clothes, but these were insufficient to secure me from the dews of night. I was a poor, helpless, miserable wretch; I knew, and could distinguish, nothing; but feeling pain inv

sat down

ess, innumerable sounds rang

my ears, and on all sides various scents saluted me; the only object that I could distinguish was the bright moon, and I fixed my eyes on that with pleasure.

"Several changes of day and night passed, and the orb of night had greatly lessened, when I began to distinguish my sensations from each other. I gradually saw plainly the clear stream that supplied me with drink and the trees that shaded me with their foliage. I was delighted when I first discovered that a pleasant sound, which often saluted my ears, proceeded from the throats of the little winged animals who had often intercepted the light from my eyes. I began also to observe, with greater accuracy, the forms that surrounded me and to perceive the boundaries of the radiant roof of light which canopied me. Sometimes I tried to imitate the pleasant songs of the birds but was unable. Sometimes I wished to express my sensations in my own mode, but the uncouth and inarticulate sounds which broke from me frightened me into silence again.

"The moon had disappeared from the night, and again, with a lessened form, showed itself, while I still remained in the forest. My sensations had by this time become distinct, and my mind received every day additional ideas. My eyes became accustomed to the light and to perceive objects in their right forms; I distinguished the insect from the herb, and by degrees, one herb from another. I found that the sparrow uttered none but harsh notes, whilst those of the blackbird and thrush were sweet and enticing.

"One day, when I was oppressed by cold, I found a fire which had been left by some wandering beggars, and was

* The moon.

overcome with delight at the warmth I experienced from it. In my joy I thrust my hand into the live embers, but quickly drew it out again with a cry of pain. How strange, I thought, that the same cause should produce such opposite effects! I examined the materials of the fire, and to my joy found it to be composed of wood. I quickly collected some branches, but they were wet and would not burn. I was pained at this and sat still watching the operation of the fire. The wet wood which I had placed near the heat dried and itself became inflamed. I reflected on this, and by touching the various branches, I discovered the cause and busied myself in collecting a great quantity of wood, that I might dry it and have a plentiful supply of fire. When night came on and brought sleep with it, I was in the greatest fear lest my fire should be extinguished. I covered it carefully with dry wood and leaves and placed wet branches upon it; and then, spreading my cloak, I lay on the ground and sank into sleep.

"It was morning when I awoke, and my first care was to visit the fire. I uncovered it, and a gentle breeze quickly fanned it into a flame. I observed this also and contrived a fan of branches, which roused the embers when they were nearly extinguished. When night came again I found, with pleasure, that the fire gave light as well as heat and that the discovery of this element was useful to me in my food, for I found some of the offals that the travellers had left had been roasted, and tasted much more savoury than the berries I gathered from the trees. I tried, therefore, to dress my food in the same manner, placing it on the live embers. I found that the berries were spoiled by this operation, and the nuts and roots much improved.

"Food, however, became scarce, and I often spent the whole day searching in vain for a few acorns to assuage the pangs of hunger. When I found this, I resolved to quit the place that I had hitherto inhabited, to seek for one where the few wants I experienced would be more easily satisfied. In this emigration I exceedingly lamented the loss of the fire which I had obtained through accident and knew not how to reproduce it. I gave several hours to the serious consideration of this difficulty, but I was obliged to relinquish all attempt to supply it, and wrapping myself up in my cloak, I struck across the wood towards the setting sun. I passed three days in these rambles and at length discovered the open country. A great fall of snow had taken place the night

a noise, and perceiving me, shrieked loudly, and quitting the hut, ran across the fields with a speed of which his debilitated form hardly appeared capable. His appearance, different from any I had ever before seen, and his flight somewhat surprised me. But I was enchanted by the appearance of the hut; here the snow and rain could not penetrate; the ground was dry; and it presented to me then as exquisite and divine a retreat as Pandemonium appeared to the demons of hell after their sufferings in the lake of fire. I greedily devoured the remnants of the shepherd's breakfast, which consisted of bread, cheese, milk, and wine; the latter, however, I did not like. Then, overcome by fatigue, I lay down among some straw and fell asleep.

"It was noon when I awoke, and allured by the warmth of the sun, which shone brightly on the white ground, I determined to recommence my travels; and, depositing the remains of the peasant's breakfast in a wallet I found, I proceeded across the fields for several hours, until at sunset I arrived at a village. How miraculous did this appear! The huts, the neater cottages, and stately houses engaged my admiration by turns. The vegetables in the gardens, the milk and cheese that I saw placed at the windows of some of the cottages, allured my appetite. One of the best of these I entered, but I had hardly placed my foot within the door before the children shrieked, and one of the women fainted. The whole village was roused; some fled, some attacked me, until, grievously bruised by stones and many other kinds of missile weapons, I escaped to the open country and fearfully took refuge in a low hovel, quite bare, and making a wretched appearance after the palaces I had beheld in the village. This hovel, however, joined a cottage of a neat and pleasant appearance, but after my late dearly bought experience, I dared not enter it. My place of refuge was constructed of wood, but so low that I could with difficulty sit upright in it. No wood, however, was placed on the earth, which formed the floor, but it was dry; and although the wind entered it by innumerable chinks, I found it an agreeable asylum from the snow and rain.

"Here, then, I retreated and lay down happy to have found a shelter, however miserable, from the inclemency of the season, and still more from the barbarity of man.

"As soon as morning dawned I crept from my kennel, that I might view the adjacent cottage and discover if I could remain in the habitation I had found. It was situated against the back of the cottage and surrounded on the sides which were exposed by a pig sty and a clear pool of water. One part was open, and by that I had crept in; but now I covered every crevice by which I might be perceived with stones and wood, yet in such a manner that I might move them on occasion to pass out; all the light I enjoyed came through the sty, and that was sufficient for me.

"Having thus arranged my dwelling and carpeted it with clean straw, I retired, for I saw the figure of a man at a distance, and I remembered too well my treatment the night before to trust myself in his power. I had first, however, provided for my sustenance for that day by a loaf of coarse bread, which I purloined, and a cup with which I could drink more conveniently than from my hand of the pure water which flowed by my retreat. The floor was a little raised, so that it was kept perfectly dry, and by its vicinity to the chimney of the cottage it was tolerably warm.

"Being thus provided, I resolved to reside in this hovel until something should occur which might alter my determination. It was indeed a paradise compared to the bleak forest, my former residence, the rain-dropping branches, and dank earth. I ate my breakfast with pleasure and was about to remove a plank to procure myself a little water when I heard a step, and looking through a small chink, I beheld a young creature, with a pail on her head, passing before my hovel. The girl was young and of gentle demeanour, unlike what I have since found cottagers and farmhouse servants to be. Yet she was meanly dressed, a coarse blue petticoat and a linen jacket being her only garb; her fair hair

was plaited but not adorned: she ~~look~~
lost sight ~~of~~

~~hou~~se and sometimes in the

"On examining my dwelling, I found that one of the windows of the cottage had formerly occupied a part of it, but the panes had been filled up with wood. In one of these was a small and almost imperceptible chink through which the eye could just penetrate. Through this crevice a small room was visible, whitewashed and clean but very bare of furniture. In one corner, near a small fire, sat an old man, leaning his head on his hands in a disconsolate attitude. The young girl was occupied in arranging the cottage; but presently she took something out of a drawer, which employed her hands, and she sat down beside the old man, who, taking up an instrument, began to play and to produce sounds sweeter than the voice of the thrush or the nightingale. It was a lovely sight, even to me, poor wretch who had never beheld aught beautiful before. The silver hair and benevolent countenance of the aged cottager won my reverence, while the gentle manners of the girl enticed my love. He played a sweet mournful air which I perceived drew tears from the eyes of his amiable companion, of which the old man took no notice, until she sobbed audibly; he then pronounced a few sounds, and the fair creature, leaving her work, knelt at his feet. He raised her and smiled with such kindness and affection that I felt sensations of a peculiar and overpowering nature; they were a mixture of pain and pleasure, such as I had never before experienced, either from hunger or cold, warmth or food; and I withdrew from the window, unable to bear these emotions.

"Soon after this the young man returned, bearing on his shoulders a load of wood. The girl met him at the door, helped to relieve him of his burden, and taking some of the fuel into the cottage, placed it on the fire; then she and the youth went apart into a nook of the cottage, and he showed her a large loaf and a piece of cheese. She seemed pleased and went into the garden for some roots and plants, which she placed in water, and then upon the fire. She afterwards continued her work, whilst the young man went into the garden and appeared busily employed in digging and pulling up roots. After he had been employed thus about an hour, the young woman joined him and they entered the cottage together.

"The old man had, in the meantime, been pensive, but on the appearance of his companions he assumed a more cheerful air, and they sat down to eat. The meal was quickly dispatched. The young woman was again occupied in arranging the cottage, the old man walked before the cottage in the sun for a few minutes, leaning on the arm of the youth. Nothing could exceed in beauty the contrast between these two excellent creatures. One was old, with silver hairs and a countenance beaming with benevolence and love; the younger was slight and graceful in his figure, and his features were moulded with the finest symmetry, yet his eyes and attitude expressed the utmost sadness and despondency. The old man returned to the cottage, and the youth, with tools different from those he had used in the morning, directed his steps across the fields.

"Night quickly shut in, but to my extreme wonder, I found that the cottagers had a means of prolonging light by the use of tapers, and was delighted to find that the setting of the sun did not put an end to the pleasure I experienced in watching my human neighbours. In the evening the young girl and her companion were employed in various occupations which I did not understand; and the old man again took up the instrument which produced the divine sounds that had enchanted me in the morning. So soon as he had finished, the youth began, not to play, but to utter sounds that were monotonous, and neither resembling the harmony of the old man's instrument nor the songs of the birds; I since found that he read aloud, but at that time I knew nothing of the science of words or letters.

"The family, after having been thus occupied for a short time, extinguished their lights and retired, as I conjectured, to rest."

my straw, but I could not sleep. I thought of the occurrences of the day. What chiefly struck me was the gentle manners of these people, and I longed to join them, but dared not. I remembered too well the treatment I had suffered the night before from the barbarous villagers, and resolved, whatever course of conduct I might hereafter think it right to pursue, that for the present I would remain quietly in my hovel, watching and endeavouring to discover the motives which influenced their actions.

"The cottagers arose the next morning before the sun. The young woman arranged the cottage and prepared the food, and the youth departed after the first meal.

"This day was passed in the same routine as that which preceded it. The young man was constantly employed out of doors, and the girl in various laborious occupations within. The old man, whom I soon perceived to be blind, employed his leisure hours on his instrument or in contemplation. Nothing could exceed the love and respect which the younger cottagers exhibited towards their venerable companion. They performed towards him every little office of affection and duty with gentleness, and he rewarded them by his benevolent smiles.

"They were not entirely happy. The young man and his companion often went apart and appeared to weep. I saw no cause for their unhappiness, but I was deeply affected by it. If such lovely creatures were miserable, it was less strange that I, an imperfect and solitary being, should be wretched. Yet why were these gentle beings unhappy? They possessed a delightful house (for such it was in my eyes) and every luxury; they had a fire to warm them when chill and delicious viands when hungry; they were dressed in excellent clothes;

and, still more, they enjoyed one another's company and speech, interchanging each day looks of affection and kindness. What did their tears imply? Did they really express pain? I was at first unable to solve these questions, but perpetual attention and time explained to me many appearances which were at first enigmatic.

"A considerable period elapsed before I discovered one of the causes of the uneasiness of this amiable family: it was poverty, and they suffered that evil in a very distressing degree. Their nourishment consisted entirely of the vegetables of their garden and the milk of one cow, which gave very little during the winter, when its masters could scarcely procure food to support it. They often, I believe, suffered the pangs of hunger very poignantly, especially the two younger cottagers, for several times they placed food before the old man when they reserved none for themselves.

"This trait of kindness moved me sensibly. I had been accustomed, during the night, to steal a part of their store for my own consumption, but when I found that in doing this I inflicted pain on the cottagers, I abstained and satisfied myself with berries, nuts, and roots which I gathered from a neighbouring wood.

"I discovered also another means through which I was enabled to assist their labours. I found that the youth spent a great part of each day in collecting wood for the family fire, and during the night I often took his tools, the use of which I quickly discovered, and brought home firing sufficient for the consumption of several days.

"I remember, the first time that I did this, the young woman, when she opened the door in the morning, appeared greatly astonished on seeing a great pile of wood on the outside. She uttered some words in a loud voice, and the youth joined her, who also expressed surprise. I observed, with pleasure, that he did not go to the forest that day, but spent it in repairing the cottage and cultivating the garden.

"By degrees I made a discovery of still greater moment. I found that these people possessed a method of communicating their experience and feelings to one another by articulate sounds. I perceived that the words they spoke sometimes produced pleasure or pain, smiles or sadness, in the minds and countenances of the hearers. This was indeed a godlike science, and I ardently desired to become

acquainted with it. But I was baffl
made for thi

the
ves. The youth and his
had each of them several names, but the old man had only one, which was 'father.' The girl was called 'sister' or 'Agatha,' and the youth 'Felix,' 'brother,' or 'son.' I cannot describe the delight I felt when I learned the ideas appropriated to each of these sounds and was able to pronounce them. I distinguished several other words without being able as yet to understand or apply them, such as 'good,' 'dearest,' 'unhappy.'

"I spent the winter in this manner. The gentle manners and beauty of the cottagers greatly endeared them to me; when they were unhappy, I felt depressed; when they rejoiced, I sympathized in their joys. I saw few human beings besides them, and if any other happened to enter the cottage, their harsh manners and rude gait only enhanced to me the superior accomplishments of my friends. The old man, I could perceive, often endeavoured to encourage his children, as sometimes I found that he called them, to cast off their melancholy. He would talk in a cheerful accent, with an expression of goodness that bestowed pleasure even upon me. Agatha listened with respect, her eyes sometimes filled with tears, which she endeavoured to wipe away unperceived; but I generally found that her countenance and tone were more cheerful after having listened to the exhortations of her father. It was not thus with Felix. He was always the saddest of the group, and even to my unpractised senses, he appeared to have suffered more deeply than his friends. But if his countenance was more sorrowful, his voice was more cheerful than that of his sister, especially when he addressed the old man.

"I could mention innumerable instances which, although slight, marked the dispositions of these amiable cottagers.

MARY W. SHELLEY

In the midst of poverty and want, Felix carried with pleasure to his sister the first little white flower that peeped out from beneath the snowy ground. Early in the morning, before she had risen, he cleared away the snow that obstructed her path to the milk-house, drew water from the well, and brought the wood from the out-house, where, to his perpetual astonishment, he found his store always replenished by an invisible hand. In the day, I believe, he worked sometimes for a neighbouring farmer, because he often went forth and did not return until dinner, yet brought no wood with him. At other times he worked in the garden, but as there was little to do in the frosty season, he read to the old man and Agatha.

"This reading had puzzled me extremely at first, but by degrees I discovered that he uttered many of the same sounds when he read as when he talked. I conjectured, therefore, that he found on the paper signs for speech which he understood, and I ardently longed to comprehend these also; but how was that possible when I did not even understand the sounds for which they stood as signs? I improved, however, sensibly in this science, but not sufficiently to follow up any kind of conversation, although I applied my whole mind to the endeavour, for I easily perceived that, although I eagerly longed to discover myself to the cottagers, I ought not to make the attempt until I had first become master of their language, which knowledge might enable me to make them overlook the deformity of my figure, for with this also the contrast perpetually presented to my eyes had made me acquainted.

"I had admired the perfect forms of my cottagers—their grace, beauty, and delicate complexions; but how was I terrified when I viewed myself in a transparent pool! At first I started back, unable to believe that it was indeed I who was reflected in the mirror; and when I became fully convinced that I was in reality the monster that I am, I was filled with the bitterest sensations of despondence and mortification. Alas! I did not yet entirely know the fatal effects of this miserable deformity.

"As the sun became warmer and the light of day longer, the snow vanished, and I beheld the bare trees and the black earth. From this time Felix was more employed, and the heart-moving indications of impending famine disappeared.

Their food, as I afterwards found

was uniform. During the morning I attended the motions of the cottagers, and when they were dispersed in various occupations, I slept; the remainder of the day was spent in observing my friends. When they had retired to rest, if there was any moon or the night was star-light, I went into the woods and collected my own food and fuel for the cottage. When I returned, as often as it was necessary, I cleared their path from the snow and performed those offices that I had seen done by Felix. I afterwards found that these labours, performed by an invisible hand, greatly astonished them; and once or twice I heard them, on these occasions, utter the words 'good spirit,' 'wonderful'; but I did not then understand the signification of these terms.

"My thoughts now became more active, and I longed to discover the motives and feelings of these lovely creatures; I was inquisitive to know why Felix appeared so miserable and Agatha so sad. I thought (foolish wretch!) that it might be in my power to restore happiness to these deserving people. When I slept or was absent, the forms of the venerable blind father, the gentle Agatha, and the excellent Felix flitted before me. I looked upon them as superior beings who would be the arbiters of my future destiny. I formed in my imagination a thousand pictures of presenting myself to them, and their reception of me. I imagined that they would be disgusted, until, by my gentle demeanour and conciliating words, I should first win their favour and afterwards their love.

"These thoughts exhilarated me and led me to apply with fresh ardour to the acquiring the art of language. My organs were indeed harsh, but supple; and although my voice was very unlike the soft music of their tones, yet I pronounced such words as I understood with tolerable ease. It was as the ass and the lap-dog; yet surely the gentle ass whose intentions were affectionate, although his manners were rude, deserved better treatment than blows and execration.

"The pleasant showers and genial warmth of spring greatly altered the aspect of the earth. Men who before this change seemed to have been hid in caves dispersed themselves and were employed in various arts of cultivation. The birds sang in more cheerful notes, and the leaves began to bud forth on the trees. Happy, happy earth! Fit habitation for gods, which, so short a time before, was bleak, damp, and unwholesome. My spirits were elevated by the enchanting appearance of nature; the past was blotted from my memory, the present was tranquil, and the future gilded by bright rays of hope and anticipations of joy."

... ... my story. I
... ... impressed me with feelings which,
from what I had been, have made me what I am.

"Spring advanced rapidly; the weather became fine and the skies cloudless. It surprised me that what before was desert and gloomy should now bloom with the most beautiful flowers and verdure. My senses were gratified and refreshed by a thousand scents of delight and a thousand sights of beauty.

"It was on one of these days, when my cottagers periodically rested from labour—the old man played on his guitar, and the children listened to him—that I observed the countenance of Felix was melancholy beyond expression; he sighed frequently, and once his father paused in his music, and I conjectured by his manner that he inquired the cause of his son's sorrow. Felix replied in a cheerful accent, and the old man was recommencing his music when someone tapped at the door.

"It was a lady on horseback, accompanied by a countryman as a guide. The lady was dressed in a dark suit and covered with a thick black veil. Agatha asked a question, to which the stranger only replied by pronouncing, in a sweet accent, the name of Felix. Her voice was musical but unlike that of either of my friends. On hearing this word, Felix came up hastily to the lady, who, when she saw him, threw up her veil, and I beheld a countenance of angelic beauty and expression. Her hair of a shining raven black, and curiously braided; her eyes were dark, but gentle, although animated; her features of a regular proportion, and her complexion wondrously fair, each cheek tinged with a lovely pink.

"Felix seemed ravished with delight when he saw her, every trait of sorrow vanished from his face, and it instantly expressed a degree of ecstatic joy, of which I could hardly have believed it capable; his eyes sparkled, as his cheek flushed with pleasure; and at that moment I thought him as beautiful as the stranger. She appeared affected by different feelings; wiping a few tears from her lovely eyes, she held out her hand to Felix, who kissed it rapturously and called her, as well as I could distinguish, his sweet Arabian. She did not appear to understand him, but smiled. He assisted her to dismount, and dismissing her guide, conducted her into the cottage. Some conversation took place between him and his father, and the young stranger knelt at the old man's feet and would have kissed his hand, but he raised her and embraced her affectionately.

"I soon perceived that although the stranger uttered articulate sounds and appeared to have a language of her own, she was neither understood by nor herself understood the cottagers. They made many signs which I did not comprehend, but I saw that her presence diffused gladness through the cottage, dispelling their sorrow as the sun dissipates the morning mists. Felix seemed peculiarly happy and with smiles of delight welcomed his Arabian. Agatha, the ever-gentle Agatha, kissed the hands of the lovely stranger, and pointing to her brother, made signs which appeared to me to mean that he had been sorrowful until she came. Some hours passed thus, while they, by their countenances, expressed joy, the cause of which I did not comprehend. Presently I found, by the frequent recurrence of some sound which the stranger repeated after them, that she was endeavouring to learn their language; and the idea instantly occurred to me that I should make use of the same instructions to the same end. The stranger learned about twenty words at the first lesson; most of them, indeed, were those which I had before understood, but I profited by the others.

"As night came on Agatha and the Arabian retired early. When they separated Felix kissed the hand of the stranger and said, 'Good night, sweet Safie.' He sat up much longer, conversing with his father, and by the frequent repetition of her name I conjectured that their lovely guest was the subject of their conversation. I ardently desired to understand

them, and bent every faculty towards ~~~~~
found it utterly ~~~~~~~~

~~~~~~~~~~~~~~~~ simple air, and her
~~~~~~~ it in sweet accents, but unlike the wondrous strain of the stranger. The old man appeared enraptured and said some words which Agatha endeavoured to explain to Safie, and by which he appeared to wish to express that she bestowed on him the greatest delight by her music.

"The days now passed as peaceably as before, with the sole alteration that joy had taken place of sadness in the countenances of my friends. Safie was always gay and happy; she and I improved rapidly in the knowledge of language, so that in two months I began to comprehend most of the words uttered by my protectors.

"In the meanwhile also the black ground was covered with herbage, and the green banks interspersed with innumerable flowers, sweet to the scent and the eyes, stars of pale radiance among the moonlight woods; the sun became warmer, the nights clear and balmy; and my nocturnal rambles were an extreme pleasure to me, although they were considerably shortened by the late setting and early rising of the sun, for I never ventured abroad during daylight, fearful of meeting with the same treatment I had formerly endured in the first village which I entered.

"My days were spent in close attention, that I might more speedily master the language; and I may boast that I improved more rapidly than the Arabian, who understood very little and conversed in broken accents, whilst I comprehended and could imitate almost every word that was spoken.

"While I improved in speech, I also learned the science of letters as it was taught to the stranger, and this opened before me a wide field for wonder and delight.

"The book from which Felix instructed Safie was Volney's *Ruins of Empires*. I should not have understood the purport of this book had not Felix, in reading it, given very minute explanations. He had chosen this work, he said, because the declamatory style was framed in imitation of the Eastern authors. Through this work I obtained a cursory knowledge of history and a view of the several empires at present existing in the world; it gave me an insight into the manners, governments, and religions of the different nations of the earth. I heard of the slothful Asiatics, of the stupendous genius and mental activity of the Grecians, of the wars and wonderful virtue of the early Romans—of their subsequent degenerating—of the decline of that mighty empire, of chivalry, Christianity, and kings. I heard of the discovery of the American hemisphere and wept with Safie over the hapless fate of its original inhabitants.

"These wonderful narrations inspired me with strange feelings. Was man, indeed, at once so powerful, so virtuous, and magnificent, yet so vicious and base? He appeared at one time a mere scion of the evil principle and at another as all that can be conceived of noble and godlike. To be a great and virtuous man appeared the highest honour that can befall a sensitive being; to be base and vicious, as many on record have been, appeared the lowest degradation, a condition more abject than that of the blind mole or harmless worm. For a long time I could not conceive how one man could go forth to murder his fellow, or even why there were laws and governments; but when I heard details of vice and bloodshed, my wonder ceased and I turned away with disgust and loathing.

"Every conversation of the cottagers now opened new wonders to me. While I listened to the instructions which Felix bestowed upon the Arabian, the strange system of human society was explained to me. I heard of the division of property, of immense wealth and squalid poverty, of rank, descent, and noble blood.

"The words induced me to turn towards myself. I learned that the possessions most esteemed by your fellow creatures were high and unsullied descent united with riches. A man might be respected with only one of these advantages, but without either he was considered, except in very rare instances, as a vagabond and a slave, doomed to waste his powers for the profits of the chosen few! And what was I? Of my creation and creator I was absolutely ignorant, but I

knew that I possessed no money, no friends, no ki...
property. I was, besides, end...

...ut sorrow

...owledge. Oh, that I had forever re-
mained in my native wood, nor known nor felt beyond the
sensations of hunger, thirst, and heat!

"Of what a strange nature is knowledge! It clings to the
mind when it has once seized on it like a lichen on the
rock. I wished sometimes to shake off all thought and feeling,
but I learned that there was but one means to overcome
the sensation of pain, and that was death—a state which I
feared yet did not understand. I admired virtue and good
feelings and loved the gentle manners and amiable qualities
of my cottagers, but I was shut out from intercourse with
them, except through means which I obtained by stealth,
when I was unseen and unknown, and which rather increased than satisfied the desire I had of becoming one among
my fellows. The gentle words of Agatha and the animated
smiles of the charming Arabian were not for me. The mild
exhortations of the old man and the lively conversation of
the loved Felix were not for me. Miserable, unhappy wretch!

"Other lessons were impressed upon me even more deeply.
I heard of the difference of sexes, and the birth and growth
of children, how the father doted on the smiles of the infant, and the lively sallies of the older child, how all the
life and cares of the mother were wrapped up in the precious
charge, how the mind of youth expanded and gained knowledge, of brother, sister, and all the various relationships
which bind one human being to another in mutual bonds.

"But where were my friends and relations? No father had
watched my infant days, no mother had blessed me with
smiles and caresses; or if they had, all my past life was now
a blot, a blind vacancy in which I distinguished nothing. From
my earliest remembrance I had been as I then was in height

and proportion. I had never yet seen a being resembling me or who claimed any intercourse with me. What was I? The question again recurred, to be answered only with groans.

"I will soon explain to what these feelings tended, but allow me now to return to the cottagers, whose story excited in me such various feelings of indignation, delight, and wonder, but which all terminated in additional love and reverence for my protectors (for so I loved, in an innocent, half-painful self-deceit, to call them)."

Loved them even though cant relate

friends. It was one which could not fail to impress itself deeply on my mind, unfolding as it did a number of circumstances, each interesting and wonderful to one so utterly inexperienced as I was.

"The name of the old man was De Lacey. He was descended from a good family in France, where he had lived for many years in affluence, respected by his superiors and beloved by his equals. His son was bred in the service of his country, and Agatha had ranked with ladies of the highest distinction. A few months before my arrival they had lived in a large and luxurious city called Paris, surrounded by friends and possessed of every enjoyment which virtue, refinement of intellect, or taste, accompanied by a moderate fortune, could afford.

"The father of Safie had been the cause of their ruin. He was a Turkish merchant and had inhabited Paris for many years, when, for some reason which I could not learn, he became obnoxious to the government. He was seized and cast into prison the very day that Safie arrived from Constantinople to join him. He was tried and condemned to death. The injustice of his sentence was very flagrant; all Paris was indignant; and it was judged that his religion and wealth rather than the crime alleged against him had been the cause of his condemnation.

"Felix had accidentally been present at the trial; his horror and indignation were uncontrollable when he heard the decision of the court. He made, at that moment, a solemn vow to deliver him and then looked around for the means. After many fruitless attempts to gain admittance to the prison, he found a strongly grated window in an unguarded part of the building, which lighted the dungeon of the unfortunate Muhammadan, who, loaded with chains, waited in despair the execution of the barbarous sentence. Felix visited the grate at night and made known to the prisoner his intentions in his favour. The Turk, amazed and delighted, endeavoured to kindle the zeal of his deliverer by promises of reward and wealth. Felix rejected his offers with contempt, yet when he saw the lovely Safie, who was allowed to visit her father and who by her gestures expressed her lively gratitude, the youth could not help owning to his own mind that the captive possessed a treasure which would fully reward his toil and hazard.

"The Turk quickly perceived the impression that his daughter had made on the heart of Felix and endeavoured to secure him more entirely in his interests by the promise of her hand in marriage so soon as he should be conveyed to a place of safety. Felix was too delicate to accept this offer, yet he looked forward to the probability of the event as to the consummation of his happiness.

"During the ensuing days, while the preparations were going forward for the escape of the merchant, the zeal of Felix was warmed by several letters that he received from this lovely girl, who found means to express her thoughts in the language of her lover by the aid of an old man, a servant of her father who understood French. She thanked him in the most ardent terms for his intended services towards her parent, and at the same time she gently deplored her own fate.

"I have copies of these letters, for I found means, during my residence in the hovel, to procure the implements of writing; and the letters were often in the hands of Felix or Agatha. Before I depart I will give them to you; they will prove the truth of my tale; but at present, as the sun is already far declined, I shall only have time to repeat the substance of them to you.

"Safie related that her mother was a Christian Arab, seized and made a slave by the Turks; recommended by her beauty, she had won the heart of the father of Safie, who married her. The young girl spoke in high and enthusiastic terms of her mother, who, born in freedom, spurned the bondage to which she was now reduced. She instructed her daughter in the tenets of her religion and taught her to aspire to higher powers of intellect and an inde~~pendent~~

~~spirit forbidden~~

~~The~~ day for the execution of the Turk was fixed, but on the night previous to it he quitted his prison and before morning was distant many leagues from Paris. Felix had procured passports in the name of his father, sister, and himself. He had previously communicated his plan to the former, who aided the deceit by quitting his house, under the pretence of a journey and concealed himself, with his daughter, in an obscure part of Paris.

"Felix conducted the fugitives through France to Lyons and across Mont Cenis to Leghorn, where the merchant had decided to wait a favourable opportunity of passing into some part of the Turkish dominions.

"Safie resolved to remain with her father until the moment of his departure, before which time the Turk renewed his promise that she should be united to his deliverer; and Felix remained with them in expectation of that event; and in the meantime he enjoyed the society of the Arabian, who exhibited towards him the simplest and tenderest affection. They conversed with one another through the means of an interpreter, and sometimes with the interpretation of looks; and Safie sang to him the divine airs of her native country.

"The Turk allowed this intimacy to take place and encouraged the hopes of the youthful lovers, while in his heart he had formed far other plans. He loathed the idea that his daughter should be united to a Christian, but he feared the resentment of Felix if he should appear lukewarm, for he knew that he was still in the power of his deliverer if he should choose to betray him to the Italian state which they inhabited. He revolved a thousand plans by which he should be enabled to prolong the deceit until it might be no longer necessary, and secretly to take his daughter with him when he departed. His plans were facilitated by the news which arrived from Paris.

"The government of France were greatly enraged at the escape of their victim and spared no pains to detect and punish his deliverer. The plot of Felix was quickly discovered, and De Lacey and Agatha were thrown into prison. The news reached Felix and roused him from his dream of pleasure. His blind and aged father and his gentle sister lay in a noisome dungeon while he enjoyed the free air and the society of her whom he loved. This idea was torture to him. He quickly arranged with the Turk that if the latter should find a favourable opportunity for escape before Felix could return to Italy, Safie should remain as a boarder at a convent at Leghorn; and then, quitting the lovely Arabian, he hastened to Paris and delivered himself up to the vengeance of the law, hoping to free De Lacey and Agatha by this proceeding.

"He did not succeed. They remained confined for five months before the trial took place, the result of which deprived them of their fortune and condemned them to a perpetual exile from their native country.

"They found a miserable asylum in the cottage in Germany, where I discovered them. Felix soon learned that the treacherous Turk, for whom he and his family endured such unheard-of oppression, on discovering that his deliverer was thus reduced to poverty and ruin, became a traitor to good feeling and honour and had quitted Italy with his daughter, insultingly sending Felix a pittance of money to aid him, as he said, in some plan of future maintenance.

"Such were the events that preyed on the heart of Felix and rendered him, when I first saw him, the most miserable of his family. He could have endured poverty, and while this distress had been the meed of his virtue, he gloried in it; but the ingratitude of the Turk and the loss of his beloved Safie were misfortunes more bitter and irreparable. The arrival of the Arabian now infused new life into his soul.

"When the news reached Leghorn that Felix was deprived of his wealth and rank, the merchant commanded his daughter to think no more of her lover, but to prepare to return to her native country. The generous nature of Safie was outraged by this command; she attempted to expostulate with her father, but he left her angrily, reiterating his tyrannical

property, which had not yet arrived at Leghorn.

"When alone, Safie resolved in her own mind the plan of conduct that it would become her to pursue in this emergency. A residence in Turkey was abhorrent to her; her religion and her feelings were alike averse to it. By some papers of her father which fell into her hands she heard of the exile of her lover and learnt the name of the spot where he then resided. She hesitated some time, but at length she formed her determination. Taking with her some jewels that belonged to her and a sum of money, she quitted Italy with an attendant, a native of Leghorn, but who understood the common language of Turkey, and departed for Germany.

"She arrived in safety at a town about twenty leagues from the cottage of De Lacey, when her attendant fell dangerously ill. Safie nursed her with the most devoted affection, but the poor girl died, and the Arabian was left alone, unacquainted with the language of the country and utterly ignorant of the customs of the world. She fell, however, into good hands. The Italian had mentioned the name of the spot for which they were bound, and after her death the woman of the house in which they had lived took care that Safie should arrive in safety at the cottage of her lover."

CHAPTER 15

"Such was the history of my beloved cottagers. It impressed me deeply. I learned, from the views of social life which it developed, to admire their virtues and to deprecate the vices of mankind.

"As yet I looked upon crime as a distant evil, benevolence and generosity were ever present before me, inciting within me a desire to become an actor in the busy scene where so many admirable qualities were called forth and displayed. But in giving an account of the progress of my intellect, I must not omit a circumstance which occurred in the beginning of the month of August of the same year.

"One night during my accustomed visit to the neighbouring wood where I collected my own food and brought home firing for my protectors, I found on the ground a leathern portmanteau containing several articles of dress and some books. I eagerly seized the prize and returned with it to my hovel. Fortunately the books were written in the language, the elements of which I had acquired at the cottage; they consisted of *Paradise Lost,* a volume of Plutarch's *Lives,* and the *Sorrows of Werter.* The possession of these treasures gave me extreme delight; I now continually studied and exercised my mind upon these histories, whilst my friends were employed in their ordinary occupations.

"I can hardly describe to you the effect of these books. They produced in me an infinity of new images and feelings, that sometimes raised me to ecstasy, but more frequently sunk me into the lowest dejection. In the *Sorrows of Werter,* besides the interest of its simple and affecting story, so many opinions are canvassed and so many lights thrown upon what had hitherto been to me obscure subjects that I found in it a never-ending source of speculation and astonishment. The gentle and domestic m̶a̶n̶n̶e̶r̶

̶c̶o̶m̶b̶i̶n̶e̶d̶ ̶w̶i̶t̶h̶

...̶p̶t̶,̶ ̶without precisely
understanding it.

"As I read, however, I applied much personally to my
own feelings and condition. I found myself similar yet at
the same time strangely unlike to the beings concerning
whom I read and to whose conversation I was a listener.
I sympathized with and partly understood them, but I was
unformed in mind; I was dependent on none and related to
none. 'The path of my departure was free,' and there was
none to lament my annihilation. My person was hideous and
my stature gigantic. What did this mean? Who was I? What
was I? Whence did I come? What was my destination? These
questions continually recurred, but I was unable to solve
them.

"The volume of Plutarch's *Lives* which I possessed contained the histories of the first founders of the ancient re-
publics. This book had a far different effect upon me from
the *Sorrows of Werter*. I learned from Werter's imaginations
despondency and gloom, but Plutarch taught me high
thoughts; he elevated me above the wretched sphere of my
own reflections, to admire and love the heroes of past ages.
Many things I read surpassed my understanding and experience. I had a very confused knowledge of kingdoms, wide
extents of country, mighty rivers, and boundless seas. But
I was perfectly unacquainted with towns and large assem-
blages of men. The cottage of my protectors had been the
only school in which I had studied human nature, but this
book developed new and mightier scenes of action. I read
of men concerned in public affairs, governing or massacring
their species. I felt the greatest ardour for virtue rise within
me, and abhorrence for vice, as far as I understood the
signification of those terms, relative as they were, as I ap-

plied them, to pleasure and pain alone. Induced by these feelings, I was of course led to admire peaceable lawgivers, Numa, Solon, and Lycurgus, in preference to Romulus and Theseus. The patriarchal lives of my protectors caused these impressions to take a firm hold on my mind; perhaps, if my first introduction to humanity had been made by a young soldier, burning for glory and slaughter, I should have been imbued with different sensations.

"But *Paradise Lost* excited different and far deeper emotions. I read it, as I had read the other volumes which had fallen into my hands, as a true history. It moved every feeling of wonder and awe that the picture of an omnipotent God warring with his creatures was capable of exciting. I often referred the several situations, as their similarity struck me, to my own. Like Adam, I was apparently united by no link to any other being in existence; but his state was far different from mine in every other respect. He had come forth from the hands of God a perfect creature, happy and prosperous, guarded by the especial care of his Creator; he was allowed to converse with and acquire knowledge from beings of a superior nature, but I was wretched, helpless, and alone. Many times I considered Satan as the fitter emblem of my condition, for often, like him, when I viewed the bliss of my protectors, the bitter gall of envy rose within me.

"Another circumstance strengthened and confirmed these feelings. Soon after my arrival in the hovel I discovered some papers in the pocket of the dress which I had taken from your laboratory. At first I had neglected them, but now that I was able to decipher the characters in which they were written, I began to study them with diligence. It was your journal of the four months that preceded my creation. You minutely described in these papers every step you took in the progress of your work; this history was mingled with accounts of domestic occurrences. You doubtless recollect these papers. Here they are. Everything is related in them which bears reference to my accursed origin; the whole detail of that series of disgusting circumstances which produced it is set in view; the minutest description of my odious and loathsome person is given, in language which painted your own horrors and rendered mine indelible. I sickened as I read. 'Hateful day when I received life!' I exclaimed in

reply to creator

agony. 'Accursed creator! Why did you f———
hideous that ...

...become acquainted with
...mation of their virtues they would compassionate
me and overlook my personal deformity. Could they turn
from their door one, however monstrous, who solicited their
compassion and friendship? I resolved, at least, not to despair, but in every way to fit myself for an interview with
them which would decide my fate. I postponed this attempt
for some months longer, for the importance attached to
its success inspired me with a dread lest I should fail.
Besides, I found that my understanding improved so much
with every day's experience that I was unwilling to commence this undertaking until a few more months should have
added to my sagacity.

"Several changes, in the meantime, took place in the cottage. The presence of Safie diffused happiness among its
inhabitants, and I also found that a greater degree of plenty
reigned there. Felix and Agatha spent more time in amusement and conversation, and were assisted in their labours by servants. They did not appear rich, but they were
contented and happy; their feelings were serene and peaceful, while mine became every day more tumultuous. Increase of knowledge only discovered to me more clearly
what a wretched outcast I was. I cherished hope, it is true,
but it vanished when I beheld my person reflected in water
or my shadow in the moonshine, even as that frail image
and that inconstant shade.

"I endeavoured to crush these fears and to fortify myself for the trial which in a few months I resolved to under-
go; and sometimes I allowed my thoughts, unchecked by
reason, to ramble in the fields of Paradise, and dared to
fancy amiable and lovely creatures sympathizing with my
feelings and cheering my gloom; their angelic countenances

Knowledge = Problems

breathed smiles of consolation. But it was all a dream; no Eve soothed my sorrows nor shared my thoughts; I was alone. I remembered Adam's supplication to his Creator. But where was mine? He had abandoned me, and in the bitterness of my heart I cursed him.

"Autumn passed thus. I saw, with surprise and grief, the leaves decay and fall, and nature again assume the barren and bleak appearance it had worn when I first beheld the woods and the lovely moon. Yet I did not heed the bleakness of the weather; I was better fitted by my conformation for the endurance of cold than heat. But my chief delights were the sight of the flowers, the birds, and all the gay apparel of summer; when those deserted me, I turned with more attention towards the cottagers. Their happiness was not decreased by the absence of summer. They loved and sympathized with one another; and their joys, depending on each other, were not interrupted by the casualties that took place around them. The more I saw of them, the greater became my desire to claim their protection and kindness; my heart yearned to be known and loved by these amiable creatures; to see their sweet looks directed towards me with affection was the utmost limit of my ambition. I dared not think that they would turn them from me with disdain and horror. The poor that stopped at their door were never driven away. I asked, it is true, for greater treasures than a little food or rest: I required kindness and sympathy; but I did not believe myself utterly unworthy of it.

"The winter advanced, and an entire revolution of the seasons had taken place since I awoke into life. My attention at this time was solely directed towards my plan of introducing myself into the cottage of my protectors. I revolved many projects, but that on which I finally fixed was to enter the dwelling when the blind old man should be alone. I had sagacity enough to discover that the unnatural hideousness of my person was the chief object of horror with those who had formerly beheld me. My voice, although harsh, had nothing terrible in it; I thought, therefore, that if in the absence of his children I could gain the good will and mediation of the old De Lacey, I might by his means be tolerated by my younger protectors.

"One day, when the sun shone on the red leaves that

strewed the ground and diffused cheerfulness, although it

trial, which would decide my hopes or realize my fears. The servants were gone to a neighbouring fair. All was silent in and around the cottage; it was an excellent opportunity; yet, when I proceeded to execute my plan, my limbs failed me and I sank to the ground. Again I rose, and exerting all the firmness of which I was master, removed the planks which I had placed before my hovel to conceal my retreat. The fresh air revived me, and with renewed determination I approached the door of their cottage.

"I knocked. 'Who is there?' said the old man. 'Come in.'

"I entered. 'Pardon this intrusion,' said I; 'I am a traveller in want of a little rest; you would greatly oblige me if you would allow me to remain a few minutes before the fire.'

" 'Enter,' said De Lacey, 'and I will try in what manner I can to relieve your wants; but, unfortunately, my children are from home, and as I am blind, I am afraid I shall find it difficult to procure food for you.'

" 'Do not trouble yourself, my kind host; I have food; it is warmth and rest only that I need.'

"I sat down, and a silence ensued. I knew that every minute was precious to me, yet I remained irresolute in what manner to commence the interview, when the old man addressed me. 'By your language, stranger, I suppose you are my countryman; are you French?'

" 'No; but I was educated by a French family and understand that language only. I am now going to claim the protection of some friends, whom I sincerely love, and of whose favour I have some hopes.'

" 'Are they Germans?'

" 'No, they are French. But let us change the subject. I am an unfortunate and deserted creature; I look around and

I have no relation or friend upon earth. These amiable people to whom I go have never seen me and know little of me. I am full of fears, for if I fail there, I am an outcast in the world forever.'

" 'Do not despair. To be friendless is indeed to be unfortunate, but the hearts of men, when unprejudiced by any obvious self-interest, are full of brotherly love and charity. Rely, therefore, on your hopes; and if these friends are good and amiable, do not despair.'

" 'They are kind—they are the most excellent creatures in the world; but, unfortunately, they are prejudiced against me. I have good dispositions; my life has been hitherto harmless and in some degree beneficial; but a fatal prejudice clouds their eyes, and where they ought to see a feeling and kind friend, they behold only a detestable monster.'

" 'That is indeed unfortunate; but if you are really blameless, cannot you undeceive them?'

" 'I am about to undertake that task; and it is on that account that I feel so many overwhelming terrors. I tenderly love these friends; I have, unknown to them, been for many months in the habits of daily kindness towards them; but they believe that I wish to injure them, and it is that prejudice which I wish to overcome.'

" 'Where do these friends reside?'

" 'Near this spot.'

"The old man paused and then continued, 'If you will unreservedly confide to me the particulars of your tale, I perhaps may be of use in undeceiving them. I am blind and cannot judge of your countenance, but there is something in your words which persuades me that you are sincere. I am poor and an exile, but it will afford me true pleasure to be in any way serviceable to a human creature.'

" 'Excellent man! I thank you and accept your generous offer. You raise me from the dust by this kindness; and I trust that, by your aid, I shall not be driven from the society and sympathy of your fellow creatures.'

" 'Heaven forbid! Even if you were really criminal, for that can only drive you to desperation, and not instigate you to virtue. I also am unfortunate; I and my family have been condemned, although innocent; judge, therefore, if I do not feel for your misfortunes.'

" 'How can I thank you, my best and only benefactor?

From your lips first have I heard the v...
rected towards me; I shall b...
present humanity ass...
whom I am o...

"...

...ment I
...nad not a mo-
...of the old man, I cried,
...and protect me! You and your
...ends whom I seek. Do not you desert me
...our of trial!'

"'Great God!' exclaimed the old man. 'Who are you?'

"At that instant the cottage door was opened, and Felix, Safie, and Agatha entered. Who can describe their horror and consternation on beholding me? Agatha fainted, and Safie, unable to attend to her friend, rushed out of the cottage. Felix darted forward, and with supernatural force tore me from his father, to whose knees I clung; in a transport of fury, he dashed me to the ground and struck me violently with a stick. I could have torn him limb from limb, as the lion rends the antelope. But my heart sank within me as with bitter sickness, and I refrained. I saw him on the point of repeating his blow, when, overcome by pain and anguish, I quitted the cottage, and in the general tumult escaped unperceived to my hovel."

Loses every thing

vs

Love

CHAPTER 16

"Cursed, cursed creator! Why did I live? Why, in that instant, did I not extinguish the spark of existence which you had so wantonly bestowed? I know not; despair had not yet taken possession of me; my feelings were those of rage and revenge. I could with pleasure have destroyed the cottage and its inhabitants and have glutted myself with their shrieks and misery.

"When night came I quitted my retreat and wandered in the wood; and now, no longer restrained by the fear of discovery, I gave vent to my anguish in fearful howlings. I was like a wild beast that had broken the toils, destroying the objects that obstructed me and ranging through the wood with a staglike swiftness. Oh! What a miserable night I passed! The cold stars shone in mockery, and the bare trees waved their branches above me; now and then the sweet voice of a bird burst forth amidst the universal stillness. All, save I, were at rest or in enjoyment; I, like the arch-fiend, bore a hell within me, and finding myself unsympathized with, wished to tear up the trees, spread havoc and destruction around me, and then to have sat down and enjoyed the ruin.

"But this was a luxury of sensation that could not endure; I became fatigued with excess of bodily exertion and sank on the damp grass in the sick impotence of despair. There was none among the myriads of men that existed who would pity or assist me; and should I feel kindness towards my enemies? No; from that moment I declared everlasting war against the species, and more than all, against him who had formed me and sent me forth to this insupportable misery.

"The sun rose; I heard the voices of men and knew that

130

monster = Satan, see

it was impossible to return to my retreat d...
Accordingly I hid...

...of his children.
... familiarized the old De Lacey to me, and by degrees to have discovered myself to the rest of his family, when they should have been prepared for my approach. But I did not believe my errors to be irretrievable, and after much consideration I resolved to return to the cottage, seek the old man, and by my representations win him to my party.

"These thoughts calmed me, and in the afternoon I sank into a profound sleep; but the fever of my blood did not allow me to be visited by peaceful dreams. The horrible scene of the preceding day was forever acting before my eyes; the females were flying and the enraged Felix tearing me from his father's feet. I awoke exhausted, and finding that it was already night, I crept forth from my hiding-place, and went in search of food.

"When my hunger was appeased, I directed my steps towards the well-known path that conducted to the cottage. All there was at peace. I crept into my hovel and remained in silent expectation of the accustomed hour when the family arose. That hour passed, the sun mounted high in the heavens, but the cottagers did not appear. I trembled violently, apprehending some dreadful misfortune. The inside of the cottage was dark, and I heard no motion; I cannot describe the agony of this suspense.

"Presently two countrymen passed by, but pausing near the cottage, they entered into conversation, using violent gesticulations; but I did not understand what they said, as they spoke the language of the country, which differed from that of my protectors. Soon after, however, Felix approached with another man; I was surprised, as I knew that he had not quitted the cottage that morning, and waited anxiously to discover from his discourse the meaning of these unusual appearances.

" 'Do you consider,' said his companion to him, 'that you will be obliged to pay three months' rent and to lose the produce of your garden? I do not wish to take any unfair advantage, and I beg therefore that you will take some days to consider of your determination.'

" 'It is utterly useless,' replied Felix; 'we can never again inhabit your cottage. The life of my father is in the greatest danger, owing to the dreadful circumstance that I have related. My wife and my sister will never recover from their horror. I entreat you not to reason with me any more. Take possession of your tenement and let me fly from this place.'

"Felix trembled violently as he said this. He and his companion entered the cottage, in which they remained for a few minutes, and then departed. I never saw any of the family of De Lacey more.

"I continued for the remainder of the day in my hovel in a state of utter and stupid despair. My protectors had departed and had broken the only link that held me to the world. For the first time the feelings of revenge and hatred filled my bosom, and I did not strive to control them, but allowing myself to be borne away by the stream, I bent my mind towards injury and death. When I thought of my friends, of the mild voice of De Lacey, the gentle eyes of Agatha, and the exquisite beauty of the Arabian, these thoughts vanished and a gush of tears somewhat soothed me. But again when I reflected that they had spurned and deserted me, anger returned, a rage of anger, and unable to injure anything human, I turned my fury towards inanimate objects. As night advanced I placed a variety of combustibles around the cottage, and after having destroyed every vestige of cultivation in the garden, I waited with forced impatience until the moon had sunk to commence my operations.

"As the night advanced, a fierce wind arose from the woods and quickly dispersed the clouds that had loitered in the heavens; the blast tore along like a mighty avalanche and produced a kind of insanity in my spirits that burst all bounds of reason and reflection. I lighted the dry branch of a tree and danced with fury around the devoted cottage, my eyes still fixed on the western horizon, the edge of which the moon nearly touched. A part of its orb was

misfortunes; but to me, hated and despised, every country must be equally horrible. At length the thought of you crossed my mind. I learned from your papers that you were my father, my creator; and to whom could I apply with more fitness than to him who had given me life? Among the lessons that Felix had bestowed upon Safie, geography had not been omitted; I had learned from these the relative situations of the different countries of the earth. You had mentioned Geneva as the name of your native town, and towards this place I resolved to proceed.

"But how was I to direct myself? I knew that I must travel in a southwesterly direction to reach my destination, but the sun was my only guide. I did not know the names of the towns that I was to pass through, nor could I ask information from a single human being; but I did not despair. From you only could I hope for succour, although towards you I felt no sentiment but that of hatred. Unfeeling, heartless creator! You had endowed me with perceptions and passions and then cast me abroad an object for the scorn and horror of mankind. But on you only had I any claim for pity and redress, and from you I determined to seek that justice which I vainly attempted to gain from any other being that wore the human form.

"My travels were long and the sufferings I endured intense. It was late in autumn when I quitted the district where I had so long resided. I travelled only at night, fearful of encountering the visage of a human being. Nature decayed around me, and the sun became heatless; rain and snow poured around me; mighty rivers were frozen; the surface of the earth was hard and chill, and bare, and I found no shelter. Oh, earth! How often did I imprecate curses on the cause of my being! The mildness of my nature had fled, and all within me was turned to gall and bitterness. The nearer I approached to your habitation, the more deeply did I feel the spirit of revenge enkindled in my heart. Snow fell, and the waters were hardened, but I rested not. A few incidents now and then directed me, and I possessed a map of the country; but I often wandered wide from my path. The agony of my feelings allowed me no respite; no incident occurred from which my rage and misery could not extract its food; but a circumstance that happened when I arrived on the confines of Switzerland, when the sun had recovered its warmth and the earth again began to look green, confirmed in an especial manner the bitterness and horror of my feelings.

"I generally rested during the day and travelled only when I was secured by night from the view of man. One morning, however, finding that my path lay through a deep wood, I ventured to continue my journey after the sun had risen; the day, which was one of the first of spring, cheered even me by the loveliness of its sunshine and the balminess of the air. I felt emotions of gentleness and pleasure, that had long appeared dead, revive within me. Half surprised by the novelty of these sensations, I allowed myself to be borne away by them, and forgetting my solitude and deformity, dared to be happy. Soft tears again bedewed my cheeks, and I even raised my humid eyes with thankfulness towards the blessed sun, which bestowed such joy upon me.

"I continued to wind among the paths of the wood, until I came to its boundary, which was skirted by a deep and rapid river, into which many of the trees bent their branches, now budding with the fresh spring. Here I paused, not exactly knowing what path to pursue, when I heard the sound of voices, that induced me to conceal myself under the shade of a cypress. I was scarcely hid when a young girl came running towards the spot where I was concealed, laughing, as if she ran from someone in sport. She continued her course along the precipitous sides of the river, when suddenly her foot slipped, and she fell into the rapid stream. I rushed from my hiding-place and with extreme labour, from the force of the current, saved her and dragged her to shore. She was senseless, and I endeavoured by every means in my power to restore animation, when I

was suddenly interrupted by the approach
was probably th

… and bone. The feelings of kindness and gentleness which I had entertained but a few moments before gave place to hellish rage and gnashing of teeth. Inflamed by pain, I vowed eternal hatred and vengeance to all mankind. But the agony of my wound overcame me; my pulses paused, and I fainted.

"For some weeks I led a miserable life in the woods, endeavouring to cure the wound which I had received. The ball had entered my shoulder, and I knew not whether it had remained there or passed through; at any rate I had no means of extracting it. My sufferings were augmented also by the oppressive sense of the injustice and ingratitude of their infliction. My daily vows rose for revenge—a deep and deadly revenge, such as would alone compensate for the outrages and anguish I had endured.

"After some weeks my wound healed, and I continued my journey. The labours I endured were no longer to be alleviated by the bright sun or gentle breezes of spring; all joy was but a mockery which insulted my desolate state and made me feel more painfully that I was not made for the enjoyment of pleasure.

"But my toils now drew near a close, and in two months from this time I reached the environs of Geneva.

"It was evening when I arrived, and I retired to a hiding-place among the fields that surround it to meditate in what manner I should apply to you. I was oppressed by fatigue and hunger and far too unhappy to enjoy the gentle breezes of evening or the prospect of the sun setting behind the stupendous mountains of Jura.

"At this time a slight sleep relieved me from the pain of reflection, which was disturbed by the approach of a beauti-

ful child, who came running into the recess I had chosen,
with all the sportiveness of infancy. Suddenly, as I gazed
on him, an idea seized me that this little creature was unprejudiced and had lived too short a time to have imbibed
a horror of deformity. If, therefore, I could seize him and
educate him as my companion and friend, I should not be
so desolate in this peopled earth.

"Urged by this impulse, I seized on the boy as he passed
and drew him towards me. As soon as he beheld my form,
he placed his hands before his eyes and uttered a shrill
scream; I drew his hand forcibly from his face and said,
'Child, what is the meaning of this? I do not intend to
hurt you; listen to me.'

"He struggled violently. 'Let me go,' he cried; 'monster!
Ugly wretch! You wish to eat me and tear me to pieces.
You are an ogre. Let me go, or I will tell my papa.'

" 'Boy, you will never see your father again; you must
come with me.'

" 'Hideous monster! Let me go. My papa is a syndic—
he is M. Frankenstein—he will punish you. You dare not
keep me.'

" 'Frankenstein! You belong then to my enemy—to him
towards whom I have sworn eternal revenge; you shall be
my first victim.'

"The child still struggled and loaded me with epithets
which carried despair to my heart; I grasped his throat to
silence him, and in a moment he lay dead at my feet.

"I gazed on my victim, and my heart swelled with exultation and hellish triumph; clapping my hands, I exclaimed,
'I too can create desolation; my enemy is not invulnerable;
this death will carry despair to him, and a thousand other
miseries shall torment and destroy him.'

"As I fixed my eyes on the child, I saw something glittering on his breast. I took it; it was a portrait of a most
lovely woman. In spite of my malignity, it softened and
attracted me. For a few moments I gazed with delight on
her dark eyes, fringed by deep lashes, and her lovely lips;
but presently my rage returned; I remembered that I was
forever deprived of the delights that such beautiful creatures
could bestow and that she whose resemblance I contemplated would, in regarding me, have changed that air of
divine benignity to one expressive of disgust and affright.

Murder

Sees beauty destroys him

agam Pl ech.

"Can you wonder that such thoughts transport~~~~
rage? I only wonder that at that ~~~~
ing my sensations i~~~~
am~~~~

~~~~ ~~~~, is one of
~~~~ are bestowed on all but
~~~~ over her and whispered, 'Awake, fairest,
~~~~ lover is near—he who would give his life but to obtain
one look of affection from thine eyes; my beloved, awake!'

"The sleeper stirred; a thrill of terror ran through me.
Should she indeed awake, and see me, and curse me, and
denounce the murderer? Thus would she assuredly act if
her darkened eyes opened and she beheld me. The thought
was madness; it stirred the fiend within me—not I, but she,
shall suffer; the murder I have committed because I am
forever robbed of all that she could give me, she shall
atone. The crime had its source in her; be hers the punishment! Thanks to the lessons of Felix and the sanguinary
laws of man, I had learned now to work mischief. I bent
over her and placed the portrait securely in one of the
folds of her dress. She moved again, and I fled.

"For some days I haunted the spot where these scenes
had taken place, sometimes wishing to see you, sometimes resolved to quit the world and its miseries forever.
At length I wandered towards these mountains, and have
ranged through their immense recesses, consumed by a
burning passion which you alone can gratify. We may not
part until you have promised to comply with my requisition.
I am alone and miserable; man will not associate with me;
but one as deformed and horrible as myself would not deny
herself to me. My companion must be of the same species
and have the same defects. This being you must create."

wants mate

Wose unsure of murder
Cannot decide goal or m.

CHAPTER 17

Block to Fighter

The being finished speaking and fixed his looks upon me in the expectation of a reply. But I was bewildered, perplexed, and unable to arrange my ideas sufficiently to understand the full extent of his proposition. He continued, "You must create a female for me with whom I can live in the interchange of those sympathies necessary for my being. This you alone can do, and I demand it of you as a right which you must not refuse to concede."

The latter part of his tale had kindled anew in me the anger that had died away while he narrated his peaceful life among the cottagers, and as he said this I could no longer suppress the rage that burned within me.

"I do refuse it," I replied; "and no torture shall ever extort a consent from me. You may render me the most miserable of men, but you shall never make me base in my own eyes. Shall I create another like yourself, whose joint wickedness might desolate the world. Begone! I have answered you; you may torture me, but I will never consent."

"You are in the wrong," replied the fiend; "and instead of threatening, I am content to reason with you. I am malicious because I am miserable. Am I not shunned and hated by all mankind? You, my creator, would tear me to pieces and triumph; remember that, and tell me why I should pity man more than he pities me? You would not call it murder if you could precipitate me into one of those ice-rifts and destroy my frame, the work of your own hands. Shall I respect man when he contemns me? Let him live with me in the interchange of kindness, and instead of injury I would bestow every benefit upon him with tears of gratitude at his acceptance. But that cannot be; the human senses are insurmountable barriers to our union. Yet mine shall not be the

Trying reason and the none

submission of abject slavery. I will revenge my injuries; if I
cannot inspire love, I will cause fear, and chiefly towards you
my arch-enemy, because my creator, do I swear inextinguishable
hatred. Have a care: I will work at your destruction, nor finish
until I desolate your heart, so that you shall curse the hour of
your birth."

A fiendish rage animated him as he said this; his face was
wrinkled into contortions too horrible for human eyes to behold;
but presently he calmed himself and proceeded—

"I intended to reason. This passion is detrimental to me, for
you do not reflect that you are the cause of its excess. If any
being felt emotions of benevolence towards me, I should return them a hundred and a hundredfold; for that one creature's sake I would make peace with the whole kind! But
I now indulge in dreams of bliss that cannot be realized.
What I ask of you is reasonable and moderate; I demand
a creature of another sex, but as hideous as myself; the gratification is small, but it is all that I can receive, and it shall
content me. It is true, we shall be monsters, cut off from
all the world; but on that account we shall be more attached
to one another. Our lives will not be happy, but they will
be harmless and free from the misery I now feel. Oh! My
creator, make me happy; let me feel gratitude towards you
for one benefit! Let me see that I excite the sympathy of
some existing thing; do not deny me my request!"

I was moved. I shuddered when I thought of the possible
consequences of my consent, but I felt that there was some
justice in his argument. His tale and the feelings he now expressed proved him to be a creature of fine sensations, and
did I not as his maker owe him all the portion of happiness
that it was in my power to bestow? He saw my change of
feeling and continued, "If you consent, neither you nor any
other human being shall ever see us again; I will go to the
vast wilds of South America. My food is not that of man;
I do not destroy the lamb and the kid to glut my appetite;
acorns and berries afford me sufficient nourishment. My companion will be of the same nature as myself and will be content with the same fare. We shall make our bed of dried
leaves; the sun will shine on us as on man and will ripen our
food. The picture I present to you is peaceful and human,
and you must feel that you could deny it only in the wanton-
ness of power and cruelty. Pitiless as you have been towards

me, I now see compassion in your eyes; let me seize the favourable moment and persuade you to promise what I so ardently desire."

"You propose," replied I, "to fly from the habitations of man, to dwell in those wilds where the beasts of the field will be your only companions. How can you, who long for the love and sympathy of man, persevere in this exile? You will return and again seek their kindness, and you will meet with their detestation; your evil passions will be renewed, and you will then have a companion to aid you in the task of destruction. This may not be; cease to argue the point, for I cannot consent."

"How inconstant are your feelings! But a moment ago you were moved by my representations, and why do you again harden yourself to my complaints? I swear to you, by the earth which I inhabit, and by you that made me, that with the companion you bestow I will quit the neighbourhood of man and dwell, as it may chance, in the most savage of places. My evil passions will have fled, for I shall meet with sympathy! My life will flow quietly away, and in my dying moments I shall not curse my maker."

His words had a strange effect upon me. I compassionated him and sometimes felt a wish to console him, but when I looked upon him, when I saw the filthy mass that moved and talked, my heart sickened and my feelings were altered to those of horror and hatred. I tried to stifle these sensations; I thought that as I could not sympathize with him, I had no right to withhold from him the small portion of happiness which was yet in my power to bestow.

"You swear," I said, "to be harmless; but have you not already shown a degree of malice that should reasonably make me distrust you? May not even this be a feint that will increase your triumph by affording a wider scope for your revenge?"

"How is this? I must not be trifled with, and I demand an answer. If I have no ties and no affections, hatred and vice must be my portion; the love of another will destroy the cause of my crimes, and I shall become a thing of whose existence everyone will be ignorant. My vices are the children of a forced solitude that I abhor, and my virtues will necessarily arise when I live in communion with an equal. I shall feel the affections of a sensitive being and become linked to

Beauty again issue

the chain of existence and events from which I am now excluded."

sessing faculties it would be vain to cope with. After a long
pause of reflection I concluded that the justice due both to
him and my fellow creatures demanded of me that I should
comply with his request. Turning to him, therefore, I said, "I
consent to your demand, on your solemn oath to quit Europe
forever, and every other place in the neighbourhood of man,
as soon as I shall deliver into your hands a female who will
accompany you in your exile."

"I swear," he cried, "by the sun, and by the blue sky of
heaven, and by the fire of love that burns my heart, that
if you grant my prayer, while they exist you shall never behold me again. Depart to your home and commence your
labours; I shall watch their progress with unutterable anxiety;
and fear not but that when you are ready I shall appear."

Saying this, he suddenly quitted me, fearful, perhaps, of
any change in my sentiments. I saw him descend the mountain with greater speed than the flight of an eagle, and quickly lost among the undulations of the sea of ice.

His tale had occupied the whole day, and the sun was upon
the verge of the horizon when he departed. I knew that
I ought to hasten my descent towards the valley, as I should
soon be encompassed in darkness; but my heart was heavy,
and my steps slow. The labour of winding among the little
paths of the mountain and fixing my feet firmly as I advanced perplexed me, occupied as I was by the emotions
which the occurrences of the day had produced. Night
was far advanced when I came to the halfway resting-place
and seated myself beside the fountain. The stars shone at
intervals as the clouds passed from over them; the dark pines
rose before me, and every here and there a broken tree lay
on the ground; it was a scene of wonderful solemnity and

Nature again   problem w/ new life

stirred strange thoughts within me. I wept bitterly, and clasping my hands in agony, I exclaimed, "Oh! Stars and clouds and winds, ye are all about to mock me; if ye really pity me, crush sensation and memory; let me become as nought; but if not, depart, depart, and leave me in darkness."

These were wild and miserable thoughts, but I cannot describe to you how the eternal twinkling of the stars weighed upon me and how I listened to every blast of wind as if it were a dull ugly siroc on its way to consume me.

Morning dawned before I arrived at the village of Chamounix; I took no rest, but returned immediately to Geneva. Even in my own heart I could give no expression to my sensations—they weighed on me with a mountain's weight and their excess destroyed my agony beneath them. Thus I returned home, and entering the house, presented myself to the family. My haggard and wild appearance awoke intense alarm, but I answered no question, scarcely did I speak. I felt as if I were placed under a ban—as if I had no right to claim their sympathies—as if never more might I enjoy companionship with them. Yet even thus I loved them to adoration; and to save them, I resolved to dedicate myself to my most abhorred task. The prospect of such an occupation made every other circumstance of existence pass before me like a dream, and that thought only had to me the reality of life.

...could not collect the courage to recommence my work. I feared the vengeance of the disappointed fiend, yet I was unable to overcome my repugnance to the task which was enjoined me. I found that I could not compose a female without again devoting several months to profound study and laborious disquisition. I had heard of some discoveries having been made by an English philosopher, the knowledge of which was material to my success, and I sometimes thought of obtaining my father's consent to visit England for this purpose; but I clung to every pretence of delay and shrank from taking the first step in an undertaking whose immediate necessity began to appear less absolute to me. A change indeed had taken place in me; my health, which had hitherto declined, was now much restored; and my spirits, when unchecked by the memory of my unhappy promise, rose proportionably. My father saw this change with pleasure, and he turned his thoughts towards the best method of eradicating the remains of my melancholy, which every now and then would return by fits, and with a devouring blackness overcast the approaching sunshine. At these moments I took refuge in the most perfect solitude. I passed whole days on the lake alone in a little boat, watching the clouds and listening to the rippling of the waves, silent and listless. But the fresh air and bright sun seldom failed to restore me to some degree of composure, and on my return I met the salutations of my friends with a readier smile and a more cheerful heart.

It was after my return from one of these rambles that my father, calling me aside, thus addressed me, "I am happy to remark, my dear son, that you have resumed your former pleasures and seem to be returning to yourself. And yet you are still unhappy and still avoid our society. For some time I was lost in conjecture as to the cause of this, but yesterday an idea struck me, and if it is well founded, I conjure you to avow it. Reserve on such a point would be not only useless, but draw down treble misery on us all."

I trembled violently at his exordium, and my father continued, "I confess, my son, that I have always looked forward to your marriage with our dear Elizabeth as the tie of our domestic comfort and the stay of my declining years. You were attached to each other from your earliest infancy; you studied together, and appeared, in dispositions and tastes, entirely suited to one another. But so blind is the experience of man that what I conceived to be the best assistants to my plan may have entirely destroyed it. You, perhaps, regard her as your sister, without any wish that she might become your wife. Nay, you may have met with another whom you may love; and considering yourself as bound in honour to Elizabeth, this struggle may occasion the poignant misery which you appear to feel."

"My dear father, reassure yourself. I love my cousin tenderly and sincerely. I never saw any woman who excited, as Elizabeth does, my warmest admiration and affection. My future hopes and prospects are entirely bound up in the expectation of our union."

"The expression of your sentiments of this subject, my dear Victor, gives me more pleasure than I have for some time experienced. If you feel thus, we shall assuredly be happy, however present events may cast a gloom over us. But it is this gloom which appears to have taken so strong a hold of your mind that I wish to dissipate. Tell me, therefore, whether you object to an immediate solemnization of the marriage. We have been unfortunate, and recent events have drawn us from that everyday tranquillity befitting my years and infirmities. You are younger; yet I do not suppose, possessed as you are of a competent fortune, that an early marriage would at all interfere with any future plans of honour and utility that you may have formed. Do not suppose, however, that I wish to dictate happiness to you or that a delay on your part would cause me any serious uneasiness. Interpret my words with candour and answer me, I conjure you, with confidence and sincerity."

I listened to my father in silence and remained f[...]
time incapable of offering [...]
[...]

[...]ate before I
[...] the delight of a union from which I
[...]ected peace.

I remembered also the necessity imposed upon me of
either journeying to England or entering into a long correspondence with those philosophers of that country whose
knowledge and discoveries were of indispensable use to me
in my present undertaking. The latter method of obtaining
the desired intelligence was dilatory and unsatisfactory; besides, I had an insurmountable aversion to the idea of engaging myself in my loathsome task in my father's house while
in habits of familiar intercourse with those I loved. I knew
that a thousand fearful accidents might occur, the slightest
of which would disclose a tale to thrill all connected with me
with horror. I was aware also that I should often lose all
self-command, all capacity of hiding the harrowing sensations
that would possess me during the progress of my unearthly
occupation. I must absent myself from all I loved while thus
employed. Once commenced, it would quickly be achieved,
and I might be restored to my family in peace and happiness. My promise fulfilled, the monster would depart forever. Or (so my fond fancy imaged) some accident might
meanwhile occur to destroy him and put an end to my slavery
forever.

These feelings dictated my answer to my father. I expressed a wish to visit England, but concealing the true
reasons of this request, I clothed my desires under a guise
which excited no suspicion, while I urged my desire with an
earnestness that easily induced my father to comply. After
so long a period of an absorbing melancholy that resembled
madness in its intensity and effects, he was glad to find that
I was capable of taking pleasure in the idea of such a journey,

and he hoped that change of scene and varied amusement would, before my return, have restored me entirely to myself.

The duration of my absence was left to my own choice; a few months, or at most a year, was the period contemplated. One paternal kind precaution he had taken to ensure my having a companion. Without previously communicating with me, he had, in concert with Elizabeth, arranged that Clerval should join me at Strasbourg. This interfered with the solitude I coveted for the prosecution of my task; yet at the commencement of my journey the presence of my friend could in no way be an impediment, and truly I rejoiced that thus I should be saved many hours of lonely, maddening reflection. Nay, Henry might stand between me and the intrusion of my foe. If I were alone, would he not at times force his abhorred presence on me to remind me of my task or to contemplate its progress?

To England, therefore, I was bound, and it was understood that my union with Elizabeth should take place immediately on my return. My father's age rendered him extremely averse to delay. For myself, there was one reward I promised myself from my detested toils—one consolation for my unparalleled sufferings; it was the prospect of that day when, enfranchised from my miserable slavery, I might claim Elizabeth and forget the past in my union with her.

I now made arrangements for my journey, but one feeling haunted me which filled me with fear and agitation. During my absence I should leave my friends unconscious of the existence of their enemy and unprotected from his attacks, exasperated as he might be by my departure. But he had promised to follow me wherever I might go, and would he not accompany me to England? This imagination was dreadful in itself, but soothing inasmuch as it supposed the safety of my friends. I was agonized with the idea of the possibility that the reverse of this might happen. But through the whole period during which I was the slave of my creature I allowed myself to be governed by the impulses of the moment; and my present sensations strongly intimated that the fiend would follow me and exempt my family from the danger of his machinations.

It was in the latter end of September that I again quitted my native country. My journey had been my own sugges-

tion, and Elizabeth therefore acquiesced . . .
with disqui. . .

. . . . only, and it was
. . . . . . anguish that I reflected on it, to order that my
chemical instruments should be packed to go with me. Filled
with dreary imaginations, I passed through many beautiful
and majestic scenes, but my eyes were fixed and unobserving.
I could only think of the bourne of my travels and the work
which was to occupy me whilst they endured.

After some days spent in listless indolence, during which
I traversed many leagues, I arrived at Strasbourg, where I
waited two days for Clerval. He came. Alas, how great was
the contrast between us! He was alive to every new scene,
joyful when he saw the beauties of the setting sun, and more
happy when he beheld it rise and recommence a new day.
He pointed out to me the shifting colours of the landscape
and the appearances of the sky. "This is what it is to live,"
he cried; "now I enjoy existence! But you, my dear Frankenstein, wherefore are you desponding and sorrowful!" In truth,
I was occupied by gloomy thoughts and neither saw the descent of the evening star nor the golden sunrise reflected in
the Rhine. And you, my friend, would be far more amused
with the journal of Clerval, who observed the scenery with
an eye of feeling and delight, than in listening to my reflections. I, a miserable wretch, haunted by a curse that shut
up every avenue to enjoyment.

We had agreed to descend the Rhine in a boat from Strasbourg to Rotterdam, whence we might take shipping for London. During this voyage we passed many willowy islands and
saw several beautiful towns. We stayed a day at Mannheim,
and on the fifth from our departure from Strasbourg, arrived
at Mainz. The course of the Rhine below Mainz becomes
much more picturesque. The river descends rapidly and winds
between hills, not high, but steep, and of beautiful forms.

We saw many ruined castles standing on the edges of precipices, surrounded by black woods, high and inaccessible. This part of the Rhine, indeed, presents a singularly variegated landscape. In one spot you view rugged hills, ruined castles overlooking tremendous precipices, with the dark Rhine rushing beneath; and on the sudden turn of a promontory, flourishing vineyards with green sloping banks and a meandering river and populous towns occupy the scene.

We travelled at the time of the vintage and heard the song of the labourers as we glided down the stream. Even I, depressed in mind, and my spirits continually agitated by gloomy feelings, even I was pleased. I lay at the bottom of the boat, and as I gazed on the cloudless blue sky, I seemed to drink in a tranquillity to which I had long been a stranger. And if these were my sensations, who can describe those of Henry? He felt as if he had been transported to fairy-land and enjoyed a happiness seldom tasted by man. "I have seen," he said, "the most beautiful scenes of my own country; I have visited the lakes of Lucerne and Uri, where the snowy mountains descend almost perpendicularly to the water, casting black and impenetrable shades, which would cause a gloomy and mournful appearance were it not for the most verdant islands that relieve the eye by their gay appearance; I have seen this lake agitated by a tempest, when the wind tore up whirlwinds of water and gave you an idea of what the water-spout must be on the great ocean; and the waves dash with fury the base of the mountain, where the priest and his mistress were overwhelmed by an avalanche and where their dying voices are still said to be heard amid the pauses of the nightly wind; I have seen the mountains of La Valais, and the Pays de Vaud; but this country, Victor, pleases me more than all those wonders. The mountains of Switzerland are more majestic and strange, but there is a charm in the banks of this divine river that I never before saw equalled. Look at that castle which overhangs yon precipice; and that also on the island, almost concealed amongst the foliage of those lovely trees; and now that group of labourers coming from among their vines; and that village half hid in the recess of the mountain. Oh, surely the spirit that inhabits and guards this place has a soul more in harmony with man than those who pile the glacier or retire to the inaccessible peaks of the mountains of our own country."

Clerval! Beloved friend! Even now it delight~
your words and t~ l~

> The sounding cataract
> Haunted him like a passion: the tall rock,
> The mountain, and the deep and gloomy wood,
> Their colours and their forms, were then to him
> An appetite; a feeling, and a love,
> That had no need of a remoter charm,
> By thought supplied, or any interest
> Unborrow'd from the eye.*

laments lk

And where does he now exist? Is this gentle and lovely being lost forever? Has this mind, so replete with ideas, imaginations fanciful and magnificent, which formed a world, whose existence depended on the life of its creator—has this mind perished? Does it now only exist in my memory? No, it is not thus; your form so divinely wrought, and beaming with beauty, has decayed, but your spirit still visits and consoles your unhappy friend.

Pardon this gush of sorrow; these ineffectual words are but a slight tribute to the unexampled worth of Henry, but they soothe my heart, overflowing with the anguish which his remembrance creates. I will proceed with my tale.

Beyond Cologne we descended to the plains of Holland; and we resolved to post the remainder of our way, for the wind was contrary and the stream of the river was too gentle to aid us.

Our journey here lost the interest arising from beautiful scenery, but we arrived in a few days at Rotterdam, whence we proceeded by sea to England. It was on a clear morning, in the latter days of December, that I first saw the white

*Wordsworth's "Tintern Abbey."

strong connection

cliffs of Britain. The banks of the Thames presented a new scene; they were flat but fertile, and almost every town was marked by the remembrance of some story. We saw Tilbury Fort and remembered the Spanish Armada, Gravesend, Woolwich, and Greenwich—places which I had heard of even in my country.

At length we saw the numerous steeples of London, St. Paul's towering above all, and the Tower famed in English history.

point of rest, we determined to remain several months in this wonderful and celebrated city. Clerval desired the intercourse of the men of genius and talent who flourished at this time, but this was with me a secondary object; I was principally occupied with the means of obtaining the information necessary for the completion of my promise and quickly availed myself of the letters of introduction that I had brought with me, addressed to the most distinguished natural philosophers.

If this journey had taken place during my days of study and happiness, it would have afforded me inexpressible pleasure. But a blight had come over my existence, and I only visited these people for the sake of the information they might give me on the subject in which my interest was so terribly profound. Company was irksome to me; when alone, I could fill my mind with the sights of heaven and earth; the voice of Henry soothed me, and I could thus cheat myself into a transitory peace. But busy, uninteresting, joyous faces brought back despair to my heart. I saw an insurmountable barrier placed between me and my fellow men; this barrier was sealed with the blood of William and Justine, and to reflect on the events connected with those names filled my soul with anguish.

But in Clerval I saw the image of my former self; he was inquisitive and anxious to gain experience and instruction. The difference of manners which he observed was to him an inexhaustible source of instruction and amusement. He was also pursuing an object he had long had in view. His design was to visit India, in the belief that he had in his knowledge of its various languages, and in the views he had taken of its society, the means of materially assisting the prog-

V's blighted existence

ress of European colonization and trade. In Britain only could he further the execution of his plan. He was forever busy, and the only check to his enjoyments was my sorrowful and dejected mind. I tried to conceal this as much as possible, that I might not debar him from the pleasures natural to one who was entering on a new scene of life, undisturbed by any care or bitter recollection. I often refused to accompany him, alleging another engagement, that I might remain alone. I now also began to collect the materials necessary for my new creation, and this was to me like the torture of single drops of water continually falling on the head. Every thought that was devoted to it was an extreme anguish, and every word that I spoke in allusion to it caused my lips to quiver, and my heart to palpitate.

After passing some months in London, we received a letter from a person in Scotland who had formerly been our visitor at Geneva. He mentioned the beauties of his native country and asked us if those were not sufficient allurements to induce us to prolong our journey as far north as Perth, where he resided. Clerval eagerly desired to accept this invitation, and I, although I abhorred society, wished to view again mountains and streams and all the wondrous works with which Nature adorns her chosen dwelling-places.

We had arrived in England at the beginning of October, and it was now February. We accordingly determined to commence our journey towards the north at the expiration of another month. In this expedition we did not intend to follow the great road to Edinburgh, but to visit Windsor, Oxford, Matlock, and the Cumberland lakes, resolving to arrive at the completion of this tour about the end of July. I packed up my chemical instruments and the materials I had collected, resolving to finish my labours in some obscure nook in the northern highlands of Scotland.

We quitted London on the 27th of March and remained a few days at Windsor, rambling in its beautiful forest. This was a new scene to us mountaineers; the majestic oaks, the quantity of game, and the herds of stately deer were all novelties to us.

From thence we proceeded to Oxford. As we entered this city our minds were filled with the remembrance of the events that had been transacted there more than a century and a half before. It was here that Charles I had collected his

forces. This city had remained faithful to him, after the
nation had forsaken his cause to join the standard of par-
liament and liberty.

...streets are al-
...sis, which flows beside it
...ows of exquisite verdure, is spread forth into
a placid expanse of waters, which reflects its majestic assemblage of towers, and spires, and domes, embosomed among
aged trees.

I enjoyed this scene, and yet my enjoyment was embittered
both by the memory of the past and the anticipation of the
future. I was formed for peaceful happiness. During my
youthful days discontent never visited my mind, and if I was
ever overcome by *ennui,* the sight of what is beautiful in
nature or the study of what is excellent and sublime in the
productions of man could always interest my heart and communicate elasticity to my spirits. But I am a blasted tree;
the bolt has entered my soul; and I felt then that I should
survive to exhibit what I shall soon cease to be—a miserable
spectacle of wrecked humanity, pitiable to others and intolerable to myself.

We passed a considerable period at Oxford, rambling
among its environs and endeavouring to identify every spot
which might relate to the most animating epoch of English
history. Our little voyages of discovery were often prolonged
by the successive objects that presented themselves. We visited the tomb of the illustrious Hampden and the field on
which that patriot fell. For a moment my soul was elevated
from its debasing and miserable fears to contemplate the
divine ideas of liberty and self-sacrifice of which these sights
were the monuments and the remembrancers. For an instant
I dared to shake off my chains and look around me with a
free and lofty spirit, but the iron had eaten into my flesh,
and I sank again, trembling and hopeless, into my miserable
self.

We left Oxford with regret and proceeded to Matlock, which was our next place of rest. The country in the neighbourhood of this village resembled, to a greater degree, the scenery of Switzerland; but everything is on a lower scale, and the green hills want the crown of distant white Alps which always attend on the piny mountains of my native country. We visited the wondrous cave and the little cabinets of natural history, where the curiosities are disposed in the same manner as in the collections at Servox and Chamounix. The latter name made me tremble when pronounced by Henry, and I hastened to quit Matlock, with which that terrible scene was thus associated.

From Derby, still journeying northwards, we passed two months in Cumberland and Westmorland. I could now almost fancy myself among the Swiss mountains. The little patches of snow which yet lingered on the northern sides of the mountains, the lakes, and the dashing of the rocky streams were all familiar and dear sights to me. Here also we made some acquaintances, who almost contrived to cheat me into happiness. The delight of Clerval was proportionably greater than mine; his mind expanded in the company of men of talent, and he found in his own nature greater capacities and resources than he could have imagined himself to have possessed while he associated with his inferiors. "I could pass my life here," said he to me; "and among these mountains I should scarcely regret Switzerland and the Rhine."

But he found that a traveller's life is one that includes much pain amidst its enjoyments. His feelings are forever on the stretch; and when he begins to sink into repose, he finds himself obliged to quit that on which he rests in pleasure for something new, which again engages his attention, and which also he forsakes for other novelties.

We had scarcely visited the various lakes of Cumberland and Westmorland and conceived an affection for some of the inhabitants when the period of our appointment with our Scotch friend approached, and we left them to travel on. For my own part I was not sorry. I had now neglected my promise for some time, and I feared the effects of the demon's disappointment. He might remain in Switzerland and wreak his vengeance on my relatives. This idea pursued me and tormented me at every moment from which I might otherwise have snatched repose and peace. I waited for my letters with

knows danger of sit.

feverish impatience; if they were delayed I was miserable and
overcome by a thousand fears: ~~~~
saw the ~~~~

~~~~or by winds done~~~~

...sited Edinburgh with languid eyes and mind; and yet
that city might have interested the most unfortunate being.
Clerval did not like it so well as Oxford, for the antiquity
of the latter city was more pleasing to him. But the beauty
and regularity of the new town of Edinburgh, its romantic
castle and its environs, the most delightful in the world,
Arthur's Seat, St. Bernard's Well, and the Pentland Hills
compensated him for the change and filled him with cheerfulness and admiration. But I was impatient to arrive at the
termination of my journey.

We left Edinburgh in a week, passing through Coupar,
St. Andrew's, and along the banks of the Tay, to Perth, where
our friend expected us. But I was in no mood to laugh and
talk with strangers or enter into their feelings of plans with
the good humour expected from a guest; and accordingly I
told Clerval that I wished to make the tour of Scotland alone.
"Do you," said I, "enjoy yourself, and let this be our ren-
dezvous. I may be absent a month or two; but do not interfere
with my motions, I entreat you; leave me to peace and solitude for a short time; and when I return, I hope it will be
with a lighter heart, more congenial to your own temper."

Henry wished to dissuade me, but seeing me bent on this
plan, ceased to remonstrate. He entreated me to write often.
"I had rather be with you," he said, "in your solitary rambles,
than with these Scotch people, whom I do not know; hasten,
then, my dear friend, to return, that I may again feel myself
somewhat at home, which I cannot do in your absence."

Having parted from my friend, I determined to visit some
remote spot of Scotland and finish my work in solitude. I
did not doubt but that the monster followed me and would

discover himself to me when I should have finished, that he might receive his companion.

With this resolution I traversed the northern highlands and fixed on one of the remotest of the Orkneys as the scene of my labours. It was a place fitted for such a work, being hardly more than a rock whose high sides were continually beaten upon by the waves. The soil was barren, scarcely affording pasture for a few miserable cows, and oatmeal for its inhabitants, which consisted of five persons, whose gaunt and scraggy limbs gave tokens of their miserable fare. Vegetables and bread, when they indulged in such luxuries, and even fresh water, was to be procured from the mainland, which was about five miles distant.

On the whole island there were but three miserable huts, and one of these was vacant when I arrived. This I hired. It contained but two rooms, and these exhibited all the squalidness of the most miserable penury. The thatch had fallen in, the walls were unplastered, and the door was off its hinges. I ordered it to be repaired, bought some furniture, and took possession, an incident which would doubtless have occasioned some surprise had not all the senses of the cottagers been benumbed by want and squalid poverty. As it was, I lived ungazed at and unmolested, hardly thanked for the pittance of food and clothes which I gave, so much does suffering blunt even the coarsest sensations of men.

In this retreat I devoted the morning to labour; but in the evening, when the weather permitted, I walked on the stony beach of the sea to listen to the waves as they roared and dashed at my feet. It was a monotonous yet ever-changing scene. I thought of Switzerland; it was far different from this desolate and appalling landscape. Its hills are covered with vines, and its cottages are scattered thickly in the plains. Its fair lakes reflect a blue and gentle sky, and when troubled by the winds, their tumult is but as the play of a lively infant when compared to the roarings of the giant ocean.

In this manner I distributed my occupations when I first arrived, but as I proceeded in my labour, it became every day more horrible and irksome to me. Sometimes I could not prevail on myself to enter my laboratory for several days, and at other times I toiled day and night in order to complete my work. It was, indeed, a filthy process in which I was engaged. During my first experiment, a kind of enthusiastic

frenzy had blinded me to the horror of my employment; my mind was intently fixed on the consummati...
and ...

... encounter the object which I so much dreaded to behold. I feared to wander from the sight of my fellow creatures lest when alone he should come to claim his companion.

In the meantime I worked on, and my labour was already considerably advanced. I looked towards its completion with a tremulous and eager hope, which I dared not trust myself to question but which was intermixed with obscure forebodings of evil that made my heart sicken in my bosom.

CHAPTER 20

forseel
prob.

I sat one evening in my laboratory; the sun had set, and the moon was just rising from the sea; I had not sufficient light for my employment, and I remained idle, in a pause of consideration of whether I should leave my labour for the night or hasten its conclusion by an unremitting attention to it. As I sat, a train of reflection occurred to me which led me to consider the effects of what I was now doing. Three years before, I was engaged in the same manner and had created a fiend whose unparalleled barbarity had desolated my heart and filled it forever with the bitterest remorse. I was now about to form another being of whose dispositions I was alike ignorant; she might become ten thousand times more malignant than her mate and delight, for its own sake, in murder and wretchedness. He had sworn to quit the neighbourhood of man and hide himself in deserts, but she had not; and she, who in all probability was to become a thinking and reasoning animal, might refuse to comply with a compact made before her creation. They might even hate each other; the creature who already lived loathed his own deformity, and might he not conceive a greater abhorrence for it when it came before his eyes in the female form? She also might turn with disgust from him to the superior beauty of man; she might quit him, and he be again alone, exasperated by the fresh provocation of being deserted by one of his own species.

Even if they were to leave Europe and inhabit the deserts of the new world, yet one of the first results of those sympathies for which the demon thirsted would be children, and a race of devils would be propagated upon the earth who might make the very existence of the species of man a condition precarious and full of terror. Had I right, for my

own benefit, to inflict this curse upon everlasting
tions?...

... lips as he gazed on
me, where I sat fulfilling the task which he had allotted
to me. Yes, he had followed me in my travels; he had
loitered in forests, hid himself in caves, or taken refuge in
wide and desert heaths; and he now came to mark my
progress and claim the fulfilment of my promise.

As I looked on him, his countenance expressed the utmost extent of malice and treachery. I thought with a sensation of madness on my promise of creating another like
to him, and trembling with passion, tore to pieces the thing
on which I was engaged. The wretch saw me destroy the
creature on whose future existence he depended for happiness, and with a howl of devilish despair and revenge,
withdrew.

I left the room, and locking the door, made a solemn
vow in my own heart never to resume my labours; and
then, with trembling steps, I sought my own apartment. I
was alone; none were near me to dissipate the gloom and
relieve me from the sickening oppression of the most terrible reveries.

Several hours passed, and I remained near my window
gazing on the sea; it was almost motionless, for the winds
were hushed, and all nature reposed under the eye of the
quiet moon. A few fishing vessels alone specked the water,
and now and then the gentle breeze wafted the sound of
voices as the fishermen called to one another. I felt the
silence, although I was hardly conscious of its extreme pro-
fundity, until my ear was suddenly arrested by the paddling
of oars near the shore, and a person landed close to my
house.

In a few minutes after, I heard the creaking of my door,
as if some one endeavoured to open it softly. I trembled

from head to foot; I felt a presentiment of who it was and wished to rouse one of the peasants who dwelt in a cottage not far from mine; but I was overcome by the sensation of helplessness, so often felt in frightful dreams, when you in vain endeavour to fly from an impending danger, and was rooted to the spot.

Presently I heard the sound of footsteps along the passage; the door opened, and the wretch whom I dreaded appeared. Shutting the door, he approached me and said in a smothered voice, "You have destroyed the work which you began; what is it that you intend? Do you dare to break your promise? I have endured toil and misery; I left Switzerland with you; I crept along the shores of the Rhine, among its willow islands and over the summits of its hills. I have dwelt many months in the heaths of England and among the deserts of Scotland. I have endured incalculable fatigue, and cold, and hunger; do you dare destroy my hopes?"

"Begone! I do break my promise; never will I create another like yourself, equal in deformity and wickedness."

"Slave, I before reasoned with you, but you have proved yourself unworthy of my condescension. Remember that I have power; you believe yourself miserable, but I can make you so wretched that the light of day will be hateful to you. You are my creator, but I am your master; obey!"

"The hour of my irresolution is past, and the period of your power is arrived. Your threats cannot move me to do an act of wickedness; but they confirm me in a determination of not creating you a companion in vice. Shall I, in cool blood, set loose upon the earth a demon whose delight is in death and wretchedness? Begone! I am firm, and your words will only exasperate my rage."

The monster saw my determination in my face and gnashed his teeth in the impotence of anger. "Shall each man," cried he, "find a wife for his bosom, and each beast have his mate, and I be alone? I had feelings of affection, and they were requited by detestation and scorn. Man! You may hate, but beware! Your hours will pass in dread and misery, and soon the bolt will fall which must ravish from you your happiness forever. Are you to be happy while I grovel in the intensity of my wretchedness? You can blast my other passions, but revenge remains—revenge, henceforth dearer than light or food! I may die, but first you, my tyrant and tormentor, shall curse the sun that

~~...started~~ forward and exclaimed, "Villain! Before you sign my death-warrant, be sure that you are yourself safe."

I would have seized him, but he eluded me and quitted the house with precipitation. In a few moments I saw him in his boat, which shot across the waters with an arrowy swiftness and was soon lost amidst the waves.

All was again silent, but his words rang in my ears. I burned with rage to pursue the murderer of my peace and precipitate him into the ocean. I walked up and down my room hastily and perturbed, while my imagination conjured up a thousand images to torment and sting me. Why had I not followed him and closed with him in mortal strife? But I had suffered him to depart, and he had directed his course towards the mainland. I shuddered to think who might be the next victim sacrificed to his insatiate revenge. And then I thought again of his words—"*I will be with you on your wedding-night.*" That, then, was the period fixed for the fulfilment of my destiny. In that hour I should die and at once satisfy and extinguish his malice. The prospect did not move me to fear; yet when I thought of my beloved Elizabeth, of her tears and endless sorrow, when she should find her lover so barbarously snatched from her, tears, the first I had shed for many months, streamed from my eyes, and I resolved not to fall before my enemy without a bitter struggle.

The night passed away, and the sun rose from the ocean; my feelings became calmer, if it may be called calmness when the violence of rage sinks into the depths of despair. I left the house, the horrid scene of the last night's contention, and walked on the beach of the sea, which I almost regarded as an insuperable barrier between me and my fellow creatures; nay, a wish that such should prove the fact stole across me. I desired that I might pass my life on that barren rock, wearily, it is true, but uninterrupted by any sudden shock of misery. If I returned, it was to be sacrificed or to see those whom I most loved die under the grasp of a demon whom I had myself created.

I walked about the isle like a restless spectre, separated from all it loved and miserable in the separation. When it became noon, and the sun rose higher, I lay down on the grass and was overpowered by a deep sleep. I had been awake the whole of the preceding night, my nerves were agitated, and my eyes inflamed by watching and misery. The sleep into which I now sank refreshed me; and when I awoke, I again felt as if I belonged to a race of human beings like myself, and I began to reflect upon what had passed with greater composure; yet still the words of the fiend rang in my ears like a death-knell; they appeared like a dream, yet distinct and oppressive as a reality.

The sun had far descended, and I still sat on the shore, satisfying my appetite, which had become ravenous, with an oaten cake, when I saw a fishing-boat land close to me, and one of the men brought me a packet; it contained letters from Geneva, and one from Clerval entreating me to join him. He said that he was wearing away his time fruitlessly where he was, that letters from the friends he had formed in London desired his return to complete the negotiation they had entered into for his Indian enterprise. He could not any longer delay his departure; but as his journey to London might be followed, even sooner than he now conjectured, by his longer voyage, he entreated me to bestow as much of my society on him as I could spare. He besought me, therefore, to leave my solitary isle and to meet him at Perth, that we might proceed southwards together. This letter in a degree recalled me to life, and I determined to quit my island at the expiration of two days.

Yet, before I departed, there was a task to perform, on which I shuddered to reflect; I must pack up my chemical instruments, and for that purpose I must enter the room which had been the scene of my odious work, and I must handle those utensils the sight of which was sickening to me. The next morning, at daybreak, I summoned sufficient courage and unlocked the door of my laboratory. The re-

mains of the half-finished creature, whom I had destroyed
lay scattered on the f...

...ging my

...apparatus.

Nothing could be more complete than the alteration that
had taken place in my feelings since the night of the appearance of the demon. I had before regarded my promise
with a gloomy despair as a thing that, with whatever consequences, must be fulfilled; but I now felt as if a film had
been taken from before my eyes and that I for the first
time saw clearly. The idea of renewing my labours did not
for one instant occur to me; the threat I had heard weighed
on my thoughts, but I did not reflect that a voluntary act
of mine could avert it. I had resolved in my own mind
that to create another like the fiend I had first made would
be an act of the basest and most atrocious selfishness, and
I banished from my mind every thought that could lead to
a different conclusion.

Between two and three in the morning the moon rose;
and I then, putting my basket aboard a little skiff, sailed
out about four miles from the shore. The scene was perfectly solitary; a few boats were returning towards land, but
I sailed away from them. I felt as if I was about the commission of a dreadful crime and avoided with shuddering
anxiety any encounter with my fellow creatures. At one time
the moon, which had before been clear, was suddenly over-
spread by a thick cloud, and I took advantage of the moment of darkness and cast my basket into the sea; I listened
to the gurgling sound as it sank and then sailed away from
the spot. The sky became clouded, but the air was pure,
although chilled by the northeast breeze that was then rising.
But it refreshed me and filled me with such agreeable sensations that I resolved to prolong my stay on the water,
and fixing the rudder in a direct position, stretched myself

at the bottom of the boat. Clouds hid the moon, everything was obscure, and I heard only the sound of the boat as its keel cut through the waves; the murmur lulled me, and in a short time I slept soundly.

I do not know how long I remained in this situation, but when I awoke I found that the sun had already mounted considerably. The wind was high, and the waves continually threatened the safety of my little skiff. I found that the wind was northeast and must have driven me far from the coast from which I had embarked. I endeavoured to change my course but quickly found that if I again made the attempt the boat would be instantly filled with water. Thus situated, my only resource was to drive before the wind. I confess that I felt a few sensations of terror. I had no compass with me and was so slenderly acquainted with the geography of this part of the world that the sun was of little benefit to me. I might be driven into the wide Atlantic and feel all the tortures of starvation or be swallowed up in the immeasurable waters that roared and buffeted around me. I had already been out many hours and felt the torment of a burning thirst, a prelude to my other sufferings. I looked on the heavens, which were covered by clouds that flew before the wind, only to be replaced by others; I looked upon the sea; it was to be my grave. "Fiend," I exclaimed, "your task is already fulfilled!" I thought of Elizabeth, of my father, and of Clerval—all left behind, on whom the monster might satisfy his sanguinary and merciless passions. This idea plunged me into a reverie so despairing and frightful that even now, when the scene is on the point of closing before me forever, I shudder to reflect on it.

Some hours passed thus; but by degrees, as the sun declined towards the horizon, the wind died away into a gentle breeze and the sea became free from breakers. But these gave place to a heavy swell; I felt sick and hardly able to hold the rudder, when suddenly I saw a line of high land towards the south.

Almost spent, as I was, by fatigue and the dreadful suspense I endured for several hours, this sudden certainty of life rushed like a flood of warm joy to my heart, and tears gushed from my eyes.

How mutable are our feelings, and how strange is that clinging love we have of life even in the excess of misery! I constructed another sail with a part of my dress and eager-

tory I perceived a small neat town and a good harbour, which I entered, my heart bounding with joy at my unexpected escape.

As I was occupied in fixing the boat and arranging the sails, several people crowded towards the spot. They seemed much surprised at my appearance, but instead of offering me any assistance, whispered together with gestures that at any other time might have produced in me a slight sensation of alarm. As it was, I merely remarked that they spoke English, and I therefore addressed them in that language. "My good friends," said I, "will you be so kind as to tell me the name of this town and inform me where I am?"

"You will know that soon enough," replied a man with a hoarse voice. "Maybe you are come to a place that will not prove much to your taste, but you will not be consulted as to your quarters, I promise you."

I was exceedingly surprised on receiving so rude an answer from a stranger, and I was also disconcerted on perceiving the frowning and angry countenances of his companions. "Why do you answer me so roughly?" I replied. "Surely it is not the custom of Englishmen to receive strangers so inhospitably."

"I do not know," said the man, "what the custom of the English may be, but it is the custom of the Irish to hate villains."

While this strange dialogue continued, I perceived the crowd rapidly increase. Their faces expressed a mixture of curiosity and anger, which annoyed and in some degree alarmed me. I inquired the way to the inn, but no one replied. I then moved forward, and a murmuring sound arose from the crowd as they followed and surrounded me, when an ill-looking man approaching tapped me on the shoulder and said, "Come, sir, you must follow me to Mr. Kirwin's to give an account of yourself."

"Who is Mr. Kirwin? Why am I to give an account of myself? Is not this a free country?"

"Ay, sir, free enough for honest folks. Mr. Kirwin is a magistrate, and you are to give an account of the death of a gentleman who was found murdered here last night."

This answer startled me, but I presently recovered myself. I was innocent; that could easily be proved; accordingly I followed my conductor in silence and was led to one of the best houses in the town. I was ready to sink from fatigue and hunger, but being surrounded by a crowd, I thought it politic to rouse all my strength, that no physical debility might be construed into apprehension or conscious guilt. Little did I then expect the calamity that was in a few moments to overwhelm me and extinguish in horror and despair all fear of ignominy or death.

I must pause here, for it requires all my fortitude to recall the memory of the frightful events which I am about to relate, in proper detail, to my recollection.

Horrible things again

upon me, however, with some degree of severity, and then,
turning towards my conductors, he asked who appeared as
witnesses on this occasion.

About half a dozen men came forward; and, one being
selected by the magistrate, he deposed that he had been out
fishing the night before with his son and brother-in-law,
Daniel Nugent, when, about ten o'clock, they observed a
strong northerly blast rising, and they accordingly put in for
port. It was a very dark night, as the moon had not yet risen;
they did not land at the harbour, but, as they had been accustomed, at a creek about two miles below. He walked on
first, carrying a part of the fishing tackle, and his companions
followed him at some distance. As he was proceeding along
the sands, he struck his foot against something and fell at his
length on the ground. His companions came up to assist
him, and by the light of their lantern they found that he had
fallen on the body of a man, who was to all appearance dead.
Their first supposition was that it was the corpse of some
person who had been drowned and was thrown on shore
by the waves, but on examination they found that the clothes
were not wet and even that the body was not then cold. They
instantly carried it to the cottage of an old woman near
the spot and endeavoured, but in vain, to restore it to life.
It appeared to be a handsome young man, about five and
twenty years of age. He had apparently been strangled, for
there was no sign of any violence except the black mark of
fingers on his neck.

The first part of this deposition did not in the least interest
me, but when the mark of the fingers was mentioned I remembered the murder of my brother and felt myself extreme-

ly agitated; my limbs trembled, and a mist came over my eyes, which obliged me to lean on a chair for support. The magistrate observed me with a keen eye and of course drew an unfavourable augury from my manner.

The son confirmed his father's account, but when Daniel Nugent was called he swore positively that just before the fall of his companion, he saw a boat, with a single man in it, at a short distance from the shore; and as far as he could judge by the light of a few stars, it was the same boat in which I had just landed.

A woman deposed that she lived near the beach and was standing at the door of her cottage, waiting for the return of the fishermen, about an hour before she heard of the discovery of the body, when she saw a boat with only one man in it push off from that part of the shore where the corpse was afterwards found.

Another woman confirmed the account of the fishermen having brought the body into her house; it was not cold. They put it into a bed and rubbed it, and Daniel went to the town for an apothecary, but life was quite gone.

Several other men were examined concerning my landing, and they agreed that, with the strong north wind that had arisen during the night, it was very probable that I had beaten about for many hours and had been obliged to return nearly to the same spot from which I had departed. Besides, they observed that it appeared that I had brought the body from another place, and it was likely that as I did not appear to know the shore, I might have put into the harbour ignorant of the distance of the town of —— from the place where I had deposited the corpse.

Mr. Kirwin, on hearing this evidence, desired that I should be taken into the room where the body lay for interment, that it might be observed what effect the sight of it would produce upon me. This idea was probably suggested by the extreme agitation I had exhibited when the mode of the murder had been described. I was accordingly conducted, by the magistrate and several other persons, to the inn. I could not help being struck by the strange coincidences that had taken place during this eventful night; but, knowing that I had been conversing with several persons in the island I had inhabited about the time that the body had been found, I was perfectly tranquil as to the consequences of the affair.

I entered the room where the corpse lay and was led up

tor—"

The human frame could no longer support the agonies that I endured, and I was carried out of the room in strong convulsions.

A fever succeeded to this. I lay for two months on the point of death; my ravings, as I afterwards heard, were frightful; I called myself the murderer of William, of Justine, and of Clerval. Sometimes I entreated my attendants to assist me in the destruction of the fiend by whom I was tormented; and at others I felt the fingers of the monster already grasping my neck, and screamed aloud with agony and terror. Fortunately, as I spoke my native language, Mr. Kirwin alone understood me; but my gestures and bitter cries were sufficient to affright the other witnesses.

Why did I not die? More miserable than man ever was before, why did I not sink into forgetfulness and rest? Death snatches away many blooming children, the only hopes of their doting parents; how many brides and youthful lovers have been one day in the bloom of health and hope, and the next a prey for worms and the decay of the tomb! Of what materials was I made that I could thus resist so many shocks, which, like the turning of the wheel, continually renewed the torture?

But I was doomed to live and in two months found myself as awaking from a dream, in a prison, stretched on a wretched bed, surrounded by jailers, turnkeys, bolts, and all the miserable apparatus of a dungeon. It was morning, I remember, when I thus awoke to understanding; I had forgotten the particulars of what had happened and only felt as if some great misfortune had suddenly overwhelmed me; but when I looked around and saw the barred windows and the squalidness of the room in which I was, all flashed across my memory and I groaned bitterly.

This sound disturbed an old woman who was sleeping in a chair beside me. She was a hired nurse, the wife of one of the turnkeys, and her countenance expressed all those bad qualities which often characterize that class. The lines of her face were hard and rude, like that of persons accustomed to see without sympathizing in sights of misery. Her tone expressed her entire indifference; she addressed me in English, and the voice struck me as one that I had heard during my sufferings. "Are you better now, sir?" said she.

I replied in the same language, with a feeble voice, "I believe I am; but if it be all true, if indeed I did not dream, I am sorry that I am still alive to feel this misery and horror."

"For that matter," replied the old woman, "if you mean about the gentleman you murdered, I believe that it were better for you if you were dead, for I fancy it will go hard with you! However, that's none of my business; I am sent to nurse you and get you well; I do my duty with a safe conscience; it were well if everybody did the same."

I turned with loathing from the woman who could utter so unfeeling a speech to a person just saved, on the very edge of death; but I felt languid and unable to reflect on all that had passed. The whole series of my life appeared to me as a dream; I sometimes doubted if indeed it were all true, for it never presented itself to my mind with the force of reality.

As the images that floated before me became more distinct, I grew feverish; a darkness pressed around me; no one was near me who soothed me with the gentle voice of love; no dear hand supported me. The physician came and prescribed medicines, and the old woman prepared them for me; but utter carelessness was visible in the first, and the expression of brutality was strongly marked in the visage of the second. Who could be interested in the fate of a murderer but the hangman who would gain his fee?

These were my first reflections, but I soon learned that Mr. Kirwin had shown me extreme kindness. He had caused the best room in the prison to be prepared for me (wretched indeed was the best); and it was he who had provided a physician and a nurse. It is true, he seldom came to see me, for although he ardently desired to relieve the sufferings of every human creature, he did not wish to be present at the agonies and miserable ravings of a murderer. He came,

ment was opened and Mr. Kirwin entered. His countenance expressed sympathy and compassion; he drew a chair close to mine and addressed me in French, "I fear that this place is very shocking to you; can I do anything to make you more comfortable?"

"I thank you, but all that you mention is nothing to me; on the whole earth there is no comfort which I am capable of receiving."

"I know that the sympathy of a stranger can be but of little relief to one borne down as you are by so strange a misfortune. But you will, I hope, soon quit this melancholy abode, for doubtless evidence can easily be brought to free you from the criminal charge."

"That is my least concern; I am, by a course of strange events, become the most miserable of mortals. Persecuted and tortured as I am and have been, can death be any evil to me?"

"Nothing indeed could be more unfortunate and agonizing than the strange chances that have lately occurred. You were thrown, by some surprising accident, on this shore, renowned for its hospitality, seized immediately, and charged with murder. The first sight that was presented to your eyes was the body of your friend, murdered in so unaccountable a manner and placed, as it were, by some fiend across your path."

As Mr. Kirwin said this, notwithstanding the agitation I endured on this retrospect of my sufferings, I also felt considerable surprise at the knowledge he seemed to possess concerning me. I suppose some astonishment was exhibited in my countenance, for Mr. Kirwin hastened to say, "Immediately upon your being taken ill, all the papers that were on your person were brought me, and I examined them that I might discover some trace by which I could send to your relations an account of your misfortune and illness. I found several letters, and, among others, one which I discovered from its commencement to be from your father. I instantly wrote to Geneva; nearly two months have elapsed since the departure of my letter. But you are ill; even now you tremble; you are unfit for agitation of any kind."

"This suspense is a thousand times worse than the most horrible event; tell me what new scene of death has been acted, and whose murder I am now to lament?"

"Your family is perfectly well," said Mr. Kirwin with gentleness; "and someone, a friend, is come to visit you."

I know not by what chain of thought the idea presented itself, but it instantly darted into my mind that the murderer had come to mock at my misery and taunt me with the death of Clerval, as a new incitement for me to comply with his hellish desires. I put my hand before my eyes, and cried out in agony, "Oh! Take him away! I cannot see him; for God's sake, do not let him enter!"

Mr. Kirwin regarded me with a troubled countenance. He could not help regarding my exclamation as a presumption of my guilt and said in rather a severe tone, "I should have thought, young man, that the presence of your father would have been welcome instead of inspiring such violent repugnance."

"My father!" cried I, while every feature and every muscle was relaxed from anguish to pleasure. "Is my father indeed come? How kind, how very kind! But where is he, why does he not hasten to me?"

My change of manner surprised and pleased the magistrate; perhaps he thought that my former exclamation was a momentary return of delirium, and now he instantly resumed his former benevolence. He rose and quitted the room with my nurse, and in a moment my father entered it.

Nothing, at this moment, could have given me greater pleasure than the arrival of my father. I stretched out my hand to him and cried, "Are you, then, safe—and Elizabeth—and Ernest?"

My father calmed me with assurances of their welfare and endeavoured, by dwelling on these subjects so interesting to my heart, to raise my desponding spirits; but he soon felt

destiny

that a prison cannot be the abode of cheerfulness. "What a place is this that you inhabit

[illegible obscured text]

. . . . . . not allowed to converse for any length of time, for the precarious state of my health rendered every precaution necessary that could ensure tranquillity. Mr. Kirwin came in and insisted that my strength should not be exhausted by too much exertion. But the appearance of my father was to me like that of my good angel, and I gradually recovered my health.

As my sickness quitted me, I was absorbed by a gloomy and black melancholy that nothing could dissipate. The image of Clerval was forever before me, ghastly and murdered. More than once the agitation into which these reflections threw me made my friends dread a dangerous relapse. Alas! Why did they preserve so miserable and detested a life? It was surely that I might fulfil my destiny, which is now drawing to a close. Soon, oh, very soon, will death extinguish these throbbings and relieve me from the mighty weight of anguish that bears me to the dust; and, in executing the award of justice, I shall also sink to rest. Then the appearance of death was distant, although the wish was ever present to my thoughts; and I often sat for hours motionless and speechless, wishing for some mighty revolution that might bury me and my destroyer in its ruins.

The season of the assizes approached. I had already been three months in prison, and although I was still weak and in continual danger of a relapse, I was obliged to travel nearly a hundred miles to the country town where the court was held. Mr. Kirwin charged himself with every care of collecting witnesses and arranging my defence. I was spared the disgrace of appearing publicly as a criminal, as the case was not brought before the court that decides on life and death. The grand jury rejected the bill, on its being proved that I was on

fate = death

the Orkney Islands at the hour the body of my friend was found; and a fortnight after my removal I was liberated from prison.

My father was enraptured on finding me freed from the vexations of a criminal charge, that I was again allowed to breathe the fresh atmosphere and permitted to return to my native country. I did not participate in these feelings, for to me the walls of a dungeon or a palace were alike hateful. The cup of life was poisoned forever, and although the sun shone upon me, as upon the happy and gay of heart, I saw around me nothing but a dense and frightful darkness, penetrated by no light but the glimmer of two eyes that glared upon me. Sometimes they were the expressive eyes of Henry, languishing in death, the dark orbs nearly covered by the lids and the long black lashes that fringed them; sometimes it was the watery, clouded eyes of the monster, as I first saw them in my chamber at Ingolstadt.

My father tried to awaken in me the feelings of affection. He talked of Geneva, which I should soon visit, of Elizabeth and Ernest; but these words only drew deep groans from me. Sometimes, indeed, I felt a wish for happiness and thought with melancholy delight of my beloved cousin or longed, with a devouring *maladie du pays,* to see once more the blue lake and rapid Rhone, that had been so dear to me in early childhood; but my general state of feeling was a torpor in which a prison was as welcome a residence as the divinest scene in nature; and these fits were seldom interrupted but by paroxysms of anguish and despair. At these moments I often endeavoured to put an end to the existence I loathed, and it required unceasing attendance and vigilance to restrain me from committing some dreadful act of violence.

Yet one duty remained to me, the recollection of which finally triumphed over my selfish despair. It was necessary that I should return without delay to Geneva, there to watch over the lives of those I so fondly loved and to lie in wait for the murderer, that if any chance led me to the place of his concealment, or if he dared again to blast me by his presence, I might, with unfailing aim, put an end to the existence of the monstrous image which I had endued with the mockery of a soul still more monstrous. My father still desired to delay our departure, fearful that I could not sustain the fatigues of a journey, for I was a shattered wreck—the shadow of a hu-

man being. My strength was gone. I was a mere skeleton,
and fever night and day

... which I was, the wind that blew me from the detested shore of Ireland, and the sea which surrounded me
told me too forcibly that I was deceived by no vision and
that Clerval, my friend and dearest companion, had fallen
a victim to me and the monster of my creation. I repassed,
in my memory, my whole life—my quiet happiness while
residing with my family in Geneva, the death of my mother,
and my departure for Ingolstadt. I remembered, shuddering,
the mad enthusiasm that hurried me on to the creation of
my hideous enemy, and I called to mind the night in which
he first lived. I was unable to pursue the train of thought;
a thousand feelings pressed upon me, and I wept bitterly.

Ever since my recovery from the fever I had been in the
custom of taking every night a small quantity of lauda-
num, for it was by means of this drug only that I was enabled
to gain the rest necessary for the preservation of life. Oppressed by the recollection of my various misfortunes, I now
swallowed double my usual quantity and soon slept pro-
foundly. But sleep did not afford me respite from thought
and misery; my dreams presented a thousand objects that
scared me. Towards morning I was possessed by a kind of
nightmare; I felt the fiend's grasp in my neck and could not
free myself from it; groans and cries rang in my ears. My
father, who was watching over me, perceiving my restless-
ness, awoke me; the dashing waves were around, the cloudy
sky above, the fiend was not here: a sense of security, a
feeling that a truce was established between the present hour
and the irresistible, disastrous future imparted to me a kind
of calm forgetfulness, of which the human mind is by its
structure peculiarly susceptible.

CHAPTER 22

The voyage came to an end. We landed, and proceeded to Paris. I soon found that I had overtaxed my strength and that I must repose before I could continue my journey. My father's care and attentions were indefatigable, but he did not know the origin of my sufferings and sought erroneous methods to remedy the incurable ill. He wished me to seek amusement in society. I abhorred the face of man. Oh, not abhorred! They were my brethren, my fellow beings, and I felt attracted even to the most repulsive among them, as to creatures of an angelic nature and celestial mechanism. But I felt that I had no right to share their intercourse. I had unchained an enemy among them whose joy it was to shed their blood and to revel in their groans. How they would, each and all, abhor me and hunt me from the world did they know my unhallowed acts and the crimes which had their source in me!

My father yielded at length to my desire to avoid society and strove by various arguments to banish my despair. Sometimes he thought that I felt deeply the degradation of being obliged to answer a charge of murder, and he endeavoured to prove to me the futility of pride.

"Alas! My father," said I, "how little do you know me. Human beings, their feelings and passions, would indeed be degraded if such a wretch as I felt pride. Justine, poor unhappy Justine, was as innocent as I, and she suffered the same charge; she died for it; and I am the cause of this— I murdered her. William, Justine, and Henry—they all died by my hands."

My father had often, during my imprisonment, heard me make the same assertion; when I thus accused myself, he sometimes seemed to desire an explanation, and at others he

won't seek sympathy out of fear of rejection

appeared to consider it as the offspring of delirium, and that during my illness, some idea of this kind

. . . . to have confided the fatal . . . . Yet, still, words like those I have recorded would burst uncontrollably from me. I could offer no explanation of them, but their truth in part relieved the burden of my mysterious woe.

Upon this occasion my father said, with an expression of unbounded wonder, "My dearest Victor, what infatuation is this? My dear son, I entreat you never to make such an assertion again."

"I am not mad," I cried energetically; "the sun and the heavens, who have viewed my operations, can bear witness of my truth. I am the assassin of those most innocent victims; they died by my machinations. A thousand times would I have shed my own blood, drop by drop, to have saved their lives; but I could not, my father, indeed I could not sacrifice the whole human race."

The conclusion of this speech convinced my father that my ideas were deranged, and he instantly changed the subject of our conversation and endeavoured to alter the course of my thoughts. He wished as much as possible to obliterate the memory of the scenes that had taken place in Ireland and never alluded to them or suffered me to speak of my misfortunes.

As time passed away I became more calm; misery had her dwelling in my heart, but I no longer talked in the same incoherent manner of my own crimes; sufficient for me was the consciousness of them. By the utmost self-violence I curbed the imperious voice of wretchedness, which sometimes desired to declare itself to the whole world, and my manners were calmer and more composed than they had ever been since my journey to the sea of ice.

Save others of woe delirious

A few days before we left Paris on our way to Switzerland I received the following letter from Elizabeth:

My dear Friend,

It gave me the greatest pleasure to receive a letter from my uncle dated at Paris; you are no longer at a formidable distance, and I may hope to see you in less than a fortnight. My poor cousin, how much you must have suffered! I expect to see you looking even more ill than when you quitted Geneva. This winter has been passed most miserably, tortured as I have been by anxious suspense; yet I hope to see peace in your countenance and to find that your heart is not totally void of comfort and tranquillity.

Yet I fear that the same feelings now exist that made you so miserable a year ago, even perhaps augmented by time. I would not disturb you at this period, when so many misfortunes weigh upon you, but a conversation that I had with my uncle previous to his departure renders some explanation necessary before we meet.

Explanation! You may possibly say, What can Elizabeth have to explain? If you really say this, my questions are answered and all my doubts satisfied. But you are distant from me, and it is possible that you may dread and yet be pleased with this explanation; and in a probability of this being the case, I dare not any longer postpone writing what, during your absence, I have often wished to express to you but have never had the courage to begin.

You well know, Victor, that our union had been the favourite plan of your parents ever since our infancy. We were told this when young, and taught to look forward to it as an event that would certainly take place. We were affectionate playfellows during childhood, and, I believe, dear and valued friends to one another as we grew older. But as brother and sister often entertain a lively affection towards each other without desiring a more intimate union, may not such also be our case? Tell me, dearest Victor. Answer me, I conjure you, by our mutual happiness, with simple truth—Do you not love another?

You have travelled; you have spent several years of your life at Ingolstadt; and I confess to you, my friend, that when I saw you last autumn so unhappy, flying to solitude from the society of every creature, I could not help supposing that you might regret our connection and believe yourself bound in honour to fulfil the wishes of your parents, although they opposed themselves to your inclinations. But this is false reasoning. ...

... miseries tenfold by being an obstacle to your wishes. Ah! Victor, be assured that your cousin and playmate has too sincere a love for you not to be made miserable by this supposition. Be happy, my friend; and if you obey me in this one request, remain satisfied that nothing on earth will have the power to interrupt my tranquillity.

Do not let this letter disturb you; do not answer tomorrow, or the next day, or even until you come, if it will give you pain. My uncle will send me news of your health, and if I see but one smile on your lips when we meet, occasioned by this or any other exertion of mine, I shall need no other happiness.

Elizabeth Lavenza

Geneva, May 18th, 17—

This letter revived in my memory what I had before forgotten, the threat of the fiend—*"I will be with you on your wedding-night!"* Such was my sentence, and on that night would the demon employ every art to destroy me and tear me from the glimpse of happiness which promised partly to console my sufferings. On that night he had determined to consummate his crimes by my death. Well, be it so; a deadly struggle would then assuredly take place, in which if he were victorious I should be at peace and his power over me be at an end. If he were vanquished, I should be a free man. Alas! What freedom? Such as the peasant enjoys when his family have been massacred before his eyes, his cottage burnt, his lands laid waste, and he is turned adrift, homeless, penniless, and alone, but free. Such would be my liberty except that in my Elizabeth I possessed a treasure, alas, balanced by those horrors of remorse and guilt which would pursue me until death.

Sweet and beloved Elizabeth! I read and reread her letter, and some softened feelings stole into my heart and dared to whisper paradisiacal dreams of love and joy; but the apple was already eaten, and the angel's arm bared to drive me from all hope. Yet I would die to make her happy. If the monster executed his threat, death was inevitable; yet, again, I considered whether my marriage would hasten my fate. My destruction might indeed arrive a few months sooner, but if my torturer should suspect that I postponed it, influenced by his menaces, he would surely find other and perhaps more dreadful means of revenge. He had vowed *to be with me on my wedding-night*, yet he did not consider that threat as binding him to peace in the meantime, for as if to show me that he was not yet satiated with blood, he had murdered Clerval immediately after the enunciation of his threats. I resolved, therefore, that if my immediate union with my cousin would conduce either to hers or my father's happiness, my adversary's designs against my life should not retard it a single hour.

In this state of mind I wrote to Elizabeth. My letter was calm and affectionate. "I fear, my beloved girl," I said, "little happiness remains for us on earth; yet all that I may one day enjoy is centred in you. Chase away your idle fears; to you alone do I consecrate my life and my endeavours for contentment. I have one secret, Elizabeth, a dreadful one; when revealed to you, it will chill your frame with horror, and then, far from being surprised at my misery, you will only wonder that I survive what I have endured. I will confide this tale of misery and terror to you the day after our marriage shall take place, for, my sweet cousin, there must be perfect confidence between us. But until then, I conjure you, do not mention or allude to it. This I most earnestly entreat, and I know you will comply."

In about a week after the arrival of Elizabeth's letter we returned to Geneva. The sweet girl welcomed me with warm affection, yet tears were in her eyes as she beheld my emaciated frame and feverish cheeks. I saw a change in her also. She was thinner and had lost much of that heavenly vivacity that had before charmed me; but her gentleness and soft looks of compassion made her a more fit companion for one blasted and miserable as I was.

The tranquillity which I now enjoyed did not endure.

Memory brought madness with it, and when I ~~what had passed~~

. . . . me with res-
. . . . for the unfortunate to be resigned,
~~but~~ for the guilty there is no peace. The agonies of remorse
poison the luxury there is otherwise sometimes found in
indulging the excess of grief.

Soon after my arrival my father spoke of my immediate
marriage with Elizabeth. I remained silent.

"Have you, then, some other attachment?"

"None on earth. I love Elizabeth and look forward to
our union with delight. Let the day therefore be fixed; and on
it I will consecrate myself, in life or death, to the happiness
of my cousin."

"My dear Victor, do not speak thus. Heavy misfortunes
have befallen us, but let us only cling closer to what remains
and transfer our love for those whom we have lost to those
who yet live. Our circle will be small but bound close
by the ties of affection and mutual misfortune. And when time
shall have softened your despair, new and dear objects of
care will be born to replace those of whom we have been
so cruelly deprived."

Such were the lessons of my father. But to me the remembrance of the threat returned; nor can you wonder that,
omnipotent as the fiend had yet been in his deeds of blood,
I should almost regard him as invincible, and that when he
had pronounced the words *"I shall be with you on your
wedding-night,"* I should regard the threatened fate as un-
avoidable. But death was no evil to me if the loss of Elizabeth
were balanced with it, and I therefore, with a contented
and even cheerful countenance, agreed with my father that
if my cousin would consent, the ceremony should take place
in ten days, and thus put, as I imagined, the seal to my
fate.

really blind to plan?

Great God! If for one instant I had thought what might be the hellish intention of my fiendish adversary, I would rather have banished myself forever from my native country and wandered a friendless outcast over the earth than have consented to this miserable marriage. But, as if possessed of magic powers, the monster had blinded me to his real intentions; and when I thought that I had prepared only my own death, I hastened that of a far dearer victim.

As the period fixed for our marriage drew nearer, whether from cowardice or a prophetic feeling, I felt my heart sink within me. But I concealed my feelings by an appearance of hilarity that brought smiles and joy to the countenance of my father, but hardly deceived the ever-watchful and nicer eye of Elizabeth. She looked forward to our union with placid contentment, not unmingled with a little fear, which past misfortunes had impressed, that what now appeared certain and tangible happiness might soon dissipate into an airy dream and leave no trace but deep and everlasting regret.

Preparations were made for the event, congratulatory visits were received, and all wore a smiling appearance. I shut up, as well as I could, in my own heart the anxiety that preyed there and entered with seeming earnestness into the plans of my father, although they might only serve as the decorations of my tragedy. Through my father's exertions a part of the inheritance of Elizabeth had been restored to her by the Austrian government. A small possession on the shores of Como belonged to her. It was agreed that, immediately after our union, we should proceed to Villa Lavenza and spend our first days of happiness beside the beautiful lake near which it stood.

In the meantime I took every precaution to defend my person in case the fiend should openly attack me. I carried pistols and a dagger constantly about me and was ever on the watch to prevent artifice, and by these means gained a greater degree of tranquillity. Indeed, as the period approached, the threat appeared more as a delusion, not to be regarded as worthy to disturb my peace, while the happiness I hoped for in my marriage wore a greater appearance of certainty as the day fixed for its solemnization drew nearer and I heard it continually spoken of as an occurrence which no accident could possibly prevent.

Elizabeth seemed happy; my tranquil demeanour contrib-

again delusion—reality

uted greatly to calm her mind. But on the day that was to

The day was fair, the wind favourable; all smiled on our nuptial embarkation.

Those were the last moments of my life during which I enjoyed the feeling of happiness. We passed rapidly along; the sun was hot, but we were sheltered from its rays by a kind of canopy while we enjoyed the beauty of the scene, sometimes on one side of the lake, where we saw Mont Salêve, the pleasant banks of Montalègre, and at a distance, surmounting all, the beautiful Mont Blanc and the assemblage of snowy mountains that in vain endeavour to emulate her; sometimes coasting the opposite banks, we saw the mighty Jura opposing its dark side to the ambition that would quit its native country, and an almost insurmountable barrier to the invader who should wish to enslave it.

I took the hand of Elizabeth. "You are sorrowful, my love. Ah! If you knew what I have suffered and what I may yet endure, you would endeavour to let me taste the quiet and freedom from despair that this one day at least permits me to enjoy."

"Be happy, my dear Victor," replied Elizabeth; "there is, I hope, nothing to distress you; and be assured that if a lively joy is not painted in my face, my heart is contented. Something whispers to me not to depend too much on the prospect that is opened before us, but I will not listen to such a sinister voice. Observe how fast we move along and how the clouds, which sometimes obscure and sometimes rise above the dome of Mont Blanc, render this scene of beauty still more interesting. Look also at the innumerable fish that are swimming in the clear waters, where we can distinguish every pebble that lies at the bottom. What a divine day! How happy and serene all nature appears!"

Thus Elizabeth endeavoured to divert her thoughts and mine from all reflection upon melancholy subjects. But her temper was fluctuating; joy for a few instants shone in her eyes, but it continually gave place to distraction and reverie.

The sun sank lower in the heavens; we passed the river Drance and observed its path through the chasms of the higher and the glens of the lower hills. The Alps here come closer to the lake, and we approached the amphitheatre of mountains which forms its eastern boundary. The spire of Evian shone under the woods that surrounded it and the range of mountain above mountain by which it was overhung.

The wind, which had hitherto carried us along with amazing rapidity, sank at sunset to a light breeze; the soft air just ruffled the water and caused a pleasant motion among the trees as we approached the shore, from which it wafted the most delightful scent of flowers and hay. The sun sank beneath the horizon as we landed, and as I touched the shore I felt those cares and fears revive which soon were to clasp me and cling to me forever.

It was eight o'clock when we landed; we walked for a short time on the shore, enjoying the transitory light, and then retired to the inn and contemplated the lovely scene of waters, woods, and mountains, obscured in darkness, yet still displaying their black outlines.

The wind, which had fallen in the south, now rose with great violence in the west. The moon had reached her summit in the heavens and was beginning to descend; the clouds swept across it swifter than the flight of the vulture and dimmed her rays, while the lake reflected the scene of the busy heavens, rendered still busier by the restless waves that were beginning to rise. Suddenly a heavy storm of rain descended.

I had been calm during the day, but so soon as night obscured the shapes of objects, a thousand fears arose in my mind. I was anxious and watchful, while my right hand grasped a pistol which was hidden in my bosom; every sound terrified me, but I resolved that I would sell my life dearly and not shrink from the conflict until my own life or that of my adversary was extinguished.

Elizabeth observed my agitation for some time in timid and fearful silence, but there was something in my glance which communicated terror to her, and trembling, she asked, "What is it that agitates you, my dear Victor? What is it you fear?"

"Oh! Peace, peace, my love," replied I; "this night, and all will be safe; but this night is dreadful, very dreadful."

I passed an hour in this state of mind, when suddenly I reflected how fearful the combat which I momentarily expected would be to my wife, and I earnestly entreated her

185

to retire, resolving not to join her until I had obtained some knowledge as to the situation of my enemy.

She left me, and I continued some time walking up and down the passages of the house and inspecting every corner that might afford a retreat to my adversary. But I discovered no trace of him and was beginning to conjecture that some fortunate chance had intervened to prevent the execution of his menaces when suddenly I heard a shrill and dreadful scream. It came from the room into which Elizabeth had retired. As I heard it, the whole truth rushed into my mind, my arms dropped, the motion of every muscle and fibre was suspended; I could feel the blood trickling in my veins and tingling in the extremities of my limbs. This state lasted but for an instant; the scream was repeated, and I rushed into the room.

Great God! Why did I not then expire! Why am I here to relate the destruction of the best hope and the purest creature of earth? She was there, lifeless and inanimate, thrown across the bed, her head hanging down and her pale and distorted features half covered by her hair. Everywhere I turn I see the same figure—her bloodless arms and relaxed form flung by the murderer on its bridal bier. Could I behold this and live? Alas! Life is obstinate and clings closest where it is most hated. For a moment only did I lose recollection; I fell senseless on the ground.

When I recovered I found myself surrounded by the people of the inn; their countenances expressed a breathless terror, but the horror of others appeared only as a mockery, a shadow of the feelings that oppressed me. I escaped from them to the room where lay the body of Elizabeth, my love, my wife, so lately living, so dear, so worthy. She had been moved from the posture in which I had first beheld her, and now, as she lay, her head upon her arm and a handkerchief thrown across her face and neck, I might have supposed her asleep. I rushed towards her and embraced her with ardour, but the deadly languor and coldness of the limbs told me that what I now held in my arms had ceased to be the Elizabeth whom I had loved and cherished. The murderous mark of the fiend's grasp was on her neck, and the breath had ceased to issue from her lips.

While I still hung over her in the agony of despair, I happened to look up. The windows of the room had before been darkened, and I felt a kind of pani...

...pointed to the spot where he had disappeared, and we followed the track with boats; nets were cast, but in vain. After passing several hours, we returned hopeless, most of my companions believing it to have been a form conjured up by my fancy. After having landed, they proceeded to search the country, parties going in different directions among the woods and vines.

I attempted to accompany them and proceeded a short distance from the house, but my head whirled round, my steps were like those of a drunken man, I fell at last in a state of utter exhaustion; a film covered my eyes, and my skin was parched with the heat of fever. In this state I was carried back and placed on a bed, hardly conscious of what had happened; my eyes wandered round the room as if to seek something that I had lost.

After an interval I arose, and as if by instinct, crawled into the room where the corpse of my beloved lay. There were women weeping around; I hung over it and joined my sad tears to theirs; all this time no distinct idea presented itself to my mind, but my thoughts rambled to various subjects, reflecting confusedly on my misfortunes and their cause. I was bewildered, in a cloud of wonder and horror. The death of William, the execution of Justine, the murder of Clerval, and lastly of my wife; even at that moment I knew not that my only remaining friends were safe from the malignity of the fiend; my father even now might be writhing under his grasp, and Ernest might be dead at his feet. This idea made me shudder and recalled me to action. I started up and resolved to return to Geneva with all possible speed.

There were no horses to be procured, and I must return by the lake; but the wind was unfavourable, and the rain fell in torrents. However, it was hardly morning, and I might reasonably hope to arrive by night. I hired men to row and took an oar myself, for I had always experienced relief from mental torment in bodily exercise. But the overflowing misery I now felt, and the excess of agitation that I endured rendered me incapable of any exertion. I threw down the oar, and leaning my head upon my hands, gave way to every gloomy idea that arose. If I looked up, I saw scenes which were familiar to me in my happier time and which I had contemplated but the day before in the company of her who was now but a shadow and a recollection. Tears streamed from my eyes. The rain had ceased for a moment, and I saw the fish play in the waters as they had done a few hours before; they had then been observed by Elizabeth. Nothing is so painful to the human mind as a great and sudden change. The sun might shine or the clouds might lower, but nothing could appear to me as it had done the day before. A fiend had snatched from me every hope of future happiness; no creature had ever been so miserable as I was; so frightful an event is single in the history of man.

But why should I dwell upon the incidents that followed this last overwhelming event? Mine has been a tale of horrors; I have reached their acme, and what I must now relate can but be tedious to you. Know that, one by one, my friends were snatched away; I was left desolate. My own strength is exhausted, and I must tell, in a few words, what remains of my hideous narration.

I arrived at Geneva. My father and Ernest yet lived, but the former sunk under the tidings that I bore. I see him now, excellent and venerable old man! His eyes wandered in vacancy, for they had lost their charm and their delight——his Elizabeth, his more than daughter, whom he doted on with all that affection which a man feels, who in the decline of life, having few affections, clings more earnestly to those that remain. Cursed, cursed be the fiend that brought misery on his grey hairs and doomed him to waste in wretchedness! He could not live under the horrors that were accumulated around him; the springs of existence suddenly gave way; he was unable to rise from his bed, and in a few days he died in my arms.

What then became of me? I know not; I lost sensation, and chains and darkness were the only objects that pressed

upon me. Sometimes, indeed, I dreamt that I wandered in
flowery meadows

...to reflect on their cause—the monster whom I had
created, the miserable demon whom I had sent abroad into
the world for my destruction. I was possessed by a maddening rage when I thought of him, and desired and ardently
prayed that I might have him within my grasp to wreak a
great and signal revenge on his cursed head.

Nor did my hate long confine itself to useless wishes; I
began to reflect on the best means of securing him; and for
this purpose, about a month after my release, I repaired to a
criminal judge in the town and told him that I had an accusa-
tion to make, that I knew the destroyer of my family, and
that I required him to exert his whole authority for the apprehension of the murderer.

The magistrate listened to me with attention and kindness.
"Be assured, sir," said he, "no pains or exertions on my
part shall be spared to discover the villain."

"I thank you," replied I; "listen, therefore, to the deposition that I have to make. It is indeed a tale so strange that
I should fear you would not credit it were there not something
in truth which, however wonderful, forces conviction. The
story is too connected to be mistaken for a dream, and I have
no motive for falsehood." My manner as I thus addressed
him was impressive but calm; I had formed in my own heart
a resolution to pursue my destroyer to death, and this purpose
quieted my agony and for an interval reconciled me to life.
I now related my history briefly but with firmness and precision, marking the dates with accuracy and never deviating
into invective or exclamation.

The magistrate appeared at first perfectly incredulous,
but as I continued he became more attentive and interested;
I saw him sometimes shudder with horror; at others a

lively surprise, unmingled with disbelief, was painted on his countenance.

When I had concluded my narration I said, "This is the being whom I accuse and for whose seizure and punishment I call upon you to exert your whole power. It is your duty as a magistrate, and I believe and hope that your feelings as a man will not revolt from the execution of those functions on this occasion."

This address caused a considerable change in the physiognomy of my own auditor. He had heard my story with that half kind of belief that is given to a tale of spirits and supernatural events; but when he was called upon to act officially in consequence, the whole tide of his incredulity returned. He, however, answered mildly, "I would willingly afford you every aid in your pursuit, but the creature of whom you speak appears to have powers which would put all my exertions to defiance. Who can follow an animal which can traverse the sea of ice and inhabit caves and dens where no man would venture to intrude? Besides, some months have elapsed since the commission of his crimes, and no one can conjecture to what place he has wandered or what region he may now inhabit."

"I do not doubt that he hovers near the spot which I inhabit, and if he has indeed taken refuge in the Alps, he may be hunted like the chamois and destroyed as a beast of prey. But I perceive your thoughts; you do not credit my narrative and do not intend to pursue my enemy with the punishment which is his desert."

As I spoke, rage sparkled in my eyes; the magistrate was intimidated. "You are mistaken," said he. "I will exert myself, and if it is in my power to seize the monster, be assured that he shall suffer punishment proportionate to his crimes. But I fear, from what you have yourself described to be his properties, that this will prove impracticable; and thus, while every proper measure is pursued, you should make up your mind to disappointment."

"That cannot be; but all that I can say will be of little avail. My revenge is of no moment to you; yet, while I allow it to be a vice, I confess that it is the devouring and only passion of my soul. My rage is unspeakable when I reflect that the murderer, whom I have turned loose upon society, still exists. You refuse my just demand; I have but one re-

source, and I devote myself, either in my life...
his destruction."

... my pride of
... know not what it is you say."

I broke from the house angry and disturbed and retired to meditate on some other mode of action.

No one helps him alone angry

CHAPTER 24

*doomed
to
wander*

My present situation was one in which all voluntary thought was swallowed up and lost. I was hurried away by fury; revenge alone endowed me with strength and composure; it moulded my feelings and allowed me to be calculating and calm at periods when otherwise delirium or death would have been my portion.

My first resolution was to quit Geneva forever; my country, which, when I was happy and beloved, was dear to me, now, in my adversity, became hateful. I provided myself with a sum of money, together with a few jewels which had belonged to my mother, and departed.

And now my wanderings began which are to cease but with life. I have traversed a vast portion of the earth and have endured all the hardships which travellers in deserts and barbarous countries are wont to meet. How I have lived I hardly know; many times have I stretched my failing limbs upon the sandy plain and prayed for death. But revenge kept me alive; I dared not die and leave my adversary in being.

When I quitted Geneva my first labour was to gain some clue by which I might trace the steps of my fiendish enemy. But my plan was unsettled, and I wandered many hours round the confines of the town, uncertain what path I should pursue. As night approached I found myself at the entrance of the cemetery where William, Elizabeth, and my father reposed. I entered it and approached the tomb which marked their graves. Everything was silent except the leaves of the trees, which were gently agitated by the wind; the night was nearly dark, and the scene would have been solemn and affecting even to an uninterested observer. The spirits of the departed seemed to flit around and to cast a shadow, which was felt but not seen, around the head of the mourner.

The deep grief which this scene had at first

gave way to rage

behold the sun and
green herbage of earth, which otherwise should
vanish from my eyes forever. And I call on you, spirits of the
dead, and on you, wandering ministers of vengeance, to aid
and conduct me in my work. Let the cursed and hellish
monster drink deep of agony; let him feel the despair
that now torments me."

I had begun my adjuration with solemnity and an awe
which almost assured me that the shades of my murdered
friends heard and approved my devotion, but the furies possessed me as I concluded, and rage choked my utterance.

I was answered through the stillness of night by a loud
and fiendish laugh. It rang on my ears long and heavily; the
mountains re-echoed it, and I felt as if all hell surrounded
me with mockery and laughter. Surely in that moment I
should have been possessed by frenzy and have destroyed my
miserable existence but that my vow was heard and that I
was reserved for vengeance. The laughter died away, when
a well-known and abhorred voice, apparently close to my ear,
addressed me in an audible whisper, "I am satisfied, miserable
wretch! You have determined to live, and I am satisfied."

I darted towards the spot from which the sound proceeded,
but the devil eluded my grasp. Suddenly the broad disk of the
moon arose and shone full upon his ghastly and distorted
shape as he fled with more than mortal speed.

I pursued him, and for many months this has been my task.
Guided by a slight clue, I followed the windings of the Rhone,
but vainly. The blue Mediterranean appeared, and by a strange
chance, I saw the fiend enter by night and hide himself in a
vessel bound for the Black Sea. I took my passage in the
same ship, but he escaped, I know not how.

Amidst the wilds of Tartary and Russia, although he still

evaded me, I have ever followed in his track. Sometimes the peasants, scared by this horrid apparition, informed me of his path; sometimes he himself, who feared that if I lost all trace of him I should despair and die, left some mark to guide me. The snows descended on my head, and I saw the print of his huge step on the white plain. To you first entering on life, to whom care is new and agony unknown, how can you understand what I have felt and still feel? Cold, want, and fatigue were the least pains which I was destined to endure; I was cursed by some devil and carried about with me my eternal hell; yet still a spirit of good followed and directed my steps and when I most murmured would suddenly extricate me from seemingly insurmountable difficulties. Sometimes, when nature, overcome by hunger, sank under the exhaustion, a repast was prepared for me in the desert that restored and inspirited me. The fare was, indeed, coarse, such as the peasants of the country ate, but I will not doubt that it was set there by the spirits that I had invoked to aid me. Often, when all was dry, the heavens cloudless, and I was parched by thirst, a slight cloud would bedim the sky, shed the few drops that revived me, and vanish.

I followed, when I could, the courses of the rivers; but the demon generally avoided these, as it was here that the population of the country chiefly collected. In other places human beings were seldom seen, and I generally subsisted on the wild animals that crossed my path. I had money with me and gained the friendship of the villagers by distributing it; or I brought with me some food that I had killed, which, after taking a small part, I always presented to those who had provided me with fire and utensils for cooking.

My life, as it passed thus, was indeed hateful to me, and it was during sleep alone that I could taste joy. O blessed sleep! Often, when most miserable, I sank to repose, and my dreams lulled me even to rapture. The spirits that guarded me had provided these moments, or rather hours, of happiness that I might retain strength to fulfil my pilgrimage. Deprived of this respite, I should have sunk under my hardships. During the day I was sustained and inspirited by the hope of night, for in sleep I saw my friends, my wife, and my beloved country; again I saw the benevolent countenance of my father, heard the silver tones of my Elizabeth's voice, and beheld Clerval enjoying health and youth. Often, when wearied by a toilsome march, I persuaded myself that

what his feelings were whom I pursued I cannot know. Sometimes, indeed, he left marks in writing on the barks of the trees or cut in stone that guided me and instigated my fury. "My reign is not yet over"—these words were legible in one of these inscriptions—"you live, and my power is complete. Follow me; I seek the everlasting ices of the north, where you will feel the misery of cold and frost, to which I am impassive. You will find near this place, if you follow not too tardily, a dead hare; eat and be refreshed. Come on, my enemy; we have yet to wrestle for our lives, but many hard and miserable hours must you endure until that period shall arrive."

Scoffing devil! Again do I vow vengeance; again do I devote thee, miserable fiend, to torture and death. Never will I give up my search until he or I perish; and then with what ecstasy shall I join my Elizabeth and my departed friends, who even now prepare for me the reward of my tedious toil and horrible pilgrimage!

As I still pursued my journey to the northward, the snows thickened and the cold increased in a degree almost too severe to support. The peasants were shut up in their hovels, and only a few of the most hardy ventured forth to seize the animals whom starvation had forced from their hiding-places to seek for prey. The rivers were covered with ice, and no fish could be procured; and thus I was cut off from my chief article of maintenance.

The triumph of my enemy increased with the difficulty of my labours. One inscription that he left was in these words: "Prepare! Your toils only begin; wrap yourself in furs and provide food, for we shall soon enter upon a journey where your sufferings will satisfy my everlasting hatred."

My courage and perseverance were invigorated by these scoffing words; I resolved not to fail in my purpose, and calling on heaven to support me, I continued with unabated fervour to traverse immense deserts, until the ocean appeared at a distance and formed the utmost boundary of the horizon. Oh! How unlike it was to the blue seasons of the south! Covered with ice, it was only to be distinguished from land by its superior wildness and ruggedness. The Greeks wept for joy when they beheld the Mediterranean from the hills of Asia, and hailed with rapture the boundary of their toils. I did not weep, but I knelt down and with a full heart thanked my guiding spirit for conducting me in safety to the place where I hoped, notwithstanding my adversary's gibe, to meet and grapple with him.

Some weeks before this period I had procured a sledge and dogs and thus traversed the snows with inconceivable speed. I know not whether the fiend possessed the same advantages, but I found that, as before I had daily lost ground in the pursuit, I now gained on him, so much so that when I first saw the ocean he was but one day's journey in advance, and I hoped to intercept him before he should reach the beach. With new courage, therefore, I pressed on, and in two days arrived at a wretched hamlet on the seashore. I inquired of the inhabitants concerning the fiend and gained accurate information. A gigantic monster, they said, had arrived the night before, armed with a gun and many pistols, putting to flight the inhabitants of a solitary cottage through fear of his terrific appearance. He had carried off their store of winter food, and placing it in a sledge, to draw which he had seized on a numerous drove of trained dogs, he had harnessed them, and the same night, to the joy of the horror-struck villagers, had pursued his journey across the sea in a direction that led to no land; and they conjectured that he must speedily be destroyed by the breaking of the ice or frozen by the eternal frosts.

On hearing this information I suffered a temporary access of despair. He had escaped me, and I must commence a destructive and almost endless journey across the mountainous ices of the ocean, amidst cold that few of the inhabitants could long endure and which I, the native of a genial and sunny climate, could not hope to survive. Yet at the idea that the fiend should live and be triumphant, my rage and

vengeance returned, and like a mighty tide ~~~~~~
every other f~~~~~~

~~~~~~ ~~~~~~ barred up my passage, and I often heard the ~~~~ rugged mountains
thunder of the ground sea, which threatened my destruction. But again the frost came and made the paths of the sea secure.

By the quantity of provision which I had consumed, I should guess that I had passed three weeks in this journey; and the continual protraction of hope, returning back upon the heart, often wrung bitter drops of despondency and grief from my eyes. Despair had indeed almost secured her prey, and I should soon have sunk beneath this misery. Once, after the poor animals that conveyed me had with incredible toil gained the summit of a sloping ice mountain, and one, sinking under his fatigue, died, I viewed the expanse before me with anguish, when suddenly my eye caught a dark speck upon the dusky plain. I strained my sight to discover what it could be and uttered a wild cry of ecstasy when I distinguished a sledge and the distorted proportions of a well-known form within. Oh! With what a burning gush did hope revisit my heart! Warm tears filled my eyes, which I hastily wiped away, that they might not intercept the view I had of the demon; but still my sight was dimmed by the burning drops, until, giving way to the emotions that oppressed me, I wept aloud.

But this was not the time for delay; I disencumbered the dogs of their dead companion, gave them a plentiful portion of food, and after an hour's rest, which was absolutely necessary, and yet which was bitterly irksome to me, I continued my route. The sledge was still visible, nor did I again lose sight of it except at the moments when for a short time some ice-rock concealed it with its intervening crags. I indeed perceptibly gained on it, and when, after nearly two days' journey, I beheld my enemy at no more than a mile distant, my heart bounded within me.

But now, when I appeared almost within grasp of my foe, my hopes were suddenly extinguished, and I lost all trace of him more utterly than I had ever done before. A ground sea was heard; the thunder of its progress, as the waters rolled and swelled beneath me, became every moment more ominous and terrific. I pressed on, but in vain. The wind arose; the sea roared; and, as with the mighty shock of an earthquake, it split and cracked with a tremendous and over-whelming sound. The work was soon finished; in a few minutes a tumultuous sea rolled between me and my enemy, and I was left drifting on a scattered piece of ice that was continually lessening and thus preparing for me a hideous death.

In this manner many appalling hours passed; several of my dogs died, and I myself was about to sink under the accumulation of distress when I saw your vessel riding at anchor and holding forth to me hopes of succour and life. I had no conception that vessels ever came so far north and was astounded at the sight. I quickly destroyed part of my sledge to construct oars, and by these means was enabled, with infinite fatigue, to move my ice raft in the direction of your ship. I had determined, if you were going south-wards, still to trust myself to the mercy of the seas rather than abandon my purpose. I hoped to induce you to grant me a boat with which I could pursue my enemy. But your direction was northwards. You took me on board when my vigour was exhausted, and I should soon have sunk under my multiplied hardships into a death which I still dread, for my task is unfulfilled.

Oh! When will my guiding spirit, in conducting me to the demon, allow me the rest I so much desire; or must I die, and he yet live? If I do, swear to me, Walton, that he shall not escape, that you will seek him and satisfy my vengeance in his death. And do I dare to ask of you to undertake my pilgrimage, to endure the hardships that I have undergone? No; I am not so selfish. Yet, when I am dead, if he should appear, if the ministers of vengeance should conduct him to you, swear that he shall not live—swear that he shall not triumph over my accumulated woes and survive to add to the list of his dark crimes. He is eloquent and persuasive, and once his words had even power over my heart; but trust him not. His soul is as hellish as his form, full of treachery and fiendlike malice. Hear him not; call on the names of

voice broken, yet piercing, uttered with difficulty the words so replete with anguish. His fine and lovely eyes were now lighted up with indignation, now subdued to downcast sorrow and quenched in infinite wretchedness. Sometimes he commanded his countenance and tones and related the most horrible incidents with a tranquil voice, suppressing every mark of agitation; then, like a volcano bursting forth, his face would suddenly change to an expression of the wildest rage as he shrieked out imprecations on his persecutor.

His tale is connected and told with an appearance of the simplest truth, yet I own to you that the letters of Felix and Safie, which he showed me, and the apparition of the monster seen from our ship, brought to me a greater conviction of the truth of his narrative than his asseverations, however earnest and connected. Such a monster has, then, really existence! I cannot doubt it, yet I am lost in surprise and admiration. Sometimes I endeavoured to gain from Frankenstein the particulars of his creature's formation, but on this point he was impenetrable.

"Are you mad, my friend?" said he. "Or whither does your senseless curiosity lead you? Would you also create for yourself and the world a demoniacal enemy? Peace, peace! Learn my miseries and do not seek to increase your own."

Frankenstein discovered that I made notes concerning his history; he asked to see them and then himself corrected and augmented them in many places, but principally in giving the life and spirit to the conversations he held with his enemy. "Since you have preserved my narration," said he, "I would not that a mutilated one should go down to posterity."

Thus has a week passed away, while I have listened to the strangest tale that ever imagination formed. My thoughts and every feeling of my soul have been drunk up by the interest for my guest which this tale and his own elevated and gentle manners have created. I wish to soothe him, yet can I counsel one so infinitely miserable, so destitute of every hope of consolation, to live? Oh, no! The only joy that he can now know will be when he composes his shattered spirit to peace and death. Yet he enjoys one comfort, the offspring of solitude and delirium; he believes that when in dreams he holds converse with his friends and derives from that communion consolation for his miseries or excitements to his vengeance, that they are not the creations of his fancy, but the beings themselves who visit him from the regions of a remote world. This faith gives a solemnity to his reveries that render them to me almost as imposing and interesting as truth.

Our conversations are not always confined to his own history and misfortunes. On every point of general literature he displays unbounded knowledge and a quick and piercing apprehension. His eloquence is forcible and touching; nor can I hear him, when he relates a pathetic incident or endeavours to move the passions of pity or love, without tears. What a glorious creature must he have been in the days of his prosperity, when he is thus noble and godlike in ruin! He seems to feel his own worth and the greatness of his fall.

"When younger," said he, "I believed myself destined for some great enterprise. My feelings are profound, but I possessed a coolness of judgment that fitted me for illustrious achievements. This sentiment of the worth of my nature supported me when others would have been oppressed, for I deemed it criminal to throw away in useless grief those talents that might be useful to my fellow creatures. When I reflected on the work I had completed, no less a one than the creation of a sensitive and rational animal, I could not rank myself with the herd of common projectors. But this thought, which supported me in the commencement of my career, now serves only to plunge me lower in the dust. All my speculations and hopes are as nothing, and like the archangel who aspired to omnipotence, I am chained in an eternal hell. My imagination was vivid, yet my powers of analysis and application were intense; by the union of these

Must I then lose this admirable being? I have longed for a friend; I have sought one who would sympathize with and love me. Behold, on these desert seas I have found such a one, but I fear I have gained him only to know his value and lose him. I would reconcile him to life, but he repulses the idea.

"I thank you, Walton," he said, "for your kind intentions towards so miserable a wretch; but when you speak of new ties and fresh affections, think you that any can replace those who are gone? Can any man be to me as Clerval was, or any woman another Elizabeth? Even where the affections are not strongly moved by any superior excellence, the companions of our childhood always possess a certain power over our minds which hardly any later friend can obtain. They know our infantine dispositions, which, however they may be afterwards modified, are never eradicated; and they can judge of our actions with more certain conclusions as to the integrity of our motives. A sister or a brother can never, unless indeed such symptoms have been shown early, suspect the other of fraud or false dealing, when another friend, however strongly he may be attached, may, in spite of himself, be contemplated with suspicion. But I enjoyed friends, dear not only through habit and association, but from their own merits; and wherever I am, the soothing voice of my Elizabeth and the conversation of Clerval will be ever whispered in my ear. They are dead, and but one feeling in such a solitude can persuade me to preserve my life. If I were engaged in any high undertaking or design, fraught with extensive utility to my fellow creatures, then could I live to fulfil it. But such is not my destiny; I must pursue and destroy the being to whom I gave existence; then my lot on earth will be fulfilled and I may die."

My beloved Sister,   September 2nd

I write to you, encompassed by peril and ignorant whether I am ever doomed to see again dear England and the dearer friends that inhabit it. I am surrounded by mountains of ice which admit of no escape and threaten every moment to crush my vessel. The brave fellows whom I have persuaded to be my companions look towards me for aid, but I have none to bestow. There is something terribly appalling in our situation, yet my courage and hopes do not desert me. Yet it is terrible to reflect that the lives of all these men are endangered through me. If we are lost, my mad schemes are the cause.

And what, Margaret, will be the state of your mind? You will not hear of my destruction, and you will anxiously await my return. Years will pass, and you will have visitings of despair and yet be tortured by hope. Oh! My beloved sister, the sickening failing of your heart-felt expectations is, in prospect, more terrible to me than my own death. But you have a husband and lovely children; you may be happy. Heaven bless you and make you so!

My unfortunate guest regards me with the tenderest compassion. He endeavours to fill me with hope and talks as if life were a possession which he valued. He reminds me how often the same accidents have happened to other navigators who have attempted this sea, and in spite of myself, he fills me with cheerful auguries. Even the sailors feel the power of his eloquence; when he speaks, they no longer despair; he rouses their energies, and while they hear his voice they believe these vast mountains of ice are mole-hills which will vanish before the resolutions of man. These feelings are transitory; each day of expectation delayed fills them with fear, and I almost dread a mutiny caused by this despair.

September 5th

A scene has just passed of such uncommon interest that, although it is highly probable that these papers may never reach you, yet I cannot forbear recording it.

We are still surrounded by mountains of ice, still in imminent danger of being crushed in their conflict. The cold is excessive, and many of my unfortunate comrades have

their leader addressed me. He told me that he and his companions had been chosen by the other sailors to come in deputation to me to make me a requisition which, in justice, I could not refuse. We were immured in ice and should probably never escape, but they feared that if, as was possible, the ice should dissipate and a free passage be opened, I should be rash enough to continue my voyage and lead them into fresh dangers, after they might happily have surmounted this. They insisted, therefore, that I should engage with a solemn promise that if the vessel should be freed I would instantly direct my course southwards.

This speech troubled me. I had not despaired, nor had I yet conceived the idea of returning if set free. Yet could I, in justice, or even in possibility, refuse this demand? I hesitated before I answered, when Frankenstein, who had at first been silent, and indeed appeared hardly to have force enough to attend, now roused himself; his eyes sparkled, and his cheeks flushed with momentary vigour. Turning towards the men, he said, "What do you mean? What do you demand of your captain? Are you, then, so easily turned from your design? Did you not call this a glorious expedition? And wherefore was it glorious? Not because the way was smooth and placid as a southern sea, but because it was full of dangers and terror, because at every new incident your fortitude was to be called forth and your courage exhibited, because danger and death surrounded it, and these you were to brave and overcome. For this was it a glorious, for this was it an honourable undertaking. You were hereafter to be hailed as the benefactors of your species, your names adored as belonging to brave men who encountered death for honour and the benefit of mankind. And now, behold, with the first imagination of danger, or, if you will, the first mighty and terrific trial of your courage, you shrink away and are content to be handed down as men who had not strength enough to endure cold and peril; and so, poor souls, they were chilly and returned to their warm firesides. Why, that requires not this preparation; ye need not have come thus far and dragged your captain to the shame of a defeat merely to prove yourselves cowards. Oh! Be men, or be more than men. Be steady to your purposes and firm as a rock. This ice is not made of such stuff as your hearts may be; it is mutable and cannot withstand you if you say that it shall not. Do not return to your families with the stigma of disgrace marked on your brows. Return as heroes who have fought and conquered and who know not what it is to turn their backs on the foe."

He spoke this with a voice so modulated to the different feelings expressed in his speech, with an eye so full of lofty design and heroism, that can you wonder that these men were moved? They looked at one another and were unable to reply. I spoke; I told them to retire and consider of what had been said, that I would not lead them farther north if they strenuously desired the contrary, but that I hoped that, with reflection, their courage would return.

They retired and I turned towards my friend, but he was sunk in languor and almost deprived of life.

How all this will terminate, I know not, but I had rather die than return shamefully, my purpose unfulfilled. Yet I fear such will be my fate; the men, unsupported by ideas of glory and honour, can never willingly continue to endure their present hardships.

September 7th

The die is cast; I have consented to return if we are not destroyed. Thus are my hopes blasted by cowardice and indecision; I come back ignorant and disappointed. It requires more philosophy than I possess to bear this injustice with patience.

September 12th

It is past; I am returning to England. I have lost my hopes of utility and glory; I have lost my friend. But I will endeavour to detail these bitter circumstances to you, my dear sister; and while I am wafted towards England

fectly free. When the sailors saw this and that their return to their native country was apparently assured, a shout of tumultuous joy broke from them, loud and long-continued. Frankenstein, who was dozing, awoke and asked the cause of the tumult. "They shout," I said, "because they will soon return to England."

"Do you, then, really return?"

"Alas! Yes; I cannot withstand their demands. I cannot lead them unwillingly to danger, and I must return."

"Do so, if you will; but I will not. You may give up your purpose, but mine is assigned to me by heaven, and I dare not. I am weak, but surely the spirits who assist my vengeance will endow me with sufficient strength." Saying this, he endeavoured to spring from the bed, but the exertion was too great for him; he fell back and fainted.

It was long before he was restored, and I often thought that life was entirely extinct. At length he opened his eyes; he breathed with difficulty and was unable to speak. The surgeon gave him a composing draught and ordered us to leave him undisturbed. In the meantime he told me that my friend had certainly not many hours to live.

His sentence was pronounced, and I could only grieve and be patient. I sat by his bed, watching him; his eyes were closed, and I thought he slept; but presently he called to me in a feeble voice, and bidding me come near, said, "Alas! The strength I relied on is gone; I feel that I shall soon die, and he, my enemy and persecutor, may still be in being. Think not, Walton, that in the last moments of my existence I feel that burning hatred and ardent desire of revenge I once expressed; but I feel myself justified in desiring the death of my adversary. During these last days I have been occupied in examining my past conduct; nor do I find it blamable. In a fit of enthusiastic madness I created a rational creature and was bound towards him to assure, as far as was in my power, his happiness and well-being. This was my duty, but there was another still paramount to that. My duties towards the beings of my own species had greater claims to my attention because they included a greater proportion of happiness or misery. Urged by this view, I refused, and I did right in refusing, to create a companion for the first creature. He showed unparalleled malignity and selfishness in evil; he destroyed my friends; he devoted to destruction beings who possessed exquisite sensations, happiness, and wisdom; nor do I know where this thirst for vengeance may end. Miserable himself that he may render no other wretched, he ought to die. The task of his destruction was mine, but I have failed. When actuated by selfish and vicious motives, I asked you to undertake my unfinished work, and I renew this request now, when I am only induced by reason and virtue.

"Yet I cannot ask you to renounce your country and friends to fulfil this task; and now that you are returning to England, you will have little chance of meeting with him. But the consideration of these points, and the well balancing of what you may esteem your duties, I leave to you; my judgment and ideas are already disturbed by the near approach of death. I dare not ask you to do what I think right, for I may still be misled by passion.

"That he should live to be an instrument of mischief disturbs me; in other respects, this hour, when I momentarily expect my release, is the only happy one which I have enjoyed for several years. The forms of the beloved dead flit before me, and I hasten to their arms. Farewell, Walton! Seek happiness in tranquillity and avoid ambition, even if it be only the apparently innocent one of distinguishing yourself in science and discoveries. Yet why do I say this? I have myself been blasted in these hopes, yet another may succeed."

His voice became fainter as he spoke, and at length, exhausted by his effort, he sank into silence. About half an hour afterwards he attempted again to speak but was unable; he pressed my hand feebly, and his eyes closed forever, while the irradiation of a gentle smile passed away from

scarcely stir. Again there is a sound as of a human voice, but hoarser; it comes from the cabin where the remains of Frankenstein still lie. I must arise and examine. Good night, my sister.

Great God! what a scene has just taken place! I am yet dizzy with the remembrance of it. I hardly know whether I shall have the power to detail it; yet the tale which I have recorded would be incomplete without this final and wonderful catastrophe.

I entered the cabin where lay the remains of my ill-fated and admirable friend. Over him hung a form which I cannot find words to describe—gigantic in stature, yet uncouth and distorted in its proportions. As he hung over the coffin, his face was concealed by long locks of ragged hair; but one vast hand was extended, in colour and apparent texture like that of a mummy. When he heard the sound of my approach, he ceased to utter exclamations of grief and horror and sprung towards the window. Never did I behold a vision so horrible as his face, of such loathsome yet appalling hideousness. I shut my eyes involuntarily and endeavoured to recollect what were my duties with regard to this destroyer. I called on him to stay.

He paused, looking on me with wonder, and again turning towards the lifeless form of his creator, he seemed to forget my presence, and every feature and gesture seemed instigated by the wildest rage of some uncontrollable passion.

"That is also my victim!" he exclaimed. "In his murder my crimes are consummated; the miserable series of my being is wound to its close! Oh, Frankenstein! Generous and self-devoted being! What does it avail that I now ask thee to pardon me? I, who irretrievably destroyed thee by

destroying all thou lovedst. Alas! He is cold, he cannot answer me."

His voice seemed suffocated, and my first impulses, which
had suggested to me the duty of obeying the dying request
of my friend in destroying his enemy, were now suspended
by a mixture of curiosity and compassion. I approached this
tremendous being; I dared not again raise my eyes to his
face, there was something so scaring and unearthly in his
ugliness. I attempted to speak, but the words died away on
my lips. The monster continued to utter wild and incoherent
self-reproaches. At length I gathered resolution to address
him in a pause of the tempest of his passion. "Your repentance," I said, "is now superfluous. If you had listened
to the voice of conscience and heeded the stings of remorse
before you had urged your diabolical vengeance to this extremity, Frankenstein would yet have lived."

"And do you dream?" said the demon. "Do you think
that I was then dead to agony and remorse? He," he continued, pointing to the corpse, "he suffered not in the
consummation of the deed. Oh! Not the ten-thousandth portion
of the anguish that was mine during the lingering detail of
its execution. A frightful selfishness hurried me on, while my
heart was poisoned with remorse. Think you that the groans
of Clerval were music to my ears? My heart was fashioned
to be susceptible of love and sympathy, and when wrenched
by misery to vice and hatred, it did not endure the violence
of the change without torture such as you cannot even
imagine.

"After the murder of Clerval I returned to Switzerland,
heart-broken and overcome. I pitied Frankenstein; my pity
amounted to horror; I abhorred myself. But when I discovered that he, the author at once of my existence and of
its unspeakable torments, dared to hope for happiness, that
while he accumulated wretchedness and despair upon me he
sought his own enjoyment in feelings and passions from the
indulgence of which I was forever barred, then impotent
envy and bitter indignation filled me with an insatiable thirst
for vengeance. I recollected my threat and resolved that it
should be accomplished. I knew that I was preparing for
myself a deadly torture, but I was the slave, not the master,
of an impulse which I detested yet could not disobey. Yet
when she died! Nay, then I was not miserable. I had cast

was rekindled within me. Wretch! I said. It is well that
you come here to whine over the desolation that you have
made. You throw a torch into a pile of buildings, and when
they are consumed, you sit among the ruins and lament the
fall. Hypocritical fiend! If he whom you mourn still lived,
still would he be the object, again would he become the
prey, of your accursed vengeance. It is not pity that you
feel; you lament only because the victim of your malignity
is withdrawn from your power."

"Oh, it is not thus—not thus," interrupted the being.
"Yet such must be the impression conveyed to you by what
appears to be the purport of my actions. Yet I seek not a
fellow feeling in my misery. No sympathy may I ever find.
When I first sought it, it was the love of virtue, the feelings
of happiness and affection with which my whole being overflowed, that I wished to be participated. But now that virtue
has become to me a shadow, and that happiness and affection are turned into bitter and loathing despair, in what
should I seek for sympathy? I am content to suffer alone
while my sufferings shall endure; when I die, I am well
satisfied that abhorrence and opprobrium should load my
memory. Once my fancy was soothed with dreams of virtue,
of fame, and of enjoyment. Once I falsely hoped to meet
with beings who, pardoning my outward form, would love
me for the excellent qualities which I was capable of unfolding. I was nourished with high thoughts of honour and
devotion. But now crime has degraded me beneath the
meanest animal. No guilt, no mischief, no malignity, no
misery, can be found comparable to mine. When I run over
the frightful catalogue of my sins, I cannot believe that I
am the same creature whose thoughts were once filled with
sublime and transcendent visions of the beauty and the maj-

esty of goodness. But it is even so; the fallen angel becomes a malignant devil. Yet even that enemy of God and man had friends and associates in his desolation; I am alone.

"You, who call Frankenstein your friend, seem to have a knowledge of my crimes and his misfortunes. But in the detail which he gave you of them he could not sum up the hours and months of misery which I endured wasting in impotent passions. For while I destroyed his hopes, I did not satisfy my own desires. They were forever ardent and craving; still I desired love and fellowship, and I was still spurned. Was there no injustice in this? Am I to be thought the only criminal, when all humankind sinned against me? Why do you not hate Felix, who drove his friend from his door with contumely? Why do you not execrate the rustic who sought to destroy the saviour of his child? Nay, these are virtuous and immaculate beings! I, the miserable and the abandoned, am an abortion, to be spurned at, and kicked, and trampled on. Even now my blood boils at the recollection of this injustice.

"But it is true that I am a wretch. I have murdered the lovely and the helpless; I have strangled the innocent as they slept and grasped to death his throat who never injured me or any other living thing. I have devoted my creator, the select specimen of all that is worthy of love and admiration among men, to misery; I have pursued him even to that irremediable ruin. There he lies, white and cold in death. You hate me, but your abhorrence cannot equal that with which I regard myself. I look on the hands which executed the deed; I think on the heart in which the imagination of it was conceived and long for the moment when these hands will meet my eyes, when that imagination will haunt my thoughts no more.

"Fear not that I shall be the instrument of future mischief. My work is nearly complete. Neither yours nor any man's death is needed to consummate the series of my being and accomplish that which must be done, but it requires my own. Do not think that I shall be slow to perform this sacrifice. I shall quit your vessel on the ice raft which brought me thither and shall seek the most northern extremity of the globe; I shall collect my funeral pile and consume to ashes this miserable frame, that its remains may afford no light to any curious and unhallowed wretch who would create such another as I have been. I shall die. I shall no longer

all to me, I should have wept to die; now it is my only consolation. Polluted by crimes and torn by the bitterest remorse, where can I find rest but in death?

"Farewell! I leave you, and in you the last of humankind whom these eyes will ever behold. Farewell, Frankenstein! If thou wert yet alive and yet cherished a desire of revenge against me, it would be better satiated in my life than in my destruction. But it was not so; thou didst seek my extinction, that I might not cause greater wretchedness; and if yet, in some mode unknown to me, thou hadst not ceased to think and feel, thou wouldst not desire against me a vengeance greater than that which I feel. Blasted as thou wert, my agony was still superior to thine, for the bitter sting of remorse will not cease to rankle in my wounds until death shall close them forever.

"But soon," he cried with sad and solemn enthusiasm, "I shall die, and what I now feel be no longer felt. Soon these burning miseries will be extinct. I shall ascend my funeral pile triumphantly and exult in the agony of the torturing flames. The light of that conflagration will fade away; my ashes will be swept into the sea by the winds. My spirit will sleep in peace, or if it thinks, it will not surely think thus. Farewell."

He sprang from the cabin window as he said this, upon the ice raft which lay close to the vessel. He was soon borne away by the waves and lost in darkness and distance.

AFTERWORD

> ... there is a fire
> And motion of the soul which will not dwell
> In its own narrow being, but aspire
> Beyond the fitting medium of desire. ...
> —Byron, *Childe Harold's Pilgrimage,*
> Canto III

> ... Ere Babylon was dust,
> The Magus Zoroaster, my dead child,
> Met his own image walking in the garden.
> That apparition, sole of men, he saw.
> For know there are two worlds of life and death:
> One that which thou beholdest; but the other
> Is underneath the grave, where do inhabit
> The shadows of all forms that think and live
> Till death unite them and they part no more...
> —Shelley, *Prometheus Unbound,*
> Act I

The motion-picture viewer who carries his obscure but still authentic taste for the sublime to the neighborhood theater, there to see the latest in an unending series of *Frankensteins,* becomes a sharer in a romantic terror now nearly one hundred and fifty years old. Mary Shelley, barely nineteen years of age when she wrote the original *Frankenstein,* was the daughter of two great intellectual rebels, William Godwin and Mary Wollstonecraft, and the second wife of Percy Bysshe Shelley, another great rebel and an unmatched lyrical poet. Had she written nothing, Mary Shelley would be remembered today. She is remembered in her own right as the author of a novel valuable in itself but also prophetic of an intellectual world to come, a novel de-

Frankenstein represents the feelings, and his nameless creature the intellect. In her view the monster has no emotion,
and "what passes for emotion . . . are really intellectual
passions arrived at through rational channels." Miss Spark
carries this argument far enough to insist that the monster
is asexual and that he demands a bride from Frankenstein
only for companionship, a conclusion evidently at variance
with the novel's text.

The antithesis between the scientist and his creature in
Frankenstein is a very complex one and can be described
more fully in the larger context of Romantic literature and
its characteristic mythology. The shadow or double of the
self is a constant conceptual image in Blake and Shelley
and a frequent image, more random and descriptive, in the
other major Romantics, especially in Byron. In *Frankenstein*
it is the dominant and recurrent image and accounts for
much of the latent power the novel possesses.

Mary Shelley's husband was a divided being, as man and
as poet, just as his friend Byron was, though in Shelley the
split was more radical. *Frankenstein: or, The Modern Prometheus* is the full title of Mrs. Shelley's novel, and while
Victor Frankenstein is *not* Shelley (Clerval is rather more
like the poet), the Modern Prometheus is a very apt term
for Shelley or for Byron. Prometheus is the mythic figure
who best suits the uses of Romantic poetry, for no other
traditional being has in him the full range of Romantic
moral sensibility and the full Romantic capacity for creation and destruction.

No Romantic writer employed the Prometheus archetype
without a full awareness of its equivocal potentialities. The
Prometheus of the ancients had been for the most part a

spiritually reprehensible figure, though frequently a sympathetic one, in terms both of his dramatic situation and in his close alliance with mankind against the gods. But this alliance had been ruinous for man in most versions of the myth, and the Titan's benevolence toward humanity was hardly sufficient recompense for the alienation of man from heaven that he had brought about. Both sides of Titanism are evident in earlier Christian references to the story. The same Prometheus who is taken as an analogue of the crucified Christ is regarded also as a type of Lucifer, a son of light justly cast out by an offended heaven.

In the Romantic readings of Milton's *Paradise Lost* (and *Frankenstein* is implicitly one such reading) this double identity of Prometheus is a vital element. Blake, whose mythic revolutionary named Orc is another version of Prometheus, saw Milton's Satan as a Prometheus gone wrong, as desire restrained until it became only the shadow of desire, a diminished double of creative energy. Shelley went further in judging Milton's Satan as an imperfect Prometheus, inadequate because his mixture of heroic and base qualities engendered in the reader's mind a "pernicious casuistry" inimical to the spirit of art.

Blake, more systematic a poet than Shelley, worked out an antithesis between symbolic figures he named Spectre and Emanation, the shadow of desire and the total form of desire, respectively. A reader of *Frankenstein*, recalling the novel's extraordinary conclusion, with its scenes of obsessional pursuit through the Arctic wastes, can recognize the same imagery applied to a similar symbolic situation in Blake's lyric on the strife of Spectre and Emanation:

> My Spectre around me night and day
> Like a Wild beast guards my way.
> My Emanation far within
> Weeps incessantly for my Sin.
>
> A Fathomless and boundless deep,
> There we wander, there we weep;
> On the hungry craving wind
> My Spectre follows thee behind.

more intellectual and more emotional than his maker; indeed he excels Frankenstein as much (and in the same ways) as Milton's Adam excels Milton's God in *Paradise Lost*. The greatest paradox and most astonishing achievement of Mary Shelley's novel is that the monster is *more human* than his creator. This nameless being, as much a Modern Adam as his creator is a Modern Prometheus, is more lovable than his creator and more hateful, more to be pitied and more to be feared, and above all more able to give the attentive reader that shock of added consciousness in which aesthetic recognition compels a heightened realization of the self. For like Blake's Spectre and Emanation or Shelley's Alastor and Epipsyche, Frankenstein and his monster are the solipsistic and generous halves of the one self. Frankenstein is the mind and emotions turned in upon themselves, and his creature is the mind and emotions turned imaginatively outward, seeking a greater humanization through a confrontation of other selves.

I am suggesting that what makes *Frankenstein* an important book, though it is only a strong, flawed novel with frequent clumsiness in its narrative and characterization, is that it contains one of the most vivid versions we have of the Romantic mythology of the self, one that resembles Blake's *Book of Urizen*, Shelley's *Prometheus Unbound*, and Byron's *Manfred*, among other works. Because it lacks the sophistication and imaginative complexity of such works, *Frankenstein* affords a unique introduction to the archetypal world of the Romantics.

William Godwin, though a tendentious novelist, was a powerful one, and the prehistory of his daughter's novel begins with his best work of fiction, *Caleb Williams* (1794).

Godwin summarized the climactic (and harrowing) final third of his novel as a pattern of flight and pursuit, "the fugitive in perpetual apprehension of being overwhelmed with the worst calamities, and the pursuer, by his ingenuity and resources, keeping his victim in a state of the most fearful alarm." Mary Shelley brilliantly reverses this pattern in the final sequence of her novel, and she takes from *Caleb Williams* also her destructive theme of the monster's war against "the whole machinery of human society," to quote the words of Caleb Williams while in prison. Muriel Spark argues that *Frankenstein* can be read as a reaction "against the rational-humanism of Godwin and Shelley," and she points to the equivocal preface that Shelley wrote to his wife's novel, in order to support this view. Certainly Shelley was worried lest the novel be taken as a warning against the inevitable moral consequences of an unchecked experimental Prometheanism and scientific materialism. The preface insists that:

> The opinions which naturally spring from the character and situation of the hero are by no means to be conceived as existing always in my own conviction; nor is any inference justly to be drawn from the following pages as prejudicing any philosophical doctrine of whatever kind.

Shelley had, throughout his own work, a constant reaction against Godwin's rational humanism, but his reaction was systematically and consciously one of heart against head. In the same summer in the Swiss Alps that saw the conception of *Frankenstein*, Shelley composed two poems that lift the thematic conflict of the novel to the level of the true sublime. In the *Hymn to Intellectual Beauty* the poet's heart interprets an inconstant grace and loveliness, always just beyond the range of the human senses, as being the only beneficent force in life, and he prays to this force to be more constant in its attendance upon him and all mankind. In a greater sister-hymn, *Mont Blanc*, an awesome meditation upon a frightening natural scene, the poet's head issues an allied but essentially contrary report. The force, or power, is there, behind or within the mountain, but its external workings upon us are either indifferent or malevolent, and this power is not to be prayed to. It can teach us, but what it teaches us is our own dangerous freedom

Prometheus, like Frankenstein, has made

this monster is Jupiter, the God of all institutional and his-
torical religions, including organized Christianity. Salvation
from this conceptual error comes through the heart's prompt-
ings, through love alone; but love in this poem, as elsewhere
in Shelley, is always closely shadowed by ruin. Indeed, what
choice spirits in Shelley perpetually encounter is ruin mas-
querading as love, pain presenting itself as pleasure. The
tentative way out of this situation in Shelley's poetry is
through the quest for a feeling mind and an understanding
heart, which is symbolized by the sexual reunion of Prometheus and his Emanation, Asia. Frederick A. Pottle sums
up *Prometheus Unbound* by observing its meaning to be
that "the head must sincerely forgive, must willingly es-
chew hatred on purely experimental grounds," while "the affections must exorcize the demons of infancy, whether personal or of the race." In the light cast by these profound
and precise summations, the reader can better understand
both Shelley's lyrical drama and his wife's narrative of the
Modern Prometheus.

There are two paradoxes at the center of Mrs. Shelley's
novel, and each illuminates a dilemma of the Promethean
imagination. The first is that Frankenstein *was* successful,
in that he did create Natural Man, not as he was, but as
the meliorists saw such a man; indeed, Frankenstein did
better than this, since his creature was, as we have seen,
more imaginative than himself. Frankenstein's tragedy stems
not from his Promethean excess but from his own moral
error, his failure to love; he *abhorred his creature*, became
terrified, and fled his responsibilities.

The second paradox is the more ironic. This either would
not have happened or would not have mattered anyway, if

Frankenstein had been an aesthetically successful maker; a beautiful "monster," or even a passable one, would not have been a monster. As the creature bitterly observes in Chapter 17:

> Shall I respect man when he contemns me? Let him live with me in the interchange of kindness, and instead of injury I would bestow every benefit upon him with tears of gratitude at his acceptance. But that cannot be; the human senses are insurmountable barriers to our union.

As the hideousness of his creature was no part of Victor Frankenstein's intention, it is worth noticing how this disastrous matter came to be.

It would not be unjust to characterize Victor Frankenstein, in his act of creation, as being momentarily a moral idiot, like so many who have done his work after him. There is an indeliberate humor in the contrast between the enormity of the scientist's discovery and the mundane emotions of the discoverer. Finding that "the minuteness of the parts" slows him down, he resolves to make his creature "about eight feet in height and proportionably large." As he works on, he allows himself to dream that "a new species would bless me as its creator and source; many happy and excellent natures would owe their being to me." Yet he knows his is a "workshop of filthy creation," and he fails the fundamental test of his own creativity. When the "dull yellow eye" of his creature opens, this creator falls from the autonomy of a supreme artificer to the terror of a child of earth: "breathless horror and disgust filled my heart." He flees his responsibility and sets in motion the events that will lead to his own Arctic immolation, a fit end for a being who has never achieved a full sense of another's existence.

Haunting Mary Shelley's novel is the demonic figure of the Ancient Mariner, Coleridge's major venture into Romantic mythology of the purgatorial self trapped in the isolation of a heightened self-consciousness. Walton, in Letter 2 introducing the novel, compares himself "to that production of the most imaginative of modern poets." As a seeker-out of an unknown passage, Walton is himself a Promethean quester, like Frankenstein, toward whom he is so compellingly drawn. Coleridge's Mariner is of the line of Cain, and

of terming the scientist a "generous and self-devoted being."
Frankenstein, the Modern Prometheus who has violated nature, receives his epitaph from the ruined second nature he
has made, the God-abandoned, who consciously echoes the
ruined Satan of *Paradise Lost* and proclaims, "Evil thenceforth became my good." It is imaginatively fitting that the
greater and more interesting consciousness of the creature
should survive his creator, for he alone in Mrs. Shelley's
novel possesses character. Frankenstein, like Coleridge's
Mariner, has no character in his own right; both figures win
a claim to our attention only by their primordial crimes
against original nature.

The monster is of course Mary Shelley's finest invention,
and his narrative (Chapters 11 through 16) forms the
highest achievement of the novel, more absorbing even than
the magnificent and almost surrealistic pursuit of the climax.
In an age so given to remarkable depictions of the dignity
of natural man, an age including the shepherds and beggars
of Wordsworth and what W. J. Bate has termed Keats's
"polar ideal of disinterestedness"—even in such a literary
time Frankenstein's hapless creature stands out as a sublime
embodiment of heroic pathos. Though Frankenstein lacks the
moral imagination to understand him, the daemon's appeal
is to what is most compassionate in us:

> Oh, Frankenstein, be not equitable to every other, and
> trample upon me alone, to whom thy justice, and even
> thy clemency and affection, is most due. Remember that
> I am thy creature; *I ought to be thy Adam, but I am
> rather the fallen angel, whom thou drivest from joy for
> no misdeed.* Everywhere I see bliss, from which I alone

am irrevocably excluded. I was benevolent and good; misery made me a fiend. Make me happy, and I shall again be virtuous."

The passage I have italicized is the imaginative kernel of the novel and is meant to remind the reader of the novel's epigraph:

> Did I request thee, Maker, from my clay
> To mold me man? Did I solicit thee
> From darkness to promote me?

That desperate plangency of the fallen Adam becomes the characteristic accent of the daemon's lamentations, with the influence of Milton cunningly built into the novel's narrative by the happy device of Frankenstein's creature receiving his education through reading *Paradise Lost* "as a true history." Already doomed because his standards are human, which makes him an outcast even to himself, his Miltonic education completes his fatal growth in self-consciousness. His story, as told to his maker, follows a familiar Romantic pattern "of the progress of my intellect," as he puts it. His first pleasure after the dawn of consciousness comes through his wonder at seeing the moon rise. Caliban-like, he responds wonderfully to music, both natural and human, and his sensitivity to the natural world has the responsiveness of an incipient poet. His awakening to a first love for other beings, the inmates of the cottage he haunts, awakens him also to the great desolation of love rejected when he attempts to reveal himself. His own duality of situation and character, caught between the states of Adam and Satan, Natural Man and his thwarted desire, is related by him directly to his reading of Milton's epic:

> It moved every feeling of wonder and awe that the picture of an omnipotent God warring with his creatures was capable of exciting. I often referred the several situations, as their similarity struck me, to my own. Like Adam, I was apparently united by no link to any other being in existence, but his state was far different from mine in every other respect. He had come forth from the hands of God a perfect creature, happy and prosperous, guarded by the especial care of his Creator; he

was allowed to converse with and acquire knowledge

terrible than the expelled Adam's. Echoing Milton, he asks
the ironic question "And now, with the world before me,
whither should I bend my steps?" to which the only possible answer is, toward his wretched Promethean creator.

If we stand back from Mary Shelley's novel in order better to view its archetypal shape, we see it as the quest of
a solitary and ravaged consciousness first for consolation,
then for revenge, and finally for a self-destruction that will
be apocalyptic, that will bring down the creator with his
creature. Though Mary Shelley may not have intended it,
her novel's prime theme is a necessary counterpoise to
Prometheanism, for Prometheanism exalts the increase in
consciousness despite all cost. Frankenstein breaks through
the barrier that separates man from God and gives apparent
life, but in doing so he gives only death-in-life. The profound
dejection endemic in Mary Shelley's novel is fundamental to
the Romantic mythology of the self, for all Romantic horrors
are diseases of excessive consciousness, of the self unable to
bear the self. Kierkegaard remarks that Satan's despair is
absolute because Satan, as pure spirit, is pure consciousness, and for Satan (and all men in his predicament) every
increase in consciousness is an increase in despair. Frankenstein's desperate creature attains the state of pure spirit
through his extraordinary situation and is racked by a consciousness in which every thought is a fresh disease.

A Romantic poet fought against self-consciousness
through the strength of what he called imagination,
a more than rational energy by which thought could seek
to heal itself. But Frankenstein's daemon, though he is in the
archetypal situation of the Romantic Wanderer or Solitary,
who sometimes was a poet, can win no release from his own

story by telling it. His desperate desire for a mate is clearly an attempt to find a Shelleyan Epipsyche or Blakean Emanation for himself, a self within the self. But as he is the nightmare actualization of Frankenstein's desire, he is himself an emanation of Promethean yearnings, and his only double is his creator and denier.

When Coleridge's Ancient Mariner progressed from the purgatory of consciousness to his very minimal control of imagination, he failed to save himself, since he remained in a cycle of remorse, but he at least became a salutary warning to others and made of the Wedding Guest a wiser and a better man. Frankenstein's creature can help neither himself nor others, for he has no natural ground to which he can return. Romantic poets liked to return to the imagery of the ocean of life and immortality, for in the eddying to and fro of the healing waters they could picture a hoped-for process of restoration, of a survival of consciousness despite all its agonies. Mary Shelley, with marvelous appropriateness, brings her Romantic novel to a demonic conclusion in a world of ice. The frozen sea is the inevitable emblem for both the wretched daemon and his obsessed creator, but the daemon is allowed a final image of reversed Prometheanism. There is a heroism fully earned in the being who cries farewell in a claim of sad triumph: "I shall ascend my funeral pile triumphantly and exult in the agony of the torturing flames." Mary Shelley could not have known how dark a prophecy this consummation of consciousness would prove to be for the two great Promethean poets who were at her side during the summer of 1816, when her novel was conceived. Byron, writing his own epitaph at Missolonghi in 1824, and perhaps thinking back to having stood at Shelley's funeral pile two years before, found an image similar to the daemon's to sum up an exhausted existence:

> The fire that on my bosom preys
> Is lone as some volcanic isle;
> No torch is kindled at its blaze—
> A funeral pile.

The fire of increased consciousness stolen from heaven ends as an isolated volcano cut off from other selves by an estranging sea. "The light of that conflagration will fade

ern Prometheus ends with a last word true, not to his accomplishment, but to his desire:

> Farewell, Walton! Seek happiness in tranquillity and avoid ambition, even if it be only the apparently innocent one of distinguishing yourself in science and discoveries. Yet why do I say this? I have myself been blasted in these hopes, yet another may succeed.

Shelley's Prometheus, crucified on his icy precipice, found his ultimate torment in a Fury's taunt: "And all best things are thus confused to ill." It seems a fitting summation for all the work done by Modern Prometheanism and might have served as an alternate epigraph for Mary Shelley's disturbing novel.

HAROLD BLOOM

SELECTED BIBLIOGRAPHY

Works by MARY WOLLSTONECRAFT SHELLEY

History of a Six Week's Tour (with P. B. Shelley), 1817   Travel
Frankenstein; or, the Modern Prometheus, 1818   Novel
  (Signet Classic 0451-520098)
Mathilda, 1819   Novella (publ. 1959)
Valperga, 1823   Novel
The Last Man, 1826   Novel
Lodore, 1835   Novel
Falkner, 1837   Novel
Letters, ed. F. L. Jones, 1944
Journal, ed. F. L. Jones, 1947
Collected Tales and Stories, ed. C. E. Robinson, 1976

Selected Biography and Criticism

Church, Richard. *Mary Shelley (1797–1851).* New York: Viking, 1928.

Grylls, R. Glynn. *Mary Shelley.* London: Oxford University Press, 1938.

Levine, George and U. C. Knoepflmacher, eds. *The Endurance of* Frankenstein: *Essays on Mary Shelley's Novel.* Berkeley: University of California Press, 1979.

Nitchie, Elizabeth. *Mary Shelley: Author of* Frankenstein. New Brunswick, N.J.: Rutgers University Press, 1953. Rpt. Westport, Conn.: Greenwood, 1970.

Norman, Sylva. "Mary Wollstonecraft Shelley." *Shelley and His Circle,* III. Ed. Kenneth N. Cameron. Cambridge, Mass.: Harvard University Press, 1970, pp. 397-422.

Spark, Muriel. *Child of Light: A Reassessment of Mary Wollstonecraft Shelley.* Hadleigh, Essex: Tower Bridge, 1951.

Walling, William. *Mary Shelley.* New York: Twayne, 1972.

A NOTE ON THE TEXT

The text of the Signet Classic *Frankenstein or, The Modern Prometheus* is that of the third edition, revised and corrected by the author and published by Henry Colburn and Richard Bentley, London, 1831. The author's Introduction, lacking in the first edition (1818) and the second (1823), was published in this edition for the first time. The text is reprinted here with permission from The Carl and Lily Pforzheimer Foundation, Inc., on behalf of The Carl H. Pforzheimer Library.

L A S   D O S   V E N E C I A S

CUARTO CRECIENTE

JOAQUÍN MORTIZ • MÉXICO

ROSARIO FERRÉ

Primera edición, marzo de 1992
© Rosario Ferré, 1992
© D. R. Editorial Joaquín Mortiz, S. A. de ...
Grupo Editorial Planeta
Insurgentes Sur 1162-3o., Col. del Vall
México, 03100, D. F.

ISBN 968-27-0508-8

Portada: John Singer Sargent,
"Puente de los suspiros" (ca. 1907)

Primera edición, marzo de 1992
© Rosario Ferré, 1992
© D. R. Editorial Joaquín Mortiz, S. A. de C. V.
Grupo Editorial Planeta
Insurgentes Sur 1162-3o. , Col. del Valle
México, 03100, D. F.

ISBN 968-27-0508-8

Portada: John Singer Sargent,
"Puente de los suspiros" (ca. 1907)

La hora nos despoja de un don inconcebible
Tan íntimo que sólo es traducible
En un sopor que la vigilia dora...
¿Quién serás esta noche en el oscuro
Sueño, del otro lado de su muro?

JORGE LUIS BORGES

¿Seré yo el puente errante
entre el sueño y la muerte?
Presente...!
¿De qué lado del mundo me
llaman, de qué frente?

JULIA DE BURGOS

Cambio de forma en tránsito constante,
nacida y transfigada a sueño, a bruma...
Agua-luz lagrimándose en diamante
diamante sollozándose en espuma.

LUIS PALÉS MATOS

ble; donde aquella oscuridad a la que tanto temía
ingresar nocturnamente se volvía una suave manta

Venecia fue antiguamente una ciudad de descubri-
dores, de gentes que se arrojaban a la buena o a la
mala ventura, sin temor a los traicioneros caminos
del agua. Marco Polo, Cristóbal Colón, Américo
Vespucci, todos visitaron en algún momento Venecia, y pusieron sus conocimientos marítimos al ser-
vicio de los Dodges de la República, cuya íntima
naturaleza residía en el derecho de la humanidad a
surcar en plena libertad los océanos y mares del
mundo. La primera vez que escuché la palabra Venecia fue en una canción de viaje que mi madre me cantaba, y que decía: "El Adriático fue mi cuna,/ una
góndola me arrulló/ y una sutil y azul laguna/ mi
tranquila niñez pasó". En aquel entonces la palabra
Venecia era para mí, al igual que el sillón de mi
madre y la cuna de la canción, un lugar de tránsito,
de paso a otras realidades: la palabra Venecia era
el pórtico que me era necesario atravesar para ingresar cotidianamente de la vigilia al sueño, del mundo
exterior al interior, a ese mundo donde lo prohibido,
lo que muchas veces me aterraba y me amenazaba
durante el día, se volvía terreno familiar y acepta-

ble; donde aquella oscuridad a la que tanto temía ingresar nocturnamente se volvía una suave manta con la que mi madre me abrigaba. Aquella V mayúscula, que se repetía tres veces (Venecia-Vaivén-Viaje) en su canto, me hacía identificarme con su sonido de una manera especial.

Mi madre había estado en Venecia en viaje de novios y hablaba siempre de ella, no como una ciudad real, sino como una "ciudad de sueño". Venecia era, por aquel entonces, el lugar predilecto de los reciencasados de buena familia de la isla, y viajar a Venecia en viaje de nupcias era algo así como verificar *in situ* que la luna nueva era, en efecto, una hojuela de harina garapiñada de miel. Pero cuando me cantaba su canción, que tenía una melodía profundamente triste, yo dudaba de que Venecia fuera tal y como ella me la describía. Intuía que para ella la verdadera Venecia no era la ciudad a la cual se llegaba en viaje de luna de miel, sino la casa paterna, la sutil y azul laguna de la niñez que ella se había visto obligada a abandonar luego de su matrimonio.

Cuando mi madre regresó a la isla de su viaje a Venecia y se instaló en su nueva casa de Ponce, no se sentía contenta. No era que estuviera desgraciada sino que vivía como en un limbo, en un estado de perpetua suspensión, esperando el momento en que regresaría de visita a casa de sus padres. Había crecido en Mayagüez, en una hermosa casa amurallada y rodeada de balcones que daban al mar Caribe, en la cual sus padres, que la adoraban, habían construido un mundo que correspondía a los ideales románticos de los terratenientes de la isla. A aquel

El viaje semanal a Mayagüez tenía sus aventuras y la que me resulta más inolvidable era el cruce del Río Loco, entre Yauco y San Germán. Para los años cuarenta Puerto Rico se desangraba en una emigración masiva hacia el continente; en un solo año (el '42) los veinte mil emigrados al año fueron creciendo hasta llegar a los setenta mil, una verdadera hemorragia de seres que huían del hambre y del desempleo durante una operación de válvula de escape designada secretamente a asegurar el futuro de los que se quedaban. Como cuando hace agua el buque y la mitad de la tripulación se arroja al mar, estando la costa engañosamente cerca y perdida toda esperanza para los que no pueden nadar, en el Puerto Rico de aquellos años los emigrantes fueron los sacrificados, y los que se beneficiaron fueron los huérfanos, los enfermos y los débiles, los que no pudieron irse, en fin, así como los privilegiados que recibían un 80 porciento del ingreso nacional.

El Río Loco permaneció sin puente a través de toda esa década, razón por la cual tuvimos que enfrentarnos a él muchas veces. Había una razón válida para que el gobierno no gastara fondos públicos en construir el puente durante una situación de crisis como aquélla. El Río Loco era llano y pocas veces cogía agua; casi siempre era posible cruzarlo en carro como si se tratara de un pedregal polvoriento, regado de huevos prehistóricos y troncos de árboles destrozados. Cuando crecía, sin embargo, se henchía como un monstruo achocolatado que arrastraba sobre su lento dorso toda suerte de escombros humanos, techos descuarrangirados, sillones desenguatados, ollas, zapatos viejos, ropa, y sobre todo innumerables cerdos, chivos y pollos flotando patas arriba e inflados por la podredumbre, cuya ...

... llevaba ese nombre precisamente por ser tan temperamental: nunca crecía cuando debía, o sea, cuando llovía en el llano y todos los ríos de la vecindad se salían de madre y se arrojaban camino al mar dando tumbos como caballos desbocados. Era un río lunático, que se hinchaba de agua cuando el sol fogueaba las cañas como una brasa y sacaba hasta a los alacranes de sus cuevas en busca de agua, y fue quizá por eso que siempre lo relacioné oscuramente con mi madre. Como al Río Loco, a ella también le daban accesos de llanto en los momentos más inesperados, cuando a su alrededor brillaba el sol y a la familia le iba mejor que nunca. Lloraba cuando llovía "allá en la altura", en el interior de su cabeza, en las quebradas ocultas de la montaña, y yo sólo podía observarla en silencio y testimoniar su llanto. Preguntarle que por qué lloraba, que por quién lloraba, me hubiese puesto a la merced de un pellizco cárdeno o de algún coscorrón resabioso y destripador de trenzas. La aventura de cruzar el río tendía entonces como un velo de alegría sobre el impasse de ver a mi madre, muda como una piedra algunos días después de nuestro regreso a casa, anegada en la corriente de su propio llanto. Verla desafiar el río, arrojarse impaciente a su conquista era como una negación de sus derrotas previas, de su incapacidad para sobreponerse a las periódicas inundaciones que la visitaban.

En primera instancia, y acabando de llegar junto al río, mi madre decidía siempre esperar a que las aguas bajaran, antes de hacer zarpar el Pontiac como un yate mofletudo sobre aquella madeja de tirijala, que halaba todo lo que se encontraba a sus orillas hacia el mar, pero la paciencia nunca le duraba. Muy pronto, sobre todo si se trataba del viaje de ida hacia la casa paterna, le ordenaba al chofer que internara a velocidad moderada el hocico del Pontiac en el río (si se iba muy rápido, el agua inundaba inmediatamente el coche), siguiendo la ruta que había tomado ante nosotros algún otro aventurero más afortunado. El Río Loco, sin embargo, era sorprendentemente ancho, y resultaba sumamente difícil cruzarlo sin caer en algún hondón que, oculto a medio camino, hacía subir drásticamente el nivel de las aguas. Inmediatamente se escuchaba escopetear el motor, el carro sufría un corto acceso de delirium tremens, y de pronto veíamos el suero achocolatado lamer en silencio los cristales rápidamente subidos hasta el techo de fieltro.

La imagen de aquel contraste, entre el mundo de miseria que flotaba lentamente fuera de nuestras ventanas, el detritus purulento y hediondo de aquel caos, y el interior del coche perfumado y lleno de golosinas, de los calderos de arroz con gandules y de arroz

niñez, en la cual tuviera todas las comodidades. A pesar de ello, mi padre no pudo nunca devolverle su paraíso. Es posible que esto se debiera a que mi madre resentía el no seguir siendo un ser íntegro, adosado al árbol patriarcal y sostenido por el ramaje externo de su populosa parentela; el verse dividida y multiplicada hacia adentro, obligada a contemplar su rostro reflejado en otros rostros y su mirada en otros ojos que se le parecían y que sin embargo eran siempre distintos y eternamente cambiantes. Se le hacía difícil aceptar que su cuerpo se convirtiese en un lugar de paso de las generaciones venideras, de sus hijos y nietos, de sus amores y sus odios. La inevitable mudanza, el tránsito incomprensible de aquella Venecia equivocada a la que había llegado, la amenazaba con la pérdida de la identidad y con la dispersión.

Mi madre remprendía nocturnamente, llevándome consigo en su sillón, ese viaje de novios que yo *no* debería de hacer, porque me conllevaría los mismos sufrimientos que le había causado a ella. Ese viaje, me alertaba en su canción, era un cruel rito de pasaje, que nos obligaba a las mujeres a cambiar de estado. De él no regresábamos nunca al lugar del cual habíamos partido, ni regresábamos de la misma manera. El canal por el cual las generaciones venideras llegarían al mundo quedaba abierto, y ese hecho nos cambiaba, nos convertía de espacios cerrados y autosuficientes, en lugares transitados. Los seres llegarían a nuestro cuerpo-puerto de lugares misteriosos y desconocidos, y partirían de él para ingresar en otros viajes, cuyos términos permanecían igualmente

angustiantes e inexplicados. Y, la razón que mi madre
jamás pronunciaba, pero que yo tenía más presente,
era que a causa de ese viaje

canción. Me casé y tuve varios hijos; por mi cuerpo
pasaron al mundo, como ella me lo había anunciado,
otros seres que entraron al vacío del tiempo, y me
sentí a mi vez amenazada por la dispersión. No fue
hasta que comencé a escribir que aquel malestar
comenzó a disiparse. Y fue a mi madre, a su canción sobre Venecia, a quien tuve que agradecérselo,
aunque para aquel entonces ya había muerto, y
nunca se lo pude decir. En la canción que ella me
cantaba, Venecia era una ciudad llena de peligros,
que era necesario evitar a toda costa, pero en la que
yo escuchaba Venecia era la palabra Venecia, el
balanceo feliz de las góndolas, el chapoteo de las
olas, la suave brisa marítima que me empujaba al
sueño. Escribir es también emprender un viaje, arrojarse a una aventura sorprendente, y mi primer viaje,
mi primera aventura, la emprendí en aquel sillón en
el cual mi madre y yo navegábamos juntas todas las
noches a Venecia. Aquel viaje tenía como propósito
curarme de todo deseo de viajar, retenerme a su lado
para siempre, pero, en lugar de ello, me inició en
la posibilidad de viajar por la palabra. Si no le temo

15

hoy a la escritura es porque esa Venecia me reconcilió al hecho de ser un lugar de tránsito y de cambio, de canales misteriosos por los cuales las vidas de otros seres, así como las palabras que intentan describirlas, fluyen y desembocan unas en otras. Gracias a la canción de mi madre me volví en mi propia descubridora, y pude, a diferencia de ella, vivir en una casa abierta y sin murallas, sin temerle a los caminos desconocidos y muchas veces traicioneros del agua. Fue así como descubrí la existencia de esa otra Venecia, tan distinta del paraíso perdido de la niñez que ella me describía en su canción; aunque quizá no tan distinta...

GUARDI

Sobre este cuerpo que tiñe la mirada
Venecia despide un celaje indetenible
como el del agua vertida sobre agua.

reflejo especular de la palabra.

Acodada sobre el reborde de la piedra
contempla, en el dédalo espejeante,
esfumarse fugaz
la propia
sombra: el tránsito
de la góndola al muelle, de la vigilia
al sueño, bajo puentes sigilosos
como párpados.

ACUARELA

El poder y la guerra nada pueden
contra su imperecedera evanescencia.
Napoleón no expolió sus tesoros,
ni bebió Atila el huno en los purpúreos
cálices de sus sagrarios, cercenada
la cabeza venerada de San Marcos
por la cólera infiel de los alfanjes.
Imposible asediar sus catedrales
que borra el tiempo, el esplendor aciago
de sus palacios, que desangran sus colores
por el borde metálico del mar, sus almenares
cautivos de la inconstante lejanía.
¿Cómo invadir un cuerpo que se hunde?
¿Cómo sitiar su errante laberinto
el clamoroso batallón del sátrapa?
Por sus corredores se esfuman los sanguinarios
cascos del enemigo, por sus muros
se extingue la inevitable hoguera
que consume periódicamente el mundo.
Venecia es una acuarela delicada
que pesa lo que el pincel sobre la página.
Sin ella la memoria del mundo se hundiría
bajo la humeante pesantez del oro
del mar ensangrentado
y de la piedra.

y [...] sobre el teclado de hilo de la mesa
centelleaban mudo desorden consumado,
y en torno a las gardenias de las urnas
giraba aún el aire grave de la fiesta.
La marea había introducido ya sus sombras
por los balaustres alabastrinos de los altane
cuando Rialta retiró su canapé
de plumas hacia las penumbras húmedas
de la sala. El efímero oro de su cuerpo
se empañaría ahora bajo las guirnaldas de fruta
que destilaban un perfume rancio,
pasado de su tiempo y de su punto
preciso de dulzor.
El grito de los pavorreales agonizó en el aire
y disparó contra el cielo sus mil ojos de cobalto.
Había *viento* y *cenizas en el viento*.
Las aguas subieron el primer escalón,
y lamieron obstinadas la puerta.
Rialta tapió la puerta, pero las aguas siguieron
subiendo. Tapió el portal, forjado a hierro
vivo, pero las aguas siguieron subiendo.
Tapió el zaguán y los salones dorados,

la salita Tintoretto y el pórtico de Palladio,
pero las aguas siguieron subiendo.
La rosetta madre, quebrada en su ajedrez
de sangre, la iluminaban rosettas aún más altas.
Madrastra de mareas armada de reflejos,
la luna enarboló indiferente su oblea
y se detuvo en el pretil de la ventana.
"Dejad en paz lo que ha sido mío", le rogó
Rialta. "Mientras su recuerdo quede como estaba,
no habré muerto enteramente."

Recorrió minuciosamente la ciudad:
su arquitectura femenina hasta en el olor
a sexo, que no se deja nunca imaginar
toda entera, poblada de pasajes
y de emblemas secretos,
el silabeo submarino que devora
sus efímeros palacios y sus plazas,
la agonía que descarna en cuarzo vivo
el soberano hundimiento del olvido.
De allí venía la luz, la oscuridad, la piedra
cifrada que deslaza sobre el agua
la noche lateral de la escritura,
así como también el tiempo unánime
que todo lo corroe y lo desgasta.
De su visita alucinada hoy le restan
un silencio antiguo, la descomposición natural
de la palabra, y el eterno gestar
de su materia orgánica.

GIOVANNI BELLINI

No huyeron a tiempo.
Ni Poe, ni Byron, ni Hoffman, ni George Sand.
Ni la puerta cancel carcomida por el agua.
Ni el león alado de relámpagos verdes.
Ni la cuadriga fogosa que sobrevivió a Nerón.
Venecia los atrapó en sus óleos fugitivos

hasta borrarlos sobre ese lienzo que transcurre
cuando el vaso del cuerpo se levanta del lecho
y derrama al alba la memoria del sueño.

y vio zarpar el esqueleto de su alma.

BARCAROLA DE HOFFMANN

En Venecia todo es mudanza, todo es pasaje.
En su dintel se anticipa cotidianamente
la despedida definitiva de la muerte.
Imposible retroceder, imposible arrepentirse
por la calle inasible que transita
el agua. Navegar es un crónico
agitar de pañuelos, eximido del eco
reconfortante de los pasos,
mientras los senderos fundamentales
quedan, por lo general,
abandonados, ante el temor de que la noche
nos sorprenda en ellos
antes de transitar
por otros.

                              ...marcos el vaporetto del
                                                    [Lido
tocaba la sirena para los bañistas
y las góndolas bailaban como delfines
                                [dieciochescos.

Los vendedores de gargantillas venecianas
colgaban sus diminutas anémonas al lóbulo de
                                [los turistas
en nostálgicas memorabilias de vidrio.

Al fondo de su campana transparente
Eurídice hilvanaba las lágrimas de Orfeo
a los largos hilos de su remordimiento.

Venecia atravesaba la palabra espejo
como viajaba el pensamiento por la palabra
Venecia.

Venecia es un vitral que se desangra en el
                                [Adriático.

CANALAUTOR

Atravesó aquel paraje en un sueño
al ritmo de calcañares y de astrágalos.
El color de las flores
se transparentaba en sus venas,
arrastradas por un agua ancestral.
Por él llegó al mundo
hasta extraer el postrer grito
que se desataba junto al cordón umbilical:
¿Cómo perseverar, el corazón de Fidelio

[intacto?

[visiones
de ese paraje aterrador a donde se apresuraba a
[ir.
¿Podía darle algo mejor el corazón de Venecia?

VENECIA GOYESCA

Gótica caverna voluptuosa;
en la noche emite vagidos guturales.
Ataúd luctuoso flotando a la deriva
al ritmo de lúgubres membranas.
Puente de líquidos suspiros
que el alma confusa desborda.
Efluvio de cloroformo y ácido fénico
destilado por entre alas de murciélago.
Falla incontinente y telúrica
alumbrada por la incontinencia de su sexo.

Rialta reconoce una vez más el canal
por el que vino al mundo.
Por sus tinieblas navega todavía,
buscándose a sí misma.

...sino de las

...s ser todo

...ella te muestre:
la dama del *trompe l'oeil*,
la del engaño pintado sobre párpados
pesados como telones operáticos, la que se dora
al sol sobre las terrazas fragantes
de los altane, la que se ata las guedejas
venenosas con el aliento del sirocco mortal,
la que se enrosca a la cintura los ritmos
de sus pámpanos de sangre, la que incita
a los hombres con la brisa musgosa que exhalan
sus axilas, abiertas como ventanas, la reina
del limo cadavérico, la corteja
de los ancianos seniles que bendicen el pan
de cada día con la hiel de la Santa Cruz,
la Dogaresa que le obsequió al Dux
el anillo áureo de su silencio
perfecto, la suicida del minarete
de marfil, la del Espejo de
la Santidad Cristiana, la del fanal
que se enciende y se persigna en las noches

tempestuosas del alma, la madre del ahogado
inmortal, la del hijo que se murió sin Dios."
Rialta, indiferente ante tan irracional
espectáculo, cumplió con desdén los edictos
de carnestolendas. Se rapó el pelo,
vistió sus carnes con un saco
de yute penitente y se calzó las sandalias
sensatas de aparcelar el alma,
antes de volver las espaldas a las celebraciones
y abandonar para siempre la ciudad.

...ia la ciudad interior.
...los tremulos acantilados de la carne
transcurrían archipiélagos musgosos,
lentos respiraderos que giraban
a la mesura de la cadera
o del abismo más alto
y genital. La madre se detuvo
y, sajado con austeridad el corpiño,
le develó a la hija la prueba
de la inconstancia del Dios;
el doble repudio de ese pecho
que se inclina, ya maduro
hacia el vértigo crepuscular del zenith
como una fruta cuyo oro
ha fundido el bochorno polvoriento del tiempo;
su preferencia por las colinas abrigadas
y aún tibias del verano, por los campos
                              [sembrados
de ajos perfumados, en los que todavía
hunde sus bocados el manso cordero pascual
goloso de tuberosas femeneidades
que comienzan a socavarlo todo bajo el sol.

"Imposible confiar en su reflejo, le dijo la madre,
en el escándalo de los cuerpos empotrados
para siempre en idéntico recuerdo
bajo las acres ceremonias del verano.
El dolor te llegará por los canales
apenas tibios de las tardes de noviembre,
la sonrisa apoyada sobre la quilla diabólica,
cada hombro una casa, la cintura
alborotada como una plaza de toros,
vaticinando alianzas de oros inciertos,
malgastados sobre la sangre irremediable,
el remo quebrado a la cintura como un asta
que destila su aljófar
perfumado, al canotier de paja
desperdigando una risa irresponsable al viento.
Imposible balancear toda la hermosura del
                                        [mundo

sobre el hombro, creer en Dios
y en sus atributos inmortales. Mejor
navegar en reverso, sobre aupadas
puntas de pie, hacia el cálido regazo materno,
hacia esa doble tibieza que te dio el ser."
La hija, densa la miel cuajada en los
panales, selló con sombra tácita los labios
de la madre, se desprendió del cuello
el dulce cilicio de sus brazos y desnudó
impaciente el azogue blanco de su cuerpo
para así mejor proclamar su entrega
al abrazo del Dios.

.... nunca
......go buscando
por los edificios olientes a ruina que reincide en
                                        [hábito
o quizá en vicio,
al pie del cielo raso encalado cuidadosamente
                            [por el restaurador,
entre las vigas de ausubo negras como el pecado
e igualmente paralelas e inevitables,
o por el ojo de buey siempre atento en lo alto
como una sandía azul recortada a pleno vuelo
                                    [contra el muro
de por lo menos cuatro brazos de espesor,
ciudad marina y a la vez celeste en la que el
                                        [cielo
se confunde día a día con el mar,
he envejecido bastante desde la primera vez
que caminé por tus calles, sin saber cuántas
veces repetiría la ceremonia.

La claridad del mar me llamaba como una
                            [enorme nostalgia
y el azul era tu color predominante.

Los cardúmenes descendían a chorros por entre
                              [tus aceras musgosas
convertidos en adoquines inquietos un día de
                              [mucha lluvia,
tus casas, de fachadas líquidas como miradas
desleían Calma y Tranquilidad en la distancia
como si contemplaran, pintiparadas sobre los
                              [tacones
de sus azulejos, las neblinosas lejanías de
                              [Villalba.
Por tu añil más recóndito viajaba el sueño
que no siempre se desprendía de la periferia del
                              [orbe,
pisar tus calles ya daban ganas de navegar
porque todo el mundo sabía que tus adoquines
habían venido de lejanas tierras
y que habían servido de lastre a las fragatas
                              [vacías
que luego regresaban a Europa como urnas
                              [perfumadas,
llenas hasta reventar las estibas de azúcar, de
                              [tabaco y de café,
balanceándose pesadamente sobre el agua.

El aire también me llamaba;
yo venía de Ponce, donde las casas eran terreras
y polvosas, asfixiadas por la miopía estéril de
                              [las tierras del Sur,
apabulladas por una gravedad de cal y canto
que las anclaba irremediablemente al valle,
donde las damas vestidas de rosa suministraban

el elixir del consuelo a los hijos enfermos,
dedicadas desinteresadamente a velar
por las pupilas encen~~...~~

~~...~~

~~[tanto~~ aire,
a aquel bautizo atrevido de espuma y sal,
al yodo rebelde ardiéndome sobre los labios,
aquel empinado subir y bajar
para de pronto divisar el mar a la vuelta
de cualquier esquina, aquel navío gigante
que se adentraba por los muros de las casas
como si les hiciera el amor
iluminado y todo vestido de gala,
al revolar de faldas y melenas
en la esquina de la Plaza de Armas,
que no nos dejaba ver mientras nos lo veían
todo, los pordioseros sentados en la acera
cuya única limosna era ver, los jóvenes
delicuescentes, víctimas del sofocante deseo
del trópico, el choferito *préparaté*
y el revendón dormitando a la sombra
de su balanza encarnada,
procurando madurar lentamente, junto a
los aguacates, las papayas y los plátanos,
el gesto lascivo que le iluminaba las
                                   [salpimentadas
mejillas, todos al acecho del deleitoso temblor

de las carnes al subir la cuesta más empinada
de Padín, sabiendo que al llegar a la cima el
                                    [viento
repetiría otra vez su impertinente revelación
y que saldríamos de nuevo remontando los aires
                              [como Marylin,
asidas a nuestras faldas como amapolas
                                    [voladoras
que el viento dispersaría suavemente
al atardecer sobre el mar.
Aquella ciudad era una borrachera de
                    [sensaciones que mareaba,
una travesía liviana, aérea
un romper con todas las amarras
de esas culpas secretas que hunden troncos
en la tierra. Cada calle era un muelle
abandonado, un duelo a muerte con la
                                    [resignación
y con la madre, restallando, como Nora
el portazo furioso con el que nos fuimos de casa.

Las lanchas de Cataño,
juguetes maravillosos de remendar el tiempo,
nos iniciaron en el hábito traicionero
del viaje. Máquinas marineras de hacer trutrú
iban suturando costa a costa nuestro destino
en una arriesgada operación de corazón abierto.
(Ya se van los Reyes, madre
bendito sea Dios,
ellos van y vienen
y nosotras no.)
Correr las olas de Norte a Sur es una experiencia

excitante, cantar canciones en castellano
y contar dinero en americano
es todavía más ...

...

... de New York
donde los bosques supuran heroína y alcohol
sobre la sien de los proscritos
que ríen, vuelan, se sienten inmortales
porque mañana han de pagar con lo que falta?
¡Por diez centavos voy y vengo, madre,
por diez centavos!
¡Como los Reyes Magos, madre,
como los Reyes Magos!
Pero cada travesía era una muerte lenta,
una proa que afila el bisturí en la noche
y separa las olas de las entretelas del alma
que nunca acaba de arribar a buen puerto.
Luego hay que zurcir las márgenes salpicadas de
                                          [sangre
de los que se fueron a cosechar panes amargos
por entre los rascacielos de acetileno y plata.

Todo puerto es adolescente en su fuero interno,
y quizá también en su seno más
tierno. Hay siempre alguna dársena
secreta que se abre, como una vena suicida,
en dirección al mar, algún callejón

que deambula por la oscuridad marina,
hacia esa fugacidad perdida que buscamos.
Todo pórtico, como la juventud,
convida a usarse, a salir por él para algún día
volver a entrar,
desafiando el tiempo impío del que se queda,
del que aguarda resentido a la orilla del camino
para ver el cuerpo de su peor enemigo pasar.
Todo embarcadero es un quicio vertical de
                                              [voces,
una madeja de lenguas que entrelazan su aliento
al trajín de ricas mercaderías
de matizados colores y texturas.
Por sus delicados agremanes de espuma
se reconcilian sutilmente las razas
y los tiempos; así quedaron bordadas
en punto en sombra y en punto en cruz
a los tapices importados de lejanas tierras,
las blancas colinas *capitolinas*
de tus siete pecados capitales,
los estamentos más negros de tus *arrabales*,
el *cuajo* y el *mondongo* de tus amanecidos
que se bendicen la cruda junto a las *alcantarillas*,
tus perros *realengos* que orean felices
su pelambre anacrónica por los caminos reales,
las almenas castizas de tu *Fortaleza*,
el laberinto mozárabe de tus *azoteas*,
Paraíso invertido de los gatos
que ensayan nocturnamente sus *salsas* operáticas,
el seráfico felino que deambula
por los abismos de tus *tragaluces*
y el mínimo demonio que vigila a *pie juntillas*

el angustiado devenir de nuestros sueños,
la submarina claridad de tus *zaguanes*

desposados al odio y al despecho,
los bailarines *siquedélicos* del *Escambrón*,
pertinaces en el arte de *brillar la hebilla*
al ritmo candente del cuatro por cuatro.

Desde los balcones coloniales del Viejo San Juan
los huesos de nuestros muertos queridos
agitan lánguidamente pañuelos cuando nos dicen
                                        [adiós,
e iluminan en las noches los arrecifes volcánicos
de su funéreo pedimento carcomido por el mar.
Noel Estrada pasea sus húmeros por las galerías
                                        [de La Luna,
entreverando nostalgias por entre los recuerdos
del alma, y en la madrugada le tararea
boleros a las prostitutas
que se han quedado varadas al borde del
                                        [orgasmo.
Los fémures de Clara Lair, fugitivos como
                                        [cuellos
de cisne, se asoman a la bahía por entre
los balaustres de su pequeño balcón español
y descuelgan guirnaldas de opio sobre el agua

en honor a Pardo Adonis (éxtasis
de caoba, de canela y de miel),
único recuerdo puro de su existencia triste.
Desde el balcón del Ocho Puertas Joe Valiente
con blancos metatarsos trenza al piano
bellas danzas de Morell y de Tavárez,
y exime el corazón de sus pesares
al ritmo melancólico de marfil con marfil.

Compañeras de Odiseo
zarpamos un día en busca de la lejana Cólchide,
construida con los cedros más perfumados del
                                        [Líbano.
Llevamos tantos años viajando,
atrás quedó la blancura insoportable
recortada contra el azul del cielo,
las calles modestas por las que bajaban
las damitas recatadas de gracia y de donaire
y las aún más agraciadas y encopetadas putas
de voces líquidas y cabelleras suntuosas
exhibiendo sus mercedes por la criollísima
                                        [Caleta
de las Monjas, el celaje rosado del atardecer en
                                        [los óleos
de Campeche, la miniatura de la Dama a
                                        [Caballo
que trenza a la crin de su alazán un relicario
                                        [que lee
"De la dulzura viene la fuerza",
el calabozo alado de San Felipe del Morro,
las murallas medievales con su crinolina de
                                        [espuma

44

bullendo al pie de la Calle del Cristo,
los escaparates criollos de la Calle San Francisco,
cada vez más destartalados por la liquidación

los adolescentes de la Calle San Sebastián
flechados por las saetas insanables del amor,
el aroma a café y a mallorcas recién horneadas,
último antojo de los moribundos que agonizan
[en capitales remotas,
San Juan Bautista
invocando el Apocalipsis con el dedo
al son del engracia baja para que veas esto,
Toribio tocando su güiro en la esquina de la
[Tanca,
los coches atrapados como peces candentes
entre la San Justo y la Tetuán,
los muelles repletos de viajeros recién llegados
o a punto de partir,
las muchedumbres vociferando su júbilo y su
[angustia
bajo el sol siderúrgico de las tres de la tarde,
la ciudadela rodeada de espejos en la que
[Narciso
ha perdido todo deseo de comunicarse con el
[mundo.

45

Pero lo cierto es que todavía no la hemos
                              [encontrado,
imposible descubrir su ubicación exacta,
el latido preciso de su longitud
geográfica, la ciudad no sufre paralelos
ni puntos de partida,
no admite vectores que tracen punto fijo
a su vertiginoso corazón.
Deshace de continuo sus muros sobre el agua,
parece hecha de harina de mar o quizá de
                              [llanto,
al atardecer se destaca con mayor nitidez
su albicante geometría
y aparece reflejada cruelmente en el espejo del
                              [alma.

Y sin embargo, no bien volvemos hacia ella la
                              [mirada,
su presencia se esfuma en un laberinto de algas.

esposa era de allí. Su padre le había regalado una avioneta Cessna de regalo de bodas y esa avioneta era, después de su mujer, la gran pasión de su vida. La mañana del accidente, mi tía le había pedido a mi tío que viajara de Ponce a la Capital a buscarle un par de zapatillas plateadas que necesitaba esa noche para un baile en el Casino.

El viaje debería tomar unos veinte minutos de ida y veinte de vuelta en avión, y mi tío, que estaba locamente enamorado de mi tía, quiso complacerla. El mismo trayecto en coche hubiese tomado cerca de cuatro horas ida y cuatro horas vuelta, debido a la topografía misteriosa de nuestra isla. Puerto Rico mide cien millas de largo por treinta y cinco de ancho, pero cruzarla en coche de costa a costa requería en esa época, cuando aún no estaba construida la autopista, de una paciencia y persistencia de siglos. Esto era así a causa de las agrestes montañas, ríos y despeñaderos que conforman su interior boscoso y hoy casi despoblado, topografía que a veces recuerda un mapa apretado por el puño iracundo de Dios y arrojado como desventurada bola de papel a los piélagos ultramarinos del Caribe.

La isla, decían, había desafiado la voluntad divina de hacernos desaparecer a causa de nuestra futura soberbia, de nuestro empecinado convencimiento de constituir un continente y no una peña pobre, un ínfimo peñón perdido en el Caribe, que le había servido a los españoles durante siglos de presidio para los prófugos de sus colonias, y que ocultaba en su seno apretado y umbroso su verdadera extensión. Y era al aventurarse por sus carreteras, que se adentraban en interminables laberintos de curvas en forma de horquilla, de horqueta, de látigo o de honda, que desafiaban todos los tiempos y distancias y producían en los viajeros un indescriptible escozor, que era posible conocer la isla en sus justas proporciones. Los viajeros descubrían entonces al término de su viaje, agobiados por el mareo, el calor y el tedio y dando un suspiro de alivio al verse por fin fuera de aquel enmarañado dédalo de curvas, abismos y cuestas del cual habían temido no salir jamás, que el tamaño de la isla era por lo menos diez veces mayor de lo que aparentaba en los mapas. En todo caso, fue por haberse servido de aquella extravagante transportación aérea que la magnanimidad de mi abuelo le había proveído para cometer el pecado de viajar de Ponce a la Capital en veinte minutos, siendo así uno de los primeros habitantes del pueblo en desafiar aquella topografía mágica de la isla que durante siglos constituyó uno de sus poderosos secretos, que mi tío pereció trágicamente en aquel viaje, al estrellarse aquel día su avioneta plateada contra el costado de una montaña.

La familia le permitió a la joven viuda enterrar los pocos restos que pudieron recoger entre los matorrales de la montaña

mente había accedido a venirse a vivir contando con que su hermano sería su vecino y compañero. A diferencia de Mayagüez, cuyas casas de balcones y medios puntos de encaje tallados en madera miraban hacia el mar o hacia los valles sembrados de caña que ondeaban a su alrededor, y que guardaba todavía en aquel tiempo el aire lírico de los pueblos decimonónicos, Ponce era una ciudad chata y caliente, de comercios poco atractivos y de calles pobladas de almacenes cuyos muros medían metro y medio de espesor. Tanto el mar como el valle se encontraban sorprendentemente distantes, como si sus habitantes les hubiesen vuelto las espaldas adrede, porque podrían distraerlos peligrosamente de sus actividades de especulación y lucro.

Durante los años subsiguientes mi madre y mi tía, que nunca se volvió a casar y le guardó luto a su marido toda la vida, visitaban juntas los domingos la tumba, y a esas visitas comenzaron a llevarme desde que cumplí un año. La bocanada de aire helado y de flores putrefactas que salía de aquella capilla cuando mi madre abría con su propia llave la cancela de hierro negro, permanece hoy uno de los recuerdos más intensos de mi niñez. Aquellas visitas fueron tomando poco a poco un cariz extraño; entre ambas mujeres, vestidas rigurosamente de negro, se estableció una competencia mórbida, que se expresaba tanto en el tamaño de los mazos de nardos y azucenas que cada cual traía consigo y colocaba semanalmente ante la cripta, como en los opulentos floreros de filigrana de plata o de porcelana francesa que traían de sus casas, para colocar en ellos sus respectivos ramos.

Guardando un silencio absoluto, que sólo quebraba el silbido de las casuarinas sembradas alrededor de la capilla, levantábamos entre las tres los floreros llenos de flores podridas de la semana anterior, los vaciábamos en el basural vecino, y luego subíamos a pie por una cuesta de piedra caliza que aún no había sido pavimentada, hasta el tope de la colina donde había otras tumbas recientes y la municipalidad había colocado una llave de agua para el público. Una vez allí, lavábamos cuidadosamente los floreros, los llenábamos de agua de nuevo, y volvíamos a bajar la cuesta para colocarlos en la capilla. Durante aquellas visitas aprendí muchas cosas: que allí, sellado en su nicho de mármol y acompañado por los ángeles de brazos cruzados sobre el pecho y ojos sellados en éxtasis que mi tía había enviado a tallar en Roma, para que lo acompañaran en su nombre en las noches, yacía mi tío, intocado por la lluvia y el sol; y también que los vivos podían odiarse a muerte por el amor de un muerto.

Mi madre adoraba a su hermano, y el duelo en

que la sumió su muerte se prolongó por diez años. Yo, a mi vez, adoraba a mi madre, y no podía comprender por qué un

mera comunión, en que a las demás niñas sus padres les hicieron imprimir alegres estampas del Niño Jesús iluminadas a colores que conmemoraban su día, a causa del luto por nuestro tío, que llevaba ya seis años de muerto, mis estampillas fueron impresas en blanco y negro, con una triste letra de esquela.

A los siete años de muerto mi tío, en presencia de mi madre todavía no se podía mencionar su nombre sin que inmediatamente se hiciera un silencio álgido, durante el cual sus ojos se llenaban de lágrimas. Solía pasarse horas contemplando el álbum en el cual guardaba los pequeños talismanes de papel que era lo único que le quedaba para recordarlo. Había recortado con infinito cuidado su silueta en todas las fotos de familia, para colocarlo solo, curiosamente sentado o flotando de pie en el vacío, intocado por la cercanía de sus seres queridos y sobre todo de mi tía. Recuerdo todavía el rictus de amargura que vi en su boca cuando le pregunté un día por qué mi tía y mis primos jamás venían a visitarnos a la casa, cuando los veíamos todos los domingos en el cementerio, y me contestó que no venían porque ella se los había prohibido, porque había sido por culpa del capricho de mi tía que su hermano había muerto, al pedirle que fuera a buscarle en avión sus tontas zapatillas de baile.

De aquel pozo de tristeza en que me sumió indirectamente la muerte de mi tío vino a sacarme, cuando cumplí siete años, Gilda Ventura. Gilda era negra, alta y delgada, y tendría escasamente diez años más que yo cuando llegó a nuestra casa. A diferencia de mi madre, tenía un temperamento alegre y se vestía siempre con trajes estampados de flores que destacaban las líneas armoniosas de su cuerpo, flexible y bronceado como un almácigo. Me gustaba sobre todo verla pintarse los labios de rojo brillante con un solo trazo experto de la mano, porque aquel gesto, y la sonrisa que lo acompañaba, me eximía de toda la aridez, de toda la incomprensible tristeza del luto de mi madre.

A Gilda le encantaba leer y terminadas las faenas de la escuela nuestra actividad favorita era escondernos de los mayores para tomar turnos leyéndonos cuentos en voz alta. Descubrí gracias a ella que en el mundo de Barba Azul un hombre podía asesinar a siete mujeres por celos antes de ser castigado por la justicia; que en el mundo de la Sirenita se podía tener el valor de salir del océano en busca del amado, a pesar de sentir los pies destrozados por cuchillos que brotaban de la tierra; y sobre todo que en el mundo de la Reina de las Nieves, mi cuento preferido, una mujer hermosísima secuestraba a una niña y se la llevaba a vivir con ella a su palacio de hielo. Como mi madre, la Reina de las Nieves había perdido a su hermano (en un accidente de trineo) y, desde aquella ocasión se le había enterrado una astilla de hielo en el corazón, y no había podido amar a

[texto ilegible]

...heroes, el que viviéramos en una isla cuya topografía misteriosa había causado la muerte de mi tío, el que mi madre viviera enamorada de su recuerdo y yo devorada por los celos, no eran entonces calamidades tan extraordinarias, y yo no debía guardar resentimiento por ello.

PRIMITIVAS

EL SUEÑO DE YADWIGHA

*El arte del aduanero Rousseau
brota del surtidor de su
encantamiento.*

JOSÉ LEZAMA LIMA

Yadwigha se ha quedado dormida al fondo del
[misterio.
Inmóvil en la brisa de la temeridad divina
eleva al cielo un índice autoritario
y decide tañer la sombra de su propio sueño.
Terciada sobre la boca la flauta iridiscente
conjura, en el contorno de su fuga, el rumor
de la selva que la cerca. El mamoncillo
de escamas de lagarto gotea sobre sus muslos
su esperma silenciosa, y el níspero balancea
sobre ella sus teticas de majá
o de faisán inaccesible. El mamey
multiplica, en su soberbio Sermón
del Paraíso, sus bienaventurados pechos
mientras gira en el empíreo sus planetas
de humeante azúcar moscabada.
Bajo la malanaga centifolia que la abriga
ruge el oro agazapado de los tigres
y el neblí alzado alumbra los juncales
a punto de ser fulminado por su grito.
Yadwigha tañe toda la noche, ebria de amanecer
y de sueño. Los bermejos, los amarantos,
los añiles, fluyen por la cintura

de su flauta y la redimen, en sus óleos
consagrados, de la grisura impenetrable de la
                                        [muerte

(Los nenúfares lluev~~~~ ~~

~~~~ ~~ suerte!
¡Hoy, gracias a ti, ha quedado eternizado
el pincel del aduanero con alas!"
Yadwigha, sorprendida, despierta
y cesa en la espesura el tañido de su flauta.
Fauna, flora, joven apolíneo
se esfuman por los bordes oleaginosos del
                                        [misterio
y su corazón reina, una vez más, supremo
sobre el silencio pre-adánico del lienzo.

EL SUEÑO DE LA GITANA

*En los poemas como en los sueños,
uno pone cosas que sabe, y cosas
que no quiere saber que sabe.*

ADRIENNE RICH

La gitana duerme como una santa de Sassetta
sobre las arenas babilónicas del desierto.
Con su brazo ha construido una rústica capilla
en la que reposa la reliquia de su rostro.
El arco iris la abriga de los vientos estériles
y arrastra tras de sí los delicados perfumes
de los incontables países reconocidos en su
                                    [marcha.
Su soledad es tan grande que ha borrado
toda huella de su paso por el páramo.
La manera que tiene de recibir la luna
me confirma que es poeta y peregrina.
A sus espaldas el río de la memoria teje
el murmullo de su derrumbe
en la corriente, y un león incandescente husmea
el nacimiento cauteloso de su cuello.
La gitana, impasible, duerme,
a su lado una guitarra y una botija de agua.
Se descuelga por el susurro verde de su sueño
como suele bajar la luna por el hilo
de la araña, a tomar su alimento acostumbrado.
El león la ronda con belfos dilatados
y chasquea su cola tensa contra el flanco

pavorosamente límpido del cielo.
La gitana saborea la sombra que la habita

_____ __ _____ ____ la distancia
de una alegría que se prolonga?
¿Es la ferocidad del poema o la del felino en
[acecho
lo que transpone la claridad del lienzo
para llegar hasta nosotros como el
desdoblamiento de un viaje en calma?
El león y el poema pasan, enigmáticos
por debajo de su sueño.

EL SUEÑO EN EL JARDIN DES PLANTES

*El Paraíso sólo puede pintarse
desde el infierno.*

EMIL NORMIL, pintor haitiano

El aduanero camina bajo el aguanieve de un
                              [atardecer plomizo
hacia los arabescos de fin de siglo del Jardin des
                              [Plantes.
A su paso el ángel de la Marsellesa sopla la
                              [trompeta
y los leones de la Plaza Denfert saludan,
                              [genuflexos.
Rémy de Gourmont, su amigo, lo cree empleado
                              [de un banco
que lo envía a cobrarle intereses Ymaginistas
a los macacos y cacatúas de la selva ecuatorial.
Su compadre Apollinaire da por ciertos los
                              [desvaríos de sus viajes
por las selvas de México y de América Central.
El aduanero hace poco le escribió una carta:
"Querido Guillaume:
Me quedan menos de cinco céntimos para el
                              [almuerzo.
¿No podrías adelantarme un franco por el
                              [retrato
de la musa coronada por los pensamientos del
                              [poeta?

62

Josephinette se muere de tisis
en el ventisquero de mi desván-atelier.
No ha podido vend

para saldar la renta del mes.
Madame la Baronne D'Oettinger me pagó quince
por el auto-retrato del pintor badelou. Esa venta
                              [me puso triste
porque me había encariñado de ese pequeño
                                        [buque
con todas las banderas desplegadas a sus
                              [espaldas..."
El aduanero navega al fondo del invernadero
                              [nacional
como un buque a la deriva en una botella
                              [vegetal.
Los pies adoloridos y el estómago recorrido por
                              [los vientos alisios
se sienta en un anónimo banco de piedra
en busca de un poco de reposo y de calor
                              [tropical.
Piensa en el Paraíso que le prometió ayer al
                              [comerciante Vollard
a cambio de los lienzos y óleos que le fió
para su última muestra en el Salon des Artistes
                              [Indépendents.

El aduanero arma con dificultad su caballete
al pie de un fugitivo helecho cuerno de alce
y remueve soñoliento frente al bastidor del lienzo
sus huesos de pequeña marioneta de leña.
El barrendero del invernadero
barre a sus pies las hojas con la punta del alma.
Cumplidor hacendoso de su deber estatal
arrincona todos los pesares del mundo
bajo el yagrumo rumboso de una gigantesca
                                      [malanga.
La cabeza del aduanero, madura por fin de
                                      [sueño
le gotea sobre las solapas polvorientas del pecho.
El hambre lo acecha en su estado bienaventurado
y le llena el estómago de musarañas.
Sueña con una familia de monos mirlitonescos
que pescan, fornican, saltan
por entre las persianas oleaginosas de los
                                      [almácigos.
Sobre su cabeza los mameyes, los pajuiles y los
                                      [plátanos
rezuman el perfume de su paradisíaco festín
al alcance aprovechable del alma.
La tormenta de aguanieve arrecia súbitamente su
                                      [furia
sobre el laberíntico palacete de cristal.
El aduanero, impasible, sigue soñando.
Sobre su cabeza aúllan mil desgracias
burladas por el frágil firmamento del Jardin des
                                      [Plantes.
Señor absoluto de su pincel sonámbulo
espiga sin temor sus óleos sobre el lienzo

en penachos verdes de puro salmo.
Una vez pintado el Paraíso
contempla con asombro su simetría

de su termo, la media luna evangélica
de su pan.

LAS ROSAS DE VAN GOGH

En el sanatorio de San Rémy
las rosas blancas que pintó Van Gogh
arden en su eterna Pascua de Resurrección
al centro de un jarro de porcelana verde
de Celadón. Espirales sin ruido,
elevan en secreto su arquitectura de hielo
sobre el mantel levemente rosado
y una hoja sombría, casi negra,
quiebra con su quemadura lívida
la aparente serenidad del ramo.
El latido de la locura acecha al fondo de esas
                                    [rosas
que se adentran implacables hacia el centro
del cuadro. Apocalipsis de nieve
que horada tiritando las tinieblas,
por ellas fluye la gracia que sepulta el ojo
en una dolorosa conglomeración
de gozo. El terror de saberse señalado
por Dios, llevó a su autor a devorar aquel día
varios pomos de albayalde blanco,
por lo que también se bebió
una lata de Kerosén, del que empleaba
para diluir la pena de sus pinceles
e iluminar la noche con su lámpara.
"Me encuentro mucho mejor", le escribió aquel
                                    [día
a su hermano Teo. "Creo que he podido por fin

dominarme, y no temerle más
a las rosas implacables de la muerte."

EL SUEÑO DE AMOR VELADO

El lenguaje
es una expiación
propiciación
al que no habla

OCTAVIO PAZ

Juana Inés duerme el sueño de Iztaccíhuatl
coronada por las rosas que se venderán
mañana, en el mercado de flores de Nepantla.
Sus pies rozan ese confín secreto donde el
                          [Volcán de Nieve
vierte invisible su humor hacia el Volcán de
                                 [Fuego,
y Popocatépetl peina sigiloso sus cabellos
en manantiales de ónix a lo largo
de su cuerpo. A cada suspiro suyo se levantan
                           [como garzas
cien tempestades de nieve por entre los
                             [ventisqueros
y en su pecho arde una llama piramidal·que
asciende, y consume en vilo el mundo.
Juana Inés despierta y, apremiada por su sueño
se dirige a grandes pasos hacia el Valle de
                             [México.
(A la vera del camino Amecameca desploma
sus perales, oferta a pleno cielo
su aromosa garganta de pomona
por entre gemela cornucopia de volcanes.)

Da tres golpes a la puerta del convento
y clama con imperiosidad ser admitida
a su labrado alcázar.

... espesura lagrimeante de los cirios
y el Arzobispo Aguiar y Seijas domeña
con dificultad el galgo albino
que le carcome solapadamente las entrañas.
Ávidos celadores de su fama
y de su alma, los prelados la amonestan
con raciocinio diverso. Láquesis
ha de guiar su pluma junto a la mecida tumba
donde se enhebra y corta sin duelo el propio
                                        [estambre
y la derecha ha de borrar fratricida el trazo de
                                        [la izquierda
sobre el mar angustiosamente arado de la
                                        [página.
Isis ha de labrar paciente peces mudos
a espumada escritura dispersa en vega llana,
ecos marinos que, amarillos de despecho amargo
coronan el corazón de abrojos y de cardos.
Juana Inés postra en hinojos, ante el Dios de las
                                        [Semillas
su pensamiento altivo en cáliz de cobalto.
Va arrojando una a una ante él sus vestiduras

hasta que, desollada en muro de cal viva
ofrece el manso cuello a la argentina esquila
de perlas gentil plinto, desamparado ahora
de rutilantes gargantillas y corales.
Observa caer, gozosa, los cabellos
que vistieron otrora en mítica alquería
cabeza tan despoblada de noticias,
y agradece la pelliza gris que apaga el cuerpo
en tosco hábito, emponzoñado
de recuerdos. Todo lo sufre Juana Inés,
todo lo sobrelleva con paciencia:
el impávido lampo del Sagrario
ojo ciclópeo que, inflamado en sangre
consume el alma inerme en tornos vanos,
los escombros de esta alcoba y de esta mano
temeraria que, obstinada, intenta
a fugitivas sombras dar alcance
por entre consonantes y vocales,
el silicio, el látigo, el escudo
el rosario, el barbote, el crucifijo
prendido al hombro como inmortal ballesta
que ha de defenderla de la tiranía del siglo,
el velo encenizado que, con vuelo presto
le amordaza melancólico la frente
combatiendo incendio raudo con secular

                                     [incendio.
Ícaro de nieve que, de propia voluntad cautivo
vuelca desaforado el pecho hacia la

                                     [incandescencia
para rendir en combustión secreta su materia,
tiende ya su alma el vuelo hacia la celda.
Serena en la inviolabilidad del claustro como

el gerifalte en su alcándara, Juana Inés
se inclina hacia sus enemigos y sonríe.

SEGUNDO SUEÑO

El discurso es un acero
que sirve por ambos cabos,
de dar muerte por la punta
por el pomo de resguardo.

SOR JUANA INÉS DE LA CRUZ

"La fama de Juana Inés crepita y lame
hasta los cimientos del mundo"
ha dicho con inquina la Marquesa,
inclinando provocativa el doble marfil del pecho
sobre el banquete irisado de faisanes.
El Marqués ha convocado, incrédulo, a su mesa
a los cuarenta sabios más ilustres del reino
para que interroguen ante él públicamente
al prodigio cortesano de Nepantla.
Pisa la joven con decisión el tabloncillo
de dorada cera, labrado ayer por la clepsidra
de su pie,
hoy por estilete raudo de su verso.
(El Oidor le ofrece ufano su butaca
damasquinada en oro y plata
y se acomoda a sus pies con mansedumbre

                                     [falsa.)

Juana Inés se pasea, Ícaro invicto
por entre los letrados sedentarios del reino.
Ora les dispara redondillas y romances
blandiendo el acero por la punta,
ora remonta el vuelo, ingenio osado

por sobre los laberintos de la física.
Sus versos giran, rehiletes de fuego
por las calzadas festivas de México

caminan tras de ella zahiriéndola a preguntas:
el misterio del Haikú, el diámetro de Antares
el orbe inmóvil de la esfera de Parménides
la facilidad con que oculta el colibrí
el suspendido diamante en el espacio,
la vesánica pupila de Gorgona
contemplando enfurecida el mundo
desde el escudo ensangrentado de Perseo,
si brota o no de los macizos del Olimpo
la misteriosa cadencia del hexámetro.
A todo responde Juana Inés con gallardía.
Vuelan a pesar de ella las maledicencias en su
                                              [torno,
agudos cortafríos que luego inscriben
sus respuestas en torvos palimpsestos
de sílex. Vuelve altiva el pabellón de las
                                              [espaldas
a la Farsalia tinta en sangre de los sabios
y abandona para siempre el banquete
y el palacio.
Desde la oscura celda de un convento
salva todos los enigmas y distancias:

se entrega al sueño
como el nadador a un gran río
y entrevera, a las espinas del caracol,
el plumaje incendiado de su alma.

Me vedarán el sueño, el epitafio
de esa noche geométrica que asciende
a cuatro puntos cardinales del vacío
por entre obeliscos y pirámides,
pero no podrán vedarme la palabra.
Me ocultarán el claro espejo que deambula
por un universo sin Dios y ardiendo en llamas
así como la gemela escala
por la que accede el cuerpo fermentado y
                                        [múltiple
al diáfano misterio de lo Unánime,
pero no podrán ocultarme la palabra.
Silenciarán el canto de la nocturna Nictimene
compañera de vuelo del insomnio
que imita el melancólico trazo de mis versos
tras los batientes lacerados de esta página,
pero no podrán silenciarme la palabra.
Me negarán el consuelo de la docta Hispasa
separada de los huesos de su carne
por las aristas nacaradas de las ostras
que blandieron contra ella los frailes
                                        [sanguinarios,

pero no podrán negarme la palabra.
Desterrarán de mi celda a Homero y a Platón,
a Safo, a Píndaro y hasta al dulce Ovidio
que plañe sobre mi rostro en las tinieblas
la verecundia feliz de su martirio,
pero no podrán desterrar a la palabra.
Me usurparán el astrolabio y el compás
la escuadra musamétrica de Kircher
el anillo que aprisiona en breve cárcel
el rostro amado que ante mí parece
ciñéndome una vez más a la esperanza
con vínculo terrible,
pero no podrán usurparme la palabra.
Abolirán el llamear de la palabra
el crepitar de la palabra
el cenizar de la palabra,
pero no podrán abolir a la palabra.
Le cercenarán los labios avinagrados a la

                                        [palabra
pero no podrán quitarme la sed de la palabra.
Sofocarán el silencio de la palabra
hasta que sólo quede la voz de la palabra
clamando en el desierto de la palabra,
pero no podrán quitarme la palabra.
Podrán quitarme la palabra
pero no el sueño de la palabra.
El día llegará, sin duda, en que todo me lo

                                        [quiten
y sólo me quede la palabra.

La trágica caída y aún más pavorosa muerte de Mohamad Almotámid Abenabad, último gran príncipe Abadí y poderoso Cadí de Sevilla, así como la de Abu Bakr Abenámar, su visir poeta, le fueron revelados a una mujer humilde en un sueño. En el pasado nuestro pueblo fue demasiado soñador y romántico: en lugar de ocuparse de la salvación del alma, vivía dedicado al alevoso quehacer de escribir versos. Todos los habitantes de Sevilla aspiraban entonces a ser poetas, y hasta sus mendigos más pobres vivían recitándose poemas unos a otros, mientras deambulaban perdidos por los caminos del reino. Alabado sea Alá, porque hoy ya nadie se atreve a escribirlos, y nuestro pueblo vive dedicado a las ablaciones sagradas y a la Guerra Santa.

En honor a Ramayquía, la muletera anónima del Guadalquivir, repetimos aquí este relato, recogido en las crónicas de Kitab Al Muchib, último gran historiador Abadí. Víctima del mal que azotaba a Sevilla, él también aspiró a ser poeta, empecinado constructor de palabras vanas. Glorificado sea Alá porque hace ya muchos años que Kitab Al Muchib depuso la pluma de ganso por la agónica media luna de su alabarda. Con ella dibuja hoy arabescos de plata sobre los cuellos de los herejes, como es su deber hacerlo desde que fue nombrado por Yusuf Abén Taxim, verdugo oficial del reino. A pesar de que Ramayquía fue una mujer pecadora, cómplice del placer y de la corrupción más vil, sus palabras estuvieron de vez en cuando inspiradas por un soplo divino, y sus versos fueron el instrumento misterioso de la justicia de Alá. Sirva su vida de ejemplo para las generaciones venideras, de que no existe sobre la tierra nieve ni lodo, sueño incandescente ni poema corrupto, que no acabe por glorificar su nombre.

Como todos los Abadíes, Mohamad Almotámid Abenabad, ilustre Rey de Sevilla, fue un Príncipe contradictorio. Su padre, Al Motámid, fue un hombre de gustos refinados, que amaba las palmeras de dátiles y los patios de naranjos y arrayanes con los cuales pobló la rumorosa Sevilla, pero fue también un Príncipe implacable. En más de una ocasión anonadó a sus enemigos más ilustres, ahogándolos en baños de agua de rosa, o crucificándolos a las puertas de la ciudad, acompañados por sus perros. Abenabad heredó esta ambivalencia de sus antepasados, y tenía la sonrisa dividida en una hilera desigual, que reflejaba las vertientes conflictivas de su alma. Por un lado era armoniosa y halagüeña, ordenada en una hilera de marfiles dignos de un ajedrez real, y por el otro era supernumeraria y violenta, capaz de la más sublime crueldad guerrera.

Mohamad Almotámid tenía un amigo, a quien amaba por sobre todas las cosas: Abenámar, el poeta pordiosero de Siles, autor de versos encomiásticos por encargo. Al Motámid, padre de Abenabad, juzgó esta amistad de su hijo con un plebeyo como

ﾍﾍﾛ ﾍﾍﾛﾍﾍﾛﾍﾍﾛﾍ de Oriente. Abenámar se convirtió en su maestro. "En la belleza, y no en la fe de Mahoma", le repetía el joven con insidia, "se oculta el secreto de una vida espléndida y eterna."

En realidad, la pasión que Abenabad sentía por su ministro no resultaba en absoluto sorprendente. Abenámar era tan hermoso que cualquier hombre o mujer se hubiese podido enamorar fácilmente de él. Tenía ojos aterciopelados de poeta, manos delicadas de músico, y la piel tersa y delicada como laca de guitarra, pero lo que más llamaba la atención era su hermosa cabellera roja, que llevaba siempre suelta sobre los hombros en señal de desafío. "El alba nos ha traído ya su blanco alcanfor", le cantaba el Cadí a su amigo, "cuando la noche aparta de nosotros su negro ámbar."

Abenabad soñaba con ser poeta, pero no un poeta cualquiera, versificador pedestre de zéjeles y muwaxajas, sino un creador de auténticas realidades imaginarias, como lo era su amigo Abenabad. Se decía que el poeta de Siles podía recitar, verso a verso y estrofa a estrofa un poema, hasta que sin proponérselo, sin ni siquiera pensar en ello, ante los ojos de los presentes aparecía, perfectamente palpable y verificable, la realidad concreta de ese poema. Abenabad jamás había observado a Abenámar llevar a cabo esta proeza, pero tenía una fe absoluta en su amigo. Un día le pidió que, en lugar de estudiar los escritos de otros poetas, le enseñara a escribir como él, y el visir estuvo de acuerdo, no sin antes advertirle que el poder de conjurar el amor, el éxtasis o el hastío sólo se lograba tras largos y pacientísimos ejercicios, durante los cuales el Príncipe debería renunciar a su pasión por la guerra. Abenabad amaba más que nada en el mundo, después de escuchar a Abenámar recitar sus poemas, asolar los campamentos del Rey Alfonso, chacal cristiano, con el relámpago de su espada. Bajo la funesta influencia de su amigo, sin embargo, Abenabad se decidió a abandonar sus deberes de Príncipe Mahometano y se dedicó a la poesía en cuerpo y alma. Su sueño era llegar a edificar sobre la tierra el Paraíso soñado por el Islam: sublime laberinto de jardines, mujeres, música y agua. Pobló su corte de poetas y de músicos, y abandonó por completo la Guerra Santa. En adelante redactó en verso todas sus cartas de batalla y se limitó a derrotar a los pedestres ejércitos y bárbaros obispos del infiel sobre taraceados campos de marfil y ónix.

Paseábanse un día ambos amigos por las afueras de la ciudad, disfrutando del frondoso paraje que crece a orillas del Guadalquivir, cuando una brisa onduló repentinamente las aceradas aguas del río. Abenabad improvisó allí mismo un verso, rogándole

jando su cabeza bajo las húmedas grutas que bordeaban el río, y pensaba que aquella precariedad le confería el derecho a ser testigo imparcial de todas las locuras y ambiciones de los hombres, así como de cantarles de cuando en cuando sus verdades. Como sus amigos, los poetas mendigos del reino, Ramayquía valoraba la libertad de pensamiento y acto por sobre todos los bienes y comodidades del mundo. Por eso a veces se iba a caminar por el reino junto a ellos, componiendo y recitando versos.

Al escuchar aquella tarde la respuesta de la joven, Abenabad se volvió al punto hacia ella, con la intención de descubrir quién podía improvisar con más prontitud que su amigo el final de un poema, pero Abenámar, tomándolo por los hombros, se lo impidió. "Conozco bien a esta joven, le dijo, famosa en tus tierras por la facilidad con la que improvisa versos. Si la miras y le hablas podrías enamorarte de ella, y eso no sería sabio, pues entorpecería tu aprendizaje. Mejor nos la llevamos a vivir a palacio, donde deberá residir entre nosotros como una presencia velada, para que nos inspire a ambos." Y, ordenándole a sus eunucos que la llevaran al Palacio, regresó con su amigo a la corte por otro camino. Algunas semanas después, sin embargo, Abenabad traicionó a Abenámar, y se amancebó con Ramayquía, haciéndola su concubina. "Me reservo el derecho a gozar de su cuerpo", le dijo entonces a su amigo con algo de vergüenza, "pero te dejo en libertad para que disfrutes de su alma. Podrás en adelante ser su amigo, y visitarla cuando quieras." A Ramayquía, por otra parte, le dijo severamente: "Te prometo que en adelante no habrá de faltarte nada y que vivirás entre nosotros como una reina, pero con una sola condición: cuando estés en presencia de Abenabad,

explicación alguna para ello. Ya no se encontraba en la calurosa Sevilla, botín codiciado por los cristianos, con sus mezquitas y bazares ruidosos, y sus calles trenzadas de incienso y de efluvios fétidos, sino en un paraje deliciosamente fresco y pulcro, alejado de toda amenaza de guerra. En ese paraje desconocido que se había esfumado al despertar, los árboles, cubiertos de nieve, ardían contra el cielo despejado como un simétrico laberinto de llamas. Ramayquía se había visto una vez más expulsada de aquel paraíso al final de su sueño. Despeñada por una pendiente de lodo, había caído una vez más en la negrura, en el infierno inconcebible por innombrable. Se despertó gritando, luchando con manos desesperadas por salir de aquel pantano que amenazaba asfixiarla.

Velada de la cabeza a los pies, como se veía obligada a hacerlo desde su llegada al Palacio, Ramayquía tocó a la puerta del gabinete de Abenabad. Éste se encontraba, como siempre, enfrascado en la composición de un nuevo poema, en compañía de su visir poeta. Hincada frente a él, Ramayquía osó quebrar por primera vez su silencio. Le contó en un poema el sueño que había tenido, y cómo se había sentido absolutamente feliz en aquel paraje nevado, que había visto en la primera parte de su sueño:

El almendro nevado me mostró sus frutos,
que parecían lágrimas ensangrentadas
por los tormentos del amor. Estaban congelados,
pero si se los fundiera, serían vino
entre las manos de mi amado.

"Quisiera más que nada en el mundo que me devolvieras la libertad", le dijo Ramayquía. "Como mulera anónima caminaré descalza hasta ese país, porque ese sueño ha despertado en mí una necesidad apremiante de conocer la nieve."

Abenabad escuchó su poema pero se negó a complacerla. Pensó que aquella era la oportunidad perfecta para demostrarle el poder de conjurar la realidad que su maestro le había enseñado. "Siento mucho no poder complacerte y dejar que te marches", le dijo, "porque Abenámar y yo disfrutamos demasiado de tu compañía. Pero te prometo que esta misma noche escribiremos para ti un poema que te hará conocer la nieve." Aquella noche los amigos trabajaron hasta muy tarde, combinando y borrando metáforas. Como la fe de Abenabad en la palabra era todavía débil y no quería decepcionar a su amada, a medianoche interrumpió su trabajo y, sin que el visir lo supiera, descendió al patio del alcázar. Cuando al amanecer Ramayquía despertó no podía creer lo que veía. Un intenso perfume a almen-

dras lo inundaba todo, y los árboles del patio al que
abrían sus habitaciones se encontraban enteramente
cubiertos de nieve. Abenabad leyó entonces en voz
alta el

"Desciende ahora a tu patio y juega con esa nieve",
le dijo el Príncipe, "imítala en todos los versos que
quieras. Tu hermoso sueño bien merecía un poema."

Ramayquía intentó aquella noche escribir un
poema en el cual aquella nieve odiosa, completa-
mente distinta a la que ella había soñado, desapare-
ciera al instante, pero al verse tan desgraciada, pri-
sionera y siempre sola dentro de los muros del
Palacio, no logró componer una sola estrofa. A los
pocos días se despertó otra vez gritando, enredada
en la maleza de sus propios sueños. Esta vez fue la
segunda parte del sueño la que se le hizo más presente. La pendiente de lodo por la cual se veía descender era ahora el foso del alcázar del Cadí, al fondo
del cual había visto a los guerreros Abadíes todos
muertos. Ramayquía entró de nuevo al gabinete de
trabajo de Abenabad y, desde su ausencia velada,
interrumpió por segunda vez su silencio. "No sé lo
que pueda significar mi sueño, ¡oh gran Cadí!",
afirmó con vehemencia, "pero te aconsejo que dejes
por un tiempo de escribir poemas y te apertreches

85

bien con tus soldados en tus castillos, porque pronto los Abadíes serán derrotados!"

Al pronunciar estas palabras, sin embargo, Ramayquía cometió un error imperdonable. Asomándose por sobre el abismo de su velo, osó mirar fijamente al hermoso Abenámar, como si fuese a él a quien dirigiese su súplica. Como poeta al fin, estaba acostumbrado a las visiones, y sabía que las suyas podrían también cumplirse. Pero Abenámar no tuvo fe en sus palabras; se limitó a sonreírle y, en lugar de apoyarla, guardó silencio.

Abenabad, por su parte, al escuchar el ruego de su concubina, se sintió carcomido por los celos. En su mente se encendieron mil sospechas, que parpadearon en las tinieblas de su sangre berberisca como nidos de fuego. Miró a Abenámar, que sostenía todavía ante él la pluma y el tintero, y miró a Ramayquía, en cuyo tocador hasta entonces sólo él había reinado y tocado, y los juzgó traidores, confabulados. "Bien", dijo con un suspiro, mientras disimulaba bajo su enjuta mejilla izquierda su sonrisa guerrera, "esta misma noche Abenámar y yo escribiremos para ti un segundo poema. Te prometo que mañana sin falta perderás tu terror al lodo."

Esa noche el Cadí trabajó nuevamente hasta muy tarde, combinando y borrando metáforas, y al amanecer bajó secretamente a los jardines del Palacio. Cuando regresó a su estudio Abenámar ya le había dado los toques finales al manuscrito, y lo había espolvoreado con ceniza hialina para que se consumiera el exceso de tinta. Entonces entraron juntos a la habitación de Ramayquía, y Abenabad le pidió a Abenámar que leyera en voz alta el poema. Mientras lo leía, las celosías de las habitaciones de la joven se fueron abriendo sobre un espectáculo aterrador.

Tu pesadilla bien merecía un segundo poema; los Abadíes jamás serán derrotados."

Abenabad desterró poco después de esto a Abenámar de la corte de Sevilla y éste se refugió en su fortaleza de Siles, confiado que en el Cadí triunfarían eventualmente los preceptos pacíficos que él le había enseñado. Al principio Abenabad lloró desconsolado su ausencia, e intentó aliviar sus penas haciendo el amor más a menudo con Ramayquía, pero esta diversión no lograba devolverle la serenidad perdida. A pesar de que el cuerpo de Ramayquía, endurecido por el sol y el viento y de miembros parejamente delicados y fuertes, como correspondía a una joven que había vivido siempre vida independiente de mancebo, le recordaban el cuerpo exquisitamente moldeado de Abenámar, holgar con su concubina nunca le resultaba lo mismo. Al abrazar en el pasado el cuerpo de su visir, Abenabad había soñado que sostenía entre sus brazos una guitarra exquisitamente pulida y sensual, sobre cuyas cuerdas podía templar a satisfacción sus versos, mientras que Ramayquía permanecía siempre en ellos muda y fría, doblegada con precisión paciente a su placer, pero cumpliendo al pie de la letra su decreto de silencio.

En un principio el que Ramayquía cumpliera a cabalidad la ley que él mismo le había impuesto lo enardecía sobremanera, imaginándose la facilidad sorprendente con que ella solía responder con sus rimas en el pasado a los poetas más expertos del reino, pero muy pronto su mansedumbre llegó a exasperarlo, incluso a humillarlo. Desnuda entre los incensarios que los eunucos del visir mecían a su alrededor, al extremo de sus largas leontinas de plata, Ramayquía se negaba siempre a contestarle, accediendo con lejana indiferencia a sus requerimientos. A pesar de aquellas heladas acogidas, sin embargo, la hermosura de su concubina, gemela sólo a la de su visir, y los recuerdos de felicidad perdida que su cuerpo despertaba en él, hacían que el Cadí se consumiese en deseos hacia ella, buscando noche a noche consuelo en su compañía.

En una ocasión Abenabad se encerró en su estudio y comenzó a componer en voz alta un poema:

No halla el corazón consuelo
ni respiro mi desgracia...

Desde la habitación contigua Ramayquía escuchó sus palabras, pronunciadas entre sollozos y suspiros, y se compadeció por primera vez de él. Pensó que, dando fe de una amistad sincera, podría quizá consolarlo, a la vez que lograr que reconociera la crueldad de ese decreto que la obligaba a ella a guar-

llas. Era por su culpa que los habitantes del reino vivían todos con la cabeza trastocada, más preocupados por engarzar nuevas perlas a sus collares de versos que por atizar las fogatas moribundas de sus campamentos.

Abenámar se sintió acosado por los remordimientos, temeroso de que la posteridad le censurase el haber sido la causa de que Sevilla pereciese. Le escribió, para la Luna de la Segunda Gumiada, la primera carta a Yusuf Abén Taxim, el piadoso, que rondaba por aquel entonces como león impaciente a las puertas de África. "Como perros asuelan las jaurías castellanas nuestras tierras, oh gran Príncipe, no quedándonos otro recurso que recurrir a Ti. En tus manos está nuestra salvación." "He descubierto que en el Alcorán ya todo estaba escrito", le confesó en una segunda carta. "Intentar componer versos que compitan con su grandeza me resulta ahora un quehacer herético y soberbio. Ven pronto. Has de traernos la bienaventuranza en este mundo y en el próximo." Poco después de recibir aquella carta Yusuf accedió a los deseos de Abenabad y cruzó el tormentoso estrecho. Con la cabeza rapada y ungida en cenizas de penitente, el Cadí fue a arrojarse a sus pies en medio del campamento. No se dolió cuando, poco después de su llegada, el Príncipe decretó que criar gansos, poseer objetos tales como tinteros o pergaminos en blanco, y hasta contemplar en las noches el temblor de las estrellas que imprimen sobre el cielo la escritura divina, eran consideradas actividades delictivas. Componer un solo zéjel, una sola muwaxaja, constituyó, desde aquel momento, un crimen de Estado.

Horrorizado por las noticias que llegaban a Siles desde Sevilla, Abenámar decidió viajar a la corte. Sabía que se jugaba la vida, pero esta certidumbre

[...]

...ps. Proclamarse de esta manera poeta frente a los cortesanos del reino equivalía, en aquel momento, a una segura sentencia de muerte, pero Abenámar sabía que Abenabad, desde su puntilloso orgullo Abadí, no se negaría a enfrentar el reto. Los ministros de Yusuf, que no compartían la confianza que su Príncipe había puesto en el Cadí, acogieron con buenos ojos el espectáculo, seguros de que en él Abenabad se comprometería. Se encontraban convencidos de que el Príncipe, a pesar de las recientes victorias que había alcanzado en el nombre sagrado de Alá, seguía siendo en su corazón un traidor y un poeta.

Envuelto en su túnica de oro, Abenabad entró a la sala de audiencias, y se sentó sobre su almohadón de terciopelo rojo. Ramayquía, enteramente velada, permaneció en la habitación contigua, para que el Cadí olvidara los deleites del Paraíso y sólo pensara en la guerra. Abenámar se despojó entonces de su albornoz raído, y todos los presentes lo reconocieron como el antiguo visir, máximo poeta del reino. De pie sobre su desconchado escabel de juglar observó a los que lo rodeaban con inconmensurable desprecio, como observa el halcón a los roedores que devoran los desperdicios de su cena que caen al pie de su alcándara. No podía perdonarles que le hubieran jurado lealtad a Yusuf, el piadoso, salvador de nuestro pobre pueblo. Un silencio sepulcral reinó en la sala y Abenabad tembló, pero muy pronto recobró su temple. Apoyado el mentón sobre la media luna de su cimitarra, inclinó ligeramente la cabeza, y le dio la señal a su antiguo amigo para que comenzara el debate.

Abenámar miró entonces a Abenabad con todo el amor del que fue capaz y recitó:

Me acordé de mi amado en el ardor de la lid.
Creí ver entre las lanzas la esbeltez de su talle,
y, cuando se inclinaron hacia mí, las abracé.

A pesar de la belleza conmovedora de aquellos versos, Abenabad permaneció impasible, y recitó en tono ferviente ese verso del Corán que afirma: "Ya lució para mí el lucero del alba, y el almuédano entona su ¡Alá es grande!" Abenámar cruzó entonces con paso firme de extremo a extremo la sala, y, afueteando sobre los hombros su melena incendiaria, se dirigió en voz sacrílega a los alfaquíes y ministros del reino. Les informó que, para que quedara allí mismo comprobado que el don creador del poeta era superior al don creador de Alá, construiría con palabras una rosa, que aparecería al punto en su mano. De no suceder así, de no ser su rosa tan roja, perfumada y perfecta como las de las mezquitas del lejano Isfahán, deberían de cortarle inmediatamente la cabeza. Abenámar recitó entonces el poema:

la frente: "En el pasado hemos sido víctimas de este ilusionista", dijo, alzando la voz por sobre el murmullo asombrado de los cortesanos. "En una ocasión me hizo creer que podía conjurar, para consentir un capricho de mi concubina, jardines de nieve y vergeles de lodo, pero éstos no fueron sino espejismos falsos. Fui yo quien, oculto bajo el manto cómplice de la noche, hice sembrar su patio de almendros florecidos y decapitar a todos los poetas-mendigos del reino. Que repita, por lo tanto, su truco, pero esta vez con un objeto de gran tamaño, que no pueda escamotear vilmente ante nosotros, ni ocultarlo al fondo de su bocamanga." Y fijando con fiereza los ojos en los de su contrincante, recitó esos versos del Corán que le dicen que todos los poetas del mundo mienten descaradamente.

Abenámar se convenció entonces de que sólo había una manera de lograr que Abenabad se traicionara, y era conjurando la presencia de algo que ambos conociesen íntimamente, el Cadí con los ojos del cuerpo y él con los del alma. Abriendo entonces los brazos como si fuese a abrazar el vacío, comenzó a enumerar, bajo los techos estucados de iconoclastas alveolos, los atributos de una mujer increíblemente hermosa, demorándose en sus rasgos más ocultos. Poro a poro, cabello a cabello, lunar a lunar, fue describiendo en voz alta su cuerpo con una familiaridad vergonzante, hasta que sus palabras resonaron por todos los salones del Palacio. Palpitaba ya la mujer entre sus brazos, desprovista de todo velo que impusiera una distancia prudente entre su desnudez y el mundo, cuando un grito terrible desgarró la sala. Abalanzándose enfurecido sobre ellos, Abenabad le arrebató entonces a Ramayquía de entre los brazos, y le cercenó de un golpe a su antiguo visir la cabeza del tronco.

Al otro día de este aterrador suceso, los cadáveres decapitados de Abenabad y de Abenámar fueron expuestos conjuntamente a las puertas de la ciudad. Abenabad, que había ejecutado a Abenámar por osar abrazar a Ramayquía en los versos de su poema, había sido a su vez decapitado por los ministros de Yusuf por creer en ese poema. Ramayquía, acusada de ser la concubina del Cadí y de su visir, recibió también aquella tarde su merecido castigo. Fue obligada a descender, con las manos atadas a la espalda, por aquella misma pendiente de lodo con la que tantas veces había soñado. Perdida definitivamente la libertad, no pareció importarle la propia muerte. Espectáculo instructivo y tremebundo fue aquél para nosotros, los antiguos súbditos de Mohamad Almotámid Abenabad, hoy fieles súbditos de Yusuf, el piadoso.

ATMOSFÉRICAS

y extingue el flamboyán su flama en el ocaso
del huracán que todo lo ha barrido con su paso.
Desprovistos de penumbra derivamos
sobre el bronce del día ya derretido
desvelados de ardor y de cansancio.
Las sombras, como ovejas descarriadas,
huyeron espantadas mar afuera,
y el cielo, atrio pulcro de pecado, arde
implacablemente azul sobre la tierra.
Un ejército de cuerpos desmembrados
yace sobre ella tendido:
caobas y samanes aguerridos,
úcares y eucaliptos animosos,
son los cadáveres de lo vivido,
los que en esforzada lid acometieron
la soledad del que ha perdido hasta su sombra.
Sobre ella perecieron, por no doblar la frente
que alberga el indomado pensamiento,
su ramaje un laberinto de quejidos
en el que anida el terror a la vida consciente;
las aceras hirsutas de voces derramadas,
la yugular a cada paso estrangulada

en teléfonos mudos como pájaros muertos.

Y sin embargo, el viejo roble de mi casa,
sobreviviente asombrado del desastre
(aunque ya desnudo de ilusiones vanas),
se ha empeñado en florecer esta mañana,
en un intento heroico por renovar la especie.

las palmas cinceladas de las panas,
volteando las malangas relucientes
bajo el furor del agua;
has dejado mi pórtico invadido de zarzales,
has inundado mi patio de murmullos
que surgen de las grietas de las piedras
y se agolpan en borbotones de silencio
en el estanque que se ahonda al fondo
del parque, desparramando sobre los aleros
fragmentos de pasado, añicos dispersos
por el polvo del tiempo, que precipitas
traidoramente de vuelco en vuelco, redoblando
entre las tejas voladoras y las ráfagas,
el llanto indetenible de mi remordimiento.

TROPICAL STORM

Tedious rain that pours
its sorrow down the secret
labyrinths of my ear, bending
backbones with its weight;
lashing ubiquitous green
over the madagascared lovers
of my screened summer porch
as it quenches the afternoon light
with its own blinding;
roaring sheet of water wrapped
around my breadfruit tree,
shaking its silvered sheaves of ash
over the bewildered palm that tugs,
distraught, at life's fragile root;
trembling torrent that shatters
my delicately varnished plantain
fans, prey to the whims of the wind;
you've left my garden flooded with murmurs
that seep from the crevices of its flagstone floor
and deepen in pools of silence
as my pond darkens at dusk;
you've spilled fragments of my past
all over my gabled windows, spreading
forgetfullness like an even mantle
over my red tiled roof,
doubling, twixt rushing leaves and
sighing streams, the tears
that flood my regret.

NÓRDICAS

de la M roja del Metro
para tomar su siesta acostumbrada.
Veterano de la guerra de Vietnam
y sobreviviente del agente naranja,
acababa de barrer por tercera vez
la esquina de la acera de su casa,
escoltado por el taconeo de los transeúntes
que atravesaban vertiginosos la calle,
vomitados por el túnel de peldaños de acero
que desenrollaba su lengua de platino
a sus espaldas. Esa butaca amarilla
de león viejo y destripado
desplomó junto a él antiguas culpabilidades
que sobrevolaron los patios del olvido.
Semiborrado por el recuerdo del exilio
Sam Roger se tendió sobre ella y entonó,
antes de dormir, su De Profundis.

RESPONSO POR LOS DESCASADOS
(WDC)

Benditos sean los descasados
los desclavados
los descalzados
los desclasados
los descavados
los sin hogar
los sin hogaza
los sin techo
los sin balcón
los sin sala
los sin comedor
los sin alcoba
los sin cama
los sin almohada
los sin colchón
los sin baño
los sin agua
los sin jabón
los sin peinilla
los sin cepillo
los sin cepillo de dientes
los sin dentista
los sin dientes
los sin comida
los sin trabajo
los sin tumba

los sin lápida
los sin temor
los sin remordimiento

CONCEPTUAL ART

It was hailing and bitter cold
and on the grate that blasts warm air
at the corner of Seventeenth
and Pennsylvania Avenue
three statues stood their ground
and stoically braved the elements.
They were burrowed in black burlap
sacks, with leper loincloths draped
over their heads in mudpacked
turbans, and from their spent
spattered cheeks you could tell
the whole world had already
driven past them. I never had
seen such a sight. The Mall
was thronged with holiday
strollers, who came and went
before the sleeping stone lions,
revelling in the gems of "Odyssey",
the latest of the National Geographic's shows,
which focused on the heroism of Tibetan Monks
who could go for thirty days
without food or drink,
and of arab warriors who,
solidly ensconced on their trawling
camels, would never need a home,
but crisscrossed the Sahara
riding barefoot over burning

sands, all their wordly belongings
slung over their backs in dried

to the Corcoran's doorstep.
No one wondered how far
they had come, or the curious
manner of their travels,
how long they had unwittingly
penanced, without Cokes
or even a hot dog, for the
inherent good of their souls,
how they had managed
to stake out their territory
from the swarm of other homeless
huddled together that windy morning
on the grates of less generous Hells.
Perhaps they expected a vent
to be always a pin up scenario
for touring Avendon vamps,
with moth white skins
and Marylin Monroe hair
skitting nervously over their skirts
as they lighted ablaze on dry ice,
or they figured it should be kept
as a stage for plaster sculptures
of the type George Segal casts

on the bodies of travelling vagabonds
so the warm air blasting upwards
will dry them out quickly,
or even as an altar for Louis Cifer himself
airing out his Paloma Picasso leather wings
after a tiresome voyage
on one of his flying cauldrons.
Nothing had prepared me for this,
the paramount indifference to the work,
to its hidden meaning,
the exquisite harmony of the composition,
as they rapidly walked by
turning their faces away just because
this was art of a different kind.

que dejaron allí olvidado los organizadores
del último cuatro de julio,
se bañó en la pileta de granito negro
frente a los Archivos de los Estados Unidos
de América, y se entretuvo leyendo
el epígrafe tallado en mármol
"The past is prologue",
sin entender exactamente
lo que quería decir.
Recogió un puñado de cobres
que cabrilleaba al fondo del agua
y se dispuso a tomar el desayuno
en el hot dog stand de la esquina.
A Sam le gusta pasearse por Washington
porque los monumentos de mármol blanco
adquieren al atardecer un ligero tinte rosado,
como si estuviesen hechos de cherry blossoms
a punto de deshojarse.
En las calles hay una luz tenuemente verde
como si se viviera dentro de una pecera
y al caminar por el Mall le parece pisar un dólar
                                        [gigante

desplegado frente al Capitolio nada más que
                              [para que él pueda
refrescar sus pies descalzos.
De igual manera, al subir las escalinatas
del monumento a Lincoln
se sueña sentado dentro de un billete de a cinco,
y cuando se pasea bajo la rotonda de Jefferson
                              [imagina
que todo su mundo es rosado y perfecto como
                              [esa bóveda
que flota al fondo del billete de a diez.
Sam Roger se siente importante
cuando desfila con su uniforme de veterano
por entre los monumentos de la Capital Imperial.
En la cabeza lleva siempre un capacete
aprovisionado con doce cepillos de dientes
que le sirven de antena para comunicarse
con las ondas del espacio sideral.
Vive persuadido de que recoger basuras
es una labor honrosa
que no todo el mundo se atreve a desempeñar.
Hay que tener valor
para echarse a la espalda un saco negro
en el que cabe todo lo que se recoge por ahí,
mondas de fruta y zapatos gastados,
desperdicios de vegetales y costillas roídas,
los compañeros que murieron en Tonkín
y los que regresaron drogadictos y aniquilados
ante la indiferencia de la nación,
abrirlo y revolverlo todo de tanto en tanto,
tratar de entender lo que pasó,
alguien tiene que hacerlo porque si no,

dígame Usted, todos acabaríamos
como los muertos vivos de Memorial Day,
los veteranos del clean cut y del crew cut,

METAFÍSICAS

...la mañana la baña con su agua
y un vaho a vainilla y a café
destila un perfume gozoso
sobre el añejo pretil de la ventana. A sus
espaldas respira la habitación de la infancia
y sobre el lecho un zarzal escarlata
crepita en llamas de brocado
su delicia terrenal aún no cumplida.
Hincado en el portal, un mensajero
le anuncia lo siguiente:
Serás la barca que rescata a los náufragos
en la ribera inalcanzable del olvido,
navegarás por las márgenes del Estigio
arrasada por una llama febril,
lo verás venir más fuerte que la noche
desafiando las trifolias de ceniza
que han de blanquear tu cuerpo en la agonía,
serás la llama que ha de nadar el agua fría
perdido todo respeto a ley
severa, el hielo escupido con desdén
sobre el artero rostro de la muerte,
serás su noche oscura, su más

abrupta selva. Navegante perdida
por el tenebroso dolor, por la ciudad doliente
vivirás para siempre a la merced del Dios."
María, sorprendida, inclina
su frente sobre la nieve de la página.
Le ruega al emisario ser eximida de todo
con tal de dar a luz por la palabra
al mandato divino que baja de lo alto.

... de humo,
que sostuvieron la perfidia de una flor
cuya promesa se disipó al infinito.

EL SUEÑO DE LIU CH'E

Todo astro se nutre del fango

El haikú que pintó Liu Ch'e en el año 304
rezuma hoy todavía su perfume
en el museo asiático de San Francisco.
Brotó en un solo trazo de su ímpetu sagrado
un opalino amanecer de enero
cuando ninguna flor hubiese podido turbar
la hialina superficie del lago.
Abrió sobre el papel su crisálida implacable
y eclipsó el brillo modesto del arroz
triturado en los traspatios por manos acólitas.
Al centro del iris un cuerpo luminoso
apareaba convexidades en la frescura glacial
como un túmulo de engranajes que se enroscan.
Liu Ch'e no pudo soportar tanta blancura.
"Polvo seremos de esos lodos"
dijo, "Polvo inmortal".

MÁS BLANC...

...latir del pezón
que hinca su fuego en el lodo primordial.
Fagocitado en vapor, el deseo
se precipita en nieve.

HOKUSAI

La ausencia es un sueño
que nos vuelve la cara
a mitad del puente.

... el corazón
de Otilia, en sus entrañas estrofas
cosedoras de inmoralidad fetal.
Así la amada madre, amargurada
quedó crucificada camino de la puna
sobre los *dos maderos curvos de su beso*.
Poe, el caballero perfecto, le ofrendó a la fama
los cinco sentidos, la cordura vertida
en una copa
de dorado etílico y un dispar deseo:
el silicio del verso
y el corazón de Virginia navegando ileso
entre la Estrella y la Sombra.

LA FUGA

El corazón del mancebo late audaz
bajo mi oído, como vuela inmóvil la piedra
en la honda de David.
Duerme, y su sangre fluye por los cauces del
                                                    [Leteo
en dirección contraria a la muerte y al olvido.
En su pecho guarda el reflejo del acero
fundido en voz, el tráfago marcial del sacerdote,
la marcha alucinante en pos del arca,
el derrumbe de los muros de la ciudad.
Su cabellera rubia me arropa
en un oleaje de avenas saludables
que me devuelven deshecha en llanto
a las playas perdidas de la niñez.
Su aliento tibio me ciñe de hielo
las sienes, mientras dispersa con veleidoso
                                                    [descuido
la nieve cruel de los cedros del Líbano.
Vive en un tiempo que yo no veré nunca.
Cuando lo abrazo, huye en un río
de leche y miel
hacia el futuro, y me arrastra tras de sí hasta su
                                                    [jardín
prohibido, donde no acaece el antes, el después,
el mientras
ni el ahora.

...pared del Ajusco.
Acomoda la mujer la espalda a dos
pechos, y exhibe su desnudez irreverente
sobre el metate ardiente de su techo.
Lleva el pubis fajado en iris de rebozo
y un hirsuto madroño que acentúa
la apretada simiente de su sexo
sobre la plancha fugitiva del segundo.
El agua de la risa se derrama
por los acantilados recónditos del sueño
al sentir germinar bajo su vientre
el tierno elote, el choclo azul, la milpa leve.
Weston, el dedo infalible en la perilla
le toma fotos bajo las nubes de México.
A sus espaldas la titánica arpa de oro
tañe el gemelo acorde de su puente
y lo conmina a regresar a la cordura,
a la esposa olvidada, a la hogaza inocente,
compartida con aliento tibio y sin recuerdos
una tarde de llovizna triste en San Francisco.

RÉQUIEM POR ROCK HUDSON

Hoy ha muerto Rock Hudson, el coloso.
Con el tejano de fieltro requintado
descendió de la pantalla diamantina
y reclinó de la cornisa de la sala
su apoteósico perfil de seis con seis.
(Las adolescentes de entonces lo soñábamos
en las penumbras del antiguo Teatro
Habana, bautizado hoy el New Broadway.)
Se sentó junto a nosotras en la fila
y nos mostró sus hectáreas sin fronteras:
el aljamiado glacis de su camisa, el confín
acantilado de su brazo, el responso
abismal de su mirada.
(Las adolescentes de entonces lo adorábamos
saboreando la batida de la vida
en gemelos sorbetes de guanábana,
al vaivén de un studebakerockanroll.)
Visitaba nuestras salas cada noche
y tarareábamos juntos los boleros
que Agustín le dedicaba a María Félix
en lo más hondo de nuestra sinfonola azul.
(Desmayadas en balances tropicales
recogíamos los bemoles subrepticios
de una ilícita ternura femenina
que se le filtraba por la piel.)
Al final de quince años de coloquio
incurrió en un insólito desliz:

apoyó el talón izquierdo, el vulnerable
en esa arista traicionera que separa
lo moral de lo inmortal.

MELOGRAFIADAS

cogiéndolo por el pomo
y por la poma, sacudiéndolo por hombros
y por pechos, y también por el antepecho,
agitando el cojitranco nazarino
por el condenado babalú del vino.
Se rumba coqueteándolo, computándolo,
la rima apretadita en una losetita,
en una sola teclita,
que nos marca el paso al sexto verso,
o a lo mejor al sexo inverso,
que nos frunce el ritmo y nos lo alitera
y también nos lo aligera,
hasta la penúltima desdicha del olvido,
hasta el último des dicho del dolor.

EL CONTABLE

Para contar hay que saber
bailar sentado y tocar
de oído, tener mesa
puesta con yunque, martillo
y estribo. Hay que saber
oír, como quien dice,
pero sobre todo como quien calla.
Sólo oyendo nos vamos siendo,
nos vamos yendo,
hasta el día en que sólo quede
la aleve lápida de la página,
tallada sobre el nacimiento
de un cuento.

ROSARIO DE CUENTOS

Lo que cuenta no es contar, es contar bien.

El que cuenta no sabe nada de cuentas.

El que cuenta no come cuentos
pero no podrá nunca vivir del cuento.

El contable cuenta lo que no cuenta,
el cuentista cuenta lo que cuenta.

No es lo mismo un rosario de cuitadas cuentas
que un rosario de cuitas bien contadas.

Para contar hay que dejar que digan por ahí.

El que cuenten es lo que cuenta,
si no cuentan es que ya no cuentas.

Para contar el cielo se necesita
una mentira grande y otra chiquita.

La ruptura de un buen cuento puede causar
la sordera eterna del tí(e)mp(an)o.

que la vida

escritor es una negación del postulado cartesiano "pienso, luego soy". El escritor dice, 'escribo, luego pienso'; o mejor 'no pienso, luego escribo'. El día que deje de escribir el escritor dejará de pensar y repetirá con Vallejo, "Vámonos, pues, por eso, a comer yerba, carne de llanto, fruta de gemido, nuestra alma melancólica en conserva".

"Se la comió", dice el que escucha un buen cuento, como si sólo fuera posible comerse el virgo de la imaginación por el tímpano del oído. Lo que se cuenta bien no ha sido jamás dicho, no ha sido jamás escuchado. Penetra el tímpano con su agudo dardo y nos deja preñados con su verbo vivificador. Nacemos a una realidad distinta, a personajes, situaciones, lugares exóticos y nunca vistos. El mal y el bien, lo bello y lo horrible, el terror y la compasión, lo masculino y lo femenino, todo entra en nosotros por el canal de lo auricular, por esa linterna mágica transitadora de ecos y sombras, y se vuelve carne bullente, verbo de gozo, carnaval de angustias y de felicidades sin tasa. Por el tímpano del cuento, ese pórtico de proporciones modestas y sagradas como pesebre navideño, damos a luz diariamente al mundo; gracias a él somos todo oídos, somos todos Dios.

menos, que sólo trabajando de sol a sol lograba ganar lo suficiente para el sustento de la familia. *Primero Rosaura y luego Lorenzo. Es una casualidad sorprendente.* Amaba aquella casa que la había visto nacer, cuyas galerías sobrevolaban los cañaverales como las de un buque orzado a toda vela. La historia de la casa alimentaba su pasión por ella, porque sobre sus almenas había tomado lugar la primera resistencia de los criollos a la invasión hacía ya casi cien años.

Al pasearse por sus salas y balcones, Don Lorenzo sentía inevitablemente encendérsele la sangre, y le parecía escuchar los truenos de los mosquetes y los gritos de guerra de quienes en ella habían muerto en defensa de la patria. En los últimos años, sin embargo, se había visto obligado a hacer sus paseos por la casa con más cautela, ya que los huecos que perforaban los pisos eran cada vez más numerosos, pudiéndose ver, al fondo abismal de los mismos, el corral de gallinas y puercos que la necesidad le obligaba a criar en los sótanos. No empece estas desventajas, a Don Lorenzo jamás se le hubiese ocurrido vender su casa o su hacienda. Como la zorra del cuento, se encontraba convencido de que un hombre podía vender la piel, la pezuña y hasta los ojos pero que la tierra, como el corazón, jamás se vende.

No debo dejar que los demás noten mi asombro, mi enorme sorpresa. Después de todo lo que nos ha pasado, venir ahora a ser víctimas de una pila de escritorcito de mierda. Como si no me bastara con la mondadera diaria de mis clientas. "Quien la viera y quien la vio", las oigo que dicen detrás de sus aba-

nicos inquietos, "la mona, aunque la vistan de seda, mona se queda". Aunque ahora ya francamente no me importa. Gracias a Lorenzo ~~~~~~~~~~~~

~~~~~~

~~~~~~

~~~~~~~~~~~~~~~~~~~~~~~~~~~~~~~~~ *más pro-*

~~~~~. Como náufrago que, braceando en el vientre tormentoso del mar, tropieza con un costillar de esa misma nave que acaba de hundirse bajo sus pies, y se aferra desesperado a él para mantenerse a flote, así se asió Don Lorenzo a las amplias caderas y aún más pletóricos senos de Rosa, la antigua modista de su mujer. Celebrado el casorio y restituida la convivencia hogareña, la risa de Don Lorenzo volvió a retumbar por toda la casa, y éste se esforzaba porque su hija también se sintiera feliz. Como era un hombre culto, amante de las artes y de las letras, no encontraba nada malo en el persistente amor de Rosaura por los libros de cuentos. Aguijoneado sin duda por el remordimiento, al recordar cómo la niña se había visto obligada a abandonar sus estudios a causa de sus malos negocios, le regalaba siempre, el día de su cumpleaños, un espléndido ejemplar de ellos.

Esto se está poniendo interesante. La manera de contar que tiene el autor me da risa, parece un firulí almidonado, un empalagoso de pueblo. Yo definitivamente no le simpatizo. Rosa era una mujer prác-

137

tica, para quien los refinamientos del pasado representaban un capricho imperdonable, y aquella manera de ser la malquistó con Rosaura. En la casa abundaban, como en los libros que leía la joven, las muñecas raídas y exquisitas, los roperos hacinados de rosas de repollo y de capas de terciopelo polvoriento, y los candelabros de cristales quebrados, que Rosaura aseguraba haber visto en las noches sostenidos en alto por deambulantes fantasmas. Poniéndose de acuerdo con el quincallero del pueblo, Rosa fue vendiendo una a una aquellas reliquias de la familia, sin sentir el menor resquemor de conciencia por ello.

El firulí se equivoca. En primer lugar, hacía tiempo que Lorenzo estaba enamorado de mí (desde mucho antes de la muerte de su mujer, junto a su lecho de enferma, me desvestía atrevidamente con los ojos) y yo sentía hacia él una mezcla de ternura y compasión. Fue por eso que me casé con él, y de ninguna manera por interés, como se ha insinuado en este infame relato. En varias ocasiones me negué a sus requerimientos, y cuando por fin accedí, mi familia lo consideró de plano una locura. Casarme con él, hacerme cargo de las labores domésticas de aquel caserón en ruinas, era una especie de suicidio profesional, ya que la fama de mis creaciones resonaba, desde mucho antes de mi boda, en las boutiques de moda más elegantes y exclusivas del pueblo. En segundo lugar, vender los cachivaches de aquella casa no sólo era saludable sicológica, sino también económicamente. En mi casa hemos sido siempre pobres y a orgullo lo tengo. Vengo de una familia

de diez hijos, pero nunca hemos pasado hambre, y el espectáculo de aquella alacena vacía, pintada enteramente de blanco y con un tragaluz en el t...
ilumin...

... que en un tiempo pertenecieron a la madre y a la abuela de Rosaura, y su frugalidad llegó a tal punto que ni siquiera los gustos moderadamente epicúreos de la familia se salvaron de ella. Desterrados para siempre de la mesa quedaron el conejo en pepitoria, el arroz con gandules y las palomas salvajes, asadas hasta su punto más tierno por debajo de las alas. Esta última medida entristeció grandemente a Don Lorenzo, que amaba más que nada en el mundo, luego de a su mujer y a su hija, esos platillos criollos cuyo espectáculo humeante le hacía expandir de buena voluntad los carrillos sobre las comisuras risueñas.

¿Quién habrá sido capaz de escribir una sarta tal de estupideces y de calumnias? Aunque hay que reconocer que, quien quiera que sea, supo escoger el título a las mil maravillas. Bien se ve que el papel aguanta todo el veneno que le escupan encima. Las virtudes económicas de Rosa la llevaban a ser candil apagado en la casa pero fanal encendido en la calle. "A mal tiempo buena cara, y no hay por qué hacerle ver al vecino que la desgracia es una desgra-

cia", decía con entusiasmo cuando se vestía con sus mejores galas para ir a misa los domingos, obligando a Don Lorenzo a hacer lo mismo. Abrió un comercio de modistilla en los bajos de la casa, que bautizó ridículamente "El alza de la Bastilla", dizque para atraerse una clientela más culta, y allí se pasaba las noches enhebrando hilos y sisando telas, invirtiendo todo lo que sacaba de la venta de los valiosos objetos de la familia en los vestidos que elaboraba para sus clientas.

Acaba de entrar a la sala la esposa del Alcalde. La saludaré sin levantarme, con una leve inclinación de cabeza. Lleva puesto uno de mis modelos exclusivos, que tuve que rehacer por lo menos diez veces, para tenerla contenta, pero aunque sé que espera que me le acerque y le diga lo bien que le queda, haciéndole mil reverencias, no me da la gana de hacerlo. Estoy cansada de servirles de incensario a las esposas de los ricos de este pueblo. En un principio les tenía compasión: verlas languidecer como flores asfixiadas tras las galerías de cristales de sus mansiones, sin nada en qué ocupar sus mentes que no fuese el bridge, el mariposear de chisme en chisme y de merienda en merienda, me daba tristeza. El aburrimiento, ese ogro de afelpada garra, había ya ultimado a varias de ellas, que habían perecido víctimas de la neurosis y de la depresión, cuando yo comencé a predicar, desde mi modesto taller de costura, la salvación por medio de la Línea y del Color. La Belleza de la moda es, no me cabe la menor duda, la virtud más sublime, el atributo más divino de las mujeres. La Belleza de la moda todo lo puede, todo lo cura, todo lo subsana. Sus seguidores son legiones, como puede verse en el fresco de la cúpula de nuestra catedral, donde los atuendos maravillosos de los ángeles sirven

...de esas capita-les. Si en el otoño se llevaba el púrpura magenta o el amaranto pastel, si en la primavera el talle se alforzaba como una alcachofa o se plisaba como un repollo de pétalo y bullón, si en el invierno los botones se usaban de carey o de nuez, todo era para mis clientas materia de dogma, artículo apasionado de fe. Mi taller pronto se volvió una colmena de actividad, tantas eran las órdenes que recibía y tantas las visitas de las damas que venían a consultarme los detalles de sus últimas "tenues".

El éxito no tardó en hacernos ricos y todo gracias a la ayuda de Lorenzo, que hizo posible el milagro vendiendo la hacienda y prestándome el capitalito que necesitaba para ampliar mi negocio. Por eso hoy, el día aciago de su sepelio, no tengo que ser fina ni considerada con nadie. Estoy cansada de tanta reverencia y de tanto halago, de tanta dama elegante que necesita ser adulada todo el tiempo para sentirse que existe. Que la esposa del Alcalde en adelante se alce su propia cola y se husmee su propio culo. Prefiero mil veces la lectura de este cuento infame a tener que

hablarle, a tener que decirle qué bien se ha combi-
nado hoy, qué maravillosamente le sientan su man-
tilla de bruja, sus zapatos de espátula, su horrible
bolso.

Don Lorenzo vendió su casa y su finca, y se trasladó con su familia a vivir al pueblo. El cambio
resultó favorable para Rosaura; recobró el buen color
y tenía ahora un sinnúmero de amigas y amigos, con
los cuales se paseaba por las alamedas y los parques.
Por primera vez en la vida dejó de interesarse por
los libros de cuentos y, cuando algunos meses más
tarde su padre le regaló el último ejemplar de ellos,
lo dejó olvidado y a medio leer sobre el velador de
la sala. A Don Lorenzo, por el contrario, se le veía
cada vez más triste, zurcido el corazón de pena por
la venta de su hacienda y de sus cañas.

Rosa, en su nuevo local, amplió su negocio y tenía
cada vez más parroquianas. El cambio de localidad
sin duda la favoreció, ocupando éste ahora por completo los bajos de la casa. Ya no tenía el corral de
gallinas y de puercos algarabeándole junto a la
puerta, y su clientela subió de categoría. Como estas
damas, sin embargo, a menudo se demoraban en
pagar sus deudas, y Rosa, por otro lado, no podía
resistir la tentación de guardar siempre para sí los
vestidos más lujosos, su taller no acababa nunca de
levantar cabeza. Fue por aquel entonces que comenzó
a martirizar a Lorenzo con lo del testamento. "Si
mueres en este momento", le dijo una noche antes
de dormir, "tendré que trabajar hasta la hora de mi
muerte sólo para pagar la deuda, ya que con la mitad
de tu herencia no me será posible ni comenzar a

hacerlo." Y como Don Lorenzo permanecía en silencio y con la cabeza baja, negándose a desheredar a su hija para beneficiarla a ella, empezó a injuriar y a insultar a Rosaura

...........e, indiferente a lo que estoy leyendo. Hay una corriente de aire frío colándose por algún lado en este cuarto y me he empezado a sentir un poco mareada, pero debe ser la tortura de este velorio interminable. No veo la hora en que saquen el ataúd por la puerta, y esta caterva de maledicentes acabe ya de largarse a su casa. Comparados a los chismes de mis clientas, los sainetes de este cuento insólito no son sino alfileterazos vulgares, que me rebotan sin que yo los sienta. Después de todo me porté bien con Lorenzo; tengo mi conciencia tranquila. Eso es lo único que importa. Insistí, es cierto, en que nos mudáramos al pueblo, y eso nos hizo mucho bien. Insistí también en que me dejara a mí el albaceazgo de todos sus bienes, porque me consideré mucho más capacitada que Rosaura, que anda siempre con la cabeza en las nubes, para administrarlos. Pero jamás lo amenacé con abandonarlo. Los asuntos de la familia iban de mal en peor, y la ruina amenazaba cada vez más de cerca a Lorenzo, pero a éste no parecía importarle. Había sido siempre un poco fantasioso y escogió pre-

cisamente esa época crítica de nuestras vidas para sentarse a escribir un libro sobre los patriotas de la lucha por la independencia.

Se pasaba las noches garabateando página tras página, desvariando en voz alta sobre nuestra identidad perdida dizque trágicamente a partir de 1898, cuando la verdad fue que nuestros habitantes recibieron a los Marines con los brazos abiertos. Es verdad que, como escribió Lorenzo en su libro, durante casi cien años después de su llegada hemos vivido al borde de la guerra civil, pero los únicos que quieren la independencia en esta isla son los ricos y los ilusos; los hacendados arruinados que todavía siguen soñando con el pasado glorioso como si se tratara de un paraíso perdido, los políticos amargados y sedientos de poder, y los escritorcitos de mierda como el autor de este cuento. Los pobres de esta isla le han tenido siempre miedo a la independencia, porque preferirían estar muertos antes de volver a verse aplastados por la egregia bota de nuestra burguesía. Sean Republicanos o Estadolibristas, todos los caciques políticos son iguales. A la hora del tasajo vuelan más rápido que una plaga de guaraguaos hambrientos; se llaman pro-americanos y amigos de los Yanquis cuando en realidad los odian y quisieran que les dejaran sus dólares y se fueran de aquí.

Al llegar el cumpleaños de su hija, Don Lorenzo le compró, como siempre, su tradicional libro de cuentos. Rosaura, por su parte, decidió cocinarle a su padre aquel día una confitura de guayaba, de las que antes solía confeccionarle su madre. Durante toda la tarde removió sobre el fogón el borbolleante líquido color sanguaza, y mientras lo hacía le pareció ver a su madre entrar y salir varias veces por pasillos y salones, transportada por el oleaje rosado de aquel perf...

...sobre el ceño de su mujer, padre e hija admiraron juntos el opulento ejemplar, cuyo grueso canto dorado hacía resaltar elegantemente el púrpura de las tapas. Inmóvil sobre su silla Rosa los observaba en silencio, con una sonrisa álgida escarchándole los labios. Llevaba puesto aquella noche su vestido más lujoso, porque asistiría con Don Lorenzo a una cena de gran cubierto en casa del Alcalde, y no quería por eso alterarse, ni perder la paciencia con Rosaura.

Don Lorenzo comenzó entonces a embromar a su mujer, y le comentó, intentando sacarla de su ensimismamiento, que los exóticos vestidos de aquellas reinas y grandes damas que aparecían en el libro de Rosaura bien podrían servirle a ella de inspiración para sus nuevos modelos. "Aunque para vestir tus opulentas carnes se necesitarían varias resmas de seda más de las que necesitaron ellas, a mí no me importaría pagarlas, porque tú eres una mujer de a deveras, y no un enclenque maniquí de cuento", le dijo pellizcándole solapadamente una nalga. *¡Pobre Lorenzo! Es evidente que me querías, sí. Con tus bro-*

mas siempre me hacías reír hasta saltárseme las lágrimas. Congelada en su silencio apático, Rosa encontró aquella broma de mal gusto, y no demostró por las ilustraciones y grabados ningún entusiasmo. Terminado por fin el examen del lujoso ejemplar, Rosaura se levantó de la mesa, para traer la fuente de aquel postre que había estado presagiándose en la mañana como un bocado de gloria por toda la casa, pero al acercársela a su padre la dejó caer, salpicando inevitablemente la falda de su madrastra.

Hacía ya rato que algo venía molestándome, y ahora me doy cuenta de lo que es. El incidente del dulce de guayaba tomó lugar hace ya muchos años, cuando todavía vivíamos en el caserón de la finca y Rosaura no era más que una niña. El firulí, o se equivoca, o ha alterado descaradamente la cronología de los hechos, haciendo ver que éstos tomaron lugar recientemente, cuando es todo lo contrario. Hace sólo unos meses que Lorenzo le regaló a Rosaura el libro que dice, en ocasión de su veinteavo aniversario, pero han pasado ya más de seis años desde que Lorenzo vendió la finca. Cualquiera diría que Rosaura es todavía niña cuando es una mangansona ya casi mayor de edad, una mujer hecha y derecha. Cada día se parece más a su madre, a las mujeres indolentes de este pueblo. Rehusa trabajar en la casa ni en la calle, alimentándose del pan honesto de los que trabajan.

Recuerdo perfectamente el suceso del dulce de guayaba. Íbamos a un coctel en casa del Alcalde, a quien tú mismo, Lorenzo, le habías propuesto que te comprara la hacienda Los Crepúsculos, como la

*llamabas nostálgicamente, y que los vecinos habían
bautizado con sorna la hacienda Los Culos Crespos,
en venganza por los humos de aristócrata que t...*

*...y en donde para colmo había que cagar a diario en
la letrina estilo Francés Provenzal que Alfonso XII le
había obsequiado a tu abuelo. Por eso aquella noche llevaba puesto aquel traje cursi, confeccionado,
como en "Gone with the Wind", con las cortinas de
brocado que el viento no se había llevado todavía,
porque era la única manera de impresionar a la insoportable mujer del Alcalde, de apelar a su arreba-
tado delirio de grandeza. Nos compraron la casa por
fin con todas las antigüedades que tenía adentro,
pero no para hacerla un museo y un parque de los
que pudiera disfrutar el pueblo, sino para disfrutarlo
ellos mismos como su lujosa casa de campo.*

Frenética y fuera de sí, Rosa se puso de pie, y con-
templó horrorizada aquellas estrías de almíbar que
descendían lentamente por su falda hasta manchar
con su líquido sanguinolento las hebillas de raso de
sus zapatos. Temblaba de ira, y al principio se le hizo
imposible llegar a pronunciar una sola palabra. Una
vez le regresó el alma al cuerpo, sin embargo, comenzó a injuriar enfurecida a Rosaura, acusándola
de pasarse la vida leyendo cuentos, mientras ella se

veía obligada a consumirse los ojos y los dedos cosiendo para ellos. Y la culpa de todo la tenían aquellos malditos libros que Don Lorenzo le regalaba, los cuales eran prueba de que a Rosaura se la tenía en mayor estima que a ella en aquella casa, y por lo cual había decidido marcharse de su lado para siempre, si éstos no eran de inmediato arrojados al patio, donde ella misma ordenaría que se encendiera con ellos una enorme fogata.

Será el humo de las velas, será el perfume de los mirtos, pero me siento cada vez más mareada. No sé por qué, he comenzado a sudar y las manos me tiemblan. La lectura de este cuento ha comenzado a enconárseme en no sé cuál lugar misterioso del cuerpo. Y no bien terminó de hablar, Rosa palideció mortalmente y, sin que nadie pudiera evitarlo, cayó redonda y sin sentido al suelo. Aterrado por el desmayo de su mujer, Don Lorenzo se arrodilló a su lado y, tomándole las manos comenzó a llorar, implorándole en una voz muy queda que volviera en sí y que no lo abandonara, porque él había decidido complacerla en todo lo que ella le había pedido. Satisfecha con la promesa que había logrado sonsacarle, Rosa abrió los ojos y lo miró risueña, permitiéndole a Rosaura, en prueba de reconciliación, guardar sus libros.

Aquella noche Rosaura derramó abundantes lágrimas, hasta que por fin se quedó dormida sobre su almohada, bajo la cual había ocultado el obsequio de su padre. Tuvo entonces un sueño extraño. Soñó que, entre los relatos de aquel libro, había uno que estaría envenenado, porque destruiría, de manera fulminante, a su primer lector. Su autor, al escribirlo, había tomado la precaución de dejar inscrita en él una señal, una manera definitiva de reconocerlo

Lorenzo pasó serenamente a mejor vida al fondo de su propia cama, consolado por los cuidos y rezos de su mujer y de su hija. Encontrábase el cuerpo rodeado de flores y de cirios, y los deudos y parientes sentados alrededor, llorando y ensalzando las virtudes del muerto, cuando Rosa entró a la habitación, sosteniendo en la mano el último libro de cuentos que Don Lorenzo le había regalado a Rosaura y que tanta controversia había causado en una ocasión entre ella y su difunto marido. Saludó a la esposa del Alcalde con una imperceptible inclinación de cabeza, y se sentó en una silla algo retirada del resto de los deudos, como si buscase un poco de silencio y sosiego. Abriendo el libro al azar sobre la falda, comenzó a hojear lentamente las páginas, admirando sus ilustraciones y pensando que, ahora que era una mujer de medios, bien podía darse el lujo de confeccionarse para sí misma uno de aquellos espléndidos atuendos de reina. Pasó varias páginas sin novedad, hasta que llegó a un relato que le llamó la atención. A diferencia del resto, no tenía ilustración alguna, y se encontraba impreso en una extraña tinta color

149

guayaba. El primer párrafo la sorprendió, porque la heroína se llamaba exactamente igual que su hijastra. Mojándose entonces el dedo del corazón con la punta de la lengua, comenzó a separar con interés aquellas páginas que, debido a la espesa tinta, se adherían molestamente unas a otras. Del estupor pasó al asombro, del asombro pasó al pasmo, y del pasmo pasó al terror, pero a pesar del creciente malestar que sentía, la curiosidad no le permitía dejar de leerlas. El relato comenzaba: "Rosaura vivía en una casa de balcones sombreados por enredaderas tupidas de trinitaria púrpura...", pero Rosa nunca llegó a enterarse de cómo terminaba.

vi el cuerpo increíblemente blanco de Doña Ana de Lanrós, nuestra primera Carmelita Descalza, incrustado en su centro. Mamá me lleva afuera y me quedo sin respiración frente al chorro de agua que baja vertiginoso del techo, lo vomita el caño de hojalata que abre su boca por la esquina de la casa, es lo mejor para el pelo antes de recortarlo, lo deja sedoso y nuevo, como acabado de sacar de la caja de González Padín, me dice Mamá. Me seca entonces la cabeza con una toalla antes de coger de la mesa las largas tijeras de acero toledano, metiendo el índice y el pulgar por entre sus ojales. Las domina desde la altura de su hombro, desde la curva carnosa del antebrazo; las mueve lentamente sobre mi nuca, como dos puñales de plata fría, y empieza delicadamente a recortarme.

—Te veo pensativa. ¿Qué soñaste?

Miro el reflejo de Mamá en el espejo del cuarto y su imagen me regresa como un celaje. Se ha borrado sobre los bancos carcomidos, sobre los lirios deshechos, sobre los manteles manchados de esperma en la capilla de la tumba de mi tío, a la que acudi-

151

mos tantas veces a rezar. He pasado la mirada tantas veces por el lugar que ocupa, por los manteles ya descosidos, por los bancos carcomidos de humedad, las azucenas marchitas y deshechas por el piso, que siento que acabará por gastarse a fuerza de deslizarle por encima los párpados. (¿Quién puso ahí ese espejo biselado por los cuatro costados que refleja tan implacablemente sobre nosotras la custodia erizada de brillantes?) De rato en rato me invaden unas ganas incontenibles de levantarme de donde estoy sentada, de hundir las manos en el espejo para tocarle a Mamá los ojos, para ver si tengo que cerrar los míos.

—¿En qué estás soñando? Cuéntame tu sueño.

El reflejo de los ojos me ciega al contemplarme en el espejo. Punto de fuga: soñar con los ojos abiertos, puesto ya el pie en el estribo. Pronto tocarán el Ángelus, sonará la campanilla del refectorio y Mamá y yo descenderemos de este escaparate que flota sobre el altar como un tiovivo antiguo. Nos alejaremos entonces de aquí, girando sobre idénticos tambores rojos, los pedales niquelados haciéndonos adelantar y retroceder con facilidad, camino del infierno o quizá del mundo. Vestidas de negro el viento embozará nuestras faldas alrededor de nuestras piernas; hará crujir nuestras faldas veloces; nos abofeteará con sus tiras negras, con sus rachas, con sus ráfagas. Nos veo a las dos, gualtrapeantes caballeras talares atravesando los montes, galgolpeando difícil y siempre de sesgo, descorriendo los misterios gozosos y los dolorosos, o anulándolo todo sobre el anular.

Estás pálida. Dime qué soñaste.

La luz atraviesa parejamente mi sueño y la mirada, me hace concordar discordias. De un tiempo acá...

...no eres tú?

Caminamos juntas por entre los panteones del cementerio, por entre ángeles aburados de yeso viejo, grisáceos y chorreados de limo negro por la espalda, por entre rosas de hierro forjado, coronas de espinas, cadenas, clavos. Un bullir de agujas de pino, un perfume a geranios quebrados que derraman una sangre seca invade mi olfato. Saltamos de tumba en tumba sobre las verjas de hierro. Son bajas, hileras de lanzas negras interrumpidas aquí y allá por jarrones de alabastro repletos de azucenas hediondas a santidad y a pudridero. Bajamos corriendo las escalinatas del panteón que reconoces, porque lo has visitado muchas veces. Cuatro columnas de granito negro, una lápida que se tañe con aldaba de bronce, coronas de flores que arrastran una caligrafía escarchada en cintas que se desgranan por el suelo. El eco de mis pasos se oye lejos, mullido por las agujas de pino. Voy bajando lentamente, cada vez más lentamente, hasta llegar a la puerta cancel. Mamá se me ha adelantado y me aguarda sentada junto a la boca de la cripta. Los pliegues de su falda negra se acumulan a sus pies en un embalse sombrío. Es exactamente igual a mi falda, sólo que está inmóvil, tallada en mármol sobre la lápida. Me mira. Me mira como yo te miro.

—Estás aterrada. Habla por fin, cuéntame el enigma de tu sueño.

—Creo que ahora podré empezar a contarlo:

postulado cartesiano "pienso, luego soy". Yo digo, 'escribo, luego pienso'; o lo que quizá sea más cierto, 'no pienso, luego escribo'. El día que deje de escribir dejaré de pensar y diré con Vallejo: "Vámonos, pues, por eso a comer yerba, carne de llanto, fruta de gemido, nuestra alma melancólica en conserva."

Escribo por un ansia de autoridad; porque necesito ser autora de mi propia vida. No me interesa adquirir poder sobre las vidas ajenas, pero sí tener el control de la mía. Vivir una vida en la cual uno no está en control es vivir de reflejo; no surge de las profundidades del propio ser. Y la vida no vale la pena vivirla si no se vive con valentía, con el valor que exige la autenticidad. Para vivir y escribir bien es necesario, como Moncha Insaurralde en el cuento "La novia robada" de Onetti, "poder atravesar con los ojos bien abiertos por las puertas del Infierno". También Mozart atravesó con los ojos abiertos por las puertas del Infierno, al compás de su *Flauta mágica*. Esta convicción es para mí fundamental y en ello radica mi desprecio por los que viven vidas de reflejo, resultado de la cobardía, del miedo. El miedo es un sentimiento profundamente humano y todos, en algún momento, somos finalmente subyugados por él. El día en que me someta a su ley inexorable, dejaré de escribir.

ÍNDICE

LAS DOS VENECIAS
SE IMPRIMIÓ EN LOS TALLERES DE
OFFSET LIBRA, S. A.
FRANCISCO I. MADERO NO. 31
COL. IXTACALCO
MÉXICO, D.F.
SE TIRARON 3 000 EJEMPLARES
Y SOBRANTES PARA REPOSICIÓN

IMPRESO Y HECHO EN MÉXICO
PRINTED AND MADE IN MEXICO